## *Praise for* THE COUNTESS

"A unique perspective on Báthory's life . . . *The Countess* walks a fine line between being a repulsive story of murder and gore and a tale of a woman defending her home and honor. Johns expertly manages that balancing act."

—Associated Press

"Johns's fictional countess is a complex, almost-but-not-quite sympathetic figure; a woman of admirable qualities who nonetheless committed acts of appalling violence."

—*Chicago Sun-Times*

"Though Johns's novel is a work of historical fiction, the details which emerge about Báthory paint a chilling portrait of a woman who, whether or not she committed the heinous acts she's credited for, emerged from a privileged if disturbed childhood and an arranged marriage with a cunning and cruelty that fit her reputation as a monster. It is easy to see how willing people were and have been to believe the worst of the Blood Countess."

—*San Francisco Book Review*

"The most lasting effect of Johns's *The Countess* is the uneasy feeling readers get that there may be a monster within each of us, concealed under veils of ethics and self-justification, and too easily overlooked."

—*Fiction Writers Review*

"The steady, calm tone of Erzsébet's narration lulls the reader along so that the first hints of madness in her girlhood engender doubt and discomfort rather than horror, and as her lack of remorse and grandiose sense of entitlement are unveiled, a matter-of-fact self-portrait of a murderer emerges . . . Carefully researched . . . gothic in tone and grimly atmospheric, with subtly handled psychology and an initially unassuming tone. Unlike most serial killer stories, this rewards patience and close reading."

—**Publishers Weekly**

"Realistic and historically accurate . . . Its understated treatment of an infamous character offers excellent potential for book club discussion."

—**Library Journal**

"*The Countess* is a fascinating look at a woman whose story has become a gruesome legend throughout time. Though Johns makes no effort to prove Báthory's innocence, which I don't believe has ever been a question, she does successfully attempt to humanize the monster that has been dramatized throughout the centuries."

—**BookBitch.com**

"Exquisitely written . . . Riveting yet disturbing."

—**HistFicChick.com**

# THE

# COUNTESS

*Also by Rebecca Johns*

ICEBERGS

# THE
# COUNTESS

❧ *A Novel of Elizabeth Báthory* ❧

*Rebecca Johns*

BROADWAY PAPERBACKS
*New York*

BROADWAY

Copyright © 2010 by Rebecca Johns
Reading Group Guide Copyright © 2011 by Rebecca Johns

Published in the United States by Broadway Paperbacks, an imprint of the
Crown Publishing Group, a division of Random House, Inc., New York.
www.crownpublishing.com

Broadway Paperbacks and its logo, a letter B bisected on the diagonal, are trademarks
of Random House, Inc.

Originally published in hardcover in slightly different form in the United States
by Crown Publishers, an imprint of the Crown Publishing Group, a division of
Random House, Inc., New York, in 2010.

Library of Congress Cataloging-in-Publication Data

Johns, Rebecca, 1971–
    The countess / by Rebecca Johns.
        p. cm.
    1. Báthory, Erzsébet, 1560-1614—Fiction.    2. Countesses—Fiction.
3. Women serial murderers—Fiction.    4. Nobility—Hungary—Fiction.    I. Title.
    PS3610.O29C68 2010
    813'.6—dc22                            2010018031

ISBN 978-0-307-58846-3
eISBN 978-0-307-58847-0

Printed in the United States of America

BOOK DESIGN BY ELINA D. NUDELMAN
COVER DESIGN BY LAURA DUFFY
COVER PHOTOGRAPHY BY ALLAN JENKINS/TREVILLION IMAGES

10   9   8   7   6   5   4   3   2   1

First Paperback Edition

*For Brandon, my ideal reader*

# DRAMATIS PERSONAE

In the countess's native language, the surname appears first, so although she is often called Elilzabeth Bathory for English-speaking audiences, she would in fact have called herself Báthory Erzsébet. In this work the characters' names are given in the order more familiar to English speakers but otherwise approximate the spelling and pronunciation the countess herself would likely have used in the late sixteenth and early seventeenth centuries. Likewise, the names of cities and towns use the Hungarian variant, including Vienna (Bécs), Prague (Prága), Bratislava (Pozsony), and Alba Iulia (Gyulafehérvár).

Pronunciation of Hungarian names puts a stronger emphasis on the vowel, as indicated by the accent mark, and softens the consonants, especially in combination: "Csejthe" thus is pronounced *CHEY-tee*, "Bicske" is *BICH-ke*, and "Pozsony" is *po-ZHONYE*. "Keresztúr" is *ker-es-TUUR* and "Sárvár" is *SHAR-var*, with a roll of the "r." More difficult for English speakers is "gy," which is pronounced with a soft *dju*, as in "adjulation."

**Erzsébet Báthory** (er-ZHAY-bet BAAH-tor-ee): a wealthy noblewoman of the kingdom of Hungary

**György Thurzó** (djuordj tuur-ZO): the palatine of Upper Hungary (1609–1616), the king's appointed representative to the Hungarian people, such as a prime minister

**Anna** (AHN-nah) **Báthory:** the countess's mother, sister to the king of Poland

*György Báthory:* the countess's father

*István* (isht-VAAN) *Báthory:* the countess's older brother

*Zsofía* (zho-FEE-a) *Báthory:* the countess's younger sister

*Klára* (KLAAR-a) *Báthory:* the countess's youngest sister

*Ferenc Nádasdy* (fer-ENTS NAA-dash-dee): the countess's husband

*Orsolya Kanizsay* (or-SHOY-yah kan-i-ZHAY): the countess's mother-in-law

*Tamás* (tam-AASH) *Nádasdy:* the countess's father-in-law, palatine of Hungary from 1559 to 1562

*Imre Megyery* (IM-ray mejd-YER-ee): steward of Sárvár and later Pál Nádasdy's tutor

*Griseldis Bánffy:* the countess's young cousin

*András* (AHN-drahsh) *Kanizsay:* a cousin of Ferenc Nádasdy

*István Bocskai* (BOTCH-kai): a noble companion to Ferenc Nádasdy, later prince of Transylvania and leader of the Bocskai Rebellion (1604–6)

*Rudolf II:* Holy Roman Emperor (1576–1612) and King of Hungary (1572–1608)

*Mátyás* (MAH-tyash) *II:* Rudolf's brother, later Holy Roman Emperor (1612–1619) and King of Hungary (1608–1619)

*Anna Nádasdy:* the countess's elder daughter

*Katalin* (Kata) *Nádasdy:* the countess's younger daughter

*Pál* (paal) *Nádasdy:* the countess's son

>×<

*Gábor* (GAAH-bore) *Báthory:* the countess's nephew, prince of Transylvania

*Miklós Zrínyi* (meek-LOSH ZREEN-yee): grandson of the Hungarian/Croatian war hero of the same name, married to the countess's daughter Anna

*György Hommonai Drugeth* (DROO-get): a wealthy nobleman married to the countess's younger daughter Katalin

*Erzsébet Czobor* (TSO-bore): Thurzó's second wife

*Anna Darvulia:* a wisewoman and healer, a servant in the Nádasdy household

*Ilona Jó* (ee-LOH-na jo): a confidential servant

*Dorottya Szentes* (dor-OTT-tee-ya SEN-tesh), known as "Dorka": a confidential servant

*Katalin Benecká* (ben-ets-KAH): a washerwoman

*Erzsi Majorosné* (er-ZHEE my-or-osh-NAY): the countess's healing woman

*Ficzkó* (FITS-ko): the countess's personal manservant

*Istók Soós* (ish-TOCK sho-USH): a steward

*Doricza* (DOR-ee-tsa): a maidservant

*Benedict Deseő* (desh-ay-OO): a steward

*István Magyari:* the Lutheran pastor of Sárvár

*Rev. Ponikenus:* the pastor of the Lutheran church at Csejthe

*Rev. Zacharias:* the pastor of Lešetice sent to hear the countess's confession during her imprisonment

*One day when the queen asked her mirror: "Mirror, mirror, on the wall, who in this land is fairest of all?" it answered: "You, my queen, are fair; it is true. But Snow-White is a thousand times fairer than you."*

*The queen took fright and turned yellow and green with envy. From that hour on whenever she looked at Snow-White her heart turned over inside her body, so great was her hatred for the girl. The envy and pride grew ever greater, like a weed in her heart, until she had no peace day and night.*

*Then she summoned a huntsman and said to him, "Take Snow-White out into the woods. I never want to see her again. Kill her, and as proof that she is dead bring her lungs and her liver back to me."*

*The huntsman obeyed and took Snow-White into the woods. He took out his hunting knife and was about to stab it into her innocent heart when she began to cry, saying, "Oh, dear huntsman, let me live. I will run into the wild woods and never come back."*

*Because she was so beautiful the huntsman took pity on her, and he said, "Run away, you poor child." He thought, "The wild animals will soon devour you anyway," but still it was as if a stone had fallen from his heart, for he would not have to kill her.*

*Just then a young boar came running by. He killed it, cut out its lungs and liver, and took them back to the queen as proof of Snow-White's death. The cook had to boil them with salt, and the wicked woman ate them, supposing that she had eaten Snow-White's lungs and liver.*

—THE BROTHERS GRIMM

# THE
# COUNTESS

*To the Reverend Eliáš Láni, Žilina*
Dominus vobiscum

It is with profound regret that I must tell you that the widow Nádasdy died last evening unrepentant and unabsolved of her crimes, despite the best efforts of myself and Rev. Ponikenus to extract her confession. At your request I have been attending that infamous lady for the past several weeks, sitting outside her door in the tower where she was a prisoner and speaking to her of the state of her immortal soul. I asked repeatedly if she felt any sorrow for the dead ones, if she knew the harm she had caused the many families that had once been under her protection, the harm she had caused her own children, but she insisted that her imprisonment was a political one engineered by the king and the palatine to steal her wealth and keep her family's influence in check. Repeatedly she contended that she had done nothing to merit the accusations against her, though she said nothing that would contradict the palatine's account of her, nor explain the presence of the dead girls found in her house at Christmastime. I knew it was your wish that she might be turned at last to the consolations of Jesus Christ, and a great victory it would have been for our cause in Hungary if she had done so, but even in the last few days, when she knew her health was failing, she would not unburden herself to me and repeatedly sent me away in the middle of my prayers. Perhaps such a woman is incapable of repentance, but I cannot help but take responsibility for the failure and hope that in the future your faith in me may be better rewarded.

Rev. Ponikenus and I were not with her when she died, so we did not hear her final words, though the guards say she was complaining of cold in her limbs and asking for her children. They heard the clattering of hooves on the tower stairs just before they found her, they say, as if the devil himself were coming to collect her. By the time the steward brought her evening bread she was already cold.

*You may be assured that the countess was every bit as intelligent and abject as your earlier reports had suggested. I often found myself bewildered by her dark wit, the breadth of her education, and the peculiar turns of her mind. I will be relieved to return to my ministry in Lešetice and leave the cold confines of the countess's household behind me. Even now I find her influence hangs over Csejthe like a cloud. The villagers whisper and stare and cross the street when I approach, as if I have been marked or marred after sitting so many hours with that dejected lady. One man, a local farmer with his cart of vegetables, stopped this morning to tell me I was not safe in the village, that the hills around the castle are still full of her followers, including an old witch named Darvulia who haunts the catacombs beneath the castle with ninety-nine cats, and who comes out at night still to conjure the countess's soul back from the realm of the dead. Much of this, I'm certain, is nothing more than local folklore, meant to frighten me away by a population who mistrusts outsiders, but nevertheless hostility hangs over the very hills, the wind, and the water. Her son-in-law Count Zrínyi is making plans to return the lady to her birthplace in Ecsed, in the east, to be buried in her family vault, for her grave will surely not be safe here, where the local people have such long memories of her misdeeds.*

*With this letter I am sending ahead some papers found among the lady's things giving an account of her life. They were discovered clasped to her breast with a note stating that in the event of her death, they were to be sent to her son at the family seat at Sárvár. I took them to read last evening, hoping they might reveal something of her that I had not already discovered, and I send them now to you that they may serve as a record of her crimes and the depth of her depravity, and of my own true and faithful efforts to bring her at last to Christ. You will notice that they become more difficult to read nearer the end, where her handwriting begins to degenerate with the onset of illness and where her cruelty becomes more apparent with every passing day. Her protestations of innocence are preposterous, and the blame she puts on the palatine, the king, and even Rev. Ponikenus for her imprisonment is nothing short of treason and blasphemy. Yet how often did I find myself, as I read, pitying that lady in her loneliness, in her disappointed hopes and plans; how often did my heart break for her! Quite honestly I was torn about what* to do with the account. The current Count Nádasdy is still a youth of sixteen who has not seen his mother in the three years since her imprisonment, so adamant was his guardian that he should not visit her for fear of sullying his name with his mother's sins. It did cross my mind to burn these pages and protect the boy from the truth, or to send them to the palatine to enter into the record against her, but I have decided to leave the sending of them to your discretion and greater experience, once you have had a chance to read them.

If it is true that Satan walks the earth wearing the most human, the most seductive of disguises, then he could find none better than Countess Báthory. I mourn for her and for the poor girls she murdered, the named and unnamed, the lowborn and the high, and for all whose lives she has blackened with her touch.

Crux sancta sit mihi lux, non draco sit mihi dux
*Rev. Nicolas Zacharias*

# PART ONE

# EXTRA HUNGARIAM
# NON EST VITA

# 1

*January 1, 1611*

The boy and his father came at dawn to shut me in, arriving from the village below the castle with their donkey and their cart and their load of tools. I was awake some hours, watching the light at the window go from black to faintly blue, so I heard them making their way across the snowy courtyard below the tower, a couple of dark figures with their heads together, whispering and shivering as they looked up toward my windows as if I were some kind of monster for men to cross themselves against.

The father spoke to the boy in words too soft to hear, but their breath, heavy from exertion or dread, lifted from their faces and spun away in the winter cold. I stood back in the darkness and did not let them see me, for I wanted no one to know I had been watching. I refused to be afraid. I paced from the window to the door and back, warming my hands by the fire and then, growing too warm, moving to the window again for a breath of cool air. When I looked again they were gone. Two lines of footprints marked the path they took— one large, for the father, and a smaller one for the boy. The patient donkey stood in his traces and stamped his small hooves, a puff of white breath rising from his mouth as well, just another of God's miserable creatures.

How every waking moment pains me until I may see you once more, Pál, speak to you once more. It grieves me that I do not have even a drawing of you or your sisters to keep me company in my prison, for the walls of my chamber are bare, having been stripped of their paintings and mirrors and weavings, any small luxury, by the palatine's soldiers when they brought me up to the castle from my house, my *kastély*, in Csejthe village two days ago. In the tower of the *vár* there is now only the bare plaster thick with frost, a rough wooden table and chairs set with a single candle, a straw mattress on the floor for a bed. Altogether the place feels and smells of a stable. A piece of stale bread sits untouched on the floor, waiting for the servant to come up and fetch it back again. I do not sleep. I try to read but am restless and pace the small space of my room instead, listening for footfalls on the stair outside my door. If only I had some embroidery, some bright bit of cloth, I might find an easier way to pass the time, but the palatine ordered the guards to take my pins and needles, my blades and scissors, as well as the mirrors and any bit of glass they could find, saying he would leave me no easy way out of my prison.

The palatine was generous enough to leave me a few books, Meister Eckhart's *Abgeschiedenheit*, Aristotle's *Politics,* though I already know them by heart.

> *Quemadmodum enim perfectum optimum animalium homo est, sic et segregatum deterius omnibus; gravissima enim habens arma. Homo autem non habens arma nascitur prudentie et virtuti; quibus ad contraria existentibus, pessima maxime.* For man, when perfected, is the best of animals, but when separated from law and justice he is the worst of all; since armed injustice is the more dangerous, and he is equipped at birth with arms meant to be used by intelligence and virtue, which he may use for the worst ends.

Never have these words seemed more true to me than they do now, as I sit isolated from all the world at the whim of György Thurzó, a man so clearly without virtue himself.

❧❧

VIRTUE SEEMS TO BE lacking in too many of the men I have known in my lifetime, Thurzó most especially.

It was only a few days ago, just after Christmas, when Thurzó snuck into Csejthe *vár* in the middle of the night with a troop of King Mátyás's guards and a scroll with King Mátyás's stamp. In the caverns under the keep, with the servant girl still warm at my feet, the palatine ordered his soldiers to take me to the tower and didn't seem to hear when I asked why he had turned against me, why he was giving credence to the falsehoods spread by my enemies. To think that I loved him once, that I took him into my bed! Then he ordered his soldiers to lead the servants away—the three old women and young Ficzkó—and there was a sound of crying in the dim light, the smell of blood and candlewax. I could hardly see for anger. He handed me the paper to read, the one with the king's seal, but I crumpled it and threw it at him. Lies, I said. Without another noble witness to testify against me, neither Thurzó nor the king have the authority to imprison me, but the palatine seemed unconcerned with such niceties. "I see the rule of law no longer applies in Hungary," I said. "What is the king giving you to turn your back on your friends?"

The gray bags under Thurzó's eyes, which had always made him look so vulnerable, now hardened into little pillows of stone. "Our friendship is the only thing saving your life right now," he said. "I suggest you say nothing that may make your situation worse than it already is." Then he laid down his sentence, there in the dim caverns beneath Csejthe, condemning me *in perpetuis carceribus*. A lifetime between stones. He left a company of his own soldiers in the keep, left me here under lock and key, taking my servants off to Bicske to stand trial for my sins, as he called them. What sins are those? I asked, but he turned away and would not answer me. I heard his carriage driving away as they took me up to the tower.

This morning I waited a long time, but the boy and his father did not come. For a moment I wondered if perhaps the palatine had thought better of his decision and sent them away again, but then their voices were outside my door, greeting the guards in the local dialect. I arranged myself to receive them into my room, determined to offer them my forgiveness as one forgives the executioner before one's head is struck off. I touched my hair, my face, did my best under the circumstances to look presentable. In a little while there was a sound of someone working at the door, and after a few minutes they had it off its hinges and set aside. The hallway was dim. A single lamp gave off a thin yellow light, but I saw the boy and his father come forward and kneel in the doorway and stepped toward them with my hand raised in friendship. At the gesture the guards threatened me with their weapons raised and ordered me back. The bigger guard, the one with the winestain on his cheek like the slap of a great hand, growled that I was not to approach the boy or his father or to make any motion of witchcraft or incantation in their direction, or the guards would finish me where I stood. "You wouldn't dare," I said.

He smiled, showing all his teeth. "Who is here to stop me?" he said.

The blood rushed to my face, and I dropped my hand. Then I could see that the masons were not offering obeisance but beginning their work, mixing the mortar and sorting out the stones in little piles, the stones that will make my prison from this day forward, for my old friend the palatine tells me that I will not leave this tower alive.

The guards ordered me to sit in a chair while the masons went to work. They sealed the windows first, closing the small slits in the wall that showed me the valley of the river Vág, the villages and farms that were a gift to me from your father on our wedding day. The mason set the stones in a circle, shutting out the light little by little, working until only a small hole remains, just large enough for me to put my hand through. Through it, if I stand on a chair, I will see little but the color of the sky, the faint cold stars, a distant smudge of hills I will never cross again.

When they finished with the windows, they retreated to the hallway and began the slow work of shutting the door to my chamber, closing me in stone by stone like Antigone in her cave. I watched them at their task. They were villagers from Csejthe, the man and his son, dressed in clean linen shirts and pants and brown homespun waistcoats. The father chose each stone carefully to fit with the one below it, frowning as if he saw something in the stone he did not like. He would not meet my gaze, though I sat not three feet away. The boy must have been ten or eleven years old, but he was a strong worker, obeying his father's every command, fetching this or that tool, mixing the mortar in a bowl. Once in a while he peeked in my direction, as if his curiosity had gotten the better of him. He had the face of the Infant himself, straw-colored hair and long-lashed eyes, the lashes throwing small sooty shadows across his pink cheeks. He reminded me in many ways of you, my love, with your shyness and your serious face, though you have your father's fierce brow and proud Nádasdy nose. I wiggled my fingers at the boy and smiled. "*Ako sa voláte?*" I asked in the local dialect. *What is your name?* I have learned two or three phrases of the language in my years in this part of the country, through many years of taking peasant girls and boys into my house as servants. My accent was not good, but the boy did not seem to notice. He stared at me with wide eyes, curiosity and fear mingled on his face. "Luki," he said, his voice high as a girl's still.

"*Teší ma,*" I answered. *Pleased to meet you.*

I was about to see if my guess was true and ask him his age when the father reached up and slapped the boy hard across the face, saying something rushed and angry. I recognized only one word: *škrata.* Witch. The father pointed at the stairs and barked an order, and young Luki took his leather strap back down the stairs, tears wetting his cheeks. Were it not for the palatine's guards, I would have slapped the mason's ugly red face myself to exact revenge for that unnecessary blow. Instead I clenched and unclenched my hands and looked away as if I had noticed nothing. I would bide my time. I am not some madwoman who does not know when and how to act, no matter what the palatine and Megyery and Ponikenus say about me. I retreated into the new darkness of my bedchamber, where I waited for my solitude to begin. The walls they lay will harden like my heart.

Then the mason's son was back with his load of stones, and the father set them tight and true. The man is a master craftsman, and the door should hold until they take it down to let me out, or else to carry me out. A gap in the stones about the span of two outstretched hands will allow the servant to pass me food and drink and take away the night jar, but otherwise I am completely without help or comfort. I am left to wash my own clothes, and clean my own room, and make up my own hair. I will not be allowed to attend church, to walk in my vineyard, to meet you or your sisters in your far-flung homes, to hear a word of kindness spoken. In a sudden rage I cursed the guards, the palatine, the mason, picking up bits of smoldering charcoal from the fire and flinging them through what was left of the door, my mouth tasting of copper. "Now, now, madam," said the winestained guard, speaking as one speaks to a bad-tempered horse, "you cannot do us any harm out here."

Looking around my room for a weapon, for anything, I grasped a burning branch from the fire, holding it out toward the straw mattress. My hand was steady and strong. "I can set the house alight," I said.

"You would not." His lips formed a thin line.

"I would. Better to burn than remain your prisoner." My limbs seemed to move without my consent, as if I were looking at myself from the outside. The flames leapt off the branch and spun away in the cold air, but the guard did not move from his post. He must have been weighing the seriousness of my threat against the lies he heard about me: that I am a whore, a witch, a vampire who bathes in the blood of maidens. After a moment he simply shrugged and smiled, turning away to speak a low word to his companion. He no longer saw me standing there with the burning branch in my hand. I dropped my arm. I am used to many reactions from many people—some pleasant, some unpleasant—but disregard is not one of them. I am not used to being invisible.

Tears stung at the edges of my vision, but I would not cry. The guards would be elated, I suppose, if I burned the castle down, for then they could go home and forget all about me, tell their drinking companions in the taverns of Bicske about the time they saw the Beast of Csejthe immolate herself out of spite. The actions of a madwoman and a criminal. As I'm a sane woman after all, I placed the branch back on the fire. I will not give the guards, or the palatine, the satisfaction of being rid of me. Not yet.

Instead I sat at my table and with shaking hands began writing these pages to you, Pál, so that you may know something of your mother besides the lies the palatine and the king and your tutor tell you. So you may know that even now, your mother thinks of you and prays for you. That she hopes you may become a better man than those she has known, and loved, during her own life.

Now I can see little but the mason's hands at work, bits of his clothing through the stone gap. I can no longer hear what the guard says in his low voice to the boy and his father, who are packing up their tools, their footsteps growing fainter as they walk back down the stairs of my tower, into the open air. The flames of the fire ebb and flicker. I will not have another. My poor servants will no doubt be submitted to torture, forced to condemn me to save themselves, because the palatine will not be merciful. He has not a drop of pity in him. He has damned me to prison for the remainder of my days—this tower, these walls, these few books, this bed. And myself, a woman alone, with nothing to do but contemplate her life.

I have done nothing that was not my right by blood and title, not to the palatine, not to anyone else. Erzsébet Báthory, widow of Ferenc Nádasdy, daughter of the most ancient noble house in Hungary, is not a witch or a madwoman, a murderess or a criminal. She has no intention of quietly accepting her fate.

# 2

The palatine, when he laid down his sentence on me, said our family was cursed with more than its share of lunatics and madmen—an unfair characterization, to say the least, and hypocritical besides, since whatever madness exists in our blood never stopped him from courting Báthory support for his political ambitions, or from loving me when it suited him. Our family has no more odd characters than anyone else's, the palatine's included.

Your grandmother, Anna, was a Báthory from the Somlyó branch of the family. When I was fifteen, her brother István, then prince of Transylvania, was elected king of Poland, where he distinguished himself as a military leader and statesman. Her other male relatives—brothers, nephews—were all distinguished leaders of men. My cousin Zsigmond Báthory, married to a Habsburg princess, was four times prince of Transylvania, and my cousin András, before he was murdered and cut into pieces, was a cardinal of the Roman church as well as prince of Transylvania and grand master of the Order of the Dragon. My father, György Báthory, was a distant cousin from the Ecsed branch of the family, a great landowner and brother to András Bonaventura Báthory, another prince of Transylvania. It was my father who owned the ladder-like fortress in the marsh where Vitus, with his lance, killed the dragon that was terrorizing the countryside and afterward was given the title *bátor*, the "bold hero." From him come our family's name and the root of our family's honor. For a thousand years Báthory sons have defended Hungary against foreign sultans and pretender kings, and Báthory daughters have bent their heads in marriage and their backs in childbearing, all in the name of national pride and filial duty. No one, myself included, has been free from the yoke of the power and glory, the servitude, of the Báthory name.

# THE COUNTESS

My mother was a learned woman, an early convert to the Calvinist faith who read and wrote Latin, who founded a school with her first husband and after his death continued the management of his estate at Erdőd, in Szathmár, championing the liberal political and religious ideals they had shared. My mother didn't long wait to marry her second husband, or, when he died quite suddenly, to succumb to the advances of her third husband, my father. She was a dedicated wife, a woman who, like many women I have known, was only happy in the marriage bed. Once, when I was six or seven years old and just learning about the future that lay in wait for me, she pressed my hands between hers and, bending down, put her face very close to mine. "You must not tell this to your sister, who is not as beautiful as you," she said, "but you will have to protect her, Erzsébet, when I'm gone. A woman who does not marry is at the mercy of the world, and your sister may never have a husband of her own. But your beauty is your blessing and your curse. You will have any man you want, so it is on you that your sister will depend. Do not forget."

For a long time I was shocked by the idea that the fate of the family would fall on me, that my little sister Zsofía would depend on me to find a husband who would love me and protect her for my sake. I could not imagine that any man would love me as my father loved my mother. I spent hours studying myself in my mother's silver-backed mirror, my great dark-brown eyes not lively enough— too much like a cow's—my forehead too high, my nose too long, my mouth too pale, twisted with wryness or mischief—not serious enough, not clever or obedient, nor supple or sensual like my mother's. Altogether I felt cloddish and awkward, crudely made, and wondered if we would all be ruined as a result—my mother and father, my brother, Zsofía, myself. We would be at the mercy of the Turks, the invaders, if I could not secure a husband with an army at his disposal and enough love to shelter us all, love like a strong roof to keep out the wind and the rain and the snow.

Later, after I had begun to grow into my looks and began to understand the uses beauty has to a woman, I overheard my mother talking to Zsofia in the garden, where they were picking herbs. All the noble-women of my acquaintance have been familiar with the herbalist's art, and my mother was an especially gifted healing woman who had undertaken to teach me and my little sister what she knew. I was sneaking out of the house to take my pony for a ride, hiding amid the bushes at the edge of the kitchen garden, and so my mother did not know I was present when she began to tell Zsofia that she was the family's one great beauty, its only hope against destitution, for women who did not marry were objects of ridicule, without protection in a world made for men. "Your sister may never marry, Zsofia," she said, "so you must protect her. Beauty such as yours will gain the attention of every man in the kingdom. When you have a husband, you must use your wealth and position to help your family." Little Zsofia had nodded solemnly, her lip trembling. As for myself, I waited until they had gone back inside, and then I made my way to the stables and kicked my pony into a hot lather, astonished at my mother's calculation and cunning.

For a long time before that, though, I had believed that my mother truly had placed all her hopes on me alone, and I had felt both privileged and terrified to be the object of her affection. Her love made me reckless. I would sometimes throw myself on her with great washes of tears, begging her to take me in her arms and stroke my hair, to reassure me that I was worthy of her affection; or else I would resent her hopes and run away and hide in the stables, or pinch my little sister until the skin on her arms turned red, or light the tails of my father's hunting dogs with a burning branch from the fireplace. When I was naughty, my mother would find me and draw me out again from inside the stable, or from under a bench, or from the confines of my bed, sighing and running her hands over my hair, and I would wrap my arms around her ribs and listen to the thudding of her heart until I was calm again and the fit had passed. Erzsébet, Erzsébet, she would say, you must not upset yourself so much. You must learn to control your passions better, my love, and save your miseries for the privacy of your own heart.

Despite her scheming, or perhaps because of it, I adored my

mother when I was a child. I used to pick up and stroke her hands, pressing her palms to my face, twisting her many rings and sometimes trying one on my own finger, imagining for a moment what it would be like to be her, a woman who had snared not one but three husbands. I begged to be in the room when my youngest sister, Klára, was born, wanting to be helpful to my mother and fearful of letting her out of my sight, lest something terrible happen during the birth. When the moment came, it all terrified me—my mother's cries of pain, the wet dark head poking out from the place between her thighs, the limp baby slithering out more piglike than human, smeared with wax and blood. I hid in the corner and would not come out, not even to hold the baby I had been so desperate to see born, not even when my mother called me to her and said there was no reason to be afraid. "You too were born like this," she said as they put Klára into her arms, but these words only frightened me more and sent me running into the hallway, where I sat on the cold boards of the wooden floor, hugging my knees to my chest and refusing to come back inside.

To my father it was upsetting for an entirely different reason. He had long been bent on producing a second son, a companion for my older brother, István, a sickly, solitary boy more given to books and prayers than statecraft or soldiering. After my father was certain that Klára and my mother were both well, he came into the hall, put his face in his hands, and wept, his head hanging and his shoulders heaving up and down. The old midwife who had overseen the birth came out and consoled him. "You should not blame yourself," she said. "There is no accounting for why some women are blessed so often and others so little, or not at all." He didn't speak, but later that day when I was brave enough to reenter my mother's room, I heard him swear to my mother that never again would she have to give birth to any child of his, boy or girl. One son, he had decided, would be enough.

My mother smiled. "Do not make promises you cannot keep, György," she said, and put her hand on his shaggy white head. He kissed her and the baby and went out again while my mother and sisters and I slept together in the big bed.

That night there was a great storm, endless flashes of lightning that came so close together it was impossible to tell one from the other. I lay shivering under the blankets while Zsofia whimpered next to me, wrapping her small arms around my neck. My mother and the new baby lay so still and quiet I bent down to check if they still breathed. Late into the night I heard the echoing voice of my father, drunk and singing, goading my brother into having a drink in the dining hall. "Here, boy," I heard him say, then István's whines of protest following. "Drink to the birth of yet another sister."

"I don't want to, Father. It smells too strong."

"Drink it. Be grateful. You'll have no brother now to share your inheritance. There, now, that wasn't so bad. Here's another. Drink it up. Look, even the angels applaud you tonight, the little lord of Ecsed."

Around us, thunder rocked the house like cannon fire, and I bent down to kiss the baby, to breathe her smell of hot milk and sleep, and pray that she would be no one's last hope, no one's only chance for salvation.

# 3

Not long before I was born most of south-central Hungary had fallen to Szulejmán, who claimed the title "the Magnificent" but whose presence was resented in the country, as outsiders have always been resented in these battle-weary lands. He took the castle at Buda without a shot, drawing out the widowed queen and her infant son on friendly pretenses and then locking the doors of the stronghold behind them. The queen, having no other choice when surrounded by the sultan's army, gathered her child and her ladies into a few carts and left the country to its fate. Whole villages fled before the sultan's janissaries, and those who had not the means or the good health to make the long journey to Habsburg lands in the west or Transylvania in the east ended up vassals of the sultan, a conquered people. The nation was left in tatters, divided into Upper Hungary, which curved along the Carpathians from the Adriatic to the borders of Transylvania, ruled by the Habsburg Ferdinand; Transylvania itself, which may have been nominally beholden to the sultan but in its heart was always wedded to Hungary; and the lower kingdom, including much of the great plains all the way north to Buda and Esztergom, which the sultan kept for himself. The conquered lands of the Alföld that had once been so rich grew deserted as the nobles fled the sultan's rule, sometimes taking their vassals with them. Farmlands turned back to grass, villages to ghost towns.

My uncle István, who would be king of Poland, was then prince of Transylvania and had great plans for reuniting Hungary against both the Turks and the Habsburgs, plans of which my father and many other nobles besides approved. My father's lands were in the far east of Upper Hungary, near the Partium with Transylvania, so he was always careful to pay attention to which way the winds were blowing. My father sent men and money to my uncle, a skilled negotiator who vied with both the Turks and the Habsburgs to see who would win his loyalty. My uncle made friends in Poland as well, marrying the Polish princess Anna Jagiellonka, since my uncle believed that country was Hungary's strongest ally and best hope against the machinations of the sultan in Constantinople and the Holy Roman Emperor in Bécs. His plans for a Hungary united with Poland against both the Turks and Austria excited many of the nobles of the old kingdom, dreaming of former glory. But after the old sultan died, the Ottomans would gradually grow less and less interested in the doings west of the Tisza, leaving Lower Hungary to a succession of pashas who never stayed long enough to make themselves at home in the palace at Buda. The nobles vied with each other, and with Bécs and Constantinople, for what was left of the old kingdom, so that no one managed to put up a serious threat to either.

Yet when I remember the Hungary of my childhood—a country torn apart by peasant revolts, by the disaster at Mohács, by the sultan's occupation—I remember not a world of dust and sorrow but the lights and music of my father's house in the marsh at Ecsed, where he and my mother entertained their friends and relatives from all over the remnants of the old kingdom. I remember the sounds of the cimbalom and the tambor, the swish of ladies' skirts as they moved in the dance, the softness of their voluminous white sleeves. I remember the servants lighting the lamps here and there in the house, illuminating the corridors, their faces glowing as if lit from within. It seemed a world full of hope still. It is a child's memory, surely colored by a brush of emotion, and yet in many ways it is more true to my experience than all the history I was to learn about later, about the sadness that came with being a Hungarian after Hungary, as we had always thought of it, had ceased to exist. When I think of your grandparents, Pál, it is always one endless celebration, days of light and music.

A few months after the birth of my youngest sister, my father hosted a tremendous gala in thanks for my mother's safe deliverance from the dangers of childbirth, and it was then that I saw how noble he really was, how good and kind a protector of his people. At that time there was a band of gypsies who camped in the village to sing and play at the festival, to dance and tell fortunes. I saw them coming down the castle bridge, speaking in the strange tongue that no outsider understands, bringing their instruments inside the great stone house with its whitewashed walls and green-tiled roof. Ecsed was crowded with family and friends. Aunts, uncles, and cousins came from Bécs, from Prága, from Pozsony and Gyulafehérvár to stay on the estate and spend nights drinking and dancing, bringing their servants and their children with them, their gifts of silk and strings of pearls and little prayers framed in gold. My cousin Griseldis

Bánffy—then just a child of seven but already so golden in her face and form that every woman in the room stopped to stroke her yellow curls—arrived with her parents in an enormous red carriage drawn by four matched white horses. Orsolya Kanizsay, the wife of the deceased palatine Tamás Nádasdy, came all the way across the country from her house at Sárvár, in the west, bringing as a gift a carpet of golden thread that had once belonged to the great king Mátyás Corvin himself. She had come to inspect me as a possible bride for her beloved only child, Ferenc Nádasdy, though I did not know it at the time.

All that week the house buzzed with preparations, with cleaning and cooking, with the baking of bread and the slaughtering of oxen and goats and capons to serve the guests. Great barrels of wine and enormous wheels of cheese were taken from the cellar, and stores of straw were brought in from the countryside to bed the many horses. For days there were voices in the corridors and the sounds of gypsy music coming from the banquet hall—the sting of a zither, the trill of a flute. The children of the other noble families, my cousins and friends, filled up the house with their shouts, their races and their games. As the eldest daughter of the house I was expected to entertain the other children, devise competitions and dances to keep them out of trouble. Little Griseldis especially I found difficult, for she was a spoiled and savage thing whose mother, having lost her other three children to the plague, indulged her every whim or desire. Every sweet Griseldis wanted, Griseldis got. Every order Griseldis gave, she expected the rest of us, no matter our superior age or position, to obey. I was patient with her for days and days, fetching her a bit of cake only minutes before the midday meal or letting her chase the puppies underfoot in the kitchen, but it was when she wrestled a doll away from Zsofia, who was a year younger and a whole head shorter, that I pinched the meat of her thigh until she cried and told her that if she didn't learn to behave like a civilized child I would lock her in a closet for the remainder of her visit. She whimpered and pouted, but after that she did what I asked without complaint, and I learned almost to enjoy her company.

She helped me the day I concocted a game of capture the flag to entertain the children's court, building small castles with bundles of firewood for the little ones to defend. I convinced István to put aside his religious tracts and instead set him the task of playing the Ottoman forces surrounding the gates of Buda, his head wrapped in a bit of old cloth for a turban, and for once he seemed to enjoy himself. The younger children, even Griseldis, laughed at how easily he fell down when they rained their blunt-tipped little arrows at him, how dramatic were his death throes, his heels beating at the dusty ground. She threw herself at him like a little *hájduk*, a bloodthirsty grin curving across her red mouth. I had to drag her away to get her to stop gleefully kicking him in the shins.

My role was to play the pasha's harem. I wrapped myself in pieces of bright gauzy silk, pouting like a wife, and demanded my "husband" pay more attention to me than to his wars, stomping my feet and threatening to kill myself for love until István would leave the castle siege and come give me a little kiss, placed tenderly on my mouth. "There," my brother said, sounding just like a husband, "that should hold you for now." Pleased with his attention, I went back to being the placated, dutiful wife for a few more minutes, but there was little for me to do except sit around and bat my eyelashes and pretend to fan myself. Eventually I gave Griseldis my piece of silk and let her do the pouting for me, which she managed only too well. Bored, I told István I was leaving him in charge while I checked on baby Klára and her wet nurse. István looked around at the little girls and boys of the children's court as they argued over the toy swords and arrows, as they cried and wrestled over the bundles of firewood, and begged me not to leave him there alone with the little savages. "Don't go, Erzsébet, for God's sake," he said. A panicked look crossed his face.

I laughed. "Don't worry," I said. "If they break anything, you can simply tie them to a post and leave them there till morning." I promised I would be right back after checking on the baby.

Once out of sight of the other children, though, I slipped down to the banqueting hall where the adults were drinking and dancing to the strains of the gypsy music and crawled under a table to keep out of sight. In the great hall the tables were set with delicate glass plates on which the servants brought meats red with paprika, great bunches of grapes like calf's brains, hot dumplings dripping with butter. The ladies, the Báthory cousins from Bécs and Prága, wore skirts of dark velvet and starched white blouses, and leather slippers too fine and soft to wear out of doors in the spring mud. But it was their faces I watched, the jealousy that stole across their countenances when they saw my mother, recovered by then from her confinement, her face flushed pink and her eyes alight under long dark lashes, bowing and smiling at a dozen men who crowded around her to offer their congratulations or beg to fetch her a glass of wine. Her ladies had dressed her hair in nets of pearls, stiffening the ruff at her neck and fastening it around her throat like a great white platter upon which to serve her beauty. She had a heart-shaped face, the face of love, my father called it. A tiny woman, no bigger than a half-grown girl and with a girl's lighthearted laugh and high, lilting voice, she was the envy of every noblewoman in the country, though she did not seek the company of the other women, preferring instead to spend her evening with the men. She conversed with her admirers in Latin or German on matters of history, philosophy, even warfare, earning her their respect and admiration even as she excited their desire. When she had entertained her guests enough, my father came and took her hand himself, and the two of them danced around the floor laughing and smiling into each other's faces. I longed to be like her, to dance and sing and be the object of everyone's attention, man and woman.

The nurse found me asleep under one of the tables, curled up on a bearskin, my stomach groaning. She took me up to bed, scolded me

roundly, and tucked me in, but long into the night I heard the gypsies playing and the throaty cry of their singing coming in through
my window. My heart thudded to the music with such happiness that
I could not sleep.

Long after midnight the party began to die down. One by one
the ladies and gentlemen fell on piles of furs or else went up to the
rooms my parents had prepared for them, falling against each other
on the stairways and in the halls in their drunken state. The gypsies
remained awake still, laughing and singing, drinking the strong apricot liquor called *pálinká* and eating the food left behind on the tables
by the fat and sleeping guests.

No one remembered afterward what started the argument. In
their drunkenness two of the gypsies began to fight, shoving and
cursing, knocking over the benches and waking the house, rousing
the servants and the guards alike. It ended when one man accused
the other of selling off his daughter to the Turks. The invaders were
feared all over the land when I was a child, particularly by girls. My
mother had told me stories of Turks snatching girls from their beds
in villages all over the country, selling them into slavery, into broth-
els, taking them back to Constantinople to hold for ransom. Nothing
was more terrible for a girl than the thought of being captured by the
Turks, and no Hungarian subject, not even a gypsy, would be permitted to collaborate with them without the direst consequences.

There were more shouts and accusations, and soon the gypsies
were calling for the lord of the house, demanding that my father
arrest the accused man then and there, have him taken in chains to
the dungeon to await trial for his crime. The accused man's friends
held him fast until my father, who as the lord of Ecsed was governor
of those lands, came down and sent for the guards. They bound his
hands and feet and transported him into the storage rooms of the
cellar, the bowels of the castle, to wait for the police.

It was near dawn, and the sky was lightening little by little in the
east. When he was gone, my father and his guests went back up to

bed, and the rest of the gypsies were sent out of the house to sleep in the fields surrounding the marsh.

When the local magistrate was brought in to preside over the trial the next morning, the accused man claimed the Turks had stolen his daughter, that he would never have sold her off. The police said they found a large amount of gold in his pockets and that the accused man had not been able to tell them where he had come by it. At first he said it was payment he'd received for selling several goats, then that he'd found it in a hollow tree along the road from Pozsony. None of it was true, of course. Saying that the man's crime could not go unpunished, and by way of making him an example to the local populace, my father asked the magistrate to sentence the gypsy to die outside the walls of the estate the next day. "For the sake of that poor girl," said my father afterward, embracing my mother as he came into her room, "there must be justice." The set of his jaw and the coldness in his expression made me shiver, for there was nothing in him in that moment of the father I knew and loved, only the great lord and landowner who was responsible for upholding the law in the village and all the surrounding lands. That my father could have more than one life—that he could be both my father and this stern authority figure, this great nobleman, at the same time—had never occurred to me before. He was father not just to me but to everyone who lived on his lands, including the wretched girl whose own flesh and blood had sold her off like a piece of livestock.

The gypsy was kept in the stables that night, locked in a stall and guarded by twelve men with guns. For long hours I could hear the condemned man standing at his window, crying and begging for mercy, his voice rising and building with wave upon wave of grief. Because I could not sleep, I stood at my windows and listened. *Save me, great lord, have pity on me,* he said in his strange accent, his voice breaking with emotion.

What would it be like, I wondered, to know you were going to die, and to know the death would not be a good one? I pictured the condemned man waiting in his cell, watching the moonlight move across the floor, marking the minutes of his last night on this earth. I pictured him alone, weeping and afraid, as I heard him calling out his despair. *Save me.* More often, though, I thought of his daughter. What might she be suffering now, if she even lived still? Her own father had handed her over to the invaders, listened with indifference as she begged him not to abandon her. *Save me.* What kind of callousness would it take for a man to accept his payment and turn away to leave with his own child crying out for him? It rent my heart. I, who was so beloved of my mother and father, could not imagine a fate worse than being made a slave, a whore, my virginity stolen, my body beaten. I tried to imagine what punishment would be fit for a man who had treated his own flesh with so much disdain. Would he have his eyes plucked out, his *heregolyó* removed with hot pincers? Would he be roasted alive atop a throne of iron, the way the rebel György Dósza had been after the peasant revolt? Nothing seemed like justice enough. I trembled with rage under my blankets, and that morning while my nurse was still asleep I slipped out of my rooms once again and down to the gate.

It was a soft misty morning in June, and the gray stone walls of the battlements were alive with bunches of greening lichen and strands of flowering ivy. Bits of white fog hovered over the house, over the wooden bridge that led away from the inner fortress. The revelers were still on the estate, and some of them had tumbled out onto the grass of the courtyard during the night and lay here and there, wrapped in cloaks and lying in piles of two and three. I hid behind the yews to avoid being seen, making my way to the front gate of the inner castle, and stepped onto the wooden bridge over the marsh. There the sun peeked through and lit the reeds with golden light, the herons moving on their long sticklike legs without a splash, searching for fish and frogs, and the insects went silent as I drew near. Finally I reached the outer battlements and then the road that led out of the marsh to a sloping grassy field. A copse of hawthorn partially hid the plain from view, but the tang of the mud and the reeds, the fertile smell of earth not yet planted, permeated everything.

In front of this idyll the place of execution was prepared. Even before I saw them I could hear the screams of the gypsy women, each word an arrow thrown at the accused man in their mysterious sharp language. A great crowd had gathered to see the condemned man's fate, and I hid among the skirts and trousers, scattering a flurry of pecking chickens as I made my way to the front of the crowd where the gypsy knelt on the ground, his hands tied behind him, the ties held by two of my father's soldiers. He seemed large to my nine-year-old eyes but was probably of medium height, with a dark pockmarked complexion and a bushy mustache that drooped at the corners with snot and tears, for he was blubbering and begging for mercy, turning his head around wildly to catch the eye of someone who would take up his cause.

Finally he addressed my father. Sir, he said, I am a guilty and sorry sinner. I have no right to ask, it's true, but please, sir, spare my life. Surely nothing good will come of killing one poor gypsy today, and so many guests still in your house. Surely you would not want such bad luck coming to your house during the celebration for the birth of your daughter.

My father would hear none of this. He said the condemned man had no right to speak of anyone's daughter, having sold his own. It was worse than the crime of Judas, a man selling his own child to the invaders. "As to bad luck," my father said, raising his great white head, "I would accept any on my house to be rid of the sight of you."

The condemned man slumped forward again, his chin against his chest in a faint. The soldiers held him by the rope that bound his wrists behind him, holding his weight at an unnatural angle, for his arms had been broken. He looked like nothing so much as the puppets my sister and I liked to play with in our rooms, sewed rags stuffed with straw and just as lifeless. My throat itched with unshed tears, but the sight of my father there and the stern tone of his voice when he addressed the man filled me with awe, so I hung back behind the skirts of the village women where no one would notice me.

A little bit away from the crowd the soldiers had taken a horse, an old and scrawny brown mare with a swayback and each of its ribs showing, and tied it to the ground with tight ropes around its legs so that even though it struggled and thrashed, it could not rise. The noise of panic it gave was the sound I had mistaken, from a distance, for the voices of the gypsy women, who were instead silent and grave at the spectacle my father had prepared.

One soldier stepped forward and slit the animal's tawny belly from front to hindquarters. It gave a scream and tried to kick out its legs, but it could not move, could not do more than shudder and heave as its bowels and blood spilled out onto the ground.

Quickly the soldiers stuffed the accused man inside the belly of the horse until only his head showed. Then one of the soldiers took a piece of cord and with a great curved needle and some rope began sewing up the horse's belly once more. The gypsy cried and begged for his life, but the soldier kept sewing. The horse was still alive but no longer had the strength to fight. Its eyes rolled back in its head, showing the whites. When the soldier was done, the man's head lay between the horse's rear legs as if the horse were birthing him, just as my sister's dark head had poked out between my mother's legs a few months before. It was the strangest sight I had ever seen—the soldiers standing around in their armor, watching a man sewed up inside a horse like a doll sewed up with its stuffing. A great bubble of laughter rose within me, a hard lump of awe and terror rising from my belly like a ball of unbaked bread that I had swallowed and would have to expel before it made me ill. Sputtering, the laugh escaped my lips. I clapped my hand over my mouth, but it was too late—I had been seen.

The man looked into my face and begged me to get a knife and cut him free, said that he had done nothing wrong. "Please, pretty child," he said in his strange, accented Hungarian, "please, I didn't hurt my daughter, you must know, she was a little girl your age, I would never hurt her. Please set me free, pretty one. I will give you a great reward." There was in his voice a malevolence that was new and strange to me, for terror ran underneath the kind words, and the look in his eyes was glittering and full of hate. What would he do to me, to the child of the man who condemned him, if I dared to set him free?

My feet were rooted to the spot, my hands clenched inside my skirt. But then my father was there, bending to scoop me up and take me back inside, scolding me for rising so early from my bed and running away from my nurse, though he could not bring himself to punish me, his favorite. He marched me back through the fortress and up to my room, scolding the nurse too for letting me slip away so easily. Then he kissed me and bade me back to sleep, which was impossible, and then closed the door after him.

I went to the window instead. Outside in the distance I could see the soldiers making their way back into the fortress, leaving the man behind to struggle and rot inside the belly of the dead horse. The other gypsies, the men who had accused him in their drunkenness, quickly packed their things and left Ecsed, ready to put the place and its sadness behind them. A few old gypsy women lingered long enough to curse and spit at the man for the sake of his vanished daughter, and then they, too, joined the rest of the gypsies in putting some distance between themselves and Ecsed village, and the estate of my mother and father, where bad luck was bound to linger.

All day I remained in my room thinking of the man inside the belly of the horse, of his thirst and pain, the smell and the flies. I ate no supper and went to bed so early and with so little fuss that my nurse told my mother I must have been ill.

Late that night I slipped out of the gate and went to the place where the man and the horse lay together, one dead and the other dying still. I found my way easily in the moonlight, following the gassy stench of entrails and old blood. The man was delirious and half mad, and at first he didn't know anyone was there, his head waving back and forth with the sudden, jerky movements of the demented and the dying. His skin was baked red and dry from a day in the sun, and his mustache was brittle with the tears and snot that had congealed there.

My footsteps were loud in the dry grass, and he turned his head back and forth to look, but I was behind him, momentarily hidden. "Is someone there?" he called out, but from where he was sewed inside the horse he could not turn his head and see me. "A drink, please," he begged. Nothing of the earlier menace remained in his voice; it was replaced with supplication, with pitiable chokes and sobs. "A sip of water is all I ask."

I stepped forward and showed myself to him in the moonlight. He roused himself and struggled. "I know you, child. You are the daughter of the lord of the house. Can you give me a little water? A sip for a dying man? I will ask nothing else, I promise, just a taste of cool water to ease my way into the next world, oh, please."

"I have no cup," I told him.

"Dip your skirt into the marsh water," he said. "You can bring it to my lips and wring it into my mouth. A drop or two is all I ask. You can do that much, can't you?"

I thought for a moment and then walked toward the edge of the marsh, where the reeds parted and a bit of dark water shone in the moonlight. I bent and let the hem of my skirt trail in the water, let the threads soak up the cool liquid. Then I walked back to the place where the condemned man lay. He beckoned me closer with a wag of his head and smiled, showing his pale gums, his strong white teeth, for he must have seen the dark stain on my skirt where I had dipped it into the water. "Yes," he said. "Yes, come closer, child, and wring that cloth into my mouth. God will reward you for showing kindness to a dying man."

I stepped forward, lifting the hem of my skirt. The gypsy opened his mouth and closed his eyes, ready for the drink, but I stood back several inches from his face and wrung my skirt out onto the dusty ground, onto the dried entrails of the poor horse that had died for the sins of the man. The water dropped onto the dust and vanished.

The man, hearing the sound, opened his eyes, struggling and cursing. I spit in his face, and the white spittle caught in his mustache and hung there like a bit of spider silk. I was never so satisfied as I was at that moment, watching him suffer. I thought of his daughter, of her fear and pain, of her sadness that no one in this world had stepped forward to protect her, not even the man who should have loved her most. I spit at him again as he wailed in his strange language about the agony of thirst, of loneliness, of death. I bent my face close to his, so close I could smell the *pálinká* on his breath still, and something else, something rotten coming up from within like old death, but I was not afraid.

"You suffer too little," I told him, and went back up to bed.

# 4

How strange are the memories that rise up when one is deprived of sleep and warmth, of all the comforts of ordinary life. I remember so well the gypsy man and the anger I felt, the exact timbre of the wail that rose from his throat, my cousin Griseldis and her yellow curls, though I cannot remember the name of the guard standing outside my door or what the old steward, Deseő, said to me this morning when he brought my tray. Perhaps I am simply growing old, thick with memories and dreams, another old woman who fears to sleep in case she will not wake again.

I remember the first time I spoke to Orsolya Kanizsay, the way she bent down to look into my face like a horse trader in the market, deciding how much to pay for this year's foals. Your grandmother was one of the grand ladies in the room the night I slipped away to the great hall to watch the guests dancing and drinking and falling in love to the sounds of the gypsy music, before drunkenness and greed spoiled the party. She must have watched me carefully all that week while I greeted the guests and helped my mother, while I entertained my sisters and cousins. Apparently she found nothing objectionable in my behavior, for the morning after I made my visit to the gypsy man my mother came to fetch me early from my bed, flinging back the shutters to let in a shaft of burning light and telling me to dress myself at once. "Half the house is already up for the day," she said, "and here you are still in bed. What will Countess Nádasdy think?"

"Why should she think anything?" I asked.

"Erzsébet," said my mother, "I need you to get up and dressed at once. The countess is the most important person at the party. She has asked to see you, and you will oblige her or so help me I will beat you with a willow switch until you cannot sit. You will be sweet and charming and dutiful, and that is all you will be."

She had the nurse wrestle me into a clean dress and yank the knots out of my hair with a comb, tears starting from my eyes with each tug. István, passing by the door, must have seen the expression of pain on my face, for he stopped to laugh at my expense, so angry was he that I had left him alone in the children's court while I snuck down to the party. My mother caught sight of him enjoying my misery and said, "Go check on your cousins, István, for God's sake. Make yourself useful." And she closed the door on his antics until I was dressed and ready for my interview with Countess Nádasdy.

When I was dressed, we hurried downstairs to my father's library, where he sat across the table from a grand lady with silvered dark hair and a dress of deepest black. A widow's dress. I had seen her at the party, of course, and knew who she was, since my mother had taken special trouble to introduce me to her the night she arrived, but I did not know what was so important that now I was summoned to speak with her and my parents alone, while the other guests were gathering for the midday meal.

I curtsyed, waiting to be spoken to as my mother had taught me, and stood back. Lead cream whitened Orsolya's spotted cheeks, giving her a waxen, carved kind of look, her reddened mouth in a round *O*, her eyebrows plucked and arched into permanent surprise. I did not like her cosmetics, having heard my mother say often that women who whitened their skin and blooded their lips were nothing but ridiculous old crones who wished to catch a young husband. Around her neck she wore a great jewel, a ruby as large as my nine-year-old fist surrounded by a circlet of gold bent into the shape of a rose. My fingers itched to stroke the delicate metalwork, the polished red surface of the ruby. Countess Nádasdy is the most important person at the party, my mother had said, and when I looked at that jewel I knew that it must be so. I curled my fingers into my palms. Without knowing entirely why, I smiled and bowed and said what an honor it was to meet her, that I had heard of the greatness of Countess Nádasdy and wished to serve her however I may. "Please," I said to my shoes, "be as one of our own family during your stay."

The countess bent and cupped my chin in her cool whitened hand. "My goodness, Anna," she said, "what a silver tongue this one has. You must be terribly proud of her. And such a face! Ferenc will love her fine dark eyes, her pretty little mouth. No, I do not think he could do any better."

My father, who loved me above all his children, first insisted that I was too young to be betrothed to anyone. "She should be at least twelve before we decide," he said, and cut a pleading look at his wife. But my mother, who knew that the young Nádasdy boy was heir not only of his father's name and title and political goodwill but his mother's vast Kanizsay fortune, took my father aside. The deal should be struck, she told him, before the groom's eye—or more important, his mother's—roamed elsewhere. So while my mother took me back upstairs, confused and relieved, Orsolya and my father struck a rich bargain: his daughter for her son, and a dowry of so much gold it could hardly be counted, so many castles and villages they could hardly be named, from one end of Upper Hungary to the other. The Báthorys and the Nádasdys would be united in marriage, in name and in blood. It would be, they thought, the beginning of a new dynasty, one that would rival the Habsburgs themselves. For two families with aspirations to independence—to a new line that would free Hungary of the Habsburgs in the west, of the Turks in the east—nothing could have been sweeter.

For myself, I understood little of what was happening in the library that afternoon. It was only later that my strange audience with Orsolya made sense to me, and I wondered again and again what would have happened that day if I had refused to climb out of bed when my mother came in that morning, if I had spoken to Orsolya like a fishwife and not the respectful daughter of a noble-man. After what my mother had told me about finding a husband to love me for my beauty, I never imagined that it would be my dowry that made the bargain, my family name and connections, my good manners and potential children. I knew only that I had passed some kind of test, and I was pleased because my mother was pleased with me. That night Orsolya and my parents toasted to the bargain, hold-ing up glasses of my father's best wine and signing their names to the paper that decided my fate, while upstairs in my bed I dreamed of gypsy music, of moonlight, of a great red jewel that hung low in the sky, always just out of my reach.

# 5

The bad luck the gypsy promised did not come until a few years afterward, but when it did, it did its work swiftly and left my family forever changed. What happened was that my father died suddenly, of a heart seizure that took him while he was dining with my mother in the evening, late, not long after Christmas. He had only picked at his food all night, complaining of heartburn, and was standing up to go to his bed when he slumped forward and hit his head on the table with such force that my mother, for many years afterward, insisted it was this injury that killed him and not the seizing of his old and soft heart. When he hit the floor—I heard the old steward swear it, the one who witnessed the whole thing—he was already dead.

I was reading to the little girls in another part of the house and heard my mother's cry, a sharp sound like the one the pigs made when their throats were slit. I went running toward it. Klára asked, "What was that, Erzsébet? What?" as she grabbed at my skirts, but I was already ahead of her, rushing away.

I reached my mother before anyone else, saw her slumped across my father's body on the floor, an overturned wineglass dripping red onto her white sleeves. I threw myself on her, thinking she had been hurt. I could not yet see my father's face, but my mother's eyes were closed, her mouth open as if she were trying to speak. The house was in an uproar, servants coming from everywhere to witness the commotion or to try to help, my mother's ladies swarming, the ancient steward helplessly picking at the bits of glass that had spread across the floor. With a greater strength than I had ever possessed I pulled my mother off my father and pinched her face, her hands, trying to get her to see me. Her skin in my fingers was cold and clammy. "*Anyu!*" I cried, calling for my mother even as the servants dragged me back, my legs beating at the air.

Finally it was my brother, István—appearing slowly on the scene as if he had known, even then, that he was already the lord of the manor—who told me at last to stop acting like a madwoman, that our mother was fine but our father was beyond our help. "He's dead," said my brother, poking our father's body with one long finger as if testing the temperature of an undesirable dish on the dinner table. "Look."

I stopped crying and gathered myself, brushing off the hands of the servants who were restraining me, breathing slowly until I felt calm again. It was true—all the color had drained from my father's large pink face, his eyes wide open and staring as if at an apparition that had come for him in the last moment, and I wondered if there could not be any peace in death, despite what the priests and my mother and father had so often insisted, no reunion of the dead with the dead, and for many nights afterward I could not sleep, thinking of the look on my father's face, thinking that perhaps there was no heaven waiting for us at all, nor hell either, but only other spirits, neither good nor evil, that came in the last moments to carry our souls away.

The old women said they would take care of my mother and father, carry my mother to her bed and my father to the winding-sheet. "Take the little ones up to bed," they said, so that was what I did. I gathered Klára and Zsófia to me, the three of us huddled on top of the blankets all night, waiting for our mother to come in, to comfort us in our sorrow. My sisters' small damp hands kept touching my face all through the night, as if making sure I lived and breathed.

We buried him a month later in the family vault, on a cold bright morning after a heavy snow, our breath stolen from us as we walked behind his corpse to the church, so that it looked like our souls, too, were being torn away. My mother had been forcibly dressed and removed from her bed by her ladies. She could barely walk and had to be supported by István, clutching at his jacket and wrapping her arms around his neck. Her hair kept straggling out of its net, and her fine pale skin was blotchy and haggard. I thought she was making a terrible spectacle of herself and shrank in embarrassment for all the guests and other mourners to see her so undone, so undignified.

Before long the procession made it inside the church. I had been told by the nurse that it was my job to keep the little girls quiet at least through the service. Think of your father, she said, and how you would want him remembered. I did as she bade me. As we took our seats I fingered the hidden sweets in my pockets—sugared dates, Klára's favorite treat, swiped from the kitchen that morning. At eight years old, Zsófia was really too old to bribe, old enough to behave herself in church at least, but at only three years old Klára could not be trusted to be quiet and would need to be paid off in sugar. Zsofía would whine if she saw Klára get something she herself did not, so I had brought enough for both of them. I could hear them chewing as the priest began his service.

The bier on which my father lay was strewn with pine boughs and mistletoe and sprinkled with droplets of fragrant oils to cover the smell that was beginning to emanate from it, a smell somehow sweet and sickening, like an uncured animal skin left too long in the sun. I couldn't connect the smell or the frozen corpse on the bier to my father, the man who had danced with my mother the night of the gypsy ball. I half expected him to come up behind me and lift me under the arms and place me on his shoulders as he used to do when he felt jolly or had been drinking, or both. It was a mistake, I felt, to have his funeral without him.

I kept looking to István, to see what he would do, but I was seated behind him, since he was my father's heir and my mother's confidant, and I could not see his face nor gauge what he was thinking while the service was beginning. In the days since my father's death I had rarely seen my brother, not even in passing in the halls or at mealtimes. My family was becoming alien to me, strange without my father there at its center to hold us all together. That morning the back of my brother's head and the shoulders of his black fur-trimmed cloak were damp with melting snow, and I could smell his familiar scent of hay and warm skin, but I felt as far from him as I did from the dead man on the bier. Suddenly my father was dead and my brother was the lord of Ecsed, in title if not in authority. Already I could see how my mother had started to depend on him, asking his advice on the funeral service and conferring with him for long hours over the eulogy and burial. He grew more solemn than usual, spent hours on his knees in prayers in the chapel of the estate, or behind the locked door of his room, scribbling away on bits of paper. At sixteen he was five years older than me and had reached his majority. He would assume my father's titles, and leave the children's court to me and to the little girls to become a real lord and master rather than a play one, and no amount of begging would persuade him otherwise. István was taking our father's place, and I my mother's, as the guardian and protector of the little girls and the myriad younger cousins who tumbled in and out of the house at Ecsed. István and I were children no longer. What my mother had said long ago was true, that the fate of the family belonged to us now.

I willed my brother to turn around, to turn and look at me, to smile or speak a word of comfort as he had always done. But his back was straight, his narrow shoulders even. He could not read my thoughts, no matter how much I wished it.

The pastor was saying that my father was a man of tremendous learning and nobility, a great lord and statesman, that Hungary had lost one of its most valuable treasures and the Báthory family its greatest hero. "His name will ring for a thousand generations," the pastor said, his face appropriately grave. At one point István looked back at me and rolled his eyes, and for that moment he was still the István I remembered and loved. I had to suppress the laugh that came up, covering my face with my hands as if to hide my tears, my shoulders shaking, and then I was ashamed, because I had loved my father and wanted to mourn him properly. Zsofía crowded in close to comfort me, and I let her. In the front row, next to István, my mother's back was as straight as a poker and just as unyielding, though I knew she had spent most of the last month prostrate with mourning. When the service was over, István, the new lord of the manor, took her arm and led her back to the sled, the little girls and I following close behind. My mother's feet left deep prints in the snow, and as I walked I stepped into them one by one, to make the going easier.

# 6

A few weeks after my father's death, Orsolya Kanizsay wrote to my mother asking if I might be sent to her house at Sárvár, where she would welcome me into the family as a daughter and finish my education as I adjusted to life among the Nádasdys. At eleven years old I would be sent away to be raised as a proper young lady, a highborn wife for Countess Nádasdy's only child. My mother called me into her room one evening to give me Orsolya's letter to read. The greeting alone took up nearly an entire page:

> *My good sister Anna, may the eternal, almighty Lord first strengthen us in the true religion by His holy faithfulness and promise, that all error be kept far from us, that we may be at one with the Christian Holy Mother Church in soul and body, and that we may walk in the true faith and in mutual love; and that He may cause you, my friend, to prosper greatly, for which I hope, and trust and believe that it will be so, and I believe of a certainty that He will wish to raise you up for trust in Him alone, amen.*

I saw the cramped, uncertain hand of a woman who had come to her education late in life, after her marriage, the awkwardly formal inflections and errors in grammar and thought that even at eleven years old I knew were the mark of an inferior mind. The words seemed kindly at least, thanking my mother in warm tones for the generosity of the dowry and for the honor of joining the house of Báthory to the house of Nádasdy, a union that would benefit both families and the country, and so on and so on. If my mother agreed to the arrangements, she wrote, she would send a carriage for me within the month.

I handed the letter back to my mother, assuming she would not consider sending me away so soon after my father's death. Girls in those days usually did not marry until fifteen or sixteen, and I had thought, after the documents were signed at the time of the gypsy ball, I would have at least five or six years at home still with my mother and father, my brother, and my little sisters before my marriage to the Nádasdy boy, in the far western part of the kingdom where I was unlikely to see them often. Though it was not unusual for girls to be sent to their mothers-in-law long before the wedding, I had always assumed that my own mother would not want me so far away from her, that I would be permitted to remain home for a while longer still.

When I said this to my mother—that I was honored, but preferred to remain home for the intervening years between that moment and the actual date of the marriage—she looked away. "Very well," she said. "I will write to her and tell her you wish to stay at home for a little while longer." Then she lay back on the pillows and closed her eyes, asking me to shut the door as I went out.

This I did, reluctantly. My mother had never taken well to my father's absences, when he would travel on matters of business or politics, and after my father's death she spent her life in bed, rarely sleeping or eating but unable to rise and face the world. She was not made for widowhood. Where other women might see the freedom that comes with the death of a husband—the release from duty and possession, the authority that comes from being a powerful widow and a landowner in her own right—my mother saw only the end of everything. It was as if she had died along with my father, for she was not the same afterward, rarely lighthearted or smiling, and the parties and balls that she and my father had so often hosted at Ecsed came to an abrupt end. She still had her immense wealth and beauty, but my father had written his will such that if she did remarry, she would lose the right to raise her children, a not-uncommon practice among the nobility of my father's acquaintance and temper but a difficult one to stomach for a woman like my mother. He did not want to see his children subjected to the whims of a stepfather, perhaps, or maybe he simply knew my mother's nature and wanted to keep her in thrall to his memory—to keep her his, body and soul, until the end of her life. Whatever his reasons, my mother was not permitted to remarry. György Báthory's widow she was, and György Báthory's widow she would remain.

Over the years I would come to see the cruelty in this decree, the jealousy and servitude. If my father had allowed her to keep her children, my mother might have rallied and found a new husband as well as some hope for what was left of her life. Instead my mother took to her bed. She ran the affairs of the estate as best she could with her head propped up against the pillows and her hair undone around her shoulders, her eyes shadowed with crying and sleepless-ness as she wrote her letters or spoke to the servants. Her jewels and fine clothes began to gather dust, her body falling abruptly into old age. She was a changed creature, hollow-eyed, her legs and arms too thin, the bones showing through her skin and her voice growing small, far away, as if it could not reach the tremendous heights of her mouth. Some women, like Orsolya, dressed in black to show the world their loss at the death of a husband. For my mother, it would be as if her spirit had cloaked itself in widow's weeds instead.

During the daylight hours she remained distant from the chil-dren who loved her so, impatient with our antics and the too-quick (to her mind) healing of our hearts over our father's death, but nights she would call to one of us to sleep with her in her bed, and even István, who was sixteen when our father died and far too old to be crawling in bed with his mother, would oblige her, wrapping his arms around her neck and letting her sleep against his shoulder. At first we went hoping for a return of the mother we knew, a brief glimpse of love, but then she would frighten us with the sounds she made in her sleep and we would steal away again and find our way to our own beds once more. Eventually we began to resent these requests, to avoid them even. István and I would bargain with each other over whose turn it was supposed to be. If he spent the night with Mother for me, I said, I would copy the verses of the Bible our tutor had given us to memorize. If I went for him, he said, he would watch

Klára and Zsofía two whole afternoons so I could take my pony outside the walls of the estate. Thus my mother's charms had worn off with her mourning, so that even her own children bribed each other to avoid her company.

Since our father's death Klára especially preferred to sleep with me, whimpering and clinging to me whenever our mother requested her presence at night, but I would take her to our mother and pull the blankets over her and whisper in her small seashell of an ear that as soon as Mother fell asleep, Klára could slide from her grasp and slip back to the bed we shared. I would kiss her and go. In the middle of the night my sister would push her small dark head under my elbow until I made way for her and took her in my arms, and then she would fall into a deep and dreamless sleep, her sweet breath on my face and her hands curled in my hair. Klára did not understand why her mother needed her so, how the loss of love can warp the spirit, and I suppose I did not blame her for preferring me. I was glad, having lost my mother to this hollow-eyed ghost, this phantom, to have another human creature to cling to.

The promised delay of my departure relieved me, though for several weeks afterward it seemed I couldn't stop hearing the name Nádasdy. It was on the lips of every servant in the house, of my brother and sisters. Zsofía clamored to know how far away the countess lived, what she looked like, how large a carriage she would send for me when the time came. The Nádasdys were there when I bathed or when I ate, when I slept or dressed or bent over my lessons. From the beginning of my engagement I had tried to shut out thoughts of Sárvár, tried not to imagine the different foods they might serve there, the different smells of the woods and streams in the far western edge of the country, on the borders with Habsburg Austria. I had been to Bécs once with my mother and father when I was small, but other than that I knew little of the part of the country in which my future family lived. Orsolya's estates at Keresztúr and Sárvár would be nothing like Bécs, so busy and crowded that one could hardly walk through the streets and squares. My new home at

Sárvár would be considerably smaller than Bécs but less remote than the marsh fortress at Ecsed. The old palatine, my betrothed's father, had brought intellectuals and musicians from as far away as Padua and Amsterdam to live and entertain at his court when he had been palatine. I hoped that Ferenc Nádasdy would be natural and outgoing and free, not stern and formal and reclusive like my brother, István, who was the same age as my husband-to-be but more than ever was becoming strange to me. I hoped Ferenc would love me enough to protect my family for my sake, that his love would be like a strong roof to keep out the rain and the wind and the snow.

Once I asked my mother to tell what she knew of the Nádasdy family that she had not already said. She had known Orsolya Kanizsay through her first husband, and they had talked many times at balls and dinners in Bécs or Pozsony. We were in my mother's room, and I was sitting on the edge of her bed staring at the shape of her feet moving underneath the blankets, like two moles disturbing a fresh grave. "Do not worry, my love," she said. "You will be married, and you will be happy. You will be as happy as I was with your father. Ferenc Nádasdy will be a powerful man, and a powerful man always needs a powerful woman by his side."

She didn't mention love, nor the fact that her own first husband had been her personal choice, a love match, and so had the second, and the third. She opened her arms for an embrace, and I went to her, because I didn't know what else to do then or how to disappoint her. The truth was that the idea of being a wife terrified me, if it meant ending up like my mother, this miserable woman, this three-time widow. I would rather have raced my pony across the fens or taken my little sisters to gather robins' eggs in the woods. I would rather have run away to Bécs, to Prága, to Paris, to dissolute Venice or sunny Rome or even cold, faraway London, where the queen who shared my name remained unmarried, a virgin still and beholden to no man.

Instead I waited until my mother released me, kissed my brow, and sent me out again. Afterward I ran out of the house to the stables, clambering up to hide in the hayloft with a book, staying there so long that I fell asleep and forgot to eat my evening meal, but it was the only place where I would not have to hear the name Ferenc Nádasdy, or think of the life that was lying in wait for me.

# 7

My mother had seen to my formal education from an early age, bringing the best instructors from the school on her first husband's estate to stay with us. With our brother, my sisters and I learned to read the works of Herodotus, of Thomas Aquinas, of Paracelsus, learned the formal inflections of Hungarian, German, Greek, and Latin at the knees of our tutor, Leopold, a stern and ugly German who was fond of beating his young charges with a green willow stick, leaving a pattern of narrow red welts on our buttocks and the backs of our legs if we didn't recite our lessons swiftly enough or in their proper order—a punishment our parents put a stop to when they learned of it, but not until I had at least three times felt the sting of Leopold's whip.

I was not a good student at first, so easily distracted by little things—a swallow that flew down the chimney into the house, or my father's hunting dogs birthing a litter of pups, or the first breaking of the sun on a cloudy day—that it was no surprise I didn't enjoy my studies. Whenever Leopold would turn his back, I would run to the stables and take my pony for a ride or hide in a corner of the kitchen, on top of the place where the linens were stored, to take an afternoon nap. Later, when I could read and write more easily, when I learned that the books I had been reluctant to open contained an escape so true, so complete that not even the tutor could prevent me from flying beyond the walls of the house, I began to appreciate what he was trying to teach me. I read—I read by firelight, by candlelight.

I read in the stables and at the table at supper, read science and astronomy, especially the works of Copernicus and the treatises of Tycho Brahe, about the order and movements of the heavens. My mother, before she was a widow, used to say I would ruin my eyes with so much reading. "You will develop a squint," she would say, kneeling down to take the volume out of my hands and set it aside. "What will you do then? No man will have you." This idea gave me pause for some little bit of time until I realized that she was teasing me and that she herself had read every book I put my hand on. Then she would laugh and give me the book back again.

After my father's death, my mother began a new instruction for me, lessons on the duties and arts of a wife that seemed often to me to be more about her own heart than mine. "Your husband will desire you," she told me, "and you must take care to keep his desire from being ever fully satisfied. Never make yourself too available to him, but always hold yourself back a little. Never tell him all the secrets of your heart, for then you will be in his power, rather than he in yours." This last was said with a little smile.

I wondered at her words, if this indeed was the philosophy of love by which she had ensnared not only one but three husbands, and I began to feel a measure of pity for my poor father, whose mind and body had been in thrall to the fierce charms of this woman, my mother.

She taught me about my monthlies, how they would come and go with the cycles of the moon until I was married and took my new husband into my bed and opened myself to him. Then I would be able to expect a child. When I gave him a son, my husband would value me above all the land in the kingdom. You will be his greatest treasure, she said, and cupped my chin in her soft hand, and for a long time I believed it.

Each day after she was done with my instruction, my mother would allow me to choose a book for my own. Despite my dislike of my lessons in the wifely arts, I thrilled in this reward and spent many hours poring over the books to pick the most beautiful or most interesting. I chose among others an ancient copy of Aristotle's *Poetics* in

Latin, the first to be printed in Europe, and a beautiful illuminated bible that had once belonged to her own mother and that I loved because the pictures of Mary, adorning the story of the birth of the Christ child, bore a striking resemblance to me. Each book I chose was a memento to take into my future life, a future I still believed was years away.

Yet it happened that only a month after the arrival of her letter, my future mother-in-law sent word that her steward Imre Megyery, her late husband's cousin and her most trusted adviser, was coming to Ecsed as my escort on her behalf, as her letter had originally stated. When I demanded that my mother hold to her promise to let me stay at home a little longer, she simply sighed and asked me to be on my best behavior and offered no explanation for her betrayal. "Please, Erzsébet," she said. "Be grateful. Your match with the Nádasdy boy is the envy of every girl in the land. The countess has asked for you, and I have no reason to deny her. She will be your family now, and you must do everything you can to please her." So Megyery was to fetch me and bring me back to my mother-in-law's estate in western Hungary, far from the comforts and familiarity of everything I had ever known, and that was the end of the discussion.

For days ahead of time the house was in an uproar, the servants cleaning the house top to bottom, the scents of baking bread and roasting meat spilling into every hall and chamber as they had not done since before my father's death. There were no gypsies and no music, but there was polished silver and good wine, and the light of many candles. The rooms echoed with the chatter of the girls in the sewing rooms, the lower answering voices of the household boys who stole to the door to watch them at their work. The house was alive again, and if the end of the festivities had not included my own departure, I would have been dancing in the halls in anticipation. But I didn't want to meet Imre Megyery, or Countess Nádasdy, or her son. I didn't want to leave my brother and my sisters, or my home. Instead, I snapped at everyone, slapped the servants, and ran away when the younger children needed me. I spent most of that week hiding beneath tables or up trees, my hair so full of bits of branches and berries it looked like a bird's nest. My brother, when he found me hiding in a hawthorn bush at the edge of the marsh, covered with owl's down, said he would cut off all my long hair if I didn't start taking care of it, like a lady should. "And if you do not start behaving like a good and grateful daughter," he said, "I will have you locked up until it's time for you to leave." I was tempted for a moment to take him up on this threat, so few were my days remaining at home, but instead I chose what little freedom I had left, promising to behave and putting on a mask of civility that I didn't feel in the least.

Imre Megyery arrived at Ecsed one afternoon when I was in the stables with the little girls. We were playing with the puppies that had recently been born, sitting in the straw and holding the bits of mewling fur in the lap of my dusty skirt, Zsofía squealing with delight as a puppy licked her face, Klára crying because one of them had scratched her with its sharp toenails. A red welt rose up in the place where the puppy had clambered too eagerly over Klára's legs, and I was bending to rub away a spot of blood when a servant came running to the stable and asked for me.

"What is it?" I asked.

"The guests are arriving, miss," she said. "Your mother sends word that you are to dress and join her in the courtyard."

I stood and went out into the courtyard, to the gate, and went up the steps to look out to the road beyond the marsh. In the distance a great carriage rattled, raising a line of fine brown dust. They would be at Ecsed within the hour, but I walked slowly into the house, refusing to rush. I was seized with a sudden desire to dash back into the stable, pick up the puppies, and bury my face in their soft fur, to climb into their nest of straw and hide among them. My heart sank as I knew my last days at home were upon me.

In the house my mother was rushing around and agitating the servants. "Erzsébet, my God, you are a disaster," she said. "Put on your good skirt, the one with the roses on it. Your mother-in-law's representative will be here any minute. He must not think you are a wild girl, with no manners or education."

I could not speak for fear of weeping. Somehow the servant girls got me dressed in a new skirt and blouse, picking the straw out of my hair and rebraiding it, but all I could see was poor little Klára who sat on a chair with her dark eyes brimming, asking if the man was coming to take me away. I stood up and kissed her. "Yes, my love," I said. "But not right away. We still have a few days together."

My little sister collapsed in a fit of tears, at which my mother threw up her hands and declared me impossible. "Why would you tell her such things, when you know it will only make her cry?"

A few minutes later I joined my mother and brother in the courtyard of the house and waited for the door to the carriage to open. The horses heaved and sweated in the sunlight, but the inside of the carriage remained shadowed, so that I could not see clearly who was inside. Imre Megyery would not officially arrive until I stood there myself to welcome him. Finally I took my place, and at some appointed signal the door opened.

"Erzsébet Báthory?"

"I am Erzsébet."

A tall gentleman, pale and froglike, with enormous bulging eyes and long, tapering fingers with small pads of fat at the tips, stepped through the door of the carriage and planted his feet like a sultan in the grassy courtyard. He was young, perhaps no more than twenty-five, but his reddish-blond hair was thin on his head already, and his beard was thick and coarse, a darker red than the hair on his head, as if his face and his scalp were competing for ugliness. I could hardly have said what I was expecting, except that it was not this reptile. He reached out one of his white hands to stroke my hair and my cheek. "She is indeed a pretty child," he said, to no one in particular, and I had to keep myself from recoiling. "I am Imre Megyery, Count Nádasdy's cousin, come to welcome you to my mistress's house."

"But we aren't yet in your mistress's house," I said, "we are in my father's. I welcome you to Ecsed and hope you will enjoy the break in your long journey while you are with us."

"Well said," Megyery answered. "My mistress will be glad to welcome you to her family."

My mother smiled at the exchange of formalities, relieved that I didn't embarrass her at this most crucial moment, that I remembered my place and fell into the role appointed for me. I have always known the role I was meant to play and could play it when it suited me, or when I knew I must, such as I did that day when I followed my brother and Megyery into the mouth of the castle at Ecsed, my home for only a few days more.

I watched the countess's man closely over those few days, trying to surmise what I could of my future husband's demeanor from his cousin's face. Megyery was known as "the Red" due to the distinctive color of his beard, my mother had told me, but such a name suited a warrior, not this tadpole bowing and scraping to do the countess's bidding. He was much reviled by my mother's female servants, who deemed him too ugly even to sleep with. "So ugly," said one, in a whisper that did not take my presence into account, "that even the vultures would spit him back out." I too had to suppress the urge to laugh at his stiff and formal demeanor when we sat at supper, or walked in the garden, or read in the evenings by candlelight. He was interested in everything I touched—what I was reading, what I was wearing, how I tended to the younger children—and had comments for me on all of them.

Once he was present when Klára came to me begging for something to eat, some little thing to quiet her stomach until suppertime. Our suppers had been later since Megyery's arrival, on account of the elaborate nature of the meals my mother had ordered. Klára, who was not yet four, had found it especially difficult waiting an extra hour or so until the cooks had finished, so when she came to me that afternoon I went out to the kitchen and found her some dried dates, which she stuffed in her mouth until she could barely talk.

Megyery, who had been reading by himself in my father's leather chair, frowned at what he must have seen as my indulgence of my sister's whims.

"Is something the matter?" I asked.

"No, my dear," he said, with the barest hint of kindness, and for a moment he seemed to go back to his reading. Then he looked up again, setting the book on his knee. "I was thinking that a little hunger wouldn't harm the child. Countess Nádasdy never gave Ferenc a sweet so soon before dinner. She would say it might spoil his appetite."

His hand was settled still on the book, as if he expected me to thank him for his officiousness in telling me how to manage my charges. "The countess sounds like a very wise lady," I said, biting off every word. "I only hope that someday I can be as learned as she."

At this he brightened at once, picking up his book and going back to his reading. "I'm sure you will be."

I said nothing else. Megyery was Orsolya's man, and she would surely hear reports of everything I said and did. My brother and mother had both taken the trouble to warn me that if I got off on the wrong foot with Orsolya my life at Sárvár would be a difficult one. Considering the man whom she had sent to me as her representative, I didn't doubt them at all. So I held my tongue and pulled Klára out of the room after me, where we might continue unseen by Megyery until suppertime.

When the day came for my departure, the courtyard filled with servants and friends and family to see me off. My small cousins were there, and my sisters. The little girls wept. My mother was there, too, her heart-shaped face shining with tears at the solemnity of this event, the leaving of her eldest daughter. The sight of her standing in the courtyard in her elegant black mourning dress trimmed in gold braid, her hair piled on her head and fastened with pearl-encrusted combs for the occasion, sobered me immediately, for I knew she thought we might never see each other again, and it was this image she was presenting to me to remember her by. Truly I was leaving

Ecsed forever. She embraced me, and I received her blessing, her hands resting on top of my hair. "Be a kind and dutiful daughter to Countess Nádasdy," she said, not missing one last opportunity for a lesson. "Give her no reason to send you home again." Then I kissed the little girls good-bye, and my brother. I put my arms around István's neck, and he embraced me too, kissing me like he had the day he played the pasha and I the pasha's harem, his expression curious, as if he were seeing me for the first time. The little girls cried and begged to go with me. I wondered when, or if, I would see any of them again.

I felt very alone as the countess's steward helped me up into the carriage before him and ordered the horses to start. Then I was waving good-bye to Ecsed, to the marsh where the dragon had roared, to the herons and frogs, to the litter of puppies barking in the straw, to my pony with its braided mane. I was moving forward, into my new life, into my future as a wife, a mother, a countess. The willow trees swayed in the wind as we passed, and a few tears fell onto the lap of my skirt. I vowed to try to love the countess and her son, but I would not let them change me or transform me into someone I was not. The hills and trees moved past me, the green tops of the wheat swaying in the wind. I would not be like the wheat, bending to any little breeze. I would be like the rocks and the hills, firm and unyielding in all things, even if I never saw my mother or my brother or my sisters again, even if I forgot my home, my language, my upbringing, the love of my mother and father, the beating of my own heart. I would live my life among strangers, and I would remember myself. I would never let them alter me.

There is a saying I learned as a child: *Extra Hungariam non est vita et si est vita, non est ita,* which means, "Beyond Hungary there is no life, and if there is life, it is not the same." To me, the familiar world of Ecsed was all of Hungary that existed.

In the carriage I dried my tears. The life I was driving toward would be mine, my own life on my own terms, even if it was not the same as the one I had known.

# 8

It took almost two weeks to reach my mother-in-law's house at Sárvár by carriage, weeks in which we sometimes climbed over mountain passes and had to get out and walk to spare the horses, or through low marshes where the wheels often stuck in the mud and needed to be pulled free, but most often through valleys of cultivated fields—fields of wheat and rye, of grapevines, of hay stacked to dry in the sun in two-legged bundles. We passed through ancient villages where statues of the madonna and child still stood in public squares, their feet strewn with flowers, villages where children came out to watch the procession of carriages wind through the center of town, shouting and chasing us for a little way. Sometimes I leaned out of the window to wave like an empress while they clapped and cheered, despite Megyery's stern disapproval.

Because of the possibility of impropriety in sending a man to escort her future daughter to the house at Sárvár, my mother-in-law had in addition sent a woman named Anna Darvulia, a servant, as my chaperone. She was a tiny creature, fearsome despite her simple clothing, with small glittering black eyes and a few white chin whiskers that gave her a fierce, badgerish look. She wore her impressive tangle of thick black hair in a knot bound at the base of her neck and spoke only when spoken to, in a voice as deep as a man's. On the first day of our journey I asked her how old she was, and she fixed me with those strange animal eyes and said she guessed at least twenty-three. "No one knows for certain," she said. "My mother never told me." What had happened to her mother? I was afraid to ask. Perhaps Darvulia was a gypsy or a Turk in disguise, or at the very least a *táltos*, a shaman born with six fingers or a full set of teeth. I kept trying to get a clear look at her hands, but I could see no hint of extra fingers. She had a way of holding herself, when she chose, that gave the impression of great strength and fortitude, as if she were waiting for the right time to throw off the roughness of her disguise and reveal the spellbound princess trapped within, although I had also seen her on several occasions stoop and deliberately make herself look sickly and old, a useful skill when asking for help from one of the soldiers in lifting a heavy trunk or buying bread from women in a rural village. Unlike Megyery, she seemed not at all interested in what I was reading or wearing or doing. After our first conversation, I worried for a time I had said something to offend her and racked my memory for what it could be, though except for asking her her age, I had said nothing other than hello the day we left on the road to Sárvár. For some reason, I very much wanted her to like me.

Besides the carriage in which I rode, our entourage included several carts carrying my dowry: chests of gold forints, silver basins, gilt and silver candelabra, ancient portraits of Báthory ancestors, my fine clothes and jewels. My mother-in-law had spared no expense in hiring enough soldiers to protect the wealth traversing the countryside, and we made a great spectacle, traveling in a long dusty line. The locals must have thought, upon seeing the carriage coming toward their villages, that we were the Turks once again on the move, not an eleven-year-old bride-to-be and her escorts.

The countryside of the Carpathian foothills was lush, sometimes rolling meadowland, sometimes marshy, but it was high summer and everywhere were green and growing things—crops of barley and oats, wildflowers, grasses that murmured in the breeze. Sometimes there were copses of birch and quaking aspen and fir or dark woods of oak and underbrush so thick the soldiers who accompanied us rode with one hand on their sword hilts, watching for movement among the trees. We avoided passage through the Turkish-occupied zones of Lower Hungary, including Buda, which I had long wanted to see, but still we had to keep a close eye out and approach any garrison with caution, for although we had letters allowing our safe passage through the lands of other noblemen friendly to my family, it was always possible to come upon a greedy officer, or an outlaw band of *hajdúks,* or gypsies who might try to fall upon the wagons and carriages and take what they could. The whole journey was conducted with the utmost of care, with the result that it took quite a long time to reach our destination, time in which I had little to do and no one for company except the redheaded tadpole Megyery, Anna Darvulia, and a few other servants.

Outside of Ecsed I knew little of the world other than what I had imagined from reading my mother's books. I had never realized what a rich and varied country I inhabited, how vast and far-flung my family's holdings were, for we passed through so many towns and villages and farms that were loyal in some way to the Báthorys that I could not name them all. The world was filled with sights so strange to my eyes that each day seemed to create the entire world anew: a man walking on stilts across a high river, a town wall thick with Turkish cannonballs, a group of soldiers leading a crying woman—a witch, Megyery told me—to a place of execution outside some little village. Suddenly my longing to see the canals of bawdy Venice, to travel to Rome or London seemed like nothing more than a childish fantasy. In truth, the place I most often longed to be during those days in the creaking, miserable, dusty carriage with the road ruts shaking my bones was at home in my bed with Klára and Zsofía curled up next to me, the sweet hot smell of their dark curls under my nose as they slept. On the road, when I drifted into an uneasy half sleep, I almost thought myself there again, until the carriage would jolt me back to myself and the sight of Megyery's thin face and bulging eyes made me remember where I was, and where I was going.

On our journey Megyery filled the air with chatter about Sárvár, about the people I would meet there and the countryside around the house, but I didn't need his blather to know where I was headed, and to whom, and why. My future husband's family was famous and powerful and wealthy, though not so famous and powerful and wealthy as my own. The old palatine Tamás Nádasdy, who died when

I was only two years old, had been learned and liberal, my mother had explained to me, a patron of the arts and literature, a convert to the Lutheran faith who set up a printing press at Sárvár to publish bibles and other books written in Hungarian. My future husband was the child of his old age, born when Tamás was fifty-eight, the longed-for heir that he and Orsolya had nearly given up hope of conceiving after many disappointments. Orsolya was a good deal younger than her husband, fourteen to his thirty-seven when they wed, heiress to a vast fortune, a beautiful, ignorant child whose education her husband had attempted as best he could after their vows were said. Their marriage was supposedly a true love match. They had pet names for each other—she was "little Mary" and he was "your grandpa"—which I would always find odd, but then the workings of other people's marriages have never made much sense to me. Even so, he was quite often away on this or that errand for the king, or to see to his holdings, and Orsolya often wrote to beg his return, especially after Ferenc was born, saying they were dying of loneliness without him. I suspect Orsolya was prone to exaggeration in her letters. She was prone to exaggeration in other areas too, which I was soon to find out.

Tamás Nádasdy would not live to see my marriage to his son. Indeed, when I arrived at Sárvár my husband-to-be had been ten years without his father, and his mother, like so many other widowed noblewomen, had sent her son to live at the court of the king, in Bécs, to finish his education. She had asked for me to come to Sárvár so that I might be her pet in her loneliness, though I knew none of that at the time. On the drive to Sárvár I had only time to resent Orsolya's sudden decision to fetch me to her, her son's need for a bride of Báthory blood, my own mother selling me off like a prize mare without any thought of what I wanted in a husband. Was Ferenc a handsome boy, I wondered, or a copy of his froggy-faced cousin, who was by then asking a number of questions about my religious upbringing, how often I prayed, and how. I suppose Megyery was trying to make certain I was a good Protestant and not some papist saboteur in disguise, or else he meant to turn me from my mother's cherished John Calvin to the teachings of Luther. I answered his questions but grew tired of his prodding, and after a few days of questions I did not engage in conversation beyond what I must answer to be polite, instead sitting and pretending to listen as he told me again and again of the goodness of the mistress of Sárvár, her simple beauty, her elegant taste.

When we came in sight of the estate at last, it was near dark, and the driver and the horses were exhausted from making the last push across the countryside so that we would not have to stop for the night. We were more than five days late arriving as it was, and Megyery had been growing increasingly anxious and irritable in the last week, lashing the driver or the captain of the guard with his sharp tongue whenever the weather or the roads or the need to change the horses held up our journey. I began to feel sorry for them. It seemed I was not the only person who had to endure the temper of the countess's stern and ambitious cousin.

It had rained most of the way to Sárvár, so of course on the day we arrived it was hot and dry, and the carriage and everything inside it was covered with a thick layer of light-brown dust that clung to my hair, my eyelashes, to every droplet of sweat on my skin and every thread on my dress. A mile outside of town, with the Nádasdy house in sight at last—a white star situated in a sunny bend in the river—Megyery made the driver stop and had Anna Darvulia take me out into the woods near the river, far from the eyes of the laughing soldiers, where she and a few ladies stripped me to my chemise and beat my clothes with their hands or dashed them against the trunks, raising clouds of dust thick as flies. Then they unbound my hair and shook it out, brushing the dust from me and rebinding the tresses again so tight that my eyes watered. Darvulia clothed me in the dress Megyery had chosen for me, a gown of dark-brown velvet like the softest mink and embroidered with elaborate white scrolls and rosettes, as well as a stiff lace ruff for around my neck. A wedding gown, because I was arriving as a bride. That night would be the first time my future husband would look upon me, and apparently he must not be disappointed.

Darvulia undressed in front of me and cleaned the dust off herself as well, bending over at the waist and shaking out her tangled black hair. Naked, she seemed far younger than I had taken her for at first. Like an ancient fairy under a bad spell, she threw off the appearance of age and poverty and exposed the delicate line of her back, the firm clear skin along her thighs. I asked her why she was changing her clothing. It seemed like a lot of bother to try to look like dewy maidens fresh from the bath after so many weeks on the road. She answered only, "My mistress does not like her guests to arrive covered in road dirt. She finds it disrespectful." I had fewer and fewer hopes of Orsolya Kanizsay all the time.

Darvulia dressed herself quickly, making herself again appear older and coarser than she really was, and then she urged me ahead of her on the path back toward the carriage. I sweated and oozed underneath the fabric—it was a winter dress, after all, and we were in high summer. But Megyery had insisted. Underneath the wide white ruff, which blocked my view of the uneven forest floor, it was all I could do to keep on my feet as I picked my way through the branches and undergrowth.

When we returned, the driver had curried the horses and wiped the walls of the carriage, opening the thick canvas curtains and beating the dust out of the velvet cushions so that they were red again instead of dun. We got in and started the last part of our grueling journey looking as fresh as if we'd been on the road no time at all.

The manor was built in the middle of an island, with a long wooden bridge connecting it to the town on the other side. As we came closer the smell of the murky black water in the moat assaulted my nose. Inside was the house itself, surrounding an inner courtyard of well-kept grass and a single bushy yew tree, dark green and pruned to within an inch of its life. The clatter of the horses' hooves when we turned from the dirt road to the wooden bridge startled the team, and when I poked my head out of the window to look, Megyery pulled again at my shoulder and turned me around. "The countess will not like it if you gape so," he said.

Our entourage pulled into the courtyard with a great deal of noise and ceremony, servants running out to greet us and shouting that we had arrived at last. Megyery stood and left the carriage, hissing that I was to remain seated until Countess Nádasdy herself came out to receive me. After so many days inside the carriage with only Megyery and Darvulia for company, I was actually glad to have arrived. I longed to stretch my legs, to run up and down the open expanse of the courtyard, to breathe a bit of fresh air, but I stayed where I was in my heavy lace-and-velvet finery, determined not to disgrace the Báthory name in this most important final moment of my journey.

The sun was going down, and the shadows in the courtyard lengthened and then dissolved as the sun dropped behind the roof of the house and tinged the sky with pink streaks and orange rosettes of cloud. All along the inner courtyard servants stopped to watch the carriage, to wait. They were shadowy figures in the growing dusk, dark and huddled as nuns in a cloister, and I could see a few young girls with their heads together, whispering and giggling in my direction. A sudden heat flooded the back of my throat, though there was nothing to be done—I would be the lady of this house someday, perhaps, but for now I was nothing more than a stranger, with no authority over even the lowest of servants. I had to endure their laughter for the moment.

Then silence settled over the courtyard, interrupted only by the satisfied rustlings of the doves in the dovecote as they settled down for the night, the twittering call and answer of a pair of swallows in the eaves. Soon Orsolya came out to greet me. She was dressed, as before, in widow's black, her silvered hair plainly done, even severe, pulling back at the sides of her face until her eyes had narrowed to little slits, and as before she was heavily made up with cosmetics, white and red. In place of the large jewel I had remembered from our first meeting she wore a small gold crucifix on a delicate chain, and she crossed her hands in front of her, just so, which gave her walk a prim, mincing kind of gait. She was nothing like my own mother had been before her widowhood, so vibrant and easygoing, an educated woman secure in herself and in her place in society. My mother-in-law, I could see clearly, was a pinched and unhappy woman, vain of a beauty that had left her long ago. Immediately my cheerful mood vanished.

Orsolya was followed by a young man with a fine jaw and a half-bored, half-amused look playing around the corners of his eyes, a young man whose expression echoed the very one I felt lurking beneath the stiff smile and calm demeanor I had arranged for the meeting of my future husband and his family. He was about sixteen or seventeen, my brother István's age, taller than his mother by a full head and shoulders, dressed in a kind of plain costume of a velvet waistcoat, white shirt, and dark leather breeches with lighter patches at the knees where some dirt had recently, and hastily, been brushed away. He also wore a sword at his waist that he tipped away from him as he walked to avoid tangling it in his legs, and I could not help but notice he had the bearing of a soldier, a young man used to the horse and the practice field. He was mannerly and polite, at least, standing back a little to let his mother go first, as a dutiful son ought. He looked up at the servants standing on the ramparts and motioned with his hand that they should keep their voices down. The girls hushed when he bade them, quieting their voices so rapidly that the only word I could think of was *reverent*. A reverent silence. Oh, he was much admired by the girls of Sárvár, my future husband—I could tell already.

Finally they stood before the carriage to await me—my future mother-in-law, my husband-to-be. Megyery bowed deeply and announced that, as promised, he had brought Count Nádasdy's bride home from Ecsed. It all felt a bit formal and overdone as I waited for them to summon me, an eleven-year-old girl with a sore backside and bitten-down nails.

Megyery opened the carriage door. I took a moment to position myself, since the leaving of carriages can make even the most graceful women look like beheaded chickens flapping in a barnyard. I would have to stoop to keep from banging my forehead on the roof of the carriage and hold up my elaborate dress, all while holding on to the side of the carriage to avoid tumbling out and landing at my new husband's feet. It was a feat I had performed many times back home at Ecsed, but never with so much finery fastened to my body, nor in so much heat. The heavy gown Darvulia had placed on me made me so hot that I nearly swooned, the world going gray for a moment as I ducked my head to leave the carriage. I was about to fall forward onto the dirt and grass below when the boy rushed forward to catch me around the waist, Megyery and the countess exclaiming and huddling around us. We stood there for a moment until I got my feet under me, the boy embarrassed at the attention of the ladies, me embarrassed and angered at my clumsiness, at being dressed up in such a ridiculous fashion. On the inner walls I could hear the servants giggling again behind their hands.

"Are you all right?" the young man asked, and I pulled myself from his grip and stood up straight.

"Yes," I said. "Thank you."

"You are quite welcome," he said, bowing to me a little more deeply than I would have thought for a son of a palatine. I wondered what he meant by it, if it was some kind of comment on his part. A joke, perhaps.

Orsolya walked forward to receive me properly, pulling me in for a stiff and awkward embrace. "Welcome to Sárvár, and to the house of Nádasdy, my dear," she said. I cringed at her use of "my dear"—it had been what my father had called my mother when he was still alive, and I could not hear it without hearing the sad echo of his voice—but Orsolya seemed not to notice. "This," she said, inclining her head toward the young man who had kept me from tumbling into the dirt, "is our cousin, András Kanizsay."

It took me a moment to realize what she had said, that the young man at her side was not, in fact, my future husband, but merely another cousin attached to the household. A soldier or a servant, perhaps, but not the man whom I was expected to marry. "You are not Ferenc Nádasdy?" I asked.

Orsolya looked dismayed. "No, of course not," she said. "Ferenc is still in Bécs, at his studies. He won't be home until his vacation, in the winter. Megyery should have told you as much on your journey." She looked to the steward, who frowned at me and blushed a deeper red.

It was the first of many times in my life I would have to mask my surprise, but I felt I did the job tolerably, arranging my face in a stiff and formal version of a smile and introducing myself with as much dignity as I had left. "I'm so glad to meet you," I said, turning all of my attention to my mother-in-law. "Thank you for welcoming me into your home, and into your family."

To the other side of me, I could see Imre Megyery scowling, still smarting over the countess's reproach, perhaps. He did tell me Ferenc was studying in Bécs, of course—I hadn't been paying attention. Then I turned to András. "And you as well, cousin," I said, trying on the word for warmth. "Thank you again for your help."

He touched his hand to his brow, and that amused expression crept again into his eyes. I was immediately sorry that I had been so warm to him, since clearly he was beneath my attention, only a servant in the house, and one inclined to tease. To him I was nothing more than a child, and a spoiled and clumsy one at that. "Welcome to Sárvár, cousin," he said.

The sun was going down. Orsolya hooked her arm through mine as if we were sisters and led me into the house, that same mincing gait she had used earlier nearly making me stumble to maintain my pace. "You must be exhausted after such a long journey," she said. "We have your room prepared, and some supper. Do you care for venison? It is very fresh and will be good for growing girls who wish to be mothers." To me this declaration was embarrassing, to say the least, but Orsolya didn't seem to notice, and once more I had to gain control of my countenance.

The house was smaller than the one in Ecsed and felt more unprotected without the sweep of the marsh around it, but inside the rooms were large and airy, the floors freshly scrubbed and gleaming. The furniture was polished wood, carved and ornate, with warm rugs on the walls and gilded candelabra on every table. In one room we passed a large portrait of a young boy of eight or nine, dressed all in black, tunic and breeches and cape thrown over one shoulder. He had a long, straight nose over a red mouth pursed and sensual, a serious, almost brooding expression in his black eyes. Orsolya stopped when she saw me looking at it. "That is Ferenc," she said. "Do you like it? I had it painted after his father's death. I sometimes thinks he looks a little sad."

"Perhaps a little," I said. It was hard for me to connect the unhappy child in the picture with a husband, a man who would love me as my father had loved my mother.

I turned to look outside, but in the darkness outside I could see little but the dim shape of the carriage that had borne me across Hungary, the occasional candle of a servant girl making her way across the courtyard. My mother-in-law's arm pulled insistently on my own, her voice prattling in my ear about the supper, my room. What kind of linens did I prefer, and did I have a favorite kind of sweet that I wanted, and what did I think of the countryside around Sárvár, wasn't it beautiful? She asked question after question while I wished, longed to be left to myself, to have a moment's peace in which to reflect on everything I had seen and heard already.

Orsolya took me up to my room, saying how eager Ferenc was to meet me, how anxious were his letters asking about my arrival. She gushed with pleasure over the details she and Megyery had arranged for me, the bed of carved wood, the candlesticks and tables and ornate trunks. One chair had a carved lion's-head back, and the candlesticks suddenly curled themselves into the shapes of dragons. The room was bright, covered in fresh white plaster—I could still smell the sting of the lime—and large, with a stone fireplace so tall I could stand inside it. The night was growing cooler, so she had a small fire built for me, and sent up a servant with a tray of hot pork and spiced apples, and a cool clean glass of well water perfumed with bits of mint. It was a welcome even my own mother would have been proud to offer, and if I had been given any choice in my coming there I might have found a reason to be happy in my new surroundings, in a beautiful house on an island in the middle of a river, where a lonely old woman had decided to take me in and make me her daughter. But that night and for a long time afterward I saw nothing but walls of plaster and stone to shut me in—the finest prison in all the land, to be sure, but a prison nonetheless.

# 9

*May 13, 1611*

It is spring in Csejthe now. The sun at the window softens and warms like a stewed apricot, and the nights are shorter, the stars clearer. The change in constellations is one of the few delights I'm still afforded by the view from my tower. I have watched as Orion has disappeared, taking his warlike club with him, to be replaced by the maiden Virgo with her golden shaft of wheat. She is sometimes called Artemis, sometimes Demeter, although I like to think of her as Persephone, who was snatched from her mother to live with Hades in the underworld, and who returns only long enough each year to see the spring come round again. Such sorrow, and such joy, are things I know only too well.

These past months in my prison—more than four, by my count—have been more difficult than any I have known before. The trial of my servants has come and gone, with no hint of what my own fate might be. The old steward, Deseő, came to tell me how the palatine had Dorka and Ilona Jó burned at the stake like common witches, their fingers pulled off with hot pincers. My little man, Ficzkó, the palatine had beheaded, and then his body too went on the fire. It was a terrible spectacle, Deseő said. The women were brought out in a little wooden cart, their hands and feet bound in chains as the local people, the palatine's servants and tenants, gathered in the fields outside Bicske *vár* and shouted insults and curses and heaped ignominy on my poor servants as the flames licked at their feet, their clothes. The local people threw their own bundles of wood on the fire, to have their part in the event. Afterward the ashes were taken away in jars like souvenirs. Only Katalin Benecká, the old washerwoman, still lives. She is being kept alive in the prison at Bicske, at least until the palatine is through humiliating her. A year, maybe two, and it's likely he will let her go home again. God only knows what her children had to promise the palatine to spare her life. God only knows what you, my dearest, must have promised to spare mine.

Meanwhile my own name has been dragged through more filth than I can imagine. They say I have eaten pieces of the maidens in my employ, beating them with my own hands until I was covered in their blood, using spells and potions against the palatine and Megyery to try to murder them. They have turned me into a human vampire, an abomination. A useful legend to use against a political enemy, and one sure to keep me here in my tower for a long time to come. Surely you must know that Thurzó and Mátyás and Megyery have much to gain by keeping me prisoner. Money, lands, power. It is your cousin Gábor they fear, and how we might help him unite the Hungarians against the Habsburgs. They think my disgrace will cause you and your sisters to fall in line to protect yourselves, your lands and position. That is why I write these pages for you. If the palatine decides to reverse his sentence and call for my head, if he continues to refuse to let me testify on my own behalf in open court, there will be no way for me to explain that I did nothing wrong, that my actions, such as they were, were within my rights as a noblewoman and landowner.

The girls who died were whores and thieves, an ulcerous cancer in my house. I had every right to punish them as I saw fit. Was I to allow licentiousness and thievery to continue under my very nose and do nothing to stop it? Should I have looked away as they stole not only my possessions but your inheritance, until we were all as destitute as a bunch of beggars? I could not. I would not.

I wish you would come to Csejthe so that I may tell you these things in person. I wish for one minute Megyery would loosen your reins, so that I may see you again, that I may kiss you and take your hand through the gap in my stone wall. You must be taller by now, I think, with maybe some of your father's breadth of shoulder, some of his height and good looks. I wish you had known him better. If your father were alive, the palatine and the king would never have dared imprison me. If your father were alive, you would be here with me now instead of miles away, under the guardianship of a man I have never trusted nor loved. We would be a family still. But God had different plans for us, it seems, and so we must endure the present as best we can, with all of his good grace.

# 10

Regardless of my mother-in-law's assurances that her son was eager to meet me, it was half a year and more that I lived in the Nádasdy household before I laid eyes on your father for the first time, when he traveled home for his Christmas vacation. In all that time Orsolya rarely left me alone. Every day there was something else of great importance she had to ask me—a manner of dress, perhaps, or a letter of thanks to write to this or that relative I had never met for some gift she had sent for me. Her instruction in childrearing was especially humorous given that my mother-in-law had raised only the one child while I myself had cared for both my little sisters and several cousins at Ecsed without much in the way of help from my mother, who had counted on my maturity from a very young age. But nothing I did was beneath Orsolya's attention. She would come into my room at all hours of the night with this or that question about how would I like the design for my new skirt, and should she have the cook make more bread for the week, and did I think she should invite this or that relative to Sárvár for a feast? In my head I was always screaming, I don't care! I don't care! But I had determined from that first day that I would be a credit to my family's honor and never speak those words aloud, though they rang often in my head those first months when Orsolya made me her pet.

By All Saints, Ferenc wrote with news of his intention to come to Sárvár for his school vacation, and his mother was so overjoyed that her interest in me grew even more intrusive. For several weeks ahead of his promised arrival Orsolya made certain to take special care with me, so that my appearance, my manners, my mode of address might be pleasing to my future husband on our first meeting. She gave instructions on my clothing and hair, my meals, even the types of pillows that adorned my bed so that I might sleep more soundly, for she often observed that I seemed tired and out of spirits in the mornings and asked whether or not I spent the nights tossing and turning or if my evenings were restful. No, I always said. I've never slept so well in my life. I never raised my voice or laughed at her, at least within her hearing, and I had the servants take her favorite glass of wine to her each evening to help her sleep, and I propped up her pillows with my own hand. Orsolya would love me, so much that, unlike my own mother, she would never send me away.

It was not only fear that inspired me. By showing duty and honor I hoped to gain a modicum of independence in my life with the widow Nádasdy and her son, the boy I was to marry. A boy whom, as my first Christmas in the Nádasdy household approached, I was finally going to meet.

It happened in November, before the first snows came. Orsolya's estate at Sárvár was her favored home because it had been her husband's favored home, only a few days' journey south of Bécs, at the far western edge of Hungary where it meets Habsburg Austria. The old palatine had built a white tower in the fortress to house the family apartments, as well as several impressive high-ceilinged halls, and it was here Orsolya chose to spend her comfortable winters, entertaining friends when she felt well and convalescing in the thermal baths when she didn't, for she suffered at times from weakness, from nausea, from frequent headaches that seemed nothing more than the ordinary complaints of advancing age. Yet she was determined every day to go to the baths, to be in better health and spirits when Ferenc arrived home. We were all expected to be at our best for Ferenc's visit, his mother included.

My fiancé arrived from Bécs one night so late in the evening that the whole house had gone to bed and didn't learn of his coming until the next day. I myself was unaware of it until Darvulia came in to stoke the fire in my room and help me get dressed. I had slept too little that night, had in fact stayed up late reading the very books Orsolya didn't want to see in my hands evenings when we sat together before her fire—Aristotle, Plato, Ptolemy. Bent on turning me from my mother's Calvinism, she preferred that I read her some passages from a recent treatise by Father Bíró, the Lutheran, whose work she greatly admired and who had been three times a guest at Sárvár. I always obliged her in her reading, knowing my place. But afterward when I returned to my own chamber, I read as much of the ancient philosophers as I liked, squinting at the words by the faint light of the candles until long after midnight, the only time in the whole of the day when I might have some peace.

At Ecsed I had been used to sleeping until dawn broke, but Orsolya, whose piety awoke her before the sun, thought dawn was too late for highborn ladies and had begun a campaign of waking me an hour before the first pink light was growing over the walls of Sárvár. So when Anna Darvulia came into the room that morning and stoked the fire and lit the candles, pulling back the curtains around my bed and turning the darkness of my chamber into a semblance of daylight, I thought it was merely another of Orsolya's attempts to make me a respectable little copy of herself. I groaned and pulled the blanket over my head. Darvulia pulled it back down again.

"The mistress requests you get up and get dressed," she said. She held out a robe for me to wear, and wearily I climbed out of bed to put it on.

I assumed my mother-in-law had more lessons for me. Besides instruction on the Bible and the teachings of her favorite scholars and priests, Orsolya filled my days with what she saw as talents necessary to women's lot—dancing, drawing, music, embroidery. The rhythms of Latin and long unbroken strings of German, the latest treatises of astronomy and physiognomy, the discoveries from the explorers combing the New World that I had learned from Leopold were all unknown at Sárvár—pursuits best saved for men, according to my mother-in-law. Instead we were to sit and sew all day. To me all these delicate occupations were an absurd waste of time. "What?" I asked Darvulia. "More embroidery? Will the kingdom fall if I do not finish another cushion?"

The servant smiled, for she was accustomed by then to my saucy tongue. She never tattled on me to the lady of the house the way the other ladies sometimes did to gain the countess's favor. She was respectful when she spoke to me and silent if she had nothing to say, which was often, but sometimes when she had a free moment she would sneak me a pomegranate or a bowl of dates, or sit and brush my hair over and over because she knew I liked it, and listen to me talk about my family and friends far away in Ecsed, or what I was reading in the evenings by candlelight, or complain about the countess's constant and unrelenting attentions. Darvulia had become, over my short time in the Nádasdy house, a kind of second mother, attentive and kind, and the only person to whom I dared show my true feelings.

Now she shook out a clean skirt for me to wear. "Your fiancé has arrived," she said. "He came very late last night. My lady asks that you join them for the evening meal. I'm to dress you for your meeting with him."

I sat up straight in front of my mirror. Darvulia would not meet my eyes, keeping her back to me as she placed the breakfast tray on my table and kicked the bearskin rug back into place on the floor. She must have known something of young Ferenc Nádasdy, having spent a few years in the countess's household, and many times I had asked her what kind of boy he was, was he handsome, was he kind? What did she know of him that she could tell me? "Nothing, miss," she always said, "except that he is a fine young man, and you will be lucky to wed him." A good diplomatic answer befitting a good diplomatic servant. And I always let the matter go, not wanting to anger the one friend I had made at Sárvár.

But that morning, when I asked her the question again and she gave the same answer—he's a fine man, you are lucky to be marrying him—I snapped at her. "Good God, Darvulia," I said at last. "I'm a servant here as much as you are, so let's have some honesty between us, shall we?"

She laughed aloud, a quick bell-like sound such as I never thought to escape from a mouth such as hers. "Yes, miss," she said. "All right then. Get dressed, and I will tell you what I know."

She dressed my hair and then bound me inside a gown of fine red Florentine silk with a pattern of stripes that I had chosen as my favorite because it brought out the color of my eyes. No more heavy brown velvet for me—I was determined the embarrassing spectacle that had happened with András Kanizsay the night I arrived at Sárvár would not repeat itself with Ferenc Nádasdy. Darvulia dressed my hair with some pearls, fine and white against the dark brown tresses, and while she worked she told me about the boy who was to become my husband. How he could read and write Hungarian at only five years old, how instead of going at once to Bécs for his schooling he had stayed with tutors at the family estate in Sárvár after his father's death and only a few years ago been sent with his cousin András Kanizsay to be educated at the king's court, where he lived with György Bocskai's family. How István Bocskai, György's son, was his dear friend and traveling companion. My future husband, it seemed, was a favorite of the Habsburg king, a golden youth marked for greatness, already named Captain of the Horse when he was eight years old in honor of his father's service to the country. A fortunate alliance, my mother would have said, whispering in my ear, if she had been witness to our conversation.

"You know more than this, surely," I said at last. "I have heard some of these reports already from Orsolya. You told me you have lived in this house for nearly ten years."

She was silent for a moment, and I wondered what game she was playing. The creases in her brow deepened as she looked at me. "I did wonder," she said, "if you meant what you said, that I should feel free to speak my mind."

"So you were testing me?"

She shrugged. "Noble ladies sometimes say they want honesty when really they want someone to flatter them, tell them how important their men are, and by extension themselves. I wasn't sure which you might be."

Impatiently I flung a piece of hair out of my eyes. "I'm meeting Ferenc for the first time, and I would like to know, in truth, what kind of man he is. Let the others flatter my vanity."

"All right then," she said, and began again.

She said that Ferenc was an honest man, a fine soldier and horseman, and more learned than most gave him credit for, given his penchant for horses and soldiering. He was known to be proud and could seem haughty at first, especially to ladies. Even his mother's company was sometimes too much for him. Orsolya would fuss and fawn over him, and he would endure it, but only just.

"She does seem to dote on him, even when he's not here," I said. "But my own mother was the same with my brother. After my father died, she hardly spoke to anyone else. I think that's only natural with mothers and sons. What is the servants' gossip?"

"Gossip?"

"I know the servants laugh about us when they think we don't notice. What do they think of Ferenc?"

She paused as if to consider what I'd said, as if weighing the worth of what she knew on some internal scale. "Some of the young ladies," she said, "have bragged in my hearing of having bedded Ferenc on various occasions. One even claims to have got a child by him, though she says she miscarried."

"Which one?"

"Judit, the seamstress."

I knew this Judit, who did the sewing in a room at the back of the house with four or five other girls of equal birth and stupidity. I had seen her smirk in my direction on more than one occasion and had wondered what I had done to offend her. Now it made sense— the laughter that had risen from the maidservants the night of my arrival, how András Kanizsay had raised a hand to shush them. "Do you think these stories any truth to them?" I asked.

She shrugged again, doubting, but it was not with enough certainty to ease my misgivings. "They could. But he is handsome, so it may be a way for them to soothe their own hurt feelings if he shows no inclination for them."

"I wonder if he will show any inclination for me."

"I'm sure he will. Any young man would be glad to have a lovely young lady like you for his bride. With your wealth and education, too, you will be more than a pretty face to him. A true companion." She picked up a brush to smooth out the tangles in my hair, wrapped an arm around my shoulders, and said, "I could not be more proud if you were my own daughter." Suffused with the warmth of her affection, I closed my eyes, enjoying the strokes of the brush as she bound my hair and tucked a fortune in pearls into the design.

Inside, though, I was busy turning over and over the things she'd told me. That the servants in Orsolya's employ would dare to spread such spiteful gossip about Ferenc was intolerable. I wanted to punish the offending girls, but I did not dare. I was not the mistress of the house yet. If Orsolya chose to surround herself with such maliciousness and dishonesty, that was her prerogative. But I began to wonder what those same servants might be saying about me. Everywhere I went in the house I seemed to come across this or that insolent maidservant smirking in my direction, her cheeks pink and her eyes full of mischief. I could hardly exit a room without peals of girlish laughter following me out the door. Did they think that Ferenc would never love me, that he would reject me and send me home to Ecsed? I could not understand why Orsolya surrounded herself with imbeciles, why she would trust her sewing or her meals or the scrubbing of her floors to giggling fools without an ounce of brains. But then some women preferred to surround themselves with stupidity, either out of pity or else because it made them feel more accomplished. I began, after a time, to wonder if Orsolya was not of the latter kind—a fool, wanting to appear learned by comparison.

Either way I began to be aware of the gossip in the court, and how the servants seemed to fear no one. Not Orsolya, not me. Only Darvulia commanded their respect, for they would cease their incessant laughter when she came into the room and remain silent, at least until that fearsome creature left them once more to their own devices. Then the chatter would begin anew, a sound that grated on my nerves more and more every day.

When Darvulia finished dressing me, I observed myself in the mirror. My skin was fine and white, smooth and unspoiled by blotches or marks—I took great care to wash my face several times a day, the way my mother had taught me—and though I didn't have her dramatic black-and-white beauty, her heart-shaped face, I did have a high clear forehead, expressive brown eyes, delicate hands that could write a fine hand in four languages or play the latest songs from Italy on the lute. I smiled, and my solemn expression transformed itself into something more lively, animated with vivacity the way my mother's had been before my father's death. A young man like Count Nádasdy might be happy to sit and talk with me. I touched my hands to my hair like I was making a prayer, like I was protecting myself and all my mother's hopes for me against what was to follow that day. All my thoughts bent toward making my husband love me, a love fine enough and large enough to protect me from anything the future might bring—wars, illness, famine. None of them would touch me if I could win Ferenc Nádasdy's love, or at least his admiration.

That evening Darvulia led me down to the dining hall as Orsolya had bidden her. I knew very well where it was, but my mother-in-law made sure I was very rarely alone in her house. The hall was lit at both ends with a bit of gray November light, but I would not let the weather distract me. I put on my sunniest expression, my best face. Some candles had been lit to dispel the gloom, and under their light I could see the figure of András Kanizsay, the wry-mouthed and insignificant cousin, sitting with his boots in the ashes of the fire. He had returned to Bécs not long after my arrival at Sárvár and had grown a little since I had seen him last, a lengthening of leg and arm and a broadening across his shoulders, and it did seem to improve him, make him seem less boyish, less handsome, a new bit of beard tempering the insolence around his mouth. He stood and bowed when I entered. I curtsied as slightly as I could.

Next to him sat a broad-shouldered young man with a shock of black hair and intense black eyes flanking a rather prominent nose, which gave him a look I was always to think of as predatory. A hunting bird, a hawk. His clothes were expensive and yet carelessly put together, rumpled and only half buttoned, as if he could not be bothered with silly matters like dressing for company, but he was especially tall and broad, so that two of me could have fit inside his frame. Next to the smaller, fairer András he was positively ferocious. He didn't look up when I entered but carried on speaking to Orsolya, who either did not see me enter or did not heed my presence. No one immediately made an effort to introduce us. Orsolya herself sat at the head of the table, her cheeks flushed and pink, her manner lively as she chatted and waved her hands about. I began to suspect that she had not been at all ill from any kind of physical ailment but had languished for want of her son, and that his appearance had improved not only her spirits but her health. After a moment, she caught my eye and stood with some little bit of aloofness to introduce me to him. "Ferenc," she said, "I am pleased to present to you Erzsébet Báthory." Immediately I realized she would not like sharing her son's attention with me. She was used to being the center of his world.

He greeted me with a nod of his head and a little noise—*ahmmm*—as he cleared his throat and spoke. "Hello," he said finally. His voice was lower than most young men of his age, as deep as a full-grown man's, but he seemed to be saddled with more shyness than other young men I'd known, for he had trouble meeting my eyes and looked from my face to the floor and back again, as if we might be expected to tumble into bed together that very moment. "It is a pleasure to meet you at last."

I would have held out my hand, but he didn't hold out his. "And I you."

"I hope we will be friends."

"I'm sure we shall." I curtsied low the way Orsolya had taught me. It was all exhaustingly polite.

András remained at Ferenc's side, but when it was clear that my fiancé had not much more to say to me, his cousin turned to me instead and inquired how I felt. "How is your health?" he said. "Are you likely to swoon again? I'm only asking so I can be ready. It wouldn't do to let you hit your head on the floor."

I frowned, trying to think of something to say in return. I didn't like being teased and was not sure how to treat him. He was not a servant, but he was not a member of the immediate family, either, and he didn't speak to me with the kind of respect that I was used to from my own small cousins, those from less well-off branches of the family whom I had looked after when I had lived at home. From Darvulia I had learned that András was a distant relative of my mother-in-law who had been taken in by the household after his father had died and his mother's money had run out. He and Ferenc were being educated together in Bécs, as was the case with so many cousins of lesser nobility. Now I asked if he didn't think himself mightily clever, if he thought he was some kind of wit. "Sarcasm," I said, "usually marks a lack of intellect as well as respect."

His manner grew faux serious. "I speak only out of genuine concern for your well-being."

"Oh, of course," said I. "I recognized your concern the moment I entered the room. It must have been there on the back of your hand, for I saw you studying your nails when I walked through the door. Looking for a bit of horse dung, perhaps, left underneath the quick?"

"So much for your pronouncements against sarcasm." I colored, but all wryness left his expression as he said that he was pleased to find that I was not the glum little girl who had met him in the courtyard at Sárvár half a year before but a young lady with intelligence and temper. "I had feared," he said, "that my cousin was marrying a solemn little nun who would plague him into an early grave."

"I'm pleased that you find me improved," I said, with as much archness as I could muster. "I wish I could say the same." András tilted his head and laughed.

Orsolya took her son by the arm and talked of how she had enjoyed the waters of Sárvár recently, when her health did not keep her confined to her bed. Ferenc settled her back into her chair, sitting down beside her to listen dutifully, though I sometimes caught him looking longingly out the window where the snow was beginning to fall, as if he would prefer to be somewhere else. He took no more notice of me. I felt abandoned by them both, my fiancé and my mother-in-law. My hopes, and my heart, sank.

"Don't mind my cousin," András said as he held out a chair for me. "Orsolya depends on him, as you can see."

"Yes," I answered. "She dotes on him completely."

He narrowed his eyes at me, though the humorous expression playing around his mouth didn't quite leave him. "Is it his part you envy, or hers?"

I sighed, feeling the mask of politeness slip a little. "Both, I suppose," I said at last. "If I'm being truthful."

András smiled again. "With me, I hope you will always be truthful, cousin." He picked up my hand and bent his head over it.

I wanted to roll my eyes, thoroughly annoyed at these niceties from the dependent cousin, the sarcastic boy, but I managed to keep my face neutral once more. "Thank you," was all I said.

All that night Orsolya plagued Ferenc with questions about his tutors and his studies and the people they knew at court, the balls and parties he attended, the friends he had there. Occasionally I would catch a name I knew and chime in with some little bit of news, hoping to impress him with my knowledge of court life and politics the way my mother had once done with her male admirers, but anytime I spoke he would stare for a moment as if I were a pig who had suddenly learned to talk, and then he would turn back to his mother without acknowledging me at all. For the most part I was forced to do nothing more than eat my soup and listen, but sometimes I spoke to András instead. He would ask me this or that question about my studies or my family back home, friends we might have in common, and sometimes he would lean over to explain to me a little background on some story Ferenc was telling his mother about the people at court—the shyness of Archduke Rudolf, lately returned from Spain, the brashness and jealousy of his younger brother, Mátyás, who thought he should have been the heir to the Habsburg throne instead of his introspective older brother. András sat so close to me that I could smell the wine on his breath, feel the warmth of his leg through the thin red silk of my skirt. He leaned in in the middle of some story about the palatine's horse to tell me how his cousin loved the theater, how he acted in theatricals with the royal family in the Hofburg afternoons when they were done with their lessons. "You should see my cousin in a wig," he said. "A blond curly wig. He looks like some kind of angry cherub. Like he should be shooting arrows from the roof of the Stephansdom at the sinners below."

I laughed in spite of myself. "Shh, cousin," I said. "I'm trying to display my good manners."

"To the devil with manners," he said, lifting his glass. "If you were my fiancée, I would pay you more attention, Erzsébet."

I lowered my head, not wanting him or his cousin to see the expression on my face. He was not my fiancé, nor ever would be. It was not his place to call me by my Christian name, nor criticize anything Ferenc said or did in regard to me. Of course I wished Ferenc would speak to me, but it was not something András should have mentioned, and I couldn't help thinking of Rudolf and Mátyás, how jealousy had colored what should have been the closeness between brothers. I turned away, sliding my chair ever so slightly away from him, and did not speak to him again for the rest of the evening.

When the meal was over, Orsolya dismissed me, and I took my leave of the young men and my mother-in-law as exhausted as if I had been on the road for two months together. Darvulia took me back to my room, where I threw myself into her arms as I would once have done with my own mother, complaining that my new husband had not even so much as glanced in my direction after that first greeting. "Don't lose heart," she said, brushing out all my long hair, her fingers deft and soothing. "He will come around in time. What man could fail to love you?"

I wanted to believe her, but I was not at all certain that Ferenc Nádasdy would even notice me. The next day I tried again, and again the next, asking about his friends and his studies, even sinking so low as to inquire about the weather and the state of the roads on his journey from Bécs. It was all in vain—Ferenc was as polite and civil to me as he was to his mother, as if I merited no more attention or consideration than courtesy demanded. All that Christmas season he rarely spoke more than two words to me at a time, attending his friends and relatives and leaving me to the attentions of András Kanizsay. I began to look for ways to avoid spending time with them, begging Darvulia to tell Orsolya I was ill, staying in bed to read or write letters home to pass the time until Ferenc went back to Bécs.

I wrote to my brother, István, who expressed alarm that Count Nádasdy seemed so little interested in his bride-to-be. It was in his Christmas letter, in fact, that István asked me how Ferenc and I were getting along, and I wrote back and confessed that we were not, that he seemed completely uninterested in my existence. *He shows me less deference than one of the servants. Even the livestock command more of his time and attention, for he spends several hours a day with the horses. He does not look at me at all, if he can help it. I begin to fear that if his mother dies before we are wed, he may send me back to Ecsed, he shows so little inclination for my company.*

My brother's letter reached me less than a month later, so that I knew how worried he was, how much the alliance between the Báthorys and Nádasdys meant to him and to my family. *You must make him look at you. You must make him forget that there are any other women in the world at all. Remember our mother, and the things she taught you. She knows how to enchant a man more than anyone I have ever seen. Make yourself pleasing, as she does, and Ferenc Nádasdy will fall madly in love with you, the good Lord willing. If he sends you home, I don't know what will become of you.*

So I did as my brother suggested. For the last week or so of the visit I tried to engage Ferenc in conversation the way I had seen my mother do with the men of her acquaintance, lowering my chin and raising my eyes to him to convey my modesty, my honor at being his betrothed; or laughing and trying to make merry, to seem both virtuous and worldly all at once. He did little except blush and stammer and find reasons to check on his horse, to speak with his steward. I tried to dazzle him with my education, to discuss the latest on the Turkish occupation of Cyprus and the pasha's defeat, the previous year, at the Battle of Lepanto. It was all in vain. At supper or in company he looked at me aslant whenever I spoke, as if I were a witch trying to put a spell on him. In our later years together, your father would come to repent those days, Pál, but it is no exaggeration to say that during the first moments of our acquaintance, from the time he arrived at Sárvár until he left again two months later, Ferenc and I stayed at opposite ends of the house and had as little to do with each other as possible.

The only one who didn't mind my attempts at being pleasing was András Kanizsay, who always sought out my company as if to make up for his cousin's disregard, smiling and joking and making me so miserable with his teasing I wished I were mistress of the house, so I could send him away. It was difficult not to compare the two of them—Ferenc so dark and serious next to András, who winked when he saw me, as if I were a favored young cousin—but I paid the insolent cousin as little attention as I could and focused on my future husband instead. Every time I met Ferenc after that first day at Sárvár, knocking into him on my way out of my bedchamber or during a chance encounter in the stables, I longed to speak with him privately so that the disguises of civility we wore might be dropped completely. But he merely blushed and bowed and went in the other direction as quickly as he could. I didn't dare seek out Ferenc Nádasdy in private, not even for the honest discourse I was wishing for, not even in the spirit of the friendship I wanted to feel for him. There were too many eyes watching us, too many foolish girls ready to believe the worst of me. There was too much at stake.

So your father and I would not be friends, not yet. The day he left Sárvár I did not even watch him go, so relieved I was to be free of the burden of Ferenc Nádasdy, to be myself once more. The young men packed their saddlebags and kissed Orsolya good-bye, and then they were off. Afterward I heard Orsolya weeping behind her chamber door but did not offer to go in and comfort her. I could not share her misery that the young men were gone. Instead I went to the music room and played a lively tune on my lute, a song for a *palotás*, a song for dancing.

# 11

My mother-in-law's love for her son was so great that she could not bear the loss of him, and a few weeks after his departure that January, Orsolya took to her bed with some pain in her legs and chest that soon moved to her head. Over the next few months she grew sickly and confused, sometimes thinking I was a young cousin she had known as a child, sometimes that I was her own mother. One night as I bent over her pillows she slapped me so violently that the servants talked of calling for a priest to perform an exorcism, but I convinced them that she was merely falling victim to the confusions of old age, that Ferenc should not hear that the servants thought his mother was possessed by the devil. Afterward she was quiet again, and slept more often, except when she complained of pains in her chest and the servants carried her down to the river on a litter so that she could take the waters.

She died one evening in her sleep not long after midsummer. The servants found her in the morning, slumped against the pillows with her eyes open, not unlike my father's had been at his own death. I had the best seamstress make a fine sheet of linen and pearls to wrap her in, and I behaved in public as if my own mother had died, keeping a serious countenance, refraining from music and spending long hours on my knees in prayer in the chapel of the estate or in conference with István Magyari, the family priest. I knew that Ferenc would hear of my actions through his steward, Imre Megyery, and in this way I hoped to show him I was a friend, an ally. There were two years between that time and when our wedding was scheduled to take place, and I knew more than ever that I must convince Ferenc that our future marriage, though arranged by our parents, could bring him some happiness.

When he returned to Sárvár for a few weeks to mourn his mother and see that she was properly placed in the family vault beside his illustrious father, my betrothed was naturally more out of spirits than ever. I spoke warmly to him on the night he arrived, telling him how happy I was to see him, even under such difficult circumstances, and said I hoped to aid him with the arrangements for his mother's funeral. All my efforts were met with nothing more than a polite nod of the head, a murmured word of thanks, and then Ferenc's quick retreat from my presence.

When he was not writing letters to this or that relative, he often went out hunting, and these excursions kept us apart for long hours every day. András Kanizsay and their friend István Bocskai often accompanied him. I made sure they had cool glasses of wine and fresh fruit on their return and took great care with my hair and dress every time I knew I was to meet them, so that Ferenc would never look on me except at my best, but in general things stayed as they had been before. When the weather grew hot, Ferenc and his retinue returned to Bécs for the rest of the summer, leaving me at Sárvár with only Darvulia and Megyery and the servants for company.

Megyery was left in Orsolya's will not only as the steward of Sárvár but as my own personal tutor in the Lutheran lessons she had so valued. I found him as officious as ever and shrank whenever he came near, and he too seemed still to resent my presence in the house, speaking to me coolly whenever we had some business matter to discuss, some lesson to study. Still angry, perhaps, that I had embarrassed him in front of his beloved Orsolya.

But that summer Megyery was struck with some sort of ague that left him feverish and delirious for a few precarious days, days in which Darvulia tended to him carefully, for among her other talents my friend was an artful healer and trusted by all the ladies around Sárvár when someone or other of them took ill. If I could not make myself useful to Ferenc, perhaps I could make myself useful to his odious cousin instead. I spoke to Darvulia, who made me her assistant, and I mixed plasters and teas and helped to collect the gore and leeches whenever Megyery was bled. I undertook these tasks with as much enthusiasm and humility as I could, reading the steward letters and notes that came in from all over, or passages from the Bible when his eyes were weak, and brought his favorite priest to sit with him and keep him company while I stole a few hours' rest. Every night I ordered him a glass of wine to improve his sleep and brought it to him with my own hands. I said nothing to offend, either in or out of his hearing, and eventually Megyery warmed to me more and more. He even said he wrote to Ferenc of how greatly my disposition had improved, which of course was my design all along.

Soon Megyery began to trust me with more responsibility, such as paying debts to the surgeon or the priest out of the estates' rent or answering the letters from the tenants in the nearby village. He had me call in the butcher's son, a certain László Bende, to question him about a fight he'd begun with one of our servants the week before. The young man—plain and nervous, with very clean, well-scrubbed hands, despite the stink of the slaughterhouse on him—endured my questions with a look of embarrassment, his chin raised, his eyes settled firmly over my left shoulder. He was not used to answering to a woman, and a very young one at that. I sent him away satisfied that he would handle future quarrels with greater decorum. It was all preparation for the day when I would be mistress of Sárvár myself, so that I would be intimately familiar with all the day-to-day needs of such a large house, such a great staff.

One day Megyery even asked me to deal personally with a squabble between two maidservants over a missing skirt. The offender was that same Judit who had said in Darvulia's hearing that she had got a child from Ferenc and lost it the summer before I arrived at Sárvár. Apparently another girl had accused Judit of stealing the favored piece of clothing, a skirt covered with beautiful and costly silk embroidery, a gift from Orsolya before her death. Judit denied taking the skirt, leading to an altercation in the sewing room that had turned violent. The girls started pulling each other's clothes and hair and even drew blood by scratching at each other with their nails. Their shouts rang through the house for several minutes before the other servants could pull them apart and send for Megyery, who sent me in his stead.

When I arrived at the scene, I dealt with the accused girl myself, questioning her in the sewing room in front of the other servants to make certain they could all see I was being fair, giving Judit every opportunity to defend herself, but she would not tell me where the skirt was hidden and denied she had taken it. "I don't have to tell you anything," she said, raising her chin to me. Already a woman with a woman's bosom and hips, where mine were still narrow as a boy's, she was coarse in dress and cleanliness but rosy and plump in complexion, and up close, with her blue eyes flashing anger at me, I could see why of all the girls on the estate, Ferenc would bed her. I thought of Ferenc's little animal eyes searching out Judit's languid blue ones and felt a strong desire to slap her impudent face. Neither whoring nor thievery could be tolerated among the servants in the Nádasdy household. Ferenc may not have thought much of me, but if I were to be mistress there, it was I who would deal with the servants on a daily basis, I who would hire them, dismiss them, keep them working harmoniously. Ferenc didn't have to love me, but by God, he would respect my position and my dignity, and so would the maidservants. They, at least, were something in the house I could control.

But how to handle it—that was the thing.

My mother would have known exactly how to deal with Judit. At Ecsed the servants had doted on my mother, though she could be severe in her treatment of them when they stepped out of line. Stealing, especially, never went unpunished, though my mother also punished girls for lasciviousness or insubordination. A devoted follower of Calvin and his concept of total depravity, the abject state of sin in which all humans live, her preferred form of punishment, especially for crimes of lust, was to have the offending maidservant stripped naked and sent to do her work in the courtyard, where every man in the house would gather round to laugh and jeer, making animal noises and crude jokes. In this way my mother would shame the girl into a new understanding of the value of modesty, of the girl's place in the sphere of the household. The girls always came back to her weeping and begging her forgiveness. She earned their loyalty by seeing to their children's education or their daughters' dowries, promising her favorites that their daughters would have places in her household when they were old enough or writing to this or that relative to see if they could use another girl. They loved her for it. My mother's servants outdid themselves in making up her clothes or bringing flowers for her room if they thought it would please her. She would reward them with presents, too—a piece of expensive cloth, a silver trinket, sometimes even a gold forint—that they hoarded like *hajdúks*. It was her particular gift, this ability to make everyone fall in love with her.

So that day I told Darvulia that Judit, who had stolen another girl's clothes, could go without her own until the evening meal, and do her work in the courtyard where everyone would see her.

Judit laughed. "Who will listen to you?" she said. "You aren't mistress here. The master doesn't even look at you."

I regarded the other maidservants in the sewing room, the seamstresses, the cook's assistant whose little girl was always underfoot. Poor women all, with few skills to recommend them, no education, no dowries. They had all come to the manor in years past, when Orsolya was mistress, it was true. Still, it would be I who saw to the future of Sárvár, I to whom they must now show allegiance. "Perhaps I'm not mistress yet," I said. "But I will be before long, and I will remember who was loyal and who was not. Anyone who thinks I'm being unfair is free to find a situation somewhere else." The servants looked at one another, but no one moved. I turned to Darvulia. "Undress her and send her into the courtyard for the remainder of the day."

When Darvulia started forward to undo the ties of the blouse around Judit's neck, all the fight went out of the girl. She began to cry, falling at my feet and begging me not to subject her to such humiliation, but I stood firm. A couple of the older seamstresses stripped her forcibly and sent her out of the house with her pieces of sewing to sit on a stone bench in the hot sun and make up her sheets blubbering and shaking. The understewards and stable boys came out to laugh at her and call out rude things in her direction, but the other maidservants would not look at her when they passed by with their buckets of soap, their bundles of clean laundry. I was rather pleased with myself for coming up with a fair punishment for both her thievery and her insolence, though I thought her reaction a bit overwrought, since she didn't do her penance for more than a single day and suffered nothing more than shame and sunburn. At the end of the day I had her brought back inside and sent Darvulia with some cream for her skin, which peeled and crisped along the pale blades of her shoulders and across the tops of her breasts. I had one of the maidservants take her a piece of roast chicken and some wine and said that she could be excused from her duties the next morning to rest, but that by afternoon I expected her back in the sewing room. She would be all right in a day or two, I knew.

Judit did not come weeping and begging my forgiveness the way my mother's maidservants had done, but the next morning the skirt magically reappeared in the trunk of the girl who had lost it, the one who had lodged the original complaint, and for many months afterward there was no trouble among the maidservants at Sárvár. A triumph, Megyery told me afterward, for now all the servants knew I was an evenhanded mistress with fairness and honesty in mind. That I would keep the peace in the house when Ferenc was gone and see to the health and well-being of everyone on the estate, as a respectable wife must. When Ferenc returned, it would be to a well-run house, and me in the center of it, ready to take my place by his side.

# 12

That autumn Sárvár was set to host an event that Orsolya had planned long before my arrival there, the party celebrating the engagement of the palatine's son to the daughter of the house of Báthory. Although the ink on the official documents had been dry for several years, it was only now that family and friends would come together to witness Ferenc put the ring on my finger and acknowledge openly what before had been merely understood.

Now that I had gained a measure of his respect, Megyery sought my advice in helping him arrange the household for the arrival of Ferenc and his retinue. It was I who oversaw the turning out of the rooms and the refreshing of the linens, had the courtyard replanted with new trees and the walls given a fresh coat of whitewash before my fiancé's arrival from the Habsburg court. More and more I tried to feel that I belonged at Sárvár, that it now was my true home. All that remained was for Ferenc Nádasdy to love me, and rejoice in our friendship and upcoming marriage.

On the afternoon they arrived I was attending Megyery in his room, receiving his last instructions regarding the furnishing in the guest quarters and how the cook should make the soup, when I heard the servants coming down the hall to announce the men's arrival. "Go, go," said the tutor, waving me off. "Don't keep him waiting. He should be pleased to see you, and how much you have improved these last months, in beauty and disposition." I hoped rather than believed this to be true as I went through the halls of Sárvár toward my future.

It was a gray day, threatening rain. I had the household servants assembled and waiting for the men in the courtyard, where Ferenc had already dismounted and was giving instructions on stabling the horses. He wore a fine yellow cloak that contrasted strongly with his dark coloring and tanned summer skin, and his longer hair gave him something of a careless appearance, though his eyes under their black brows looked even more fierce than I remembered. Strands of black hair stuck to his brow with sweat. "Welcome home, sir," I said.

"Thank you, Erzsébet," he said. It was the first time he had ever called me by my given name. He gave a curt bow and looked back toward his companions. "It's good to be home." He patted the flanks of his black horse and said something low to István Bocskai that was not meant for my ears, because they both laughed, a peppery sound full of private nuance and history. I was already forgotten. I turned to András Kanizsay and with as much formality as I could, I said, "Welcome, cousin. I hope your journey was not too tiresome."

His face broke into a smile as he looked me over. "Your lady has grown since last winter, Ferenc," he said. "And look here—see how her bosom has increased! She will make you a fine wife after all."

I blushed, a deep red that began in my belly and spread to the very tips of my hair, but Ferenc only glanced at me and looked away again. Either he was as embarrassed as I, or else the thirteen-year-old girl in front of him was not of much interest, either her face or her mediocre excuse for a bosom. Instead he spoke at length to one of the stable boys about his horse, which he suspected had a lame foot. András lowered his eyes and in a more serious tone said, "Forgive me, cousin. I didn't mean to offend you."

"Think nothing of it."

"It is a pleasure to see you again. No, don't look so angry. I've ridden long hours from Bécs, and in all that time I have never seen anything so lovely as the sight of you."

"Thank you, cousin. Your compliments do me great honor."

"Then why do you sound so offended?"

"I'm not. I'm sorry. We have so little company here that I some-times forget my manners." I looked at Ferenc. "My lord too seems to forget himself whenever he comes home. One might receive as little as a glance from him."

"My cousin is distracted at present with the trouble with the king. Old Maximilian has been ill lately, and it weighs on Ferenc." He frowned. "Is everything all right, miss? Have you been crying?"

I wiped my face. "Not at all. It's only a drop of rain."

On the balcony ringing the inner courtyard the assembled ranks of maidservants and cooks, valets and stable boys were watching carefully to see how Ferenc would treat me after the trouble with Judit, and now I saw him look up to the rail where the girl herself stood with her chin raised, her eyes gray and hot as ash, looking from him to me. It was not quite enough to serve as a confirmation of his fondness for her, but it was enough to leave a little sliver of ice in my heart that would not melt. In the count's eyes I was still a child, a bride who was being foisted upon him against his will, and now the servants knew it too. I wondered if Judit would be in Ferenc's bed the moment I was out of his sight.

András relieved my misery by offering me his arm and leading me inside out of the weather. His arm, under my hands, was quite warm and pleasant, like horse's flesh. Ferenc followed, regaling István Bocskai in a low voice with some story of a young woman of their acquaintance in Bécs, a maidservant in a noble house who had found herself with child after some friend of theirs had apparently paid her too much attention. She had been dismissed from her place, they heard, after the mistress of the house learned of the trouble. I walked in the house to the sound of their laughter, my back straight. What did they say about me, I wondered, over their cups at the end of the day? What did the maidservants of Bécs overhear about me, the child bride of Ferenc Nádasdy, in the dark of their rooms at night?

More and more I believed that our marriage would be nothing but a political match, with no joy in it for either of us. I remembered my parents' own marriage, their fondness for each other and for their children, with increasing pangs of loneliness. I didn't love Ferenc any more than he loved me, but I had hoped that we might be friends at least, companions who could enjoy each other's company as well as the power and wealth the match would bring us both. There was no one else in the Nádasdy household near my own age except for András. Darvulia was a dear friend, but I could hardly turn to the lesser servant girls for companionship—the seamstresses, the laundresses, the cooks, the housemaids, with no nobility or education to speak of. But no matter what I said or did, Ferenc never sought my company, and little by little the efforts I had begun to win his love began to seem ridiculous, even contemptible.

Inside the house I made certain the gentlemen had enough food and drink to last the evening, and then, bowing to show more respect than I really felt, I retired for the night, grateful for the air cooling my hot face. In the halls I stood back in the darkness to avoid the looks of the servant girls, the titters of the understewards, so that no one would have to witness my shame.

# 13

October saw the arrival of my mother and brother, along with many of our friends and relatives, nobles from all over Upper Hungary, in preparation for the engagement ceremony. I was overjoyed to see István again and dashed headlong through the halls and across the courtyard the moment I heard the familiar notes of my brother's voice through my window. He was barely off his horse before I had my arms around his neck, and when he kissed my forehead with all tenderness, I remembered our games in the children's court, when he had played the pasha and I the pasha's harem, threatening violence for his love. "Erzsébet, my God," he said. "Is it really you? You're so tall, and a woman now."

My mother climbed down from her carriage. She was much changed in the year and a half since I had seen her last, gray around the temples and ashen in her complexion, but she embraced me for a long time, and I waited until she let me go. "Look at you," she said. "Every woman in the country will be envious of your beauty." It was the greatest praise she could offer. I beamed and let her kiss me, and then I led them up and into the house.

We were suffering all that week under the oppression of a late heat wave, in which the crops turned brown and the rivers receded more than usual from their grassy banks, exposing stinking pools of dying fish and cracking mud. Every day the men went out into the town, first to visit the baths and then across the river where they might find a house where they could drink and play cards to escape the heat. I was glad to be without them, without the sorrow of Ferenc, the annoyance of András, though their excursions did take my brother, István, away from me also. Then came those hot, still evenings during which the whole world seemed to arrest its movement and the wandering stars to stop moving through the firmament, while the insects whirred in the grasses outside and the frogs croaked in the ditches to protest the heat. My mother and Darvulia and I, escaping to one of the lower sitting rooms where it was cooler, pulled our skirts up over our knees and fanned ourselves and sucked pieces of ice that the servants brought up from the cool house, little bits of chill winter saved in sawdust for these most uncomfortable days. I ordered a number of the candles blown out to reduce the heat as well, so the rooms were dimmer than usual, and little more than the dark head of Darvulia was visible to me across the room as we waited for Ferenc and András and my brother to come home.

The men came back well after midnight, drunk and singing, and I went down to them to wish them good evening and make certain they had everything they needed before I went off to bed. Ferenc followed me, as he did every night, I playing hostess and leading him by the light of my single candle to the door of his room. At no moment did we speak to each other, but I think he was aware, as I was, that it would not be much longer before he and I would be master and mistress of this house. He was an orphan, I nearly so, and far from the watchful eyes of our chaperones. Alone, for the present.

I stopped at the door and would have bade him good night with all politeness, as usual, but when I looked into his black eyes, his handsome rapacious face, I put my hand on his arm and leaned in more closely, speaking in a private voice that, until then, I had not known I possessed. "Good night," I said. Under my hand his skin was hot. It was the first time I had ever touched him. It was more pleasant than I had imagined, warm and close and full of expectation. "I hope your sleep is restful."

He took a step back, his face all over crimson and angry. "What are you doing?" he said. "Go back to your room, miss, and remember who and where you are." Now I was *miss* again, not Erzsébet. His face was half shadowed and stern in the dim light, the hawk-faced look of a priest reprimanding a harlot. If he encouraged wantonness in his maidservants, it appeared he would have none in his bride-to-be. To him I was to be only chaste, obedient, and modest, my eyes lowered always like those old statues of the Virgin hidden in chests and cupboards and cellars wherever the new faith had supplanted the old. There was no husband in those images, I realized now—only mother and child. No earthly love, but only submission to the will of God.

He took another step and another, opening the door as the candlelight grew and stretched between us, lengthening our shadows there. In a moment Ferenc closed the door to his chamber behind him. I could hear the click of the lock, and then I was alone on the stairs of the tower.

In the light of my single candle, which did little to dispel the darkness in that part of the house, I felt myself more lonely than ever. Ferenc would marry me, and I would become his property, that much was clear. My name and dowry, my very self, would all belong to the house of Nádasdy, but your father's heart, Pál, was something I could not hope to touch, not then. Around me the house went dim and still, and I heard the night noises of Ferenc's valet speaking to him in a low hum, the distant murmur of the young men still in the main hall, drinking by the light of the fire, the skirts of the maidservants as they swished to and fro combining with the hot shameful beating of my own heart. For a moment I raised my hand as if to pound on Ferenc's door, and then dropped it again and stood trembling in the dark, unsure where to go or what to do next.

Below there was a noise, a shuffling as of feet on wooden boards. Where the candle shone faintly through the doorway, I could see a dark figure—András Kanizsay, trying to hide in the shadows. His face was turned up to me, and for a moment I thought I saw a look of pleasure curling the corners of his mouth. What he was doing there I couldn't imagine. In a moment I heard his footsteps retreating, saw his back turning away. That he should have seen my humiliation was intolerable, and I sprinted down the opposite hall to my own bedchamber, where the white bed waited with its rugs and curtains, its cushions and down mattress, a nest fit for an empress, but one who would sleep, as always, alone.

My ladies undid the laces of my gown, took down the combs and pearls from my hair. Darvulia came in with a concoction of figs soaked in brandy that she said would help me sleep. I threw myself into her arms and wept. She said nothing about what had transpired in the hall, though I didn't doubt that somehow word was already making its way around Sárvár, to the maidservants who laughed and smirked whenever I passed, to the men down in the hall with their wine and their singing. I drank her cup dry and closed my eyes while she brushed out all my long dark-brown hair, falling afterward into a restless half sleep in which I was always seeing the change of Ferenc's countenance, his expression turning over and over to fear and revulsion. The room spun from the brandy, the strong drink.

I was still more awake than asleep long after midnight when my door opened a crack, revealing faintly a darker shape against the wall, the shadow of someone coming into the room. The ropes holding my mattress creaked beneath me. I was sitting up in bed. "Darvulia?" I asked.

"Hardly," said a male voice. Then he was inside, and the door was shut. We were alone in the darkness, a little moonlight coming through the shutters turning the shapes in the room to monstrous forms, the lion-backed chair to a beast with dripping jaws, the table in the corner to a catafalque. The rugs on the bed lay on my limbs like earth on a new grave, but I was afraid to throw them off. The room tilted and then righted itself, the liquor still buzzing in my veins. I realized I was holding my breath and let it out again with a little sigh, the only sound either of us made in that space, that wet ephemeral darkness while his steps on the floor came toward me.

"You must be lonely in here by yourself," said András Kanizsay.

I pulled the cloth closer around me. I was afraid of him, afraid of myself with him. I had a strange desire to ask him to stay, to wrap my arms around his neck and press my mouth to the warm skin there, though I knew that was impossible. "Go away," I hissed.

"I don't think you mean that at all. I think you want me here."

"Go back to your own room, András. I do mean it." This time my voice was firmer, more sure of itself, more mindful of the danger I was in.

He was standing next to the bed, so close I could smell the *pálinká* on his breath, sweet and coppery and full of sugar. I knew I should have called for the guards, but he was already in my room—the taint of him would be on me no matter what I did. We were already guilty by association. No one would believe me if I said that nothing had happened. No one would believe him if he said he did not force himself on me.

The room was stifling in the October heat, and when he came and sat on the edge of the bed, the oily sweat of his skin mingled with my own, and the slightly acrid smell of his armpits, the sweeter scent of his hair, mixed with the sugar of his breath. I held myself entirely still, listening to the blood rush in my ears. Despite my mother's tutoring in the wifely arts, I did not know what I should do. I was not yet a wife. Any movement, I felt, would endanger us both further. A faint outline of him was visible in the weak light coming through the window. The wryness was gone, replaced by a sad kind of drunken earnestness that made me pity him a little. The insignificant cousin, made significant for a moment.

"You are so beautiful," he said.

"Ferenc doesn't think so."

"Ferenc doesn't see you. *I* see you. If I had been the palatine's son, if I had been a count with enough estates for a kingdom, I could have been your husband."

"Stop talking about things that will never happen. Ferenc is going to be my husband."

"Not yet he isn't." He came closer, pressing me down into the mattress. "From the first moment I saw you, when you tumbled out of the carriage into my arms, I knew you were for me."

That made me laugh. "I thought I was a child, with a chest as flat as a boy's, a serious little nun who would plague your cousin into his grave."

"You don't have a boy's chest now. I see you looking at me. Ferenc doesn't know you. He has his swordplay and his horses and his great name to live up to. And his maidservants, and his friends. He doesn't have time for his lovely little fiancée."

His hands were rougher than I would have thought, calloused from holding the sword and the reins, and they pressed down on my wrists, down into the softness of the bed. "I'll scream," I said, but the words were weightless, like a sigh.

"No, you won't. You want me here as much as I want to be here. You'll be sweet and good, and let me be your husband tonight."

If I had wanted, I might have fought him off. Even then I could have kicked and slapped and overturned the furniture, called for the guards, called for Ferenc. Perhaps I should have. But Ferenc did not want me, and András did. Here was pleasure and friendship, instead of loneliness and resentment. Here was a man who would love me not for my dowry and family connections, not for my future children, but for myself.

If I had known then the kind of man András really was, if I had known how he would turn his back on me, I would have sent him away at once. But that night, God help me, I wanted him there, his weight pressing down the bed, his hands in my hair. His attentions had always pleased me more than they should have, and now, in darkness, I was sure I loved him. With a child's innocence, I thought if I could not have the man who was supposed to want me, I would have the other instead.

His hands were on my shift, pulling it up, and I was nowhere, I was darkness. From someplace I felt a sharp pain, and he was nothing but a shadow over me, insubstantial, like a spirit I dreamed into being. It was already too late to send him away. Willingly then I put my arms around his neck and my hands into his hair, fine and soft and smelling of woodsmoke, but the place where his whiskers burned against my face left it raw and red, so that in the morning Darvulia, who said nothing about my appearance, had to bring me some ointment for the soft parts of me, slashed, burning, an occupied country.

# 14

Thus are the seeds of trouble sown. I have often thought of that night, Pál, the girl I was then, the little fool who thought she was in love, who thought she had chosen for herself a man who would love her. Who nearly ruined everything over a moment of despair.

When Ferenc and I stood in front of our friends and family for the engagement ceremony, when I held up my hand in front of our friends and family and let him put on it the ring of gold and ruby that had once belonged to his mother, my belly was already full of András Kanizsay's child. The red dress my mother and Darvulia had bound me into that morning felt so tight across my ribs I thought I would faint, and I was so pale and green that Ferenc asked in my ear if I wouldn't like to delay a day or so until I felt better. "Of course not," I said, more sharply than I should have, and for the rest of the day he scowled, saying nothing to me, not even "good night" at the end of the evening. Instead I danced with István Bocskai, Ferenc's friend from the imperial court and an ally to my own Báthory uncles in Transylvania, his arm around my waist as he spun me around to the lively strains of a *palotás*. The eyes of everyone in the room were on us, including those of my András, who did not ask me to dance.

Instead he watched, and drank, and teased his cousin about me, all as he had before. His coldness frightened me, made me think that perhaps our night together had been a single moment only, a drunken mistake that in the light of day he meant to deny. I tried to convince myself that I no longer cared for him, that his love or lack of it meant nothing to me, but I could not stop the warmth that came over me whenever I caught his eye, the sudden twist in my entrails that felt like love. He said nothing more to me than "Good evening, miss," all night, and I went to bed that evening puzzling over the way he smiled whenever he caught me staring.

I had nearly made up my mind to forget about him, to shut the door to him forever, when he came to my room once more under cover of darkness, swearing that his actions that evening had been for my protection. "I must be aloof in public," he said, "or else I will have to declare my love for you in front of everyone, and give us both away." Awash in relief, I believed him. I wept and covered him with kisses, begged him never to turn his back on me, and once again showed him the love that his cousin would not or could not accept.

In company András and I continued much as we had before—I pretending to annoyance, András keeping up what appeared to be his usual good-natured teasing. No one looked closely enough to see that my annoyance now hid a kernel of fear that someone would discover our secret, or that his teasing masked what I thought were his more tender feelings. He made no more comments about my bosom or my age, at least, either in front of Ferenc or privately to me. He came to my bed two or three more times that month, when it seemed like it would be safe to do so, murmuring endearments and bringing me such little presents as he could afford—a comb for my hair, a bit of ribbon he'd bought in the market. I made sure, every evening, to leave the door unlocked for him and pretended surprise whenever I woke to find his sweet breath crushing against my mouth, thrilling at having a secret of my own to keep, at having someone of my own choosing to love. He would stay an hour, maybe two, and slip out again before Darvulia came in with my breakfast each morning. We thought we were being so clever. In public we might be good and honorable, but the night, he said, was ours alone. No one would ever know our secret.

It was two months or more before I noticed my monthlies had ceased. They had always been infrequent, and I too young to miss them. But I did notice how smells changed: the honeysuckle so sweet and cloying under my window that I asked the gardener to chop it down, the smell of baking bread as strong as the scent of manure in the stables. After a few weeks, food became so disagreeable I could keep nothing down except broth and a little pale beer. I hardly left my room at all, claiming an infectious fever. There was so much sickness in the country then that no one suspected, or if they did they knew better, at least, than to say anything to me.

More than once I thought of telling András, wondering what he would say, if he would be proud, if he would be frightened. If he would denounce me, let my secret slip in a moment of drunkenness or fear. If he would ask me to come away with him, take what money and possessions we could and disappear. We could go to Venice, to Rome, to the Habsburg lands in Spain, even to the New World if we chose. I imagined a flight in the dark, changing our names, the bucking decks of ships at sea, a new life in unknown lands.

All this I dreamed, but when I told him at last, when I gathered my courage one night and told him that I was expecting his child, he laughed and said he had been wondering. I looked so green all the time. Did I not know how to prevent a child? he asked. Did my mother teach me nothing useful?

Of course she did, I said, though she had done nothing of the kind. My mother must have thought any child I bore would be from my noble marriage and not a tryst with a lesser-born cousin. That there were ways to prevent a child, and that András knew about them while I did not, disturbed me even more than his indifference to my condition. For the first time I wondered if I could not trust him. He kissed me with as much warmth as ever, but he went away that night without making any of the promises or plans I hoped for—no carriages or ships, no desperate flights through the darkness toward an unknown fate.

A few days later, when my mother demanded the truth, and I knew I would not be able to hide it from her much longer, I told her privately that I had given myself to László Bende, the butcher's son whom I had reprimanded for fighting, a boy to whom I had spoken no more than eight or ten words in my life. No one could know the real identity of the man I had loved, not if I was to protect him. My brother was furious, saying I had debased myself and threatened a match that would be the making of all of us, but he promised to keep my secret, and to help me make arrangements to get out of Sárvár until the child was born. In the strictest secrecy my mother made plans to take me away to the Nádasdy house at Léka under the pretense of tending my illness herself, with a mother's loving attention. We dared not return home to Ecsed, where the truth would not stay hidden for long. Léka, with its healthful mountain air, its remoteness, would make an excellent place to hide my shame. I was not without hope even then. Perhaps after an absence András would reconsider his options and decide to come for me and the child. Perhaps my removal would make him remember that he loved me, and that my shame was his as well.

We left on a cool bright morning, my mother bundling me into rugs for the journey in her cart, bringing with us only Darvulia, the *táltos*, and her medicinal powders and drinks. Both her talent with the healing arts and the deep friendship I felt for her meant I would not leave her behind. She helped me climb into the carriage and settled the rug across my lap while my mother spoke to the driver about the road into the mountains. Megyery came to see us off, shading his bulging frog's eyes against the sun and wishing my health much improved. I thanked him and looked in the dark places of the courtyard, to see if there might be a young man who was sorry to see me go, but there were only servants carrying trunks, and the stable master checking the traces, and a maidservant taking the white sheets from my bed to the laundry, her eyes flicking to me and down again as she hurried past.

"Don't look for him, miss," Darvulia said. "He won't be there, and it won't look right if you get upset. You're supposed to be ill."

I looked down at the hands in my lap. "One might think he would come to see me off at least. We are supposed to be married next year."

"It wasn't the master I was speaking of, miss. You know the other does not dare come to wish you farewell when your fiancé does not."

So she had guessed the identity of my night visitor, that crafty creature. I should have known. Nothing ever slipped past Darvulia's notice. From that moment I knew I could trust her with anything, with my most secret self, and never again would there be anything but complete trust between Darvulia and myself.

In a moment Megyery helped my mother into the carriage. She settled herself down beside me and put the rug over her knees. The driver spoke a word to the horses, which lurched forward with one sickening motion, toward Léka, where three women could tend to the future in silence.

# 15

My mother, Darvulia, and I spent the whole of that winter by ourselves in a private wing of the expansive *vár* at Léka, a many-level keep on a hill in the mountains north of Sárvár, circled by mists coming off the river, cool even in the heat of summer. There we watched my belly expand, tending the fire ourselves, making the meals with the help of only Darvulia, since we didn't dare bring an entire retinue of servants who were not likely to keep gossip to themselves. That part of Hungary was suffering an outbreak of smallpox, so that we had a good excuse to hide away, with little contact from the stable master and the small group of maids who came and went around the castle when it was unoccupied by the Nádasdy court. We were kept active with the endless chores necessary for daily living and didn't speak of the business at hand, the child within me. As I felt it stretch and kick I remembered the feel of András's weight pressing me down into the bed and wondered what would have happened if Ferenc, and not András, had come to me that night when all the lights were out.

The first pains of labor began one morning in the middle of the summer. I woke clutching my hands to my belly, afraid, remembering the sight of my sister Klára being born, the wet head and the blood and my mother's cries. A wave of pain swept over me briefly and then went away again. I thought if I didn't move or speak it might lessen, so I didn't wake my mother on the other side of the bed or Darvulia from where she slept on a pallet near the window. The room was small and too warm. I kicked the rug off me and went to the window, opening it a crack. The sky bucked and wavered, and a thin trail of mist crept up from the river and into the courtyard. Below I could see a man in a blue coat and long beard leading a white horse, dancing and skittering on the paving stones. He looked up, briefly, and waved. I waved back, wondering if I were seeing a real man and horse or an apparition.

Then my mother was beside me, pulling closed the shutter. "Don't stand at the window," she said. "You'll be seen." I looked down, but the man and the horse were gone.

My mother fetched me breakfast, bread and fruit, but I wasn't hungry, nor did I want to sit still and listen while she read to me from her favorite bit of Calvin, or embroider the waistcoat I had been working on, or play the lute for my mother's amusement. The pain did not return for several hours, but I was restless, and moved from the window to the bed and back like a dog circling for a place to lie down. Still I would not tell them that the pains had begun. "Erzsébet, my God," my mother said. "Sit down before you make me dizzy."

The truth was that I was afraid. Many women I knew had died in childbirth. I was young and strong, but so had been many others who had gone before me. I did not want to die delivering András Kanizsay's child. I thought of the stories of the Virgin, who gave birth in a stable with only her husband to attend her. At least I wasn't as unfortunate as she. I had good help with me, and better on the way, for several months before my mother had sent for a midwife, a woman named Birgitta whom she trusted. This midwife had borne four children herself, all of whom had died. Of sickness, my mother was quick to explain, not the delivery itself. But Birgitta had not yet arrived that morning when the pains started. She was due soon, I knew, but not yet, not yet.

I got up again and went to the window. The mist was beginning to burn off, revealing the road that followed the line of the river, the opposite side where the hills mounted toward the sky, but there was no sign of the midwife's carriage. The heaviness in my belly increased moment by moment, and another pain came. I closed my eyes. I would not cry out. If I didn't cry, if I did not admit my suffering, the child would not come. I would be safe.

My mother was looking at me strangely. I could feel her large black eyes over my face, her knowing eyes. Another pain came, and another.

"It's started," she said. "Darvulia, get her into bed. It's time for her confinement."

"The midwife isn't here, Mother."

"Darvulia and I can deliver you if we must."

"The midwife isn't here. The baby can't come until the midwife arrives."

"Erzsébet, get into bed, my love. It's time."

A gush of green fluid fell from my body, splashing along the wooden boards and staining my shift, my feet. There was so much of it I thought at first that Darvulia had spilled a bucket of water across the floor. But my belly tightened, and I could feel the outlines of the child under my skin. Moving.

"Green," Darvulia said. "We have to be especially careful."

My mother looked grim. I didn't know what the green water meant, but I stood still while Darvulia pulled the shift off me and helped me into bed. My mother readied the birthing chair in the corner, a wooden stool with a hole in the middle on which I would have to squat. My mother had explained everything to me already, but I still felt completely unprepared as I climbed into bed, as the pains grew in frequency and the room around me closed in tighter and tighter, until there was nothing but myself and the color of pain, bright red, and a pressing, gasping need that moved lower and lower into my belly as the day wore on.

At one point I heard a new voice in the room: the midwife had arrived, come rushing up the stairs with her cloak still on, barking directions at the two women in the room and at me, her face lined and dark but kind. She helped me from the bed to the birthing chair, which was hard-backed and stiff as a confessional. She knelt before me and gave me orders. Push now. Push now, Erzsébet, or the child will die. Push.

*Save me.*

I curled around my belly and pushed and pushed, and then there was a popping and a release, and then the child slid free of me, a healthy girl with a shock of dark hair like my own, with my own great dark eyes and long, distinctive Báthory nose. The midwife cleaned out her mouth and nose with a swift and efficient finger, and then I heard her cry, a wail that circled round my head as Darvulia wiped my face and waited for the afterbirth, which she carried away like a dead child into the bowels of the castle. What she did with it I didn't know, nor did I want to know. She was a *táltos* and had her own way of doing things.

My mother put the baby briefly into my arms. She was so light after the heaviness I had felt in my belly all those months, her limbs pink and white and so warm it was like she had been taken from inside a hot oven. "Her name will be Erzsébet, after her mother," said my mother, "but that is all the inheritance she will receive from you." Then she took the child from me and gave her to the midwife, who cooed and spoke to my daughter in a strange tongue I did not understand. To this Birgitta my mother also handed over a great deal of gold, enough for a pasha's ransom, on the condition that she take the child away and never return to Hungary in this life, or contact the Báthory or Nádasdy families again. The midwife agreed. While I wept and struggled to rise from my bed, while I slapped at the hands that tried to restrain me and swore that I hated my mother and would never forgive her, that it was too much to bear, Birgitta put on her cloak and carried my baby from the castle of Léka, disappearing back to her native land, and I never saw either of them again.

My mother watched over me for several more weeks, until I was well recovered, and then she arranged to have me sent back to Sárvár with Darvulia as my chaperone. She kissed me before putting me in the carriage, a cold dry kiss on my cheek that I did not return. I would not thank her. I would show her no love for what had been done to me and my child for the sake of her ambitions. "Ferenc Nádasdy is a good man," she said, her voice weary. "He is only young and will learn in time what love is. Do your best to make him love you, and you will both be happy." I did not tell her how little hope I had of his love, nor how little desire to marry him, not when my heart was still full of András Kanizsay. Then my mother stood back to let the horses pull me away to my new life, all evidence of my sin washed as clean as if it had never been. She would be dead a few weeks later of the smallpox that was ravaging the villages of Upper Hungary, her face scarred and unrecognizable at the last by the pustules that marked that terrible disease, and afterward Darvulia and I alone would be left witness to what had passed in my rooms at Léká.

Years later I would forgive my mother, understanding that none of us who were present that day had any choice in the matter. Just as my mother had sent me to my future, I sent my secret daughter to hers, wishing that whatever joy she might find in this life would be hers, that she would have the ability to choose it for herself, and the courage to take it.

# 16

After my confinement at Léka I was sent back to Sárvár, to my tiresome chaperonage under Imre Megyery. The men were gone, having returned to Bécs during my absence, so there was little to amuse me at the Nádasdy house. I missed András but did not dare to write him. Instead I spent those months toiling over the last of my formal lessons, enduring fittings for my trousseau, writing letters to my sisters and brother and our cousins back home at Ecsed, sharing our sorrow over my mother's death.

After a few months of this we left for the Nádasdy estate at Varannó, which lay at the far eastern part of the kingdom not far from my family's house at Ecsed. There I was to be married off on the eighth of May in the year 1575, with nearly five thousand guests in attendance. Among the invited was the Holy Roman Emperor Maximilian II himself, as well as the greatest noble families from all over Hungary, Austria, and Transylvania: Batthyánys, Esterházys, Zrínyis,

Rákóczis, Drugeths, and Pálffys would crowd into the *kastély,* and the Nádasdy court would fill with more gaiety than I had ever known before, or was likely to know after.

Everything in the months leading up to the wedding itself was done with the greatest ceremony and decorum. Megyery arranged to take me from Sárvár to Varannó with a large retinue of servants, including Darvulia and some ladies, young cousins of the Báthory and Nádasdy families, crowded into carriages and chattering on and on about the young men at court, the latest gossip from Prága or Pozsony. I looked forward to the wedding not for the sake of my marriage to Ferenc but because I was certain to see András again, as well as my brother and sisters, those who really loved me and whom I loved without reservation. My life had been filled with so much solemnity of late—the birth of the child, the death of my mother—that I felt a kind of desperation for joy. I would dance until my shoes fell apart, and drink wine, and listen to endless strains of music made for my enjoyment. As we made the long trek by carriage back across Hungary Megyery told me more than once to quit fidgeting and leaning out the window like a gypsy and behave instead like a young woman on the verge of her greatest triumph. At night I would fall into Darvulia's arms and beg her to sing to me, to soothe me against my anxiety. She attended everything I needed with the greatest care, giving me a tonic that calmed my nerves and let me sleep a little in the rocking carriage, so that I was not always irritating Megyery with my impatience.

Everywhere we went there were sights that gave me pleasure. Farmers along the Carpathian foothills walked through the fields sowing their spring wheat in the turned earth, and in villages children chased the carriage through the streets, shouting for us to throw a few coins out the window in their direction, in which I, as the bride, obliged them. A shower of glittering *fillér* fell wherever we passed, scooped up by children who waved and shouted blessings in our direction as if the Virgin herself had been spotted among them.

When we arrived at the palace of Varannó—one of the smallest and most far-flung of the Nádasdy estates, chosen to be closer to my own family's holdings at Ecsed and Szathmár—it was already filled with people who had come to prepare for the wedding. Two dozen master chefs and more than a dozen wedding stewards were hired to manage the house and entertain the many guests who would soon arrive. Dressmakers, cooks, housemaids, and laundresses were brought in from the countryside, where the local peasantry rejoiced to have such profitable work, and musicians from Prága and Bécs, from as far away as Venice and Florence, came to perform for the entertainment of the noble families of Hungary. The marriage of the house of Báthory to the house of Nádasdy was a state affair, something sanctioned by the king and smiled on by God himself, who in his wisdom set the nobility as the protectors and defenders of the people. Both our families knew the necessity of outshining the neighbors in the splendor of the arrangements and spent lavishly to make it possible—Ferenc, as head of his family, and my brother as head of mine.

From my first moment at Varannó I felt myself at the center of a dance that seemed to go on whether I wanted it to or not, though I—or rather my family name and fortune, and the children I would be expected to bear on behalf of both—was the object of it all. When I stood on a box in dressmaker's pieces in a room full of windows, faint with hunger while the ladies pinned the pieces of silk and lace, the servants scurried in and out of the house carrying flour, nutmeg, honey, eggs, oranges, lemons, figs, soft-skinned apricots, bright red pomegranates, pale plucked chickens. The butchers skinned steers and boiled hogs, and kitchen boys rolled barrels of wine and great wheels of cheese up from the cellars. All around me women young and old swept and scrubbed, kneaded and whisked, and outside young men mucked the stables and mended the livery and gave the walls a fresh coat of whitewash, so that the castle gleamed in the sunlight that rose each morning as if it had been ordered especially for me. Gypsies in colorful dress came in from the countryside to play music outside the palace walls for the local people who gathered there to join the celebration and strain for a glimpse of the Hungarian grandees coming and going, reminding me of the gypsy man I had seen executed as a child. I had the wedding stewards arrange for great pig roasts on the plains near the riverbank, where long into the night the people drank and danced by torchlight until dawn. The palace of Varannó turned for a time into a city as large and splendid as Bécs itself.

At night I could hardly sleep for the sweet strains of music out the window, or for the anticipation that soon my loneliness and sorrow would end, and I would see András Kanizsay once more. The fact that I was shortly to be Ferenc Nádasdy's bride hardly factored into my thinking at all, so centered was I on the object of my desire. Ferenc and I had to wed—it was decided for us long ago and could not be set aside without dire consequences on both sides—but my heart in those days was a thing he would not, could not touch.

By custom my own family traveled first from Ecsed to be with me for the wedding preparations. They arrived one afternoon in the same great creaking wooden carriage that had once carried me across Hungary to Sárvár, my sisters leaning out the window as it crossed the bridge into the castle to wave at me. I came down to the courtyard to meet them, hardly able to stand still long enough to hear the rattle of the wheels on the boards of the drawbridge, much less wait for some steward to climb the stairs to my room and tell me they had arrived. In a moment the carriage door opened and my sisters tumbled out to embrace me, grown in loveliness and health in the three years since I had seen them last. Little Klára, whose birth those many years ago had frightened me so much, had inherited our mother's tiny frame, making her look younger even than her six years. Dark-eyed Zsofía, at nearly twelve, was the image of our mother, but my sister smiled much more easily than our mother had the last time I had seen her, so that the resemblance quickly faded, along with the stab of pain at my heart. She teased me immediately on reaching up to place her arms around my neck. "Ferenc Nádasdy will have to stand on tiptoe to kiss you, sister," she said. "Or is he really as tall as they say? A giant of a man in more than height alone?"

I rebuked her with a glance and a word. "I see your confessors have a great deal of work before them," I said. "Unless they have given you up already as a lost cause, a wild girl with no manners and no hope of redemption."

But then I touched her lovely dark hair, black as deep water, and she said, "It is good to see you again," and it was as if no time at all had passed since we had seen each other.

Next István stepped forward and embraced me, his shoulders hunched despite his increased height, several inches at least in the year or so since I had seen him last, the white line of his mouth pressed together. How solemn he had grown. He had always shown an inclination toward quiet contemplation and isolation, toward books and prayer, but it must have cost him a great deal of sadness to leave home so soon after the death of our mother. I had not been able to go to Ecsed for the funeral ceremony, since it was so close to my wedding date and because my mother needed to be buried swiftly after the smallpox took her, so István and I had not seen each other since I had left for Léka, to bear my illegitimate child in secrecy.

I asked if he was well, and he kissed me with warmth and assured me he was. "I apologize," he said. "It is only that I wish our mother were here. But I'm happy for you. We will think only of you and your marriage." Then he took my arm and led me once more into the house. I had a sense of us grown up and grave, István in my father's place now and I in my mother's, and my heart broke for my poor brother, whose grief since our mother's death must have been deep indeed.

We had little time to dwell on our family sorrows. Soon there were numerous wedding traditions to see to, first among those being the arrival of the groom's messengers to come greet us and tell us of Ferenc's approach. We had a servant posted to watch out for them for several days before their expected arrival, and every rider who approached the gates stirred in me old hopes and desires, old wishes and fears, as Ferenc Nádasdy and his retinue made the long journey from Bécs to Varannó.

I had not seen András Kanizsay since the end of the previous fall, since before my mother had taken me off to Léka with his child in my belly. I remembered how after I told him about the child his attitude toward me had changed utterly. He no longer teased Ferenc for his lack of interest in me, or me for the change from girlhood to young woman, all as he had before. He hardly looked at me, speaking to me rarely, finding excuses to leave whenever I entered the room. He had justified his behavior at the time by telling me we needed to give no hints or clues that would make anyone suspect what had passed between us, but now I was not so sure. How would he be when he saw me again? Would he be glad to see me? Would he be cold, and laugh at me as he had the night I told him about the child? He had not written to me during my absence, nor I to him, despite the anguish I felt at our separation. I wrote to Ferenc once or twice, as expected, but my letters were all politeness, containing as little of my heart as possible—my studies, my travels, the sickness stalking the woods and fields around Léka, my own health, as well as the expected formal expressions of joy at the prospect of our upcoming union. I mentioned András in my letters not at all, except to have Ferenc wish his friends and family well for me in my absence, as uninterested a pose as I could manage. Ferenc wrote to me to tell me he was well, that life in Bécs continued to be busy and amusing, but he never mentioned András in his letters to me. That the wedding would allow me a chance to see András once more filled me with far more apprehension than my upcoming marriage vows to Ferenc Nádasdy.

On the day the servant came and said the groom's heralds had been spotted on the road to Varannó, I sent for István to go down to greet them as the head of the family and waited in my rooms for the steward to come up to fetch me. I picked up some bits of embroidery to hide the fact that my hands were shaking and felt a little throb of gratitude toward Orsolya, whose patience I had tried by deriding embroidery as nothing more than a pursuit for uneducated ladies, but now I saw it kept the hands and eyes busy and the outward demeanor calm while the mind was free to travel elsewhere. I pictured András riding toward Varannó and did not know if I would be able to sit still.

My impatient sisters went to the window again and again to report the progress of the riders toward the chateau, calling news over their shoulders and looking at me to see if I blushed. The chance to meet friends of Ferenc, young men of a marriageable age and situation, made them bold. Now they were at the edge of the village, Klára said, now approaching the river, now riding up the castle hill and across the drawbridge, now dismounting their horses and slapping the dust from their thighs. "I cannot see who they are from here," she said. "But they are both young men."

"Thank heavens," answered Zsofía, standing up to look. "At least Nádasdy didn't send us two old grandpas without teeth." She was already engaged by then to András Fígedy and thus felt free to indulge in speculation over the identities of the two messengers without embarrassment. She said they were handsome, at least from several stories up. Would I come to the window and see?

No, I said, but I managed to smile at their teasing. I didn't dare go to the window but kept at the embroidery, pretending not to care in the least about the identity of the messengers. With my needle I made a stab of blue into the white cloth of a handkerchief, but my hand shook and I missed my spot, making a dent in the side of a cornflower. I had to pull it back out again and start afresh, but missed again and stuck the needle into my own finger. "Look how nervous she is," said Zsofía. "I have never seen you so lacking in composure, Erzsébet. You must be afraid of the wedding night."

"Not at all," I said.

"I hear it is not as terrible as everyone says. That with the right man it could even be pleasurable."

"Just watch the window, little sister," I said, sucking the blood from my finger. "Perhaps you will see your own future husband there, unless he thinks the better of it upon catching sight of you, and runs away again."

After a decent interval, a servant came up to fetch us, and I was able to put the embroidery aside. I paused to smooth a hand over my hair at the mirror and compose my face, as I had the day I arrived at Sárvár and learned that the young man with my mother-in-law was not Ferenc Nádasdy but his cousin. I went slowly down the stairs though I wanted to fly, followed by my own entourage of ladies, who flanked my back and my sides as we entered the great hall at Varannó. The two gentlemen were already there waiting for us, changed into clean clothes, speaking quietly but with evident pleasure to my brother, István, who seemed to know them. My heart lifted for a moment. Then they turned, and quickly I arranged my face to hide my disappointment. I recognized István Bocskai, Ferenc's closest friend from Bécs, who was as pleasant as Ferenc was cold. He seemed taller than he had since we danced at the engagement ceremony, quite well grown, and I composed my expression into a look of pleasure, bowed, and said how genuinely happy I was to see him again after my winter away from the court. "We missed you at Christmas at Sárvár this year," he said. "Ferenc was quite bereft without you."

A hint of sarcasm crept into my voice as I answered, "Yes, he must have been."

"I hope your health has improved since the winter. I can see that it has."

I searched his face for any sign of knowledge, for any hint of a secret lorded over me, but there was none, just the honest expression of a true friend. "Thank you," I said, warm with gratitude and nearly ready to weep with relief, "I am feeling very well recovered."

My brother turned my attention to the other messenger, a thin poker of a man whose narrow, uneven shoulders belied his relative youth, and deep gray bags under both eyes that I would later learn were a permanent fixture of his pleasant but unhandsome face. He was a complete stranger to me. He bowed, his back a little more stiff than Bocskai's, his dress too elegant for the occasion—all gold braid and polish, as if he were trying to impress others above his company—but his eyes roamed around the room, speaking of restlessness and impatience. A man of my own temper, surely. "Erzsébet," said my brother, "may I introduce György Thurzó, a friend from Bécs and one of your husband's newer comrades-in-arms."

"Welcome. I hope we may be friends."

"Thank you," he said, taking my hand. His hand was warm and closed over mine a little too tightly. "I'm sure we will. I have heard of the celebrated beauty of Nádasdy's bride-to-be. None of it has been exaggerated."

I could not tell if he was in earnest but thanked him nevertheless. His name was familiar to me—he was the scion of a mining family, wealthy moneylenders and landowners who had risen to power financing the Spanish wars, recently elevated to the nobility—but otherwise I knew nothing of him. At a disadvantage for real topics of conversation, I reverted to small talk. "How did you leave Ferenc?"

His tired eyes crinkled in the corners, just a hint of mirth, but I could not tell at what. "Very well. He does seem to enjoy his time in the saddle. He jousts, and races, and drinks enough for three men."

"You sound as if you don't approve."

"It's not my place to approve or disapprove. But he certainly has the king's favor. Old Maximilian adores his antics."

"And you envy him that. No, don't argue. I can see it in your face." He ducked his head, but I had caught it—the stench of jealousy. "Well, Ferenc does as he chooses. I am glad the king favors him."

"And through him, yourself."

"I suppose so. A woman can rise in position through her husband, but the reverse is true as well."

He bent over my hand. "Then may both your families benefit from your union," he said, and left me to rejoin his friend Bocskai on the other side of the room, his thin shoulders giving even more of an impression of youth and inexperience as he walked away. Why Ferenc chose to surround himself with men who envied his wealth and position I would never know, but it seemed to point to a weakness in him that reminded me of his mother. Orsolya too had surrounded herself with incompetents, hangers-on and weaklings. There would be none in the Nádasdy household after I was mistress there, I would see to it.

I had the stewards bring wine for our parched guests, and later musicians for dancing—all the formal ceremony of wedding preparations, as expected. That night I danced a *palotás* with Bocskai, who as an old acquaintance claimed the first dance with me. He was an excellent dancer, slapping his thighs with such enthusiasm that I had to smile. The newcomer, Thurzó, danced first with my sister Zsofía, who smiled and chatted with rather too much zeal. She would seem too eager, give offense to Thurzó, or else to her future in-laws, the Fígedys, who might hear of her behavior. But Thurzó didn't seem offended as he spun Zsofía around and around the floor, and so I turned my attention back to my own partner and asked him what music they were playing at the court of the king, and pressed him for details on the private lives of the imperial cubs, with whom Bocskai and Ferenc were intimately acquainted. He told me all with a liveliness of temper that matched my own, for we were very fond of each other, István Bocskai and me, like a brother to his sister. His ties to my Transylvanian uncles made him a great favorite of Báthorys everywhere. His family expected great things from him, and I had no doubt even then that he would fulfill those expectations and make himself a famous name that would live for a hundred generations.

After the first dance was over, we changed partners, and I found myself this time with Thurzó. It was only right that the groom's messengers should both dance with the bride, so he spun me around the floor and conversed safely about my journey from Sárvár, the friends we had in common. It seemed he knew my brother, too, from Bécs, where they had sometimes crossed paths at court. In a moment of gravity he told me how sorry he was to hear of the death of my mother, both for my own sake and for my brother's. He looked to where István sat alone at the table, watching the proceedings from a distance and flipping through a book he'd brought to keep himself occupied during the revelries. "István seems to take the loss of her very hard," he said.

"He does," I answered, touched that Thurzó would take such interest in my family. "They were very close, especially after my father died. My mother relied on him a great deal. I don't know how he will bear such a loss, and I will be so far away that I cannot help him."

"And who will help you in your own grief?" he asked.

I thought this a strange question, but I answered, "My husband will be my comfort, of course."

"Of course," he said, but I could not read his expression or his voice, to tell what he meant by such a statement. If he were making an offer, or a threat.

In a little while the dancing ended, and the men got back on their horses to return to Ferenc's retinue, their formal duties performed. "The groom will be at Varannó in two days' time," said Bocskai, "and he is eager to make you his wife."

"As I am to become his wife," I said. Such politeness I endured, such rituals that were meant to give a sense of romance to the occasion of a marriage in which there was likely to be none. I could almost have laughed at it, if I had not been so occupied with my own feelings, my own wishes and fears. "Thank you for coming, gentlemen," I said. "Please give my love to my husband, and send him with all speed to my side."

They said they would, and we settled in to watch and wait.

# 17

On the day Ferenc arrived with his retinue, his guests and companions and their servants, and took up residence in one of the opposite wings of the *vár*, I kept to myself. The conversation I'd had with Thurzó a few days before made me wary, so I avoided the male voices I heard in the halls, afraid that if I saw András I might forget my place and my purpose and make a spectacle that would destroy the match my mother had made for me, a match with a young man of wealth and consequence, not a poor dependent cousin without a penny to his name. Everywhere I felt an impending sense of possession, of myself as something that had been bought for Ferenc, my name and my family, my money, my future. The dressing, the dancing, the feasts and music—all was celebration, but with the appearance of gaiety more than the substance of it, a play that Ferenc and I were acting for the benefit of our families and friends.

We sat together at dinner, and when the music began, my betrothed turned to me with his face unreadable and asked if I would join him for a dance. I was surprised at the request, since it was the first time he'd ever shown much interest in me, but I agreed. He put his hand on the small of my back and led me out onto the floor, a gesture of intimacy that gave me an unexpected rush of warmth. His face was utterly calm and still and intensely focused. He was at least a head taller than me, so that when I faced forward I looked directly into the middle of his chest. As we turned around the floor I strained my eyes for András Kanizsay, my husband for only a month, and though I saw many young men of Ferenc's acquaintance from Bécs and Pozsony— including Bocskai and our new friend Thurzó—I didn't see András anywhere. Nor at the tournaments, the races. I began to wonder if he had not come. Perhaps he could not bear to see me wed to his cousin.

The day of the wedding came at last, hot and dry and with a heavy southerly wind, so that the flags flying from the battlements snapped and whipped like dogs worrying their tails, and the ladies had to keep tight hold of their skirts to retain their modesty. Outside the walls of the *vár* one of the fires burning on the plain got loose from its pit and set fire to the dry grass outside, surrounding the palace with smoke for a few hours until a fire brigade could be assembled to take buckets from the river to put it out, but our clothes smelled of the smoke, and the taste of smoke filled my mouth long after the fires had died out. Along the castle walls the colorful shutters thumped in the wind, lending a cacophony to the events of the day, thudding underneath the sweeter strains of music meant for the celebration like a persistent call to arms.

Before the ceremony I sent my brother as my representative to Ferenc with my gifts to him. First there were some fine clothes, including a great cloak trimmed in white ermine to wear during the cold winter months, then the small Spanish dagger that my father had treasured when he was alive. Finally István himself carried to my new husband the sword of the Báthory family hero Vitus, one of our most cherished possessions, signaling the joining of the Nádasdy line to the Báthory. All these, István said, my betrothed accepted with pleasure.

For his part, Ferenc sent to me, via Bocskai and Thurzó, a Milanese gown of yellow silk that pleased me very well, as well as a costly necklace made of fine yellow gold in a rose pattern containing a glowing red cabochon—the same jewel I had seen on his mother's neck the first time I had met her at Ecsed. This I placed around my neck to wear with my wedding gown, to show my pleasure at his gift. Then Bocskai handed me a scroll, closed with wax and bearing the Nádasdy seal. I unwrapped the document. It was the deed to my own piece of land in northwestern Hungary, a two days' ride from the capital at Pozsony. This scroll named me the sole owner of the Nádasdy estate at the stronghold of Csejthe, as well as the seventeen villages surrounding the castle, to keep or dispose of at my wish. As I read the document and realized what it was I held in my hands, I felt a rush of warmth toward Ferenc Nádasdy. At the moment when all my possessions, my dowry and lands, even my very self, were to become his, the richest gift any husband could have given to his bride was a place in the world to call her own. That he recognized such a fact spoke of more feeling than I had ever before given him credit of being capable. The scroll trembled in my hands. I thanked Bocskai and Thurzó and sent them back to Ferenc to express my profound gratitude.

After I was dressed, we were joined by my brother and the male members of the family, and at the appointed hour we went out together to meet my husband. The wedding was to take place in a new hall Orsolya, before her death, had ordered built for the occasion, a wedding annex constructed over the past two years inside the cramped walls of the chateau, and in the late afternoon, when the sun was already past its zenith, I went down with my sisters and brother and a great retinue to the wedding hall. Around the keep gun salutes sounded, and musicians played sweet strains of music, and on the plains outside the walls people shouted and cheered and called the bride forth. My sisters kept the hem of my dress—a heavy Florentine silk brocade with threads of real gold—out of the dust that rose and coated everything.

Inside the pavilion the guests were assembled. Then, as we were approaching the front door, Bocskai, as best man, stepped forward to greet us on Ferenc's behalf. Ferenc himself—almost unbearably handsome in velvet breeches the color of blood, a matching jacket with gold buttons, and soft yellow calfskin boots—stood back a little, surrounded by his friends. Among them I recognized András, the lighthearted tilt at the corners of his eyes the same as it used to be. Green-jeweled eyes, the color of jealousy. He glanced at me only once. At first I thought he was merely being prudent, keeping his feelings a secret still. But some strange expression—was it joy?—

played over the corners of his mouth as he stared at the place where my cousin Griseldis Bánffy stood blushing behind one of my elbows. Until that moment I hardly remembered she was there.

By that time little Griseldis was a thickheaded but pretty girl with her mother's exotic coloring—long tresses the color of August wheat, pale gray eyes. A chest flat as a shield, Zsofía had joked that morning, to keep the men at bay. She had no education to speak of, but Griseldis was the sole surviving child in a family with several small but profitable holdings in the west, including a good vineyard and croplands and a small *kastély*, and I had heard the speculation among the ladies in the past few days about who would be lucky enough to secure her and her small fortune, her yellow curls and plump red mouth. Now I heard whispers and giggling behind me, the other ladies teasing young Griseldis about her betrothal to the elegant young cousin of Ferenc Nádasdy.

For a moment I felt faint and reached out to Zsofía to steady myself. My sister took my elbow and in a whisper asked if it was too hot, if the sun and the dust were in my eyes. No, I said—I only lost my balance for a moment. The little Italian shoes I wore under my gown took some practice. I stood up straight again, but Zsofía kept hold of my elbow, just in case. I could not quite make out Ferenc's expression, if he were amused and delighted by the proceedings, or if, as usual, he endured all this fuss and ceremony with the barest of tolerance for the sake of his departed mother and all her grand ambitions for him.

Bocskai bowed, the edges of his elegant cloak touching the ground, his eyes twinkling for the bit of teasing that he was about to undertake, the good-hearted bit of fun that the bride's party enacted to test the groom before the wedding, a long-standing tradition that both parties had anticipated with pleasure. "Welcome," Bocskai said, hailing the assembled Báthory clan and wishing us health and happiness. "Would the bride kindly step forward to be married to this man?"

At this appointed signal, each of my ladies came forward one by one to offer herself as a bride to Ferenc Nádasdy, bowing and smiling and making a great show of being worthy of the attention of such a great man and noble warrior, the first man of Hungary. On and on the accolades piled up. I felt ill, watching the flags on the battlements snapping so hard and fast that I thought I would be dizzy. Griseldis and some other cousins went first, then my sisters—first Klára, then Zsofía, each elegantly coiffed and dressed in golden cloth, more beautiful than I had ever seen them. At the approach of each lady, Ferenc bowed, then shook his head. "No, she is not the one," he said, and the bridesmaid would return to her place at my side.

Soon each of my ladies had taken her turn, and then it was up to me. I stepped forward and bowed and smiled at Ferenc Nádasdy, complimented the greatness of his family name and honor, then offered myself as his bride. My eyes flicked ever so briefly to András, to see if I could find any gesture of pain on his face at this moment, but he was not looking in my direction at all. Ferenc stepped forward and raised the veil over my face. His expression was utterly unreadable—what there was of joy or hope, of amusement or anticipation, I could not tell. But then he leaned forward and pressed his lips to my cheek, and said, "Here she is, the lady of my heart." He took me by the elbow and pulled me to his side, whispering, "Are you all right, miss? Is something wrong?"

"No, nothing is wrong," I answered.

"Of course not. What could be wrong on such a grand occasion, the marriage of the house of Nádasdy to the house of Báthory?" There was resentment in his voice, a resentment I had felt myself until that morning, when he had given me a place in the world of my own and filled me momentarily with hope. Now Ferenc's voice dripped like cold water from the roof of a cave. He had no more desire to be sold in marriage than I did. Perhaps he might have chosen someone else, if the decision had been left up to him. Judit, or someone like her. "I think our parents would be pleased if they could have been here to see it. Don't you think?" he asked.

"Yes," I whispered, keeping my voice measured, my outward demeanor as calm as possible despite the turmoil in my breast. "I think they would have been very happy for us."

"I'm sure they would have been," he said. "A great day for Hungary, isn't it?" Then Ferenc took my arm and led me into the chapel before the assembled guests, the grand families of Hungary, our friends and relations. We stood before the priest and were married according to the holy rites, and Ferenc kissed me again before that grand assembly, to joyous shouts, to the stamping of feet. "Congratulations, Countess," my new husband said in my ear. "God has now sanctioned the schemes of family and fortune. Pray he knows what he is doing."

# 18

For the first ten years of our marriage Ferenc and I would rarely see each other, so involved was he in the wars across Europe, intent on making himself a great hero and soldier the way his father had been a great statesman. There were plenty of troubles with which he could distinguish himself. The election of my uncle István as the new king of Poland raised tensions between the Habsburg Maximilian and our family, since my uncle believed Poland was Hungary's strongest ally and best hope against the schemes of the sultan in Constantinople, the king in Bécs. My uncle's plans for a Hungary united with Poland against both the Turks and Austria excited many of the nobles of the old kingdom, dreaming of former glory. So when the previously elected Polish king, Henri of Valois, abdicated in favor of the French throne, my uncle—now married to the Polish queen—claimed the support of most of the country. The Polish primate, however, defied the will of the people and supported the Catholic

Maximilian against my uncle's legal rights. There was threat of civil war. Ferenc—newly united to the Báthory family but still on friendly terms with Maximilian—went to the king to try to ease the tensions between those factions, taking his friends with him: István Bocskai, György Thurzó, Miklós Zrínyi, Ádám Batthyány. András Kanizsay. They left one morning before daylight, to get a good start before the weather turned, eager to distinguish themselves as their fathers had, joking and bragging who would be the greatest among them. I watched them ride out in a column from Sárvár, turning up a white cloud of dust in the darkness, my hand raised to no one in particular. All of them at once.

Ferenc and I had spent many difficult months together after our marriage, putting on a show for our friends and relations as we traveled from Varannó to Csejthe, Csejthe to Sárvár, but it was clear that marriage had not warmed Ferenc to me. He would take my hand in public or kiss my cheek at the teasing of his friends, but in private he was indifferent to me, more given to drinking and falling into his own bed in his own room long after I'd blown out my lamp. Even the night of our wedding, when Darvulia had dressed me in a white linen shift and armed me with a small vial of oxblood to mask my missing virginity, Ferenc could hardly bring himself to touch me. After all the feasting and dancing, he had come in that night to the bawdy cheers of his friends outside the door, staggering a little from the effects of the wine, smiled at me where I sat on the edge of the bed with my arms crossed over my breasts and ordered that I lie back to accept what God and country, duty and honor demanded of both of us. When it was over, he fell asleep as soon as he touched the pillow and never noticed the vial of blood I tipped out onto the bedclothes. I spent that night at the far edge of the bed, unable to get any rest due to the sound of my new husband's bone-rattling snore, and in the morning my ladies displayed the bloody sheet as proof of my maidenhood. No one who knew the truth would dare betray it now, Darvulia for the sake of our friendship, András for the sake of his profitable betrothal. He was a lucky man with a small fortune and a lovely young bride awaiting him. Even the day of the wedding he said nothing more than "congratulations" to me, his eyes never meeting mine, and then he moved away to laugh and joke with his companions about his incredible luck at finding a beauty with a good dowry and a mother eager for her grandchildren to bear the illustrious Kanizsay name. I watched him turn my cousin around and around the floor in a dance, no longer envious of his cousin's marriage and fortune, perhaps, now that he had defiled both. If I had been the palatine's son, he'd once said to me, I could have been your husband, Erzsébet. At the time I had thought he was only speaking of love. That night, his triumph complete, András forgot all about me. He and Griseldis were all secret smiles and public modesty, he proud, she blushing as he took her hand, bowing to his betrothed and asking her for a dance, while I sat on the dais in my gown of gold-shot silk and thought I might rip myself apart from bitterness.

After the return to Sárvár and Ferenc's removal to court life, I settled into the routine of life as the new mistress of the many Nádasdy estates. There was always a great deal of business to attend to—servants to manage, furnishings to repair, livestock to breed, crops to sow. Like many women of my station I cared for all the family holdings while my husband was away, though I had far more properties to see to than they. The larger estates at Keresztúr, Varannó, Léka, Sárvár, and my own Csejthe required constant vigilance and attention in those warlike times. Scarcely a day went by when I didn't have a letter to answer to some relative or other, or a tenant who refused to pay his tithe, a dispute with a neighbor over this or that border. Sometimes a poorer neighbor, thinking me vulnerable with my husband away, would occupy one of my husband's estates, and I would have to send soldiers to throw off the squatters and restore the house to order. I was no weak-willed wife sitting at home and waiting for the men to come back and rescue me. It was I who protected what marriage and blood had bought, I who was master and mistress both.

For three years I wrote to Ferenc to let him know the business at hand, both for his approval and so that he would never feel I was overstepping my role as mistress of the house. It was a careful game I played. My husband wrote me back on occasion with an answer to a question or a bit of praise for how I had handled a dispute or tended a sick relation, but for the most part he was much engaged with politics and didn't come home if he could help it. I saw him mostly at Christmas, when he returned with his friends for the winter, and occasionally in the heat of summer, but only when the wars brought him within a day or two of Sárvár's whitewashed walls. Whenever Ferenc came home he slept in his rooms, and I in mine. Seldom did he try to pretend that my presence in his house was anything more than a political decision made for us by our ambitious families. He went to his bed always alone, and if he found companionship among the ladies of the house or my maidservants, I did not know nor want to know.

The maidservants, as I had suspected, proved to be a constant source of discord. Like many other noblewomen I often took into my home the daughters of poorer relations, girls with little education and no money who might find a place in my house and my favor, and whom I would reward by arranging for them modest dowries, honorable marriages. I would teach them to sing and play, to read bible verses and write their own names. My own mother had taken in dozens, perhaps hundreds, of such girls at Ecsed. Now it was my duty as mistress of all the Nádasdy estates to see to the health and well-being of everyone within my reach. As I had learned in my first days at Sárvár, however, the presence of such a large number of young women of marriageable age and little education was a route to trouble.

One such bit of trouble came in the form of a maidservant named Amália, a pretty little thing with reddish curls that hung to her waist and a lush, expectant expression that left her looking always like she had just been either kissed or slapped. Her mother was a distant cousin of Orsolya's whose husband had emptied the family coffers for his drinking and left the women destitute. Thus she came to me, and I took her in, glad for her companionship. Amália often attended my toilette, helping me bathe and dress, and I had favored her because she could be sweet to me and would sing in a high, clear voice like pure silver while she worked. I had given her a hand mirror, a bit of glass backed with polished brass in the shape of a dragon and his tail, because she had admired herself in it one day, turning it over and over in her pretty little hand. "You keep it," I said. "Your face in it is lovelier than mine, at any rate, and will suit it better."

"Oh, no, mistress," she said, the proper answer for a girl who wished to keep her place, "I could never be as beautiful as you." But she seemed pleased with the gift and kept it close to her. Often I would find her gazing into it, pressing her lips together to make them more plump, pinching her cheeks to give herself a blush. She was aware of her beauty and flaunted it before the other servants, turning the eyes of the handsomest boys who worked in and around Sárvár, throwing herself at the beaus of the other girls because she could. More than one young woman had come to me in tears because this or that young man had fallen prey to the allure of the red hair. I tried to intervene, tried to impress on her the importance of modesty when it came to the attentions of young men—a lesson I had learned too late, it seemed—but I could see her always looking away, looking bored, thinking, What does the mistress know about any young man? What does she know of love, when her husband spurns her bed?

At that time Ferenc came home during the summer months, riding from Bécs with some of his companions—Bocskai, Thurzó—to rest and refresh themselves after a difficult summer on the road. He had not sent word ahead that he was coming, so on the day he arrived the servants and I had much to do to see that he was comfortable, his rooms cleaned and spread with fresh bedclothes, the meals lavish and tasteful. I made a special effort to dress in a pleasing way and make up my hair in the latest fashion, but other than politeness at the evening meal he did not seek me out, nor I him.

A few days later Darvulia came early to see me where I sat writing a letter, saying that two of the servant girls had been in an argument that morning, yanking the silver hand mirror back and forth between them, shouting curses and slapping each other. Apparently my sweet little Amália had declared in front of several other girls that she had snared the attention of Ferenc Nádasdy himself, that she visited his bed at night. Perhaps she would give the count a son, she'd said, since it appeared he showed no interest in his wife. Perhaps it would be she who would be mistress of the house someday, she said, and not Erzsébet Báthory. It had happened before. Old wives died, and new wives took their place.

One of the fellow servants to whom she made this outrageous boast was a young laundress, a plain thing with a face marked by pox and a heart scarred by jealousy, who proceeded to run to Darvulia and complain. Surely she should be punished, said the plain girl. Surely the lady of the house would be grateful to know that among her servants there was one so disloyal, with designs on my place in the household. Now Darvulia stood before me where I sat at my table, calmly asking how she should handle the disciplining of Amália, while the quill trembled in my hand and drops of ink spattered the letter I was writing to my friend Countess Zrínyi. I looked down to see the stain spreading, blotting out the words I had been writing just a moment before. Amália had betrayed me. The ink stain spread until all I could see was black.

I had often left the choice of punishment to Darvulia, whom the servant girls respected and feared as women had always feared that imposing creature. She had an ability with a pair of scissors across the palm of a thief or with the sharp prick of a pin through the finger of a girl who dawdled at her sewing. Leaving the punishment to Darvulia allowed me some distance from day-to-day trouble while still maintaining the order necessary among a gaggle of unruly, uneducated girls, and I had grown to trust her to handle it most of the time without interference from me. But this time one of them had gone too far, threatening not just the happiness of a servant girl but the stability of the entire household. My position, my pride. Laughing at me, and wishing for my demise, and putting her own ignorant little behind in my place. Let her see what it means to be a countess, then, if she were so intent on being a nobleman's wife. I told Darvulia I would see to her myself.

She seemed surprised, but only asked, "What will you do?"

I remembered Judit, how the vanished skirt had reappeared after she had borne her humiliation in the courtyard. There could be no restitution of a stolen item this time, for what was taken was my husband's affection, my own good name and reputation. "I will know when I see her," I said.

"You must not be too soft on her," Darvulia said. "If they think you are threatened by her, you will lose the ability to manage them. They will say whatever they like about you to anyone who will listen."

"Don't fear. She will know who her mistress is."

The house was unusually quiet as I crossed the courtyard to the servants' quarters. The men were out hunting for the day, and so the servants, sensing the oncoming quarrel, followed me through the house and into the sewing room, where Amália and her fellows were gathered. A half circle of maidservants waited for me there, seamstresses, scullery maids, even the pockmarked little brat who had caused all the trouble in the first place with her tattling. They were speaking in sharp angry voices—I could hear them as I came down the hall—but a hush preceded me into the room, as if the house itself were drawing in its breath.

I spoke, keeping my voice as free from emotion as I could. "Amália," I said, "I understand you have been visiting the count at night since he's been home. That you think you might give him a son, if his wife will not. I understand you openly wished for my death, so that you might take my place."

"I never said so, madam. The others lie about me." She colored.

"Perhaps they do," I said, looking at Amália's accuser, at her face full of scars, at her sallow complexion and crooked teeth, a poor creature unlikely ever to leave the laundry, who probably couldn't even get the stable boys to look at her. It was always possible she had made up a lie about Amália, that she had invented the whole story as a matter of revenge, but even if she had I could not let the story spread, could not let it linger unattended like an unwelcome houseguest, or more would come after. The laundress would not look at anyone in the room. Having caused all the trouble, she had sense at least to act ashamed of herself, studying her shoes.

Amália, however, looked me full in the face, defiant, the mirror still in her hand. "You do think too much of yourself," I said. "I blame myself for encouraging your vanity. Why don't you give me the mirror?"

"It was a gift, mistress." She clutched it to her bosom. "You gave it to me."

"Since it was mine to begin with," I said, more demanding now, "it is mine to take back again."

She shot one or two of the other girls a pleading look, as if asking them to step forward and defend her, or else to join her in defying my will. For a moment I thought they might do so: to hit at me and slap me, to rend my clothes and scratch at my eyes, to take my jewels and fine possessions. There were many of them and only one of me. They could have done it, I knew. I waited, meeting their eyes, saying nothing. One by one the other girls in the room looked at their shoes, at the windows or the walls. Somewhere a candle flickered, and from outside came the sound of men laughing, telling stories. No one looked at Amália where she stood opposite me. She was not there; she did not exist. The servants valued my favor, perhaps, or perhaps they simply knew what would happen to them if any of them raised a hand against a noblewoman. Their will was weak, but mine was strong. In a moment they would know how strong.

At last Amália held out the mirror in front of her, and I took it and smashed it on the stone floor, shattering the glass and breaking the silver handle from the frame. A general gasp went up from among the servant girls, and one of them, the plain one who had coveted it in the first place, began to cry. "This is what comes from vanity and braggadocio," I said. "The next hour you boast of the count's love for you will be your last in this house."

Amália herself didn't cry or fall on her knees to beg for forgiveness, as I thought she might have done, but instead coiled into a rage—mouth pursed in a thin line, eyes burning. So there was a viper in her after all. "Mistress," she said, very slowly, "I never said such a thing. I would never mean to offend you."

"Of course you did. Such words are always meant to offend. I have more sense than to believe your lies, but nor can I let your behavior go unpunished." At a gesture I had Darvulia and the head seamstress, a woman three times my age, take her by the arms. "Strip her naked. Then have the guard take her out into the courtyard to work the rest of the day in the hot sun," I said. "If you act like a whore, I will treat you like one."

Amália pleaded her innocence, saying that her accuser spoke falsely, that she never said anything about the count falling in love with her. The other girls, she claimed, envied her the beautiful mirror, her friendship with the lady of the house, and told lies to ruin her reputation. Unfair, she said. Unjust. Would the countess believe anything some jealous girl said to her and make the others suffer for it? Would the educated lady of the house believe the lies of a prattling laundress with cracked hands?

On and on she went, struggling, cursing. I looked not at the pretty little thing whose company I had always enjoyed but just over her shoulder, where I would not have to see her jealousy and anger, where I could keep my face calm and stop the tears that had begun to pool at the corners of my vision. Having started this business, I must see it through to the end. I kept hoping she would relent, confess her offense and beg my forgiveness and put all the trouble behind us. She had been my favorite, after all. If she had only confessed her crime, if she had told me with her own lips that she had offended me, that she had been vain and selfish, and begged forgiveness, I would have stopped it all at once. I would have brought her a fresh gown and dressed her with my own hands and petted and comforted her. Instead she stormed and cursed in the courtyard all that morning while the sun came up hot over the walls of the keep, then hotter. A small crowd of men and boys gathered to watch her, to shout insults and throw stones that hit her on the cheek and drew blood, left marks on her buttocks. Whenever I passed the courtyard on this or that errand I saw her standing still and straight under the hot sunlight, sunburn creeping along the fair skin of her shoulders and across the tops of her breasts, so that her skin and hair were the same mottled reddish color. She didn't dare speak to me, but her eyes blazed. Even then she didn't have the good sense to be contrite. She had used my love for her own advantage, had turned on me the minute my back was turned, and all my love for her shrank and burned away the longer she stood in the courtyard.

At midday, thoroughly exhausted by the ordeals of the morning, I went down again, hoping to put an end to it. A crowd gathered in the courtyard to watch, men and girls both, the tools of their work still in their hands. Amália gathered herself to standing and crossed her hands over her breasts, as if newly ashamed of her nakedness. "Why did you speak against me?" I asked again. Again she said she had not, that the others were jealous of her, they hated her because the men in the house looked at her and not at them. When it was clear she would not relent, I decided to increase her punishment. I had Darvulia bring a jar of honey, and while the guards held the girl by the arms Darvulia poured the honey over her, over her head, down her shoulders, over her breasts. It dripped in the light, coating her with gold. Before the guards even released her arms the honey was drawing every insect at Sárvár. Flies and bees and gnats bit and stung her. Red welts appeared along her arms and legs, the tender flesh of her belly, the line of white skin around her hair and under her neck. She swatted and scratched, running through the dust and creating a racket, falling on her knees and begging me to let her bathe, to wash the sweetness away. Then she wept, and her tears drew more flies, and her eyes swelled. By the late afternoon she had collapsed in a corner, half delirious. The other servant girls, who at first had been so amused by the sight of their tormentor being tormented, quietly filed away during the course of the rest of the afternoon and went back to their work.

When Ferenc came in that evening from town, dismounting in the creeping dusk, he passed the girl in the courtyard and stopped for a moment to look. By then she was a quivering lump, red from the sun and covered with welts and stings, her lips parched with thirst, the honey on her breasts and arms thick with dust and trapped insects. An ugly thing, twisted by vanity. What a spectacle she must have made as my husband came inside the house for the evening, her face unrecognizable, her beauty burned away so that Ferenc would have to have asked one of the servants who she was. I was nearly ready to send Darvulia out to have the girl brought in and washed, and her stings and bites treated, when Ferenc came into my room and asked what she had done. I thought he meant to reprimand me for taking aim at his current favorite and was prepared to defend my actions. "She was tormenting the other girls over the gift I gave her, a little silver mirror," I said. "There was a quarrel, and none of the maids were doing their work." I added, "And she was spreading some malicious gossip around the house."

"About you?"

"And—about you as well."

"I see." Ferenc seemed to consider a moment, though he didn't ask what she said. Perhaps he knew. Perhaps he knew precisely. "She will certainly think twice before doing so again. And did she cry, and scratch, and try to protect herself from the insects?"

"She made a terrible noise. It's been distracting the other servants from their work all day."

"Next time," Ferenc said, "have her chained in the courtyard. There are shackles for use around the fetlocks of the horses when they are being treated for illness. Use those. If she cries, you should bind her mouth as well. She should endure the punishment she's earned, not make everyone else in the house suffer as well."

"I will remember that."

"And Erzsébet?"

"Yes?"

"Well done, my dear. A general could not have done better."

"Thank you."

He smiled, his hawklike expression growing ever more preda-tory, and considered me for a moment, as if he were deciding just how much he might be able to tell me, how much he might trust me to understand. As if I might be more than a name and an alliance with whom he had to share a house, but a friend and companion. A wife. "If you'd like, I can show you a few tricks that may come in useful in the future, battlefield techniques I have found very instructive."

"What techniques are those?"

"I will revive her for you. Watch." He took a slip of paper from his pocket, tore it in several pieces, and dipped them in oil. Then he went outside to the courtyard, and leaning down, set the oiled paper between the girl's toes. He took a twig from the ground, lit it on a torch, and set it to the pieces of paper, which went up in quick orange bursts of flame. Even in her half-conscious state the girl jumped to her feet with a little yelp of pain and shook her feet to dislodge the papers. She looked around like a horse that had stepped on a snake.

"There," he said, and looked at me with more pleasure than I had ever before seen on his face—his dark-bearded, dark-eyed, hand-some face. My husband. "You see? It is called 'star-kicking.' Now she can walk inside under her own power, and spare the backs of those who would have to carry her. Or she could endure further punish-ment, if you think she's not had enough."

In the darkening space of the courtyard, with the tang of burn-ing oil in my nostrils, I felt something in him open up to me, to the possibility of me. "Tell me more," I said.

# 19

Afterward Ferenc began to take more notice of me. It was as if before I had been a shadow in his eyes, and only now did I take on solid form and substance, when he discovered we had a common interest—he the war abroad, I the battle at home, both of us equally dedicated to victory. Several times over the next few days I caught my husband staring at me with a kind of delight over the supper table in the evenings, over cards before the fire. If I spoke harshly to the cook over the roast or slapped the face of the girl who dropped a bottle of wine, shattering it all over the rug, I would look up and see him watching me, judging all my actions anew. I could not tell if it were the heat of summer or something more delicious that lit the coals in his eyes, but I remembered my mother's advice to me, that husbands desire their wives, but that wives must take care to keep those desires from being ever fully satisfied. They must never be too ready to please, she'd said, but remain a mystery their husbands long to solve. Perhaps after the punishment of Amália, Ferenc had decided that my mysteries were something he wanted, at long last, to unravel himself.

One night I decided to prepare a special meal for my husband, sending the cook out of the house and preparing everything myself—the game birds dressed with cloves and stuffed with onions, the platters of sugary beets and vinegary olives, the loaves of bread studded with rye seeds, the candied citrons and cherries. For an entire day I worked in the hot kitchen until I could hardly stand, and when Ferenc and his friends Bocskai and Thurzó came in that night and sat at our table under candelabra polished to a blinding brightness, I served him from dishes I carried myself to show my pleasure at his visit, bustling in and out of the kitchen with a pot of butter in a silver bowl, a gilded plate with sliced beef and dumplings in dark gravy speckled with herbs. He ate it all with relish and leaned back after each course to pat his stomach and compliment the cooking. "Perhaps I should come home more often," he said.

"I would like that very much," I said, and smiled, to try to show that I was sincere, that there was no sarcasm in the sentiment. When I came around the table again, he touched the hem of my skirt as I paused beside him, rubbing the fabric between his fingers, and the smell of him—new sweat, old horse, damp hair and lye—rose up and combined with the rich brown smell of the food. My eyes swam. It had been too long since any man had looked at me with affection, much less love. All through the night his enjoyment seemed to increase, his compliments growing in lavishness and his manners warming to me. His eyes followed my movements around the table, the intensity of his gaze increasing so much that when I came at last to the table with the platter of capon to offer him the first piece, he caught me by the wrist. I could feel the warmth from his body through his waistcoat, the heat from the palm of his hand encircling my arm. "Erzsébet," he said in a low voice, so that only I heard him. "My Erzsébet."

He was drunk—the bottle of dark wine I had brought to him when he first sat down was already half empty—but only a little. He would need to drink a great deal more before he would be lost in his drunkenness. Instead his cheeks were flushed, and he tipped his head back to look up into my face, where I stood over his chair. My husband was noticing me. I nodded to him to let him know that I understood, and then set the platter down and gave him a piece of the meat, dripping with juices and small green bits of the mistletoe that my mother had said would excite a man's desire. I had been right to follow her advice from long ago, as well as the herb lore she had imparted to me. At last my humiliation would be at an end.

All that evening I watched him watching me.

He wore a dark red waistcoat and breeches, his black boots polished to a glossy sheen that matched his black hair and eyes, his white cheeks flushed with red warmth. Across my neck and under my blouse a warm bloom began like the first days of summer, so that I wondered if the herbs had had an effect on me as well, but later I would know it was simply the desire that comes from being desired oneself.

His eyes under their heavy black brows moved like an animal's, finding my face and then holding it, as if daring me to make a move, to slip away. His mouth and tongue were stained a rich red from the wine. Sometimes Thurzó, sensing Ferenc's attention was diverted away from him, would tell a joke and make my husband laugh, but then Ferenc would find my face again and hold my eyes, and for the first time in my life I felt myself blush, a creeping warmth that grew up my neck, across my face and into the dark roots of my hair.

Later in the evening, when the men were boisterous and pounding the table in a lively argument, I announced I was tired. I left to go up to my room as usual, glancing back only once to see if his eyes were following me. His look—face lowered, eyes raised—pierced me from across the room. I felt a little relief when I slipped into the cool air of the darkened stairwell, like I had been close to smothering and could breathe freely once more.

In my room Darvulia helped me undress and undo the braids in my hair, brushing it out in long, dark waves, framing the pale skin of my face, the tops of my breasts. I sat in bed with a book and read a little by candlelight, expecting at any moment for Ferenc to come to me. I read one page, then read it again, realizing I had not retained a word of what I was seeing. Still he didn't come. I wondered if I had been mistaken in his looks, his intentions. It was only when I gave up and blew out the candle that I heard the door to my chamber open and saw the dark figure of my husband come in from the hallway outside. "Erzsébet?" he said.

"Here," I said. "Here, follow my voice."

In the dark he stumbled into a chest of drawers, a wooden chair with a carved dragon's head, and cried out. "And here I thought I would surprise you."

"You do." I had been careful to drink little that night, retaining full control of my faculties, and now I chose my words as carefully, for the slightest misstep would ruin everything. He needed to trust me. "I have never been so surprised."

"So you are glad that I'm here?"

There was an uncertainty in his voice I recognized as shyness, as fear that I might send him away. He was still a new husband, after all, twenty-two years old, still learning what a wife could offer. His uncertainty, his shyness, warmed my heart toward him. "I have been waiting for this since we first met, when I thought you the handsomest man in the kingdom."

"You flatter me." Sullen now. He thought I teased him.

I took a breath and relaxed back into the pillows, weighing my words carefully. "I flatter only myself, as the wife of such a man," I said. "Will you stay?"

He leaned over and pressed his mouth on mine, his soft red mouth with the taste of the wine on it still. His hand moved over my hair, down to my collarbone and toward my breast. He sighed and said that he had been glad after all that our parents had matched us—that we were more alike than different, but it had taken him this long to realize it. "I did not know," he said, "that you were a woman of so much passion, that you had feelings like my own. I thought you wanted me only for my name and position, my title, and I did not think I could love you. Can you forgive me?"

In answer I raised the blankets and took him to me. At last my husband's love would be enough to shelter me, a love fine enough and large enough to protect me from anything the future might bring—wars, illness, even death itself.

# SIDEREUS NUNCIUS

# 1

Outside my tower the world turns the green and gold of summer, the hills and valleys echoing with the calls of sheep sent out to graze and the rattle of farm carts traveling the Vág road toward Buda. More than a year I have been in my prison, and though the air at my window is sweet and soft as eiderdown, the inside of my room remains stale. The straw in my mattress needs to be changed, the floor swept. Mice visit me at night to take away the crumbs they find along the cracks in the floor, and zephyrs stir the long-cold ashes of the fire. Rev. Ponikenus, who once denounced me in public, comes to visit me sometimes, sitting outside my door and trying to gauge the state of my immortal soul, but only my letters from you and your sisters, Pál, give me any kind of joy. I am always pleased to know how well you do with your studies, how your German and Latin have improved since I saw you last. I have worked hard and suffered much to ensure that your education is even broader and more complete than my own. Gratefully I read the book you sent me describing the movement of the Mediciean stars, those bodies in orbit around Jupiter. As a girl I read Aristotle's *De Caelo* and studied the movement of his crystalline spheres, but this mathematician, this Galilei, says the existence of these new bodies proves that there are many stars in the heavens that are all in motion around each other. That the sun is the center of the universe, and not the earth. I would like to see that with my own eyes, I think—to peer through the mathematician's glass and look on other worlds, other heavens.

This morning the wheezy old steward, Benedict Deseő, came up to the tower nearly an hour past his usual breakfast visit, so that my stomach was groaning. He set down the tray with its crusts of bread, its cup of cooked fruit, out of breath and heaving like a plow ox. "At last," I said. "Where have you been?"

"There are important visitors in Csejthe. The palatine and his wife are here."

My hand found my throat. "Where?" I asked.

"In the courtyard, even now."

Now this was remarkable news. That Thurzó would condescend to come to Csejthe now was no small matter. Eighteen months I have been in my tower, and I have not been able to convince the palatine to do so much as answer a letter. What game was he playing at? Surely he would not make the journey from Bicske without at least stopping to see me, either out of curiosity or triumph. Or perhaps he thought that now I was a prisoner, any notice of me was beneath him.

He didn't think so before. He loved me once, and I him.

His voice trembling with outrage or fear, Deseő told me that Erzsébet Czobor, the palatine's young wife, had come up to Csejthe *vár* that morning and demanded that he open the treasury to her. In addition to my wedding gown and jewels, which I had said in my will that I wanted to keep during my lifetime, the treasury holds a small amount of gold for the purchase of food and supplies, for the pay of the few servants who remain. The little thief had her servants pack everything up and load the treasure into her own carriage. Apparently she then went down to the *kastély* and did the same thing there, going through the trunks and chests that remained behind during my imprisonment. With the wedding of her stepdaughter Borbála approaching, she must have thought my fine jewels would suit her own neck. "The guards would not stop her, madam," said the servant. "She laughed at me when I said she had no authority to take them away."

"And what did she tell you in return?"

"I don't wish to say."

"Please," I said, though the word was like ash in my mouth, "I have no other way of learning what has passed."

He shifted from one foot to another as if preparing to flee. "She said, 'Tell your mistress that my authority comes from God, who hates all sinners.'"

Stunned at the malice of Thurzó's wife, at her pettiness and spite, I paced back and forth across my cell. Her husband's design in having me locked away was brazen and calculated, with as many personal incentives as political, but that Lady Thurzó should behave with so little charity, so much cruelty toward me and my children, was nothing less than unforgivable. And after her husband had urged me, with all tenderness, to make her my friend, and which I had done for his sake! Someday she too could be a wealthy widow at the mercy of her neighbors and relatives, the subject of vicious rumors and specu-lation, with no husband or grown sons to take up her cause. I know it was she who poisoned the palatine against me, who whispered the malicious gossip in his ear that he has chosen to believe. Perhaps she knows that her husband loved me once, and hates me for it.

In a rage I cursed her name and prayed to the devil to plague her and the palatine with sickness, with death. To let me out of my tower for only a moment, to place my hands around her lying, thiev-ing, scheming little throat.

I stood on a chair and tried to look out my window. The court-yard was invisible to me below, but for a moment I thought I heard a voice—Thurzó's—speaking to someone, a higher voice answering. "Tell the palatine I wish to speak with him," I said. "Tell him I have an urgent commission for him, something he alone can manage. Ask him in the name of the friendship we once shared."

When the servant was gone, I looked around my room. There were no weapons, nothing but a quill and some paper, my own two hands. My fingernails were broken and jagged, the quill dulled with my writing and stained black with ink, but it could serve well enough. Breaking it in half, I hid the sharpened end in my palm. If the pala-tine came close enough to my stone gap, if he put his face down to speak with me, I could sink it into an eye, or perhaps even his throat, before the guards would have a chance to cut me down. That would be one way of escaping my tower, at least.

Deseő came back up the stairs, out of breath, alone. The palatine would not come. He and Lady Thurzó were preparing to leave Csejthe. "He said there is no request you can make that he would now grant."

No request I could make, he said. So I had ceased to exist after all.

A sharp pain sliced my hand, the blunt end of the quill biting into my palm. Blood flowed, staining my shift. With my other hand I took it out again and sank to the floor, put my face in my hands, smearing gore on my cheeks. A moment later the faint noise of hooves on cobblestone reached me, the creak of a carriage. The palatine and his ignorant little wife were leaving just as they chose, without so much as a word to the mistress of the house. Singing like pirates, too, probably.

The wind banged the shutters against the walls of the *vár*, and the kites called to each other, lonely cries as they hunted mice in the fields. Deseő said my name, but when I did not answer, he stole away quietly and left me to my solitary grief, where I think only of you, Pál, and how far away you seem to me, how orphaned and defenseless. Be careful whom you love, my dearest. There is no cure for deceit, not in Hungary or anywhere in this old and broken world.

# 2

All through the long years when I was busy tending our fortune, seeing to the management and upkeep of the Nádasdy estates, your father was away at war with Thurzó and Bocskai and his other comrades-in-arms, building a wall of Christian soldiers against the Turkish skirmishes that continued to threaten Hungary's borders, preparing for the war that everyone knew was coming. When it arrived at long last, the combined forces of my uncle Zsigmond

Báthory, prince of Transylvania, and the Habsburg king Rudolf would recapture the strongholds of Esztergom and Győr from the sultan's forces, and many more besides. Through it all Ferenc Nádasdy won praise from the king in Bécs and respect from the Turks, who nicknamed him the Black Bey of Hungary. Each victory brought both of us more esteem in the king's eye, and when Ferenc considered whether to lend the royal treasury a vast sum—more than thirty thousand forints for the war effort—I encouraged him, despite the strain it put on our personal finances, the improvements that had to be put off, the fields that had to lie fallow. I wrote him: *It is always useful to have a king in your debt. Rudolf will remember his friends when the time comes.*

It did not seem out of the question that your father could be palatine himself someday, if he lived long enough and kept the king's favor. The thought of being a palatine's wife pleased me, especially since I had won Ferenc's affection at last and would not have to endure the taunts of insolent maids, since I had taken my proper place in your father's heart. I often wondered how proud my mother would have been if she had seen how well the match she had made suited us, once we had reconciled ourselves to it.

Yet there were regrets, too, because for the first ten years of our marriage we had no children, and until there were children, all our victories were temporary. Your father did not blame me the way many husbands do, but I felt his desperation. Time and again I endured disappointment as five years turned to seven, then nine. The few times every year that Ferenc was able to get away from the war, anxious to share my bed, nothing came of it. He took me to a doctor in Bécs who poked and prodded me with sharp instruments and cold hands, tying me to the bed to keep me still as he threaded long needles inside me, trying to push my body open with awls and pieces of pig iron so that it would admit the seeds that would make a child. Afterward I would bleed for days and days, so much I could barely rise from my bed. Ferenc even sent to Padua for the doctor who had helped his own mother and father conceive, who was by then an old man. He treated me more gently, but he spent several months with us without success. Ferenc felt guilty afterward and said he would no longer send doctors to me, though he did write to Prága and even as far away as Paris for special potions that were supposed to improve my chances at conceiving, and which Darvulia coaxed me into drinking morning and evening through my tears and objections.

I feared the only real remedy was to have Ferenc home more often by my side and told him so, though I was careful not to weep, not to make myself ridiculous with tears the way some wives did. He must never think, even then, that his absence could undo me, or I would be in his power rather than he in mine. He must come home three, four times a year at least, I said.

"I wish I could," he said. "Nothing would make me happier. But the king depends on me."

"The king does not need you as much as I do."

"Thurzó has not been home to his wife more than four times in the last three years, and Zrínyi even less. You've seen me more often than that."

"Thurzó and Zrínyi have children already. Four daughters and a son between them."

"We will have our children, don't fret," he said, but I could tell he was trying to convince me of something he didn't quite believe himself. "Perhaps Darvulia could help. She knows every herb and charm in these lands."

"Perhaps," I said. I didn't tell him that Darvulia had already given me several of her remedies, but none of them had worked. Pomegranates squeezed for their juice. Puncture-vine drunk in a tea, then ground into a paste and spread on that dark opening in my body. The sight of a cat licking itself clean while I recited a prayer to the Virgin.

"I want you to have your children, my dear. I will move heaven and earth for you. I swear it." He brushed my hair from my face and touched my hand most tenderly. But then he would leave again, and I would not see him for many months at a time, months of much waiting and little hope.

Rarely did I allow myself to think of my vanished daughter, taken off by the midwife. I could not search for them, having no idea where the midwife came from or where she had taken the child. Poor thing, to be born a girl. If she had been a son, I might have dared to tell Ferenc and hoped that in time he might accept the child, tell people it was his. But a girl was a burden unless she had a family name and a dowry to protect her. My baby, born in secret, could have neither. My daughter would never know me, or know of me.

Her father, who knew of her existence, showed no interest in what had happened to the child, in what had happened to me in bearing his child. During those brief interludes when I would see András Kanizsay at court gatherings, family holidays, I would think of our daughter. Still handsome, still elegant and humorous to his companions, András was always barely civil in my presence, as if ashamed now of the intimacies we had shared, our secret past. I could not engage him in any kind of pleasant conversation, not on the subject of his upcoming marriage or his plans for the new estate he would inherit when he and Griseldis were wed—anything. András did not seem to notice when I lavished Ferenc with affection, or hear me when I invited him and Griseldis to Sárvár at Christmas for the luxurious parties we always held there, for a chance for good wine and fine company. He would always look through me and find someone else who needed his attention, somewhere else he needed to be. Excuse me, Countess, I hear someone calling me, he would say, and then I would hear the sound of his footsteps retreating down the dark passageways, away from me, while I burned with hatred for him, for what had been done to me for the sake of his petty jealousy. As the years wore on, it became obvious that all his love for me was now at an end. At his wedding in Bécs, which I attended with Ferenc and many of our friends and family, the rapt look on his face as he stood before the priest and promised to be faithful only to Griseldis nearly made me weep, for I could see that he loved her, that he thought only of her in that moment and not of me at all.

András married Griseldis, and then he fathered children with her.

His fine masculine form and Griseldis's golden beauty made for lovely children—downy-limbed, jewel-eyed children, five daughters in eight years, all healthy, all living. God's blessing on their union, everyone said. Everyone except me. Whenever I saw my cousin with her gaggle of unruly brats, I searched their faces for a hint of my own vanished little one, wondering what she would look like now, and their small faces would seem to turn into hers, though I knew it was preposterous. My baby had had my darker coloring, my distinctive Báthory nose. She would not look like these half siblings at all. She was mine in memory, mine in beauty and temperament, and there she would remain.

So when your sister Anna was born at last, in the fall of 1585, on a bright warm day, it was as if the sun had come out on all our hopes. A child would guarantee our futures, your father's and mine, and let us forget the regrets of the past.

The labor was difficult—I had been ill for much of my pregnancy, and my strength was sapped to the end—but Darvulia sat by my side along with the doctor Ferenc had brought from Grác to tend to me. When the babe's strong wail broke the heat, your father burst into the room and clasped it to his breast, still wet and waxy. "A girl," he said. To mask his disappointment he declared her the most beautiful child who had ever been born, a future queen, the comfort of our old age. He touched one fingertip to her downy lip and handed her immediately back to me. He was not unkind, but bewildered, as if he did not know what to do with her. "As for a son," he said, "we can always try again later."

The night my sister Klára had been born, my father had sat in the hall and put his head in his hands and wept. Now I cradled my own child in my arms. Our little daughter had my mother's black-and-white beauty, as if my dead mother were staring back at me, softly blinking. The baby turned her head and nuzzled me, and when I didn't immediately open my shift and put her to my breast, she opened her small pink rosebud of a mouth and emitted a piercing scream. I handed her to the wet nurse, a widow named Ilona Jó whom I had brought to tend the child. She was my own age, twenty-five, but already she was old in spirit, a thin, humorless woman in gray homespun who spooked like a feral cat whenever I spoke to her. Her husband had died of cholera the previous winter, and her own baby daughter, recently weaned, lived now with her grandmother in a small village outside Thurzó's estate at Tokaj. Thurzó's wife, Zsofía Forgách—whom I counted as a dear friend, my companion at balls and parties in Pozsony, in Bécs—had sent her highly recommended.

Ilona Jó—bone thin from nursing, but with thick heavy wrists like a man's—opened her blouse and set the child to her breast. The baby latched on and began to suck, her strong little mouth taking in the milk greedily. "Her name is Anna," said Ferenc, "for your mother." I watched her suckle at the breast of the nurse, her little hands kneading at the other woman's bare skin, and felt a strong fist of grief squeeze the air from me. No noblewoman of my rank would stoop to nursing her child, but I could not help but feel sorrow that once again I had given my daughter away at the moment of her birth, even if it was only to a wet nurse, and a dour and ugly one at that. I began to weep, a slow, steady rolling that divided my face, separating me from myself. Ferenc sat on the bed and embraced me. "Don't worry, my love," he said, and kissed my brow. "You did well. You will do even better the next time." I didn't tell him I hardly dared to hope for a next time, that I felt I was cursed to lose all my children as punishment for the one whom I had given away.

# 3

After Anna we had Orsika, then Katalin, a passel of beautiful daughters who filled up our house and our days with their bright voices, their small hands, and their swift little feet. Anna, whose looks continued to favor my mother as she grew up, was a quick learner and walked before her first birthday, though she was a wary child who would cling to Ilona Jó even after she had been weaned, gazing at me with distrust in her lovely little black eyes, especially when I would not give her the toy she asked for or the special sweet she thought she deserved. I often had the feeling that she had judged me and found me wanting, as I myself felt I was wanting. I was hurt that she didn't love me as I had loved my own mother, so unconditionally, but did not know what I could do to earn it.

Orsika looked like her namesake, my mother-in-law, her little bow of a mouth and her arching eyebrows giving her a look of permanent surprise, but she was an active, affectionate child who would climb into my lap or her father's as easily as the wet nurse's. Even Darvulia, whom the other children feared, she treated like a favorite aunt. Outgoing, with a natural charm that her older sister could never possess, Orsika was followed two years later by Katalin, the sickly one, whose constant toothaches and colds meant long nights for myself and Darvulia as we treated this or that illness with philters down her throat and poultices on her chest. She often needed to see the surgeon for a rotting tooth and clung to me like the devil when he drew near, clawing at my neck when the old man brought his burning iron into her mouth to cauterize the wound. I hated to hold her down to let him do his work, because it reminded me of my own days with the doctors who had tried to cure me of childlessness, but I tried to soothe her with kisses and promises beforehand and tears and medicine afterward, giving her a bit of brandy so she would not suffer so greatly. Perhaps as a result of this constant attention, Kata was the most loving of my daughters, the most likely to call for me in the middle of the night or climb into my bed. I used to call her my little parasite, since I could barely walk down the halls of Sárvár or Csejthe without her clinging to my leg, begging to be picked up. She was always in my things—my mirrors and brushes, my clothes and books. The love I sometimes had trouble feeling for her older sister, the mistrustful child, I had no problem lavishing on little Kata.

Yet after all these blessings, still your father hoped for a boy. At every visit home he came to my bed to try for an heir who would bear the Nádasdy name. At the birth of each daughter he did his best to rejoice, but I could always sense the hole in the middle of his happiness. Ferenc would cradle each child and declare her even more beautiful than the last, while saying there was always the next time. His hope was so deeply felt, so rooted within the man he was, that nothing I said would dissuade him. I would do my best to give him a son.

In the winter of our twentieth year of marriage, when I was already thirty-five, I felt the signs of impending motherhood in me once more—the listlessness, the need for sleep, the hatred of food and strong light and unusual smells. I let Darvulia fuss and fret over me for months while the child grew within me, taking her teas for my stomach, her lotions to keep my skin supple while it stretched taut as a fermenting wineskin. Ferenc was away those months commanding his army and didn't see me during the whole of my pregnancy, though he wrote often to inquire how I was feeling and if I needed doctors sent to me to be certain the new child came safely into the world. As a veteran of four labors I didn't fear childbirth and settled in to wait for the child's arrival with the greatest anticipation that this time Ferenc would have his longed-for son.

By my calculation the child was due in mid-September, but my pains began one night in early August, in the midst of a drought that wilted the crops in the fields and the grapes on the vine. It was a terrible time in Sárvár. A hot wind was blowing that year from Constantinople, bringing with it the news of war as well as the stinking breath of the plague. Some of the servants had caught the disease, and though Darvulia had them quarantined in a storeroom outside the walls of the estate, it was too late to keep it out of Sárvár entirely. During a few bad weeks in July and August, the bells of the church tolled endlessly for the victims of the contagion. The burning of bodies went on day and night, the wind blowing the stench into the windows and walls no matter how tightly we nailed the shutters closed. I put Darvulia in charge of managing the estate for me, which she did tolerably well, though once or twice she had to take the whip to this or that maidservant who shirked her duty, or send away some blubbering fool who had got herself with child. For myself, I kept to my bed, so hot and uncomfortable as the child moved within me that I could not sleep day or night.

The baby arrived on a night of thunder and hot rain, and when Darvulia caught him and told me we had our son at last, I cradled him in my arms and wept for joy. Ferenc had written that if the child were a boy, he should be named after his paternal grandfather, and so this is what I did. Tamás was small, smaller than any of his sisters had been, a little scrawny thing with yellowish skin and delicate features, frail little arms and legs like green willow twigs, but I was relieved still. Everything we had would be safe now that there was a Nádasdy boy to protect it—his sisters, myself.

The babe did well at first, sucking his milk greedily, his skin growing pinker every day. His sister Orsika especially loved to hold him and would beg to be allowed to cradle him for a few minutes, stroking his soft cheek with one of her tiny fingers. The child lifted all our spirits.

Eventually the closeness and confinement began to wear on all of us. Ilona Jó and the dry nurse who tended the older children, an enormous brute of a woman named Dorottya Szentes, were always angling for my favor, snapping at each other over which of them would get to place a cool cloth on my head, which would massage my swollen feet. Both were afraid of Darvulia. Whenever my friend came into the room, the other two women would find employment in sewing or cleaning, in distracting the children or changing the baby. I knew they respected me as the lady of the house, but Darvulia they feared. They feared the creak of the wood under her soles, the low rich notes of her voice, so like a man's. The long black-and-silver hairs that fell sometimes from the tangle she kept at the back of her head, and which would sometimes pop up on pieces of clothing or blankets, they would scoop up and throw into the fire like a couple of superstitious old witches. But little Tamás was doing well, and my strength was returning. We expected the contagion to pass any day, so I decided to say nothing of their ignorance when we were all so close and hot and tired of looking at one another.

One day the baby was fussing more than usual, so that I thought he had soiled himself, but when I opened the diaper I saw it—a hard little bump in his groin announcing the beginning of the plague. In a day or two his face was black with it. Darvulia gave him a drink of something that smelled vile and which she said might halt the advancement of the disease, but a few hours later he was dead. Little Orsika—the one who had so loved her brother and doted on him—followed a few days later, her beautiful pale skin bruised a terrible black. I held her in my arms when she took her last rattling breaths and cursed God that ever I had been born a woman. Only Darvulia could pry the child from my hands and take her stiff little body to the cellars to dress her for the grave.

The other two—Ilona Jó, Dorka—whispered that Darvulia had something to do with their deaths, that she had put a spell on the children. I saw them with their heads together and heard their whispers. Darvulia did it, they said. The mistress should send her away before she kills the other children. Those crones, clawing at my own children like two wolves with a flock of lambs—how hateful they were to me, how coarse and vulgar, how much I hated them in that moment, when they turned on Darvulia. I flew at them in a fury, my hands like birds' talons. No one, I said, was to speak ill of Darvulia in my presence, Darvulia who for years had been my closest companion, Darvulia whom I loved as much as ever I loved my own mother. She had done everything she could to save my poor babies, I said, and the other two would do well to remember it. Get out of my sight, I said. The women went muttering from my presence, throwing distrustful glances behind them at Darvulia, at me. When they were gone, it was quiet, at least.

Like my own mother after my father's death, I took to my bed, but I didn't weep for my dead ones. I stared at the mirror on the far wall, at the wild-haired, squint-eyed madwoman who stared back at me. How would I explain this to Ferenc—the plague coming into our house, and taking our son and little daughter with it, and so quickly, too? Rage and grief strained inside me, threatening always to burst free. The servant girl who left wet spots on the floor of my room, so that Kata slipped and bumped her head against a table, I thrashed with the heavy end of a candlestick, keeping my blows to the arms and legs the way Ferenc had taught me so that she might endure a longer beating. The cook who burned the fine piece of salted fish someone sent as a gift I whipped in the courtyard until her blood spattered my white blouse and I had to change into a new one. The servants shrank at the sound of my voice, rushing away at my footfalls in the halls and the courtyards, but I didn't care. They were worse than useless, nothing but lazy whores who ate my food and gossiped about me and rutted like dogs when my back was turned, letting disease and death into my house. They cared nothing, nothing for the sufferings of me and my children. Let them all be damned, if I must be.

I had Darvulia bring my two living children in to me, as my own mother had once done, and cradled them close, whether they wanted to be with me or not. Anna especially didn't seem to know what to make of me in my grief. She made herself small in my arms, cringing as if she blamed me for what had happened to her brother and sister and could not bear my touch. Kata, only three years old herself, seemed not to notice and went about her baby business still, bringing me items from my dressing table to play with, showing me her puppets, picking up my hands and kissing them with her little bow-shaped mouth. "Where is Orsika?" she asked, and I pulled her to me but could hardly feel her in my arms, could not smell her baby smell, for she kept turning into someone else. Orsika. Tamás. The other daughter, the vanished one. I saw strange visions of a horse on its back birthing a human child, a dark-haired child with a mustache and fear in its voice. *Save me*, it said. I clutched at Kata until she whimpered, and Anna snatched her sister away and kept her from me until Darvulia threatened to lock her in the cellars with the bats if she did not start obeying her mother, whose heart was broken. Don't you see your mother needs you now? she asked, and Anna came back to me, reluctant, and settled herself near me on the bed, her lovely black eyes full of distrust.

Ferenc, having heard the news of the child's birth and illness, rushed home to be with us, but it was too late—he would not see little Tamás alive. A few days later we buried our darlings. Orsika I dressed in a white shift encrusted with tiny pearls, and baby Tamás, the heir we had hoped for, I wound in a fine linen sheet embroidered with gold thread. A little prince, even in death. We invited no one to the funeral. Plague funerals were not public funerals, and even if they had been, we preferred to mourn together, out of the eye of the public, when it came to the deaths of our children.

Your father wanted to try for another child right away, but I couldn't bear to think of it. For nearly a year I would not let him into my bed, saying that I would not bring another child into the world only to see it die before my eyes. Ferenc tried to be patient with me, wrapping his great arms around me until I felt I would disappear, but sometimes he would press himself on me further, and I would beg him—no, please. No more children, Ferenc. I could not endure it. He said that we still had two children living, that there was no reason to think another child would not live. The plague had been bad luck, he said, but bad luck doesn't last forever. I remembered the gypsy man who had died in the belly of the horse, and how his people had left him there, where bad luck was bound to linger. I wondered if perhaps it had landed, of all places, on me. I remembered the child I had given away, and how I had felt doomed to lose all my children as punishment for giving up the one. But I didn't speak of my anguish to Ferenc, whose heart was breaking with want. Instead I let him into my bed, in a fog of desperation and grief that must have looked like love. Even the chance of a son, an heir, the protection of our old age, lifted his spirits, and when it was over I held him against me and thought that if God were so merciful as to give me another child, another son, I would give anything I had—everything—to see him grow to manhood. My very self.

# 4

Our little Pál was born on a morning in the spring of 1598, a cool morning of mist and rain. You were the most easy and well behaved of my children from the beginning, since I had barely an hour between the beginning of my lying-in and the moment of your birth. The moment you fell free of me your father held you aloft, counted your fingers and toes, and laughed so long that tears squeezed from his eyes. "His name is Pál," he said. Darvulia could hardly snatch you back from his hands long enough to wipe the blood and wax from your plump, pink little body. A healthy child, a son. Our prayers answered at last.

Afterward your father hosted a great celebration, a feast that lasted more than a week, with enough food and wine and dancing for an army, as my own father had once done for my sister Klára and my mother. Friends and family came from all over Hungary to celebrate with us the birth of the Nádasdy heir, the palatine's grandson, on whom we lavished all our hopes. Thurzó came from Bicske, though he left my friend Zsofía Forgách and their two daughters at home, where they were recovering from a long and difficult illness. Your uncle István came all the way from Ecsed despite his own troubled health, bringing little Gábor and Anna with him, the two Báthory orphans he had adopted after he and Fruzsina Drugeth had given up hope of children of their own. Gábor especially was a pleasure, a teasing, lighthearted boy who preferred dancing and games to the serious pursuits my brother tried to bend him to, scholarship and philosophy, the great questions of our day. Anna and Kata were delighted to meet their little cousins and ran up and down the halls squealing so much that your father told them, only half in jest, that if they did not quiet down he would have their mouths sewn shut until the celebration was over. I told them to play outside, out of earshot of their father, and they went giggling into the garden to continue their games.

My cousin Griseldis, newly widowed, wrote that she could not make the trip to Sárvár, though she thanked me for my invitation nevertheless. Her husband, who had taken a wound fighting at Mezőkeresztes and suffered for some time afterward of a lingering illness, had finally died, she wrote, leaving Griseldis in charge of the small estates they had inherited. This news, which at one time would have broken me in two, now left me unmoved. András Kanizsay was dead. A lesser man than Ferenc Nádasdy, after all.

Afterward, she wrote, her two sons-in-law, along with a couple of her wealthy neighbors, had joined forces and turned on her, seizing her croplands and vineyards, the little *kastély* that had been promised them in her will. They had been unwilling, apparently, to wait for her death to possess it. The younger children had been sent to live with their older sisters, and my cousin sent to a nunnery. Her letter complained bitterly how ill her daughters treated her, how lonely she was in her present state.

The other nobles were scandalized by these actions, but no one lifted a finger to defend her. Such was life, they said. She should not have tried to keep the *kastély* for herself when she had promised it to the sons-in-law. I sent her some fine blankets and a few bottles of wine, some good cheese and other small kindnesses, but I had little sympathy for a woman like Griseldis. If her neighbors and relations felt they could treat her like a joke, an obstacle to be pushed aside, I thought, it was her own fault by proving them correct. How was I to know that in time my friends and family, my own sons-in-law and my neighbors, would do the same to me?

In Sárvár we gathered our friends to us to celebrate our good fortune. My friends among the noblewomen came to sit with me in my rooms and fuss and fret over you—my husband's aunt, Margit Choron; Countess Zrínyi; Countess Batthyány—all the women who had once pitied me for my childlessness, who had whispered about me, had flaunted their many children in front of me like prizes they had won. My sisters came too, with their little children, and my sister-in-law, your aunt Fruzsina Drugeth, held you and cooed over you longer than anyone, she who had adopted her children when they were already half-grown. How lovely it was then to sit in the white room at Sárvár surrounded by my sisters and friends and hold my little son in my arms and feel their admiration now that my happiness was complete. They rejoiced with me and prayed with me that after all our sorrows you, at least, would grow to manhood and strength, the heir that every family wanted and needed.

All that week I wrapped you in the softest linens and showed you off to our many guests. Your father held you up in front of his comrades-in-arms and declared that the sultan in Constantinople had better beware, for another Nádasdy had come to plague him into his grave. As fine and strong a boy as ever was born, the envy of all our relatives and friends. Your father gave me a ring, a large yellow diamond in a gold band, as a gift for producing his heir, and I remembered what my mother had said to me, that when I gave my husband a son he would value me above all his possessions. Your father's gaze never landed on me in those days but he looked pleased, more pleased than I had ever seen him.

It was during that time that I began to notice Thurzó's eyes on me too. As Ferenc's dearest friend he claimed a seat close to me at meals, smiling at me over his silver cup. He would lean in so close that, at times, I could feel his lips brush against my ear, so that I would wonder what he was up to, what he had in mind. One night during dinner he came forward to ask about the troubles with my uncle Zsigmond in Transylvania, who had separated from his Habsburg wife and abdicated in favor of my cousin, the Catholic cardinal András Báthory. I was picking up my glass of wine when he brushed a strand of hair away from my ear and leaned forward to ask me in a low voice whether I heard anything from my Transylvanian cousins. How did they do lately? he asked, his breath smelling of herbs and wine. I shook my head and laughed, though the question was no joke. Perhaps Thurzó was trying to pry some family secrets from me to use against my uncle and his supporters. I changed the subject to his wife and children at home, asking after their health. He studied me for a moment, as if deciding how much he could trust me. Zsofía Forgách, he said, growing melancholy, was more ill than most people knew. "I do not expect her to live out the year," he said, sighing, and set down his cup.

I put my hand on his arm, which was thinner than Ferenc's, even under his coat. Zsofía Forgách had been his stepsister before she was his wife. They had grown up together and knew from the very beginning they were meant for each other. The thought of losing her must have been hard for him. "I am so sorry to hear it," I said. "I hope you will take her a letter from me when you return. I have some herbs, too, that might help her, if you will give them to her."

Now his hand was over mine, rough and calloused from many years in the saddle, but pleasant and warm nonetheless. I had not always trusted him, but we had been friends a long time, Thurzó and I. "Thank you, yes. She would be glad to hear from you. It would lift her spirits, if not heal her body."

He seemed about to say something more, but then Ferenc was by our side, his black brows moving up and down in half-drunken merriment. I could smell the *pálinká* on his breath, the spiced meats and fruit, and I knew that he would suffer from indigestion long into the night. He had stayed away from my bed since the birth of our son, but still I knew him well enough to know his suffering. If Thurzó had not been sitting there, I might have scolded him to take his drink in more moderation, but I would not want to shame him in front of his friend, so I said nothing, only removing my hand from Thurzó's and folding it in my lap.

"What's this?" Ferenc said. "Moving in on my property, are you, old friend?"

"Not at all," I said, with a little more heat than was merited, for I never liked to think of myself as any man's property. "Thurzó was just telling me of his wife's illness."

Ferenc's face grew serious. He knew how much Zsofía Forgách meant to Thurzó. He mustered a semblance of sobriety and said, "Is there anything we may do?"

Thurzó sighed, and looked away, at the servants moving around the hall, the young girls in their brightly colored skirts, the stewards dressed in black, as if someone there might know the secret that would save her. He picked up his cup and took a long drink from it. "Thank you, but I think not. Perhaps I will return home a little early to be with her. It might do us both some good. I will say good night, my friends." He drained his drink and set the cup down. I motioned for one of the servants to take him a candle to lead him to his room, so that he might find some rest before his journey, and wondered what it was that Thurzó might have said to me if Ferenc had not interrupted him.

After he was gone, Ferenc leaned heavily against me, calling for more wine, more music, laughing when I urged him to moderation. He was still calling for more of everything when the sun broke over the horizon and the revelers were asleep in their furs, bodies piled here and there around the halls of Sárvár like the aftermath of a little war. I put his arm around my shoulders and led him up to bed.

# 5

Your sisters grew into lovely young ladies, and I often set them the task of watching their little brother, a serious boy with his father's heavy brow and bone-black eyes. Kata was an eager little mother who loved to pick you up under the arms and carry you around the house. Of course this manhandling made you cry, especially when you had been in the middle of some game or other from which your sister was taking you away. Anna, my responsible eldest child, would scold her sister that the baby was not a puppet to play with, but Kata could not resist something smaller than herself after having been the baby of the family. Like a moth to a candle she went at you again and again, until you began to cling to me or Ilona Jó whenever you saw your sister coming. "*Anyu!*" you would say, loudly, and hold up your round little arms for me to rescue you. But Kata would wait until I was not looking, or until her brother became distracted, and try again. She was never one to give up easily.

Anna grew more serene as she got older, less mischievous, but my eldest never came to me with her secrets or clambered into my lap as her sister did as I sat writing my letters or reading a book. She was well named, for she had my mother's cool eye, her calculating temperament, as well as her extraordinary beauty. A dangerous combination. Whenever I would see her move past the servant boys at home at Sárvár, the street boys in front of our house in Bécs— how she watched them watching her, how she lifted her hand just so to smooth her dress, to pat her hair, to bring attention to the parts of herself she liked best and that would make them shudder with want—I sometimes fancied I was looking at a small version of my own mother as she might have been before my own birth, relentless, self-contained, and completely aware of the power of her charm. At thirteen Anna drew the attention of every man in the room at festivals held in Pozsony, in the new Habsburg capital at Prága, even old grandfathers three times her age. Whenever she lifted her lashes, a sigh moved through the male quarter of the room, and her nurse—the heavyset, beetle-browed Dorottya Szentes—would spin her around by the shoulder and march her back out again with as much ferocity as any captain with an inexperienced and troublesome soldier.

Ferenc began to talk of betrothing Anna to the son of his old friend Miklós Zrínyi, a young man of sixteen with his father's name and his father's warlike interests. She was a good age to be betrothed, older than I had been when our parents made our match, and his mother was my dear friend, but for Anna's sake I had hoped Ferenc would choose someone less likely to be away at war year after year than the son of Zrínyi. I had thought she might make a good wife for my nephew Gábor, whom I had seen whispering with Anna in the halls at Sárvár more than once, a couple of young conspirators. The thought of my daughter as the mistress of Ecsed filled me with joy, remembering my own happy childhood there. Still, I could not deny that when your father approached her about the match with Zrínyi, Anna seemed pleased. The younger Zrínyi was broad shouldered and slender hipped like his rich and famous Croatian father, and Anna did seem to favor him more than the others, sitting closest to him at dinner, offering him the first olives, the first glass of wine. Once I even caught her reaching for his leg under the table at a feast, her soft little fingers nimbly moving across the fabric of his breeches, his face dreamy, my alarm growing with every moment until I called her name, sharply, and saw her snatch her hand back. So at last I approved of the match. She needed a husband, and quickly, too.

We celebrated their engagement on her fourteenth birthday with a great deal of wine and music, the young people blushing at each other as they exchanged rings. A handsome couple, said Ferenc to me, and everyone agreed.

Anna left for the Zrínyi house not long after, and I held her to me and wished her well, remembering the day my mother had sent me to Sárvár with Megyery and Darvulia for company. My daughter wore the red silk dress I myself had worn the night I first met Ferenc, richly colored still and fine, and with her hair combed into a great nest, her delicate face so young beneath it that I was seized with fear for her, for her future. She seemed too young and stubborn for such a vital undertaking, the uniting of two wealthy and influential families. For a moment, if I had dared, I would have snatched her back and kept her at home. But the match was made, and none of us had any choices now. I bent and whispered in her ear that she should be a good and useful daughter to the Zrínyis, and write home when she could, and remember always that she was a Nádasdy and a Báthory, no matter whom she married. *Extra Hungariam non est vita et si est vita, non est ita.* How often had I thought of those words in the years since I had left my own mother, since I had come to Sárvár when I was still a child, how long it seemed since then, and yet as I stood in the dusty courtyard of the house with my own daughter dressed in red for her journey, I saw that nothing had changed. Mothers sent their daughters out into the world, to become mothers themselves.

Anna kissed me dutifully and climbed into the carriage, but she did not cry, not even when she waved to you and Kata out the window, and the horses took her into her future, away from our sight. I knew she would be happy with young Zrínyi for a while at least, until his charm, or hers, began to wear thin. But I knew my friend Countess Zrínyi, her future mother-in-law, would help her understand her place in the family, and Anna would make herself useful there as I had done in the Nádasdy household. A woman could find great satisfaction in making a home and a life, even if it didn't always turn out exactly as she expected.

Meanwhile, with an uneasy peace settled between the king and Constantinople, I watched and waited for your father's return. He came at last in the winter of 1599, not long before Christmas, bringing his friends Thurzó and Bocskai, Zrínyi and Batthyány with him, and they in turn brought their wives, my good friends and companions. Together we spent several days drinking and feasting at Sárvár, the men teasing each other with games and good-natured violence: taking a drunken friend outside on his cot and leaving him to sleep in the snow; betting who could hang the longest off the side of his horse at a full gallop without falling; dunking each other in the icy water of the river and then running back to the house, where the last man to the door would be shut out to freeze until his lips were blue and he begged the others to have mercy on him. The more danger they faced in battle, the more violence crept into their games, as if they had lost all their fear of death and were daring God to take them. At night the ladies and I would have a chance to visit with them and hear firsthand the stories of their adventures at the front, the fierceness of the sultan's men, the blood that ran through fields of this or that strategic town, the smell of burnt flesh that rose into the air with the funeral pyres after every skirmish. I would watch the eyes of our friends as they looked with envy around Sárvár, at the house the old palatine had built with its rich carpets, its gold and silver treasures. How many of them had grown poorer in the years of fighting, while Ferenc's fields and vineyards had done so well? None of the wives of the other noblemen were as accomplished at managing their estates, at keeping them safe and prosperous, as I was. It was a point of pride that while Ferenc had been fighting for Hungary, I had been fighting for Ferenc, and for our children. Even without the money we had lent the royal treasury, I had managed to put together a sizable dowry for Anna, and money for Pál's education. Kata's dowry was still in the king's hands, but Ferenc assured me that Rudolf would repay us, with interest, now that the fighting was over. Still, the Nádasdy estates were the envy of the Hungarian nobility. Even my brother István told me so, whenever he was well enough to write. *You have done well, little sister. Everyone who sees your vineyard and fields, your houses and stables, says how beautiful they are, how lucky Ferenc is to have you by his side. Our mother would be proud.*

It was during one of these evenings of wine and companionship that Thurzó came to see me, leaving the pleasant company and good fire in the great hall to come to the library, where I kept a great wooden desk and my cask of important papers and deeds. I was writing a letter to Anna about some little piece of advice she had asked me when I heard his step at the door and looked up to see his heavily bagged eyes, his unhandsome face. He looked more tired than usual. Zsofia Forgách had died in the spring, and since then I had noticed a change in him, a subtle shift from merriment to contemplation, from engaging in the games the men played to an almost womanish need to stand back and watch with an appraising eye, as if his companions were people he had never seen before and did not know how to place. "Is everything all right, Thurzó?" I asked, and all at once I knew that nothing was right with him. He sagged somewhat against the door frame, the graying hair, thinner than it had been, tucked behind his large pale ears, giving him a rabbitlike, hunted look.

He leaned forward to see what I was writing—a bit presumptuous of him, and instinctively I put my arm over the paper for I was still somewhat wary of him, uncertain of his intentions. "I'm sorry," he said. "Your letter is none of my business. How are the children?"

"Kata has trouble with her teeth still, which sometimes keeps her from her books, but Anna is doing very well. Her mother-in-law says she is a credit to the household and looks after all the little cousins there better than their own mothers could do. And Pál has begun talking, as you've probably noticed. One can hardly get him to stop."

"I'm glad to hear it. You are so blessed." Again I felt the undercurrent of jealousy in him, a hint of resentment against his friend's good fortune. Thurzó himself had no son but only two daughters. The eldest was married, but the younger, Borbála, was Kata's age, only six and too young to be betrothed. She lived with his old mother at the estate at Biscke while Thurzó was away at the front.

"You may have a son still one day."

"Perhaps not. I'm getting too old to think about such things." He sagged more, and I wondered again if he were the kind of man to marry only once. I sensed that he was somewhat uncomfortable around women now that his wife was dead, with little sense of how to talk to them, what his place in a woman's life might be.

"You're not too old," I said, and put my hand on his arm, wanting to offer him some comfort. He had been always a worthy companion to Ferenc, even if I had not always trusted him. "You're only forty. Ferenc has still not given up the idea of another son."

"Ferenc has a beautiful wife and a fine heir. He has reason to hope for the future."

"Oh, György—" I began, and lowered my head. It wasn't right for Thurzó to say such things to his friend's wife, and I was immediately aware of the brass bell of Ferenc's voice in the house, laughing at something or other Zrínyi was saying. Thurzó was as ugly a man as I'd ever seen, certainly not a candidate for romance, even if I had been in a temper to take a lover. Yet we had both suffered so many losses, so much heartbreak, how could I fail to try to console him? There was nothing I could say that would be appropriate under the circumstances, or that would ease his suffering. There was hardly a family in Hungary that did not have a similar cross to bear. He wanted to say something else to me, I could feel it. But then we heard the footsteps of some servant coming down the hall, and Thurzó sagged against the door frame, the declaration dead on his lips. I wondered for a long time afterward what it was he had wanted to say to me, what he was thinking. "I'll leave you to your work, Countess," he said, and went back to rejoin his friends.

# 6

For all his bravery and heroism during the Turkish wars, Ferenc had not escaped unscathed. He had been wounded several times, receiving cuts on his arms and back and face at Buda that festered and putrefied, requiring the doctor to cauterize the wounds with the hot blade of a dagger. One cut on his face sliced his right eyebrow into two pieces, like a black caterpillar run over by a carriage wheel. At Esztergom he took an arrow in the shoulder, which healed well, but at Pápa his great black horse, struck down by a gunshot, rolled onto his left leg and broke it in several places. Thurzó and Bocskai had carried him all the way home to Sárvár on a stretcher, drunk and singing of victory.

Despite being reset by a good surgeon, the bones of his leg never healed properly. The skin turned black in patches, and the opposite leg—which bore the brunt of his weight when he could not stand on the other—gave him great pains. His surgeons told him to stay home and let his wife tend to him, but Ferenc wouldn't stay off his feet when he was supposed to and often went riding off on this or that errand. The leg had to be rebroken and reset several times. It was gruesome business. The last time I held my husband down with my own hands while the surgeon took a club to his limb. "Press down with all your might, Erzsébet," Ferenc said. "I might struggle, and I don't want to hurt you." The surgeon gave him some brandy to dull the pain, and then I climbed on his chest, pressing into his muscled shoulders with my thin hands and whispering in his ear that this position might be an excellent one for lovemaking. "If you're up to it later, that is," I said. He blushed—the surgeon might overhear us talking of bedroom matters—but I didn't care. I was trying to keep his mind off what was about to happen. I looked down into my husband's face, my body blocking his view of the surgeon's club, so that only I saw how the pain moved through him when the bone split and the surgeon snapped it back into place with a sickening crunch. Your father, I am proud to say, never made a sound. Afterward I bound the wounds myself, forbidding him from traveling to Prága to see the king until they had healed. As I plied him with valerian to ease the pain and help him sleep, he smiled and patted my hand. "It is lucky for me," he said, "that you have a strong stomach."

"It is," I said, "for otherwise you would have to be tended by old Darvulia. She might try to kiss you, tickling you with her whiskers while you slept."

He gave a mock shudder and sank into valerian-induced torpor. I didn't tell him that Darvulia came to his bedside when I needed to rest, nor that the surgeon had threatened that if Ferenc rebroke his leg one more time, they might have to remove it for good. It would do no good for him to worry about such things before they came to pass.

For days I fed him valerian to keep him asleep. If he slept, he could not try to stand and walk on the injured leg. It healed much better this time, and a few weeks after that he was up again, moving about slowly but with increasing strength. A few weeks later he was well enough to ride and went off again before I could make good on my threat to tie him to his bed to keep him from leaving the house.

In the meantime I kept up my work on the Nádasdy estates, increasing the demands on the tenant farmers for oats and barley, for wine and livestock that we could sell to Bécs or Gyulafehérvár. The tenants complained, but I would not relent. Kata's dowry needed to be set aside, for the day would soon come when we would have to find her a husband. Your father did not want to sell off the estates if he could help it, wanting to save them for you, Pál, when you were grown. Ferenc had already asked Rudolf for a return of the money he had lent for the war, but the king insisted he was stretched too thin after the war, and my husband would have to wait a while longer for his loan to be repaid. Ferenc wrote home to me complaining that Rudolf had enough money for his alchemists, for his poets and astronomers and architects, but not enough to settle his debts with the nobles. *The king is a king in name only. The power in the kingdom shifts, and we must be ready when the change comes.*

He went to Mátyás, whose power was growing in opposition to his brother, but officially the archduke told my husband he could not authorize payment if his brother would not. Privately, he told Ferenc that if my husband would support his bid to remove Rudolf from power, Mátyás would see his loan repaid. Ferenc preferred not to come between the two brothers, friends and allies both, but secretly he agreed that Rudolf's rule was fading and that Mátyás would make a better king, more engaged in the life outside his palace walls. Ferenc agreed to do what he could to support Mátyás, if Mátyás would agree to return the loan.

Ferenc asked me my opinion on the matter, and I told him that his support for Mátyás seemed like a wise course. Without the repayment of the thirty thousand forints owed to us by the king, I worried that our accounts would fall short and we would be forced to sell off one of the estates, Léka perhaps, or my own Csejthe, to pay Kata's dowry. Without a rich dowry, our little Kata, our beloved daughter, might have to go without a husband altogether, and women who did not marry were at the mercy of the world. After the war there were fewer eligible bachelors than ever among the higher-ranking nobility. Something would have to be done for Kata, and quickly, too.

Four years after we had packed Anna up and sent her to the Zrínyi house to her future mother-in-law, Ferenc fell ill once more and took to his bed in the house at Sárvár with some pains in his legs and coldness in his extremities. His health had been plaguing him off and on in recent months, especially a fatigue that seemed alarming given that he was no longer a young man of twenty with endless energy for the Turkish wars but a father of nearly forty-eight who had spent most of his life on horseback with a sword in his hand.

One terrible night I recall clearly. I made certain he had a comfortable chair and gave him a plump cushion to place under his feet before the fire. He didn't seem to think there was much to worry about, so I went myself to bed, where I fell into a deep and dreamless sleep. Later your father told me that he woke in the night with a need to relieve himself and threw the blankets off to visit the latrine, but when he tried to stand his leg went out from under him, and he crumpled to the floor. His legs were so weak they could not bear his weight, and when he tried again to stand, holding on to the back of a chair, the pain was so terrible that he bit his tongue and made it bleed. The maidservant who had been in his bed that night called for Darvulia, who fetched me, bending over me so closely her chin whiskers tickled my cheek. "What is it?" I asked.

"The count has fallen," said my old friend, "and I can't lift him. He won't let me call for the valet."

"Where is he?"

"In his bedchamber."

I found him in the middle of the floor with sweat on his brow and a wild expression in his black eyes that made him look like a calf about to be branded. In a corner of the room a young thing not even as old as my own daughter Anna with breasts as small as honey-suckle buds pulled her shift close to her. There was a moment when I paused to consider whether to have Darvulia take the girl to the cellars and have her horsewhipped. If the maidservants were going to debase themselves with my husband, they could at least have the good taste to hide it from me. But at the moment I had other, more pressing matters to attend to. "What are you standing there for?" I asked. "Go back to your own bed. I'll find you in the morning." I heard her running away in her bare feet, loud enough to wake the entire house.

At my feet Ferenc panted and strained. I had never seen my husband look so helpless—Ferenc Nádasdy, the Black Bey of Hungary, could not stand on his own two feet. "I need your help, Erzsébet," he said. "I cannot bear for the menservants to see me like this. Will you help me kneel so that I can relieve myself? My bladder is about to burst."

I brought him the chamberpot and knelt beside him, moved and frightened that he would ask me for help, since he would never have asked if he could have managed it without me. He pulled himself upright, and when he finished, Darvulia and I helped him stand and half carried him to the bed. When he was in bed once more, I covered him with a bearskin, for he said the cold was so terrible it burned him, and called for Darvulia to bring her bag of herbs, her powders and potions. She and I sat with him all night and tended him until his fever broke. Only then did I see to the girl who had been so stupid as to allow herself to be caught in the count's bedroom in the middle of the night. I made certain she would not make the same mistake again.

Ferenc spent several weeks in bed that winter. By the spring the illness seemed to go away gradually, though there would be days when he would feel poorly again and spend time in bed with his legs propped on a great tower of cushions. He was again in good health for Anna's wedding and feasted and danced as much as anyone, proud of the match he'd made between his daughter and the son of his friend. He and old Zrínyi and Thurzó spent most of the celebration in a corner, outdoing themselves with wine and *pálinká* the way only old friends can do. They told stories and reenacted several battles scenes, complete with sounds of cannon fire, and Zrínyi's wife and I laughed and rolled our eyes, having heard these stories many times before. Each time the number of heads they took, the number of enemy, increased at least threefold. But no one dared correct them when they were enjoying themselves so much.

But the following winter, after another brutal summer riding across the kingdom to see to the king's business and our many estates, Ferenc came home suffering more pain than ever. His black hair seemed suddenly streaked with more gray, his eyes sunk into dull red pits like stones in a cherry. I feared, when I met him in the courtyard to welcome him home, that he would fall off his horse; when he embraced me, I could sense how thin he had grown, frail even, for a man who had once stood so tall and broad that two of me could have fit inside his frame. I could count his ribs through his waistcoat. I made certain his bed was ready and took him to it straightaway, telling the valet I would see to my husband myself, please, on this, the first night of his return.

Ferenc tried to rally, even coming down to dinner that evening— saying that he could not refuse the quality of my hospitality, and remembering the night I peppered his food with mistletoe, I smiled a moment—but he went up again to his own chamber sooner than usual and spent a good part of the next several days on his back, eating little, sleeping much. His legs hurt him, he said, and when I removed his breeches I could feel that they were ice cold to the touch, pale as death. Below the knees he said he had no feeling at all. As the weeks wore on, the numbness and cold crept up to his hips, and his hands too felt the effects of it. He could hardly hold a pen to write and had to have his secretary compose his letters, and a new will that now seemed to be a dire necessity. Through it all Ferenc sat propped up with pillows, a servant rubbing his cold hands, his numb legs, with pepper and cloves to try to stimulate the blood to flow through them again. Darvulia brought him herbs from the fields to dress the bedsores that festered and oozed all along his limbs, and pine boughs to help drive the smell of death from the room, a smell that deepened and grew worse no matter what we did to stave it off.

By midwinter my husband knew the worst was upon him and asked for his secretary to write a letter to Thurzó: *Take care of my wife and children. For the sake of our old friendship, look after them when I am gone.*

He named Thurzó your official guardian, Pál, and Imre Megyery your tutor and caretaker. A man must do these offices, I knew, and yet I was bitter that Ferenc had not asked me whom I would prefer, since it was a decision I would have to live with. Anyone but Megyery, I would have told him. But it was done, and afterward there was nothing I could do to change it.

Ferenc could not lift the pen to sign the letter himself but had the secretary do so for him. I nearly wept to see him so reduced. I kissed his brow and asked him if there was anything I could do to help him, to give him comfort.

"Yes," he said. "Stay with me, Erzsébet. Put your arms around my neck and stroke my hair. Yes, like that. You remember when you did that, the night I came to you after so many years of foolishness?"

"I do remember. I remember it well. You said you were glad after all that our parents matched us. That we were more alike than different."

"It is true. We were both stubborn and didn't want to be married at first. But are you glad now? Are you sorry that you've spent your life with me?"

"No, dearest. Not sorry at all."

"I'm glad of it. I want you to do something for me."

"What?"

"Marry again. Don't let your beauty go with me to the grave. You should have a companion for your middle years."

"No one could take your place, my dearest," I said.

He seemed not to hear this, or heed it. "Don't let Pál grow up without a father. Marry again. Marry Thurzó, if you could have anyone. I've seen the way he looks at you. He would be good to you, and to Pál and the girls. He will protect you and the children."

"Don't talk so," I said. The thought of Thurzó as a husband—sad-eyed, gray-faced Thurzó—did not appeal to me in the least. "Rest, and in the morning you'll feel better."

I stroked his hair and fell asleep on the bed beside him. The next morning, when I opened my eyes, he was cold in my arms.

Carefully, so as not to disturb his body, I slid out from beneath him and called the servants to come. I stood and went to the window, where the morning light was coming in. Outside the air was clean with the scent of coming snow. I had Darvulia brew me a cup of strong tea and sat watching the stable boys muck out the stalls, the kitchen maids with the morning's fresh milk, and I wandered down to the kitchen to watch the scullery maids polishing the copper pots that would hold the butter and the bread, the way the light in the center of the bowl caught and sent a beam back toward the wall. The cat in the corner, seeing the spot of light, stopped licking herself and went to chase it, batting at something that she could never catch. In a few moments I would have to tell the children their father was dead, and I would have to begin my letters to Ferenc's friends and family—György Thurzó, István Bocskai—as well as a letter to the king himself. "Ferenc Nádasdy is dead." I would write it over and over again, as if to constantly remind myself, as if to burn it into my memory. But for that moment in the kitchen I was content to watch the cat at her game, and breathe the quiet of my first hours as a widow, the innocent domesticity, the cautious looks of the servants. The start of the second part of my life.

A few weeks later we buried him in the churchyard at Sárvár.

The priest praised Ferenc as the kindest lord and master, the greatest general and count, a nobleman of the highest order. The great families of Hungary assembled at the service wished for my family's health and safety, kissing me and wishing me well. Their eyes didn't find mine. I saw them looking behind me, looking around at the graceful high-ceilinged halls of Sárvár, the silver and the silk, the fields and vineyards and orchards. I saw the greed in their eyes. Now that Ferenc was gone and you, my son, were still a child, they coveted what Ferenc and I had built together, and I began to fear for it, and for you.

It would be up to me to protect myself and my family now that Ferenc was gone. A woman who does not marry is at the mercy of the world, my mother had told me, but a wealthy widow with a very young son, a son too young to take up his father's arms and titles, has nearly as much to lose. Greedy relatives or neighbors might try to wrest the estates from me, marching on Léka, on Keresztúr, on Csejthe, even Sárvár itself. The other nobles might be scandalized, but no one would lift a finger to help me. Even my husband's closest friends—Zrínyi, Thurzó—might get greedy enough to turn their eyes to my lands before you were grown. I did not want to end up like my cousin Griseldis, with the shaved head and frostbitten feet of a mendicant, locked up and forgotten while her sons-in-law and neighbors divided up her clothes and jewels, her lands and houses. Nothing terrified me more than the idea of the nunnery, locked up and forgotten by all the world, with nothing to occupy me but prayers and tears. A half-life, a living death. If I were to keep what was mine, I would need powerful friends on my side, a protector among my friends of rank and situation, and soon.

I would go to Bécs. I would go to Thurzó.

# 7

The two days on the road to Bécs from Sárvár were an agony, a combination of a bone-rattling carriage ride and mindless arguments between two of the young seamstresses I had brought along for company for myself and my daughter. The girls, like most of my servants, were distant relations to either my late husband or myself whose mothers had sent them to me in the hopes of arranging for them dowries and decent husbands, or in the absence of husbands at least a useful profession. The wars with the Turks had depleted the ranks of marriageable young men so significantly that many young women who came to me would never marry. Yet still their mothers sent them, and still they hoped.

The two girls, new to my household and both nearly grown at fourteen years old, sat together on the bench opposite Darvulia and Kata and myself, where instead of working at their sewing they persisted in elbowing each other. The younger one, a pretty blonde with cheekbones like two round yellow apples, complained that the other was taking up too much of her part of the bench with her fat behind. The other, a large slow-witted girl named Doricza who had been with me only a few months, pushed back whenever her companion's elbow jostled her, saying that the little blonde's bony elbows made her rib cage black and blue. More than once I told them to keep their mouths shut if they had nothing pleasant to say, and they would be quiet for a few minutes, at least until one or the other of them started complaining again.

We were all uncomfortable in the cramped space inside the carriage, in the bumps and stones along the road that jolted the carriage frame, but neither Darvulia nor Kata nor myself went on and on in such a tiresome fashion about the ache in our bones, the need to share the carriage bench, the water we had to hold until the horses took their next rest. I was sorry I had asked for the girls to ride in my own carriage and wished thin-faced Ilona Jó, the old wet nurse whom I had kept on for her loyalty, or beetle-browed Dorottya Szentes were there instead. After many years in my service, they had gained my trust, and if Darvulia was occupied, I often sought out their company before the fire or at meals in the evenings, inviting them to dine with me at my table when no one else was home. They, at least, knew how to hold their tongues in their mistress's presence.

At one point Darvulia brought out a little food, some bread and bitter dark-brown beer, a little cheese, and passed it around the carriage. We ate in silence for a while, and then the little blonde began to whine again. How uncomfortable it was, she said, when another person's flesh pressed so closely up against your own. "Maybe I should take your lunch, Doricza," she said, smirking, "since you have clearly eaten enough for two people already."

It was then that I reached over, grabbed the needle out of the bit of lace she'd been sewing, and jabbed it into the girl's pink finger, in the soft pad at the tip where her dirty jagged fingernail ended. The little twit howled and asked why I treated her thus. I said I would not listen to one more minute of her nattering, that she had best remember where she was and whom she was with. She cried out and snatched her hand back, her eyes filling with tears, but after that, at least, we were able to eat our small meal in relative peace.

The next day, when we continued on our way, the two girls sat on their bench and did their work without complaining. In fact they were so quiet that they made poor company, and when we stopped to change the horses I switched them around so Ilona Jó and Dorka could ride in the carriage with myself and Kata and Darvulia, and the two young seamstresses went in back with a couple of chambermaids and young Ficzkó, an orphan boy of fifteen whom I had taken in as my personal factotum and who liked to look at the pretty girls, to pick which of them to flirt with. The two older servants were better company, chatting more amiably about the sights along the road, about the problems of husbands and raising good children, about the pain and infirmities of growing older. If there were any complaints from the rear carriage, at least I would no longer have to listen to them.

The rolling hills of the western kingdom that year were covered with old bits of snow and damp patches of mud, the detritus of last year's failed harvest, for the weather had been so cool and damp the previous summer that nothing had ripened. Oats had rotted in the fields, and tomatoes had blackened on the vine. Blight had affected the fields far and wide. The end of the war had made us all look forward to a peaceful harvest, but it had not come, and the tenant farmers had not been able to pay their due once again. I had to let servants go at Sárvár, at Csejthe, and still the Nádasdy coffers grew thin. There would be no way to raise Kata's dowry this year, or the next or the next, if the king did not repay his debt. At nearly eleven years old, she would need that dowry all too soon. I put an arm around her shoulder and clutched her to me, my dear daughter, who might have to go without a husband if the king would not hear me.

We were all out of spirits, shriveling in the winter cool. Darvulia too seemed especially pale. Her features, which had never been beautiful, seemed more shrunken, her eyes more tired, with the faint bluish-white haze that announced the oncoming failure of eyesight. The whiskers on her chin had gone from black to white. Suddenly my friend looked very much like the most ancient of old crones, wizened beyond the span of ordinary mortals. It had never occurred to me before that I might lose her sometime, that she might actually be subject to the same process of growing old as everyone else. "Are you all right, dearest?" I asked, and she said she was, but I did not believe her in the least. She was to go right to bed when we arrived in the city, I said, and no arguments, though of course she tried to argue with me anyway, saying that I needed her help in setting up the house, for she thought always of my comfort before her own. "Go to bed, Darvulia," I said. "Surely you've earned the right to rest when you're ill, if anyone has. Let the others take on some of your duties for a change."

"All right, madam," she said, but I could tell she indulged me. They all did.

That second day we pushed hard for the north, and as the sun was sinking in the west and the sky turning a soft shade of gold, we passed around a hill and beheld the walls of Bécs. The icy Duna snaked around the edge of the city, the zigzag tiled roof and brown spire of the Stephansdom rising from the center like the trunk of a lightning-struck tree, while inside the new walls clusters of red-tiled roofs caught the last of the sunlight and turned the heart of the city to ocher. Outside the walls the plane trees and willows deepened to black in the far distance, the farms and fields fading into darkness one by one. The carriage wheels rattled beneath us when the horses came to the drawbridge and drew us into the city, through the great southern gate and up into the streets, where people and animals and the smell of both crowded in close. As we passed, the locals strained to look inside the carriages as if the king himself might be passing through, though Rudolf had moved his capital to Prága after ascending the throne, surrounding himself with artists and mathematicians, botching his relations with Hungary and Transylvania so much that my old friend István Bocskai led an insurrection against the Catholic Rudolf and his attempt to deny the Hungarian Protestants their religious freedom. Word came that Rudolf was ill, and his power was failing. Because Rudolf had no legitimate children, all the empire, Bécs included, drew in its breath to wait.

Beside me Dorka made a small noise in her throat and leaned out the window to gape. It was her first visit to the city. "My God," she said—she who had lived all her life in the small towns of Transdanubia—"it's like Jerusalem itself."

"I certainly hope so," I said, for I was thinking of salvation—my own, and my children's. To protect them now that Ferenc was dead, I would have to take my petition directly to the king's own brother, Mátyás. The archduke's power in Bécs, Ferenc had said, grew with every day Rudolf was absent. I was depending on it.

In the weeks since I buried my husband I had not been able

to stomach the view of the world from Sárvár, with nothing but work and solitude to look forward to. The period of my mourning stretched before me like a year of winters, and even my children could not make the spring come for me in those first days, when we all settled into life without our husband and father. Anna was gone to her mother-in-law's house, but even Kata snapped at you, and hid your tin soldiers in order to make you cry. You, Pál, who had always been such an active, high-spirited boy—jumping onto the back of your pony from a low wall, attacking your cousins with your little wooden sword with glee—were so listless that you often spent whole days under the shadow of my arm, avoiding the tutelage of Megyery, the old steward, whom you and I both disliked but who at least kept you at home in Sárvár instead of away at Prága in the king's court like so many other noble sons. You would run away and hide in corners of the house the way I had done as a child, curling up for a nap under a table or in the hollow of a crumbling wall, laughing at Megyery whenever he tried to get you to mind your lessons. But it was your father's wish that you study Latin and German, become a learned man the way he had been, so I relented. Once you were handed into Megyery's keeping I resolved to take your sister with me and spend some time at our house on Lobkowitz Square. Despite the impropriety of appearing at Mátyás's court while I was in mourning, I had business to discuss with the archduke, which provided ample excuse for escape.

In Bécs, too, there were friends who might help me in my cause. Thurzó had told me at Ferenc's funeral ceremony that he planned to spend much of the spring at court, for he was a confidant of both Rudolf and Mátyás, a Habsburg man through and through. If anyone could help me convince the king to repay the money owed us, it would be Thurzó. Perhaps, too, he would be a friend to me now that my husband was dead, and we both of us were the loneliest creatures in the world.

At last we arrived at Lobkowitz Square, at the house on the corner where Ferenc had lived as a young man studying at court, where he and I always stayed when we came into Austria. It was an elegant building of three stories built in the Italian style with stone arches around a central courtyard, in the middle of which stood a plane tree with a twisted trunk, covered now with snow in the last part of winter. Above rose two tiers of glass windows that looked down into the courtyard, so that at the sound of carriage wheels on cobblestones every member of the household could look out to see who had arrived. The manor had been built by my father-in-law, the old palatine, for his own stays in the city, so it was quite near the Hofburg, and several times a day companies of soldiers on muscular white Lipician horses would clatter between the manor and the practice ring in Josefplatz a few blocks away. An Augustinian church and monastery stood hard against the walls of the manor, and sometimes very early in the morning or late at night we could hear the chanting of the monks at their prayers, a low sonorous moan that permeated the walls and kept me up nights. The monks, whenever I and my ladies passed by on the street, eyed us warily, as if we might suddenly place our arms around their necks and plant tempting kisses on their faces. I admit the thought did cross my mind at times, never more so than the first night I arrived as a widow and saw them scurrying away from the carriage like the Hebrews out of Egypt.

In the house the servants had thrown open the shutters, aired out the rooms, put fresh linens on the beds, polished the silver, set torches and candles alight in the passageways, uncorked the wine. Here and there were reminders of Ferenc—the gleaming swords hanging on one wall, the chair he had liked to sit in by the fire after dinner, a bundle of letters he had left behind—but each time I lighted on something that conjured my dead husband I would have one of the servants remove it, and afterward I stood at the open window and breathed in the night air. Outside a servant emptied a night jar, and a horse in harness pissed insistently on the street. Somewhere distant there were voices arguing, and the lamplighters came along the street with their torches, but a hint of snow tinged the cool night air, and from my hair came a strong scent of the lavender oil that

Dorka had use to dress it that morning. With the majority of the royal court removed to Prága, the city was quieter than it might have been, but there would still be friends to see, and dinners and balls to attend with this or that noble family, and wives and daughters to wait on in the afternoons, and very little time to sit on my hands. In Bécs, unlike Sárvár, no one would think of me as the poor, pitied widow locked behind her castle walls and dressed eternally in black, pining for her lost husband. In Bécs I was still a woman worth noticing.

Late that night, not long after most of the house had gone to bed, there was an argument in the servants' quarters. The little blonde and Doricza were having at it again, this time over a forint I had given the fat Doricza for finishing twenty pieces of lace on the journey, for I always rewarded industriousness in my servants. The blonde said she should share in the coin, since she claimed to have done some of the work, and so she had taken the coin from Doricza's pocket and hidden it in a hollow of her heel. Doricza found it, of course, and started a row. Dorka and Ilona Jó were holding them apart when I arrived in the servants' quarters, called by the noise from my soft warm bed. "Now look what you've done," said Ilona Jó, her thin face so sour I could nearly taste it. "You've woken the mistress and upset the whole house."

Peace among the servant girls, even in good times, came rarely. Ferenc had taught me well after the incident with Amália so many years ago, not only how to revive an unconscious girl by "star-kicking" but how to administer a beating so that the beaten one could still perform her duties afterward, even how to hide the marks of a beating so that no outward evidence would show, even to a lover. The punishment of Amália had been the making of our marriage, the first time Ferenc had looked at me as someone with whom he might share more than a roof. I had proven a willing student for the techniques he wished to teach me, and he entirely trusting to let me employ them as I saw fit. Never once did he interfere with my running of the house, not even when my stick fell on the back of one of his favorites. It was, I think, his way of showing his respect for me.

After I had punished his most recent favorite, he would find a new one, and I a reason to send the offending girl away—a new house that needed a servant, or marriage to a poor relation with a minor dowry. Peace would return, for a while at least, until the new favorite forgot her place and had the audacity to flaunt my husband's favor in front of the others. Then I would again have to make an example of her, to remind them all that while Ferenc might bed them, it was I who ran the household, I upon whom their livelihoods depended. What was I to do—allow their insolence to proliferate? To let myself become a laughingstock in my own house? If they dared to bed my husband and then have the cheek to parade it in front of me, I would make certain they did not do so twice. It was my right as a noble-woman, as a wife.

Thievery, too, was a constant problem. I had a system in place to keep track of all our fine dishes, our clothing and paintings and coins. I kept ledgers hidden in my cask of papers and often took inventory of the household without telling anyone I was doing so. When I discovered some item missing—a candlestick, a cup—I would have the house searched until it was found again in a trunk or under a mattress. The poor dumb things did not realize until it was too late that their mistress was such a careful housekeeper, and I would have to educate them at the end of my stick, as much to make an example of them as punishment for the offense. A few minutes in the court-yard with my stick or the end of my whip and the entire household would be quiet for months afterward, with no theft, no drunkenness or fornication, just whispered gratitude and modest hard work.

Now it seemed another reminder was in order. In the servants' quarters of my house in Lobkowitz Square I took the blonde by the wrist in front of her fellows and handed the stolen coin to Ilona Jó, asking her to heat it in the grate of the fire that burned at one end of the room. The child was little but strong, and she twisted this way and that, kicking and striking out at me to try to get away. "Don't," she said, "don't." I held her fast. When the coin was white-hot, Ilona Jó picked it up with the tongs and placed it in the girl's outstretched palm. Dorka and I kept her still while the flesh burned for a few seconds, her body shuddering and heaving, but we were stronger than she. At last she screamed and dropped the coin on the floor, clutching her hand to her breast, the hand that now bore the likeness of the king's face marked in the center of her palm. Around her the other girls murmured and looked at their shoes. For the remainder of our time in Bécs, I knew the other girls, at least, would cause no more trouble.

Afterward I had Dorka and Ilona Jó take the girl down to the laundry to dress the wound. It would not do to have the injury fester and threaten the girl's ability to do her work, and I was not so cruel that I wanted to see her suffering continue. I was not a madwoman who enjoyed the suffering of others but a fair mistress who had meted out her punishment under the eyes of everyone in the house, who had nothing to hide. "Take her and give her something for the pain," I said to the old women, "and then wrap the burn and put her to bed." They went, the girl still clutching her hand, her face dirty and streaked with the tracks of tears, her eyes full of anger as she passed me. I went back up to bed and tried to rest, but I was bewildered by the girl's looks, how she seemed to blame me when it was she who had caused all the trouble to begin with. I had a feeling that she would cause more trouble before she was done.

Sometime during the night I heard her cry out once, then again. Dressing, I went down to the laundry to see what was the matter, furious that my rest had been disturbed for a second time in a single night. There I found the girl crouched in a corner, half dressed, hissing like a feral cat. "What's this racket?" I asked. "You're waking the whole neighborhood. If you had an ounce of brains, you would learn to keep silent. Every time I have to speak to you, you make it worse on yourself."

"She won't let me near her, mistress," said Dorka, her voice tinged with no little bit of resentment. "I told her I need to dress that wound before it festers. She says she'll write to her mother and say how we mistreat her. She threatened to go to the palatine himself to speak against you and show him the wound. She keeps coming at me, so that I needed this to defend myself." She held up the poker she had taken from the dead fire.

"She was beating me with it," said the girl. "Not defending herself at all."

"I see." I turned to Dorka. "Is that true? Were you beating her?"

"I hit her once, but it was to keep her from scratching out my eyes, just so. She's gone wild. See for yourself."

So it seemed I was expected to choose sides in this argument—the girl, or Dorka. The child had just about worn out my patience. Wearily I asked her if Dorka spoke the truth: Did she say she would go to the palatine and tell him we mistreated her?

"I did," said the girl, too young and stupid to know when to hold her tongue. "I'll go to the palatine and tell him what happens in this house. I'll tell him how you stabbed me with the needle in the carriage when all I did was poke fun at that fat Doricza. I'll tell him about the girls you beat when you find out they're with child. I'll tell him how the old women keep us locked up at night without food and water when we don't work fast enough. It isn't right. Even rich noblewomen aren't above the law. I'll tell him everything, I swear it."

The walls went dark, and the light in the room narrowed to a small white tunnel with the child at one end and myself at the other. "I think you won't," I said. In my ears there was a sound like water rushing. I took the poker out of Dorka's hand and went toward the girl, who curled into a little ball, and brought the poker down on her back once, twice. I threw all my weight into the blow, all my anger that she would blame me for her own failures, that she would take my kindness and turn it into something ugly. Who had taken her in and given her a place? Who had shown her favor by placing her in my own carriage? Who had shown her mercy in having her wounds treated? She had mutilated my kindness to her, made it ugly. The poker fell on her back again and again, making a heavy thump like the sound of the cook beating a piece of beef to make it tender. An awful noise rose out of the girl's mouth, and I hit her again, harder.

She would say nothing to the palatine, to anyone. She would shut her insolent mouth, or I would shut it for her.

At length she fell and was silent. "Do you have anything else to say," I asked, "or have you learned finally to hold your tongue?" She lay still, her chest rising and falling with her breath, and said nothing.

It was so quiet that from the monastery next door I heard someone throw a pot against the wall of the house, a loud *clank* that echoed in the otherwise quiet nighttime streets. A complaint for all the noise. In the morning one of the scullery maids would find the pot the monks had thrown in the street and bring it back, though the monks would not accept it, as if it had been tainted. I would have a mind to speak to the abbot, to tell him to mind his people better, but I would have enough to do without worrying about the monks and their silly superstitions. For the present I handed the poker back to Dorka and told her to keep the girl in the laundry until she regained consciousness. I said Dorka should tend to her in secret so that the sight of her would not upset the other maidservants, for the child was all over black and blue, and a thin trickle of blood came out of her nose. She had provoked me beyond the limit of what I could endure. Next time she would know better.

With Dorka in charge I went myself back up to bed and slept more soundly that night than I had in some time, since before Ferenc's death at least. When she came to me in the morning and told me the girl had died in the night, I felt a strange curiosity at what had happened, that it was I who had killed her, although I had not meant to do so. The light came into my room in long yellow strips like golden cloth and fell across the bedclothes, but otherwise I saw nothing, felt nothing. The girl was dead. She would trouble me, or anyone else, no longer. I would not have to find a place for her in someone else's house. I would not have to pay for her dowry out of my own pocket, nor listen to another minute of her outrageous ingratitude. I washed my hands of her, and all the others like her.

The next evening, under cover of darkness, I had my servants take the body to our Lutheran priest and bury her in the churchyard in a plain box, along with a coin or two for the priest's coffers. Though Dorka and Ilona Jó complained that someone else should be made to do it—the boy Ficzkó, perhaps, who was younger and stronger than they—they did as I bade them and removed the body from the laundry. I told them I did not trust anyone else to do it, which pleased them so much they stopped complaining, and afterward I gave them each a fine dress of silk for their troubles. I thought no more about the girl. She had been a thief, a disturbance in my house, and a weakling besides, who could not even take a beating without rousing all of Bécs in the middle of the night. I could not afford to keep such troublemakers among my maidservants, to let their greed and jealousy infect everyone around them. Let them go to the churchyard, then, where they could be no more trouble to anyone.

# 8

Once the trunks were unpacked and we were settled into the city, the first thing I did was to send word to György Thurzó that we had arrived in town. Thurzó spent many months each year in Austria with his Habsburg friends, and he especially loved winter in the capital, with its music, and dances, and pretty young things in satin and velvet and lace, though he never seemed to indulge in the little affairs and speculations the way some of the other nobles did. He certainly seemed forlorn since Zsofía Forgách had died, and I wondered whether he would marry again. He might find ample companionship in me, I began to think, if he looked carefully enough.

The next day Thurzó responded to my letter—with astonishment, because widows were expected to stay at home for at least a year—but then with pleasure, too, urging me to come to him at my first opportunity. *My dear madam, I am surprised and gladdened to hear that you have arrived at court and rejoice, along with all the citizens of the city, that you walk among us. Please accept, at your earliest convenience, an invitation to dine at my house . . .*

His note pleased me, not because dinner at Thurzó's house would be a grand affair—as a widower he did not oversee the quality of his hospitality nearly as much as he had when his wife was alive—but because the swiftness of his reply hinted that I had not been wrong to think he would welcome my company. I responded that I would join him the following week and set about making certain that the impression I made on Count Thurzó on this occasion would be a meaningful one.

The seamstresses I had brought with me from Sárvár worked for several days to make me a new dress to wear especially to Thurzó's invitation. It must not seem too ostentatious—I was still a new widow, which no one was likely to forget—but it should be becoming in color and style. I settled on an oxblood satin with a wide collar to frame my face, and a pair of new calfskin slippers so fine and soft that even walking downstairs to climb in the carriage might wear them out too soon. I dressed all my long hair in rose oil, spreading it out to dry by the fire. Afterward Darvulia and Ilona Jó helped me to braid it, using a special new coif that hid my ears and framed my eyes with little wisps of curls. A net of pearls stood out like dewdrops in my dark brown tresses, and the fat little seamstress Doricza brought down the new lace ruff she had made, larger and finer than any I had owned before. I thanked her and patted her arm, telling her she had done well, and went to press a silver *tallér* into her hand, which she refused with a great deal of modesty, saying that I had given her enough, that she was not worthy of so much attention. Dorka shuttled her out of the room before I could tell her how pleased I was to see that my punishment of the other girl, the little blonde, had made such an impression on her.

I took my time at my toilette that evening, not wanting to appear too anxious. The longer Thurzó had to wait, the more he would anticipate my arrival.

When I was ready, Darvulia had the carriage brought. Before I stepped inside, my old friend tucked a piece of parchment into my hand. "A prayer," she said. "To bring you what you want."

I unrolled the parchment. As always, Darvulia knew what occupied my thoughts. "Will it work?"

"It has always worked for me."

I smiled. "Has it?" I wondered what it was that Darvulia had wanted and got for herself that she had not told me. The inner workings of that creature had always been something of a mystery to me, no matter how I much I loved her. The other two, Ilona Jó and Dorka, frowned and put their heads together, but they had the good sense at least to remain silent on the subject of Darvulia, after the many times I had made it clear how much I loved her. "How many times must I repeat this prayer to make it work?" I asked.

"As many as you can between now and the moment when you set eyes on the one you desire. Then afterward, when you have left his sight, repeat it three more times."

Thurzó was no Ferenc Nádasdy. It would take more than mistletoe and magic to make him love me, but I decided to trust Darvulia once more. *Little cloud, grant me your favor. Holy Trinity, protect Erzsébet in her time of need, and grant your daughter your love.* I whispered it again and again, under my breath.

At last I stepped up into the carriage, being careful not to crush my new dress, and we were off through the torchlit streets of peacetime Bécs. Music fell down from the windows we passed and landed in my lap like droplets of silver. The darkness in the streets flowed around the carriage, and I felt myself awash in hope and possibility in the imperial city, which had withstood even the onslaught of the Turks following the disaster of Mohács, the siege of the sultan as he moved north and west through the kingdom in the years before

I was born. Like the sultan I would now besiege the city and its inhabitants—Archduke Mátyás, György Thurzó. Unlike the sultan I hoped to achieve my aim and return home victorious.

Thurzó's house, a newer affair with marble columns and dark brickwork, was close enough for me to walk to, though it was unimaginable that a noblewoman would traverse the city on foot. We passed the red roofs of the Hofburg rising along the walls of the city, quiet now with its master the king away in Prága, but here and there a window showed a light. In a very few minutes we passed under an archway into a courtyard that opened into a small tier of windows where candles were lit, and maidservants scurried in and out carrying bouquets of flowers, polished silver, gilded candelabra scrubbed of their wax. Thurzó himself came out to greet me and open the carriage door, his deep-set eyes even more tired-looking than usual, the bags beneath them stuffed full as two down cushions. I wondered if it was the trouble with Rudolf that pained him, or if it was the loneliness that comes with the death of a spouse, loneliness that I had come to know too well in the preceding weeks. He took both my small hands in his large ones and placed a gentlemanlike kiss on my cheek, the length of beard ticklish against my mouth. "Welcome, cousin," he said. The endearment warmed me, for although there was no blood shared between us, we were distant relations by marriage, as most of the nobility of Hungary were. I didn't blush but looked at him with clear steady eyes and said how happy I was that he could receive me, what an honor it was for a poor widow to be a guest at the Thurzó house.

He laughed. "Poor, indeed. You look remarkably well," he said. "One might even think that widowhood agrees with you. Is that a new dress?"

"It is," I said, pleased he had been paying attention. "One cannot go around Bécs looking like an old crone, widow or not."

"One can," Thurzó said, "but *you* cannot. I think you have never spent an ugly day in your life."

I laughed. "Thank you for that," I said. "An old woman always needs to hear a little untruth every day. It keeps the mind sharp."

"You will paint me as a liar, madam," said Thurzó, looking aghast, but he smiled at this old game. Feint and counterfeint. A politician through and through. He would be still my trusted friend, or else a most worthy adversary. "What brings you to town?"

"Sárvár grows a bit small for me. There has been so little pleasure there lately, now that Ferenc is gone and my elder girl is married. I was so desperate for company that I simply had to bring Kata to town. You were the first person I thought of when I arrived, since I knew you would find some way to amuse me."

"I'm certain I can. Shall we go in?" He offered me his arm, and I took it and went inside.

All that night we dined and enjoyed each other's company. He sat near me at the head of the table in his private dining room and leaned on his hands when I spoke, his eyes lighting up at some joke or bit of news about some mutual acquaintance. He did seem to be lonely, for even after the food was finished and I might have taken my leave for the evening he kept ordering the servants to bring more and more wine, as if to keep me there a little bit longer. He leaned in close to listen when I asked him questions about our friend Bocskai's troubles with the king, so close his head nearly touched my own. How unfortunate, he said, that István Bocskai would choose now to side with the Hungarian nationalists and the Transylvanians against the king.

But surely on the question of religion, I said, it was best that the Hungarians be able to choose their own faith, rather than have it imposed by the Catholic Habsburgs. As a Lutheran himself, Thurzó must see that.

"It is possible to overlook matters of faith for the good of the state," Thurzó said. "The Habsburgs remain Hungary's best hope against Constantinople. Bocskai makes a mistake by forgetting that. Rudolf's ties to Rome are not as strong as his ties to Hungary."

I said the fact that Thurzó managed to retain both the trust of

Rudolf and of Mátyás in such turbulent times was testament to his shrewdness of mind, his great ability in sorting out the affairs of men. He laughed, because he was no fool—he knew what a woman's flattery was worth. But my interest in his affairs, and praise for his decisions, seemed to please him nevertheless.

"Rudolf is a friend of yours, isn't he?" I asked.

"He is. A worthy king, very learned."

"Not unlike you yourself."

"His interests are different from mine, but I like to think myself the intellectual equal of any man."

*Or woman.* "He spends much time with his artists and astronomers, from what I hear. Even Kepler is there now as his court mathematician. It must cost him a fortune."

"A fair bit. Many of his Spanish friends come to seek his advice and encouragement, and the great minds of Europe, too, find no better friend than Rudolf. Hungary needs such a patron, if she is ever to be the equal of the great empires of the west."

"And the king needs such an ally in you, I think, if he is to manage such a transformation."

Thurzó smiled, but his heavily bagged eyes narrowed to take me in, to consider me afresh. "And so what are you after, Countess? I have never known you to offer a compliment that didn't need to be repaid somehow."

"Can I not offer a compliment to an old friend?"

"Yes, you may, but I wonder how high the price will be in the end."

I smiled. He was a man after my own heart, after all. "You may remember that my younger daughter is very nearly of an age to be betrothed. There are several decent suitors I would consider, if I were in a position to do so. The estate is somewhat short on funds of late that I might use for her dowry."

The corners of his mouth turned up, his voice rich with sarcasm. "Yes, I can see how you struggle, Countess. May we all have such monetary difficulties. You do not want me to lend you some forints? A few gold pieces to see you through your hardship?"

"Not at all, my friend, and you can remove that tone from your voice. Perhaps you know that my poor Ferenc lent the royal treasury a great deal of money ten years ago, when his majesty was embroiled in the Turkish wars. Now that the Turks are sent back, I was hoping that he might remember us, and repay his debt."

"You want me to petition the king on your behalf?"

"I merely thought you might help me arrange a meeting with the archduke. I understand he holds a bit more sway here in Bécs than does the absent king, and such a request might be better served coming from a friend rather than a woman he hardly knows."

Thurzó laughed. "You are a shrewd woman, too shrewd perhaps. Very well. I will arrange your meeting with Mátyás. I will even go with you to plead your case."

"Thank you. I knew you would serve me well in this matter."

He paused, looking at me with such frankness that I blinked and lowered my eyes, taking up the cup of wine and sipping at it. Thurzó had always been an unhandsome man, unlike my dear Ferenc, but men of power and authority always had qualities that made up for the lack of physical beauty.

He asked, "How would you be willing to show your gratitude, do you think?"

Without reservation I placed my hand on his arm. The sleeve of his coat was cool to the touch, more roughly made than the ones Ferenc had worn. When I had the chance, I would have a finer one made for him, one of such softness that to run one's hand down its length would be a delight. But for now I simply said, "How would I not?"

Whores, both of us. But honest ones, at least.

# 9

Thurzó took me in the autumn to see the archduke, transporting me
in his own carriage from the house on Lobkowitz Square into the
Hofburg, to the Schweizerhof—the Swiss Gate—with its ornate
gate and gilded letters declaring the worth of Ferdinand, Rudolf's
grandfather, the old king who had built it. We sat together, the count
absently stroking the fingers of my hand, looking out the windows
and away, for we had grown so comfortable together over the previous weeks that often we didn't need to speak at all. As we passed out
of the stone courtyard into the streets of the city I felt a surge of happiness overtake me, the joy that came from loving, for the first time
in nearly thirty years, a man of my own choosing.

That summer, while Bocskai had been fomenting his rebellion,
my poor brother István had died. His health had never been good
even when he was a child, and it seemed that the sickness in the eastern part of the country had sapped the last of my brother's strength.
He died of a rattling cough in the middle of a hot summer. The family stronghold in the marsh at Ecsed passed on to my nephew Gábor
and his younger sister, Anna, the orphaned children—Báthory
cousins both—my brother and his wife had adopted as their own.
Gábor Báthory was sixteen, nearly a man already, and one who could
defend the massive keep in the event of trouble. But still I worried
about him, and about his sister, and Kata and Pál.

As soon as I heard the news of István's death I made plans to
go to Ecsed for my brother's funeral. Thurzó, however, deemed it
unwise for me to cross the Duna and return to Ecsed while Bocskai
and his *hajdúks* were on the move. I might be vulnerable, he said,
since the Báthorys had such strong ties to Transylvania, and to Bocskai. Thurzó said it would be better for me if I remained in the city for

the time being and showed my loyalty to the king and the empire. Partly Thurzó wanted to keep me where he could keep an eye on me, I knew, but he also thought staying in the city was the wisest course if I wanted the return of the king's money. Thurzó was willing to offer me the strength of his protection and friendship, as well as his love, so I agreed. I would remain in Bécs at least until the following spring, when the roads improved, and then go on to Csejthe for the summer, stopping to see to an estate that my brother had left me in his will along the way. I wrote to Gábor that I was sorry I could not join them for the funeral rites, and stayed at the house in Lobkowitz Square. Perhaps it was a mistake to do so, but even more than my desire for his help, I had learned to enjoy the presence of György Thurzó in my bed, and I was reluctant to give him up so soon. Anything that kept me closer to him was agreeable to me then.

For months Thurzó and I had spent our evenings in each other's company. Three or four times a week we would dine together before the fire, dismissing the servants before the meal was over so that our intimacies would not be observed. He would lean over and take my hand in his, kiss it, then run his fingers up into my hair to pull a strand or two loose, preferring it down over my shoulders. Like a deep pool of still water, he said. After a few such evenings, I began having Darvulia pile it up more simply, so that a single tug of Thurzó's might bring it down. He would pick it up with his hands and kiss the ends, and then I would go to him and press my lips to the cool bags under his eyes, the tired-looking mouth. He was gorgeous in his ugliness, I saw then, a thing of exquisite tenderness and simplicity, like a frog prince. I began to think that my mother had been right to have more than one husband. As we turned into the courtyard of the Hofburg, with Thurzó pressing my hand inside the belly of the carriage to reassure me, it occurred to me that a second husband might be the happiness I had sought all my life.

The drawing room where Archduke Mátyás would receive us was plain but stylish, with small glass windows in wooden frames and white-plaster walls, though the ceilings were much higher than ordinary, and the windows let in a good deal of light. In the center of the room sat an ornate wooden table set with the richest silver I had ever seen, heavy and bright and newly polished, over which the smell of good wine, freshly poured, hung in the air, and on the walls were dozens of paintings, including one of the king himself, red-haired and heavyset, with a closely cropped beard and an imperious expression. Next to it, a similar one of his brother Mátyás, in a black jacket and white ruff and voluminous red-and-gold pleated pants, showed the two to be brothers not only in looks but in expression, haughty and stony-faced. From what Thurzó had told me, the similarities ended there, for while Rudolf was a dreamer, more poet than prince, Mátyás was a man of action. I had met him once or twice before, when Ferenc was alive, but we had never spoken in depth, and I didn't know how he would respond to a request from a woman. I would have to watch myself with him, that was certain.

Near the portrait hung a curious, brightly lit canvas, about the span of my outstretched arms, showing a coastline with a ship under sail, the yellow sun like a jewel above the deep blue water and the white hills in the distance, where clouds gathered. In the foreground a farmer with his plow and horse made furrows in the earth, and a shepherd with his flock looked up at the gathering storm. In the bottom-right corner, tiny, the white legs of what looked to be a boy falling into the water went unnoticed by anyone. I leaned over to study it more closely. Yes—the boy's flailing legs were just about to slip underneath the waves, but no one in the painting seemed to pay the least amount of attention. The plowman, the shepherd, the fisherman on the cliff above, the sailors on the ship all went about their mundane business as if nothing at all were happening.

"Icarus," said a voice behind me. "Do you like it?"

I turned, and there before me was Archduke Mátyás, who looked considerably older than in his portrait. He wore a black suit with polished brass buttons and a narrow white lace collar, and around his shoulders hung a long gold chain. His hair was short, in the German style, and reddish like his brother's, streaked through with gray, and a few deep lines had settled in around his eyes and across his brow. His face was serious even when he smiled to show his pleasure at my inspection of the painting.

"I do," I said. "It's cleverly done, to make the event such a minor moment. Icarus, who had flown so high, now falls so low, while the world takes no notice of him."

"Hmm," said the archduke. "My brother has curious taste in art. I never liked it myself. I always thought Icarus should be the center of the painting, not such an afterthought. But I suppose it is the way of great men to be unnoticed in their own time." He leaned down and squinted at it a moment, then stood back. "And what may I do for you, Lady Nádasdy?"

I noted the use of *lady* instead of *countess* but decided not to remark on it. "I have come to pay my respects, though I would wish it were under better circumstances."

"Yes. I am sorry for the loss of your husband. He was a brave soldier, the very best of us, and a good friend. He will be sorely missed." I thanked him. The archduke waved his hand in the air as if thanks were unnecessary, then said, "My friend Thurzó here would not tell me why you wanted to speak to me, though he said I would find your company most delightful. I see in that, at least, he has not been mistaken."

I bowed again in thanks. "I come to ask for your help. I am seeking repayment of the loans my late husband made the royal treasury while the country was at war. Your brother in Prága would not answer the repeated entreaties my husband made him while he was alive. I was hoping you might be able to convince him to help me now."

"The country is still at war. Your husband's friend Bocskai now sees that the Hungarians rise up against us. We must use every resource at our disposal to put down the revolt."

"I am very sorry for it, but as I am a widow now, it is up to me to see to the estate my husband left behind. My daughter is of a marriageable age, and my son is not yet grown. They depend on me to make certain their inheritance is secured."

"Of course they do. But the royal treasury is stretched very thin at the moment. It might be best to wait a while longer, until this business with Bocskai is behind us. I would not dare put such a request to my brother before then."

I was not about to be refused so easily. "Your grace—" I began, but Thurzó put his hand on my arm to stop my protests.

"You have our continued gratitude for your husband's faithful service in the wars against the Turks," said the archduke, "but I'm afraid the repayment will have to wait a while."

"Perhaps I myself should write to the king," I said, almost a question, as if I were more curious than threatening. "He might be able to find the funds, especially when he has money for court musicians, and mathematicians, and artists."

Mátyás's face tightened, a look of annoyance crossed with no little bit of caution. He didn't like his authority being superseded by his brother's, and I knew I was risking much by threatening to go directly to the king. Thurzó had told me Mátyás thought his brother a fool, a weak and ineffectual leader who had deserted Hungary and whose neglect had brought about the rift with Bocskai in the first place. It might not be long before the absent king remained absent for good, and Mátyás—or, if the situation turned, even István Bocskai—wore the crown of Hungary. Times changed; power abandoned one man and settled on another. But Rudolf was still king for now, and I needed that money. Kata needed it. I would do what I must to get it back.

"You may do as you wish," said the archduke. "But do not expect Rudolf to pay much attention. He is far too busy with his astronomers and painters to mind the affairs of state. You will learn as much if you press him in this matter. But write him if you choose." He waved his hand again, and I had the distinct feeling that he was literally brushing me away. "Thank you for coming, madam. It is always amusing to see you in Bécs."

Thurzó's hand on my arm was an insistent pressure, a warning. It reminded me of the way my mother would squeeze my arm in church whenever I succumbed to a fit of laughter. He was not about to let me push the matter further, to what he saw as my detriment, and perhaps his own. The pressure on my arm told me I was to remember my place. And so I would—for now.

"Thank you," I said, but in my heart the matter was not at all closed. Rage lapped at me. How dare he dismiss me so easily? Rudolf would hear from me about the repayment of his debt, that was certain. A man who could afford to fill his walls with such heavy silver, so many paintings, could surely afford to repay me the few thousand forints my husband had lent him.

The archduke, having dismissed us, now turned away to look at the painting once more, at poor Icarus disappearing unnoticed into the sea. "Such a shame," he said. "It could have been a good painting." His finger brushed it lightly, tilting it out of alignment as he swept past us, out of the room.

In a moment we were alone together. The danger past, Thurzó's hand dropped from my arm, and he sighed. "You should not risk making an enemy of Mátyás."

"I don't have the luxury of waiting until the archduke is in a better humor. My children are still young, and they have lost their father. If I don't fight for their rights, who will?"

"Do not alienate your friends. If you were more patient, and showed more humility, you might win more favor."

"As you do? How long might the king and the archduke put me off, if I do not make certain they remember their obligations?"

"There are ways to remind them without sacrificing their friendship." His hands went around my waist now and clasped me to him.

"What?" I asked, tilting my head up to look him in the eyes. "Are you offering to share me with Mátyás? Perhaps you can use Solomon's approach and divide me between you."

His mouth was against my hair. "Never," he said. "I would share you with no man, Erzsébet."

"Then I'm reduced to threats, I'm afraid." I sighed. "But perhaps when you are through with me, Mátyás might want me in the bargain."

He laughed. "Perhaps when you have got what you wanted, you will be through with me."

"Then perhaps we should marry, and seal the bargain now before either of us is through with the other."

"A second husband? Wouldn't that be terribly inconvenient for you, now that you have the estates all to yourself? He might get in the way of your plans for Nádasdy glory."

"The only glory for the Nádasdys at the moment," I said, placing my hand on his neck, "is with you, dearest."

He laughed. "Well said, my lady."

I allowed him to kiss me there, in the king's own reception room, before the white figure of Icarus drowning in the sea. Afterward we returned to the carriage, riding out again under the Swiss Gate where the guard stood watch over nothing at all, for the king was away in Prága, and didn't think of Bécs, or of Hungary, but only of the new Paris he was building in the north with my daughter's money. With my children's inheritance, the king was making himself a great patron of artists and scientists. He had not heard the last of me.

# 10

All that winter I stayed with Thurzó in Bécs, sending letters home to Megyery asking about your studies, Pál, and requesting that your tutor sell off some lands for me in the far western part of the kingdom to pay for Kata's dowry. She would be twelve soon, and I no longer had the option of waiting. That year I formally betrothed your sister to György Homonnai Drugeth, son of the count of the same name and my brother's nephew by marriage. The Drugeths were an old Magyar family, distinguished statesmen and warriors, and György, whose lavish estate at Homonna was the envy of the kingdom, had lobbied hard for Kata's hand. I refused him more than once, which increased his love for her all the more, exactly as I had intended. He sent letters, gifts. He wrote appalling love poems to Kata—to her eyes, her lips. I put him off as long as possible, but then Kata started in as well, telling me what a worthy young man Drugeth was, how much wealth and honor would be heaped on the family through such a marriage, so that I thought the boy might have been coaching her. "Please, Mother," she begged, flinging herself on me in my rooms at night. "If I cannot have him, I would rather have no one at all. I would rather die alone and childless than marry someone else."

Later I would laugh over her theatrics. Were we, I said to Thurzó, ever so young and wretched, threatening to kill ourselves for love? He laughed, and said he hoped not. But I watched Kata and Drugeth dancing together one evening at a party at Thurzó's house and saw the utter adoration my daughter lavished on the boy. He reminded me of András Kanizsay when I first knew him—wry, self-possessed, fully aware that every woman in the room looked up when he entered, and most of the men, too. I worried about marrying my dearest Kata to a boy who was already in love with himself, but at least her choice had some tangible merits: young Drugeth had money and position as well as youth and good looks. Thurzó opposed the match, wanting to join Kata to one of the Forgách boys to whom he was related by marriage, but in this matter I would not put my daughter's feelings aside: I signed the papers that summer and wrote to Megyery to dispose of Lendva, one of the smaller estates, to pay the dowry. I was still angry that the king would not honor his debt, since it was from your pocket, Pál, he was stealing, but at least Kata would not have to go without.

At every moment I felt the precarious nature of my situation, how easily the peace and prosperity I had built, the future I had planned for myself and my children, could come flying apart. I had finally come into my own authority as a noblewoman, now with no husband to whose wishes I had to bow, but without a husband I would be vulnerable still, and thus you would as well, Pál. At balls and parties where I met my friends among the nobility, the statesmen of Hungary and their wives, I watched for plots, for schemes, listening around corners, catching the eyes of the jealous, the ambitious, wondering who of my friends I could trust still. Would my friend Countess Zrínyi be the one to turn me out of Sárvár, if her husband set his sights on taking it? Would Margit Choron, my husband's aunt, use her family claims against me? Would Thurzó decide to annex Keresztúr, so close to his own estate at Tokaj? I did not know whom to trust. I knew only I must do everything in my power to see that your inheritance would still be there when you came of age, that I would have failed you as your mother, Pál, if I lost any part of what your father had gained for you.

Thurzó and I continued to spend most of our evenings together—discreetly, of course, to keep the servants' gossip to a minimum. After our quiet evening meals at his house or mine, we would say good night and pretend to go our separate ways, but then he would come to my rooms, or I to his, and we would enjoy each other under cover of darkness, rising to leave before the dawn broke and the house began to stir. In our shared bed he would whisper his plans for the future, how we would meet again at Csejthe or Bicske during the summer months for secret trysts. He talked of wedding you to his younger daughter, Borbála, though I thought she was too old to be a good match for you. Thurzó pushed at the subject continually. The joining of the house of Nádasdy to the house of Thurzó would be a great honor on both of us, he said, and though I tried to put him off the topic for your sake, since you were only seven years old and very far from being ready for a betrothal, I began to wonder in all seriousness if it was ourselves he was thinking of rather than our children. If he had his eye on a second wife, a second marriage to live out his remaining days, he could have found no one more willing than me. The thought of being Thurzó's wife pleased me, for even though he was one of the ugliest men I had ever met, his companionship was beyond compare. I could even say I loved him. He was a shrewd politician, more so than Ferenc had been, and more cautious with his loyalties—unlikely to bed the maidservants, or to flaunt them in front of me if he did. We were well suited to each other, György Thurzó and myself, in age and temper. Too old to be foolish, too young to be alone. The remainder of my life opened up before me like a great door into a new house, brightly lit and full of possibility.

When the hot weather was upon us and the roads dry, I began making preparations for the journey north to Csejthe with Kata and my ladies, where I planned to escape the summer miasmas of the city. The night before we left Thurzó and I dined together one last time at his house in town, in his private dining room, where he pressed me repeatedly to make certain that I would not make an enemy of Mátyás by demanding too much, or too often, during the time I was away, so that I wondered what Mátyás must have said to him after our meeting to make him worry so. It amused me that the archduke's nose was out of joint. So was mine, after all—he owed me a fortune. But I knew better than to say so to Thurzó.

He too was about to embark on his summer trip to Biscke, and then south to deal with the trouble with István Bocskai, but he promised he would be back in Bécs in November when I arrived for the winter. The few months we would spend apart, he said, would merely serve to strengthen the new bond between us. He leaned over to press his lips into my hair and said he had no desire to be so long away from me, but that the continuing trouble with Bocskai put him in a terrible position. His job was to convince his old friend to stand down his war against the Habsburgs—or in the absence of that, to meet him on the battlefield. Thurzó was facing many months on horseback between Bécs and Transylvania, many months of dust and heat. I was surprised that the king held Thurzó in such high esteem that he would trust him with something this important, putting an end to the rebellion, and even more surprised that Thurzó would agree to it. I had known that they were friends and held each other in high regard, but not that Thurzó was so deeply ingrained with the

Austrians that he would serve as their instrument against the rebellion led by his old friend István Bocskai.

But that night, with the candles throwing a yellow glow over the room, and the smell of the lavender oil my ladies had used to dress my hair, Thurzó told me it was me, and not István Bocskai, who occupied his thoughts, and the long separation ahead of us. "You will forget me before we meet again," he said, sighing with such sad conviction that for a moment I believed him. "A woman like you will have many suitors."

"Perhaps," I said, for I didn't want to let him think I was easily won over, nor that I believed him entirely sincere, "but perhaps I prefer you to any other."

"I hope you will still, when we meet again," he said. "I have half a mind to take a new wife, you see."

"Only half a mind?"

"The other half says she might not be worth the trouble, if she does not learn to hold her tongue."

"I thought it was my tongue you liked best. Now will you kiss me before you go, or will you keep talking like this all night?"

He laughed and wrapped me in his arms, planting a fervent kiss on my mouth. His breath tasted of wine, his skin of cloves. When his mouth moved to my neck, I tipped back my head and sighed with pleasure. It would be too long before we would meet again.

## 11

My ladies and I left Bécs the next morning by the Duna road, making the trek south toward the Hungarian capital at Pozsony, which the Germans who lived in that city called Pressburg. In the still-dark hours we tramped out of the house and into the waiting carriages.

Darvulia, moving slowly and using always the cane that she had adopted since we had arrived in Bécs, climbed in beside me, and I settled the blanket across her knees myself. Next came Kata, glowing now that she was betrothed, and after her the fat Doricza took her place and her sewing without so much as a grunt when she settled her haunches on the bench.

Next came Gizela Modl, a German girl who had come to Sárvár with her mother looking for work a few years back. We were short of girls then, and I had taken her in because her mother talked so tearfully about the family's poverty that I feared she would have half her children on my doorstep unless I took in Gizela, the eldest of a family that included nine girls and three boys.

From the first the Modl girl's looks gave me pause. Her apricot-skin complexion, her large brown eyes fringed by deep black lashes, made her seem both vulnerable and steely, like the blade of a knife bent almost to breaking. She was slender and fragile about the wrists and neck but with a womanly bosom that seemed always on display under soft white blouses and too-tight bodices. She had not been in my house more than a week before the stable boys were neglecting their chores to watch her beat the rugs in the courtyard, and even my husband's former valet smiled and flirted with her, doing sword tricks and inflating his service to my husband in the Turkish wars to make himself seem braver than the ten-year-old squire he had been at the time. It hardly mattered—Gizela Modl batted her eyelashes at all of them.

Yet there was an iron core in her that revealed itself once she had established herself in my house and that the young men who fawned over her rarely got to see. She knew very little Hungarian except curse words and vulgarities, which she sprinkled liberally in her speech even in front of my children, damning this and that, even the stones in the floor, the sheets on the bed. In my presence she wore a perpetual smirk, so that most often I wanted to slap her and send her crying from my sight. I restrained myself from doing so only as long as she did her work well, which was not often. After a month or two of this behavior, Darvulia had been obliged to find her new employment in the laundry to keep her out of trouble. In the time since then she had been quiet and hardworking, and I had heard so little of her from Darvulia or Dorka or the other maids that it seemed she had amended her ways, and I promptly forgot all about her.

As we were leaving the house in Bécs, however, I decided, seeing her modest expression, her downcast eyes, to reward the Modl girl with a little bit of company while we drove across the countryside, and so she climbed in the carriage and took her place opposite Darvulia with all the meekness of a trussed lamb.

Before us went a set of smartly dressed soldiers, and behind three or four more carriages bearing ladies, and trunks full of supplies bought to take with us to the summer house at Csejthe. Behind them went the rest of the company of soldiers who regularly traveled with me, in light armor and with swords gleaming. It was an impressive sight, the procession we made as we passed back through the gates of Bécs and out into the countryside, kicking up dust as we went.

Often in the carriage I would read to my ladies from the books I carried, or teach them their letters on a piece of slate to pass the time. Only a few men of my acquaintance were truly educated—Ferenc and Thurzó were the most notable examples—and even fewer of the women. Maidservants especially often had little chance of an education, and although there had been some young ladies who rolled their eyes at my attempts to make them write *A*, and *Á*, and *B*, most were glad for the chance and paid attention long enough to at least learn to write their own names. Any woman, I told them, needed to know that much, no matter her station in life, her marriage status. Doricza and the Modl girl kept their eyes on their lessons or made chitchat about the scenery as we passed but said little else, and in that way we had a pleasant journey along the Duna road, with the river on our left and the whole of Hungary before us, on our way to the fortress at Dévény, where I had business.

My brother had left me a few of his properties in his will, including the *vár* at Dévény, just north of the capital at Pozsony. The castle perched on a high outcropping of white limestone, a single tower rising dramatically from the naked rock, turreted and alone, so that it looked like one of the old gods perched on the lip of Olympus and scowling at its demesne below. It was a highly valuable and strategically placed property, situated as it was between Pozsony and Bécs at the confluence of the Duna and the Morva rivers, and I intended to look it over with my ladies and my retainers, introducing myself to the steward and spending a few nights as the new owner, to see what was needed for the upkeep of the place. Letters had gone ahead of us so that the servants could prepare for our coming.

Thurzó had tried to caution me against stopping there, saying it would only anger the king and Mátyás at a difficult time between Austria and Hungary. My brother, before his death, had been an ardent supporter of our friend István Bocskai and his revolt against the Habsburgs, a believer in a Hungary reunited against both the Turks and the Habsburgs, and Mátyás knew I was friendly still to both Bocskai and our friends and family in Transylvania, despite my close relationship to Thurzó. My nephew Gábor, whose support inside Transylvania was growing, also supported Bocskai's efforts against the repression of the Habsburgs. Thurzó said it was a mistake to make a show of ownership over Dévény when so many of my family ties were anti-Habsburg, and my own personal loyalties unknown. But I was determined to stop at Dévény before heading north to Csejthe and make myself known there among the servants as the new mistress of the place.

As we followed the river road, the blurred shapes and purple hills in the distance settled into clearer objects, the stone cliffs and trees of the town of Dévény, and soon we could see the fortress itself, the white outcropping of stone shaped like a clenched fist where from Roman times lookouts had been posted for enemy on the march. After the Turks had occupied the center of the old kingdom all the way to Buda and Eger, Dévény had become more significant than ever to keeping the peace, and now that Bocskai was on the move and my nephew Gábor was cementing his power in Transylvania, it would be so again. I was thoroughly gratified that István had thought to give it to me, because I planned to give it to you, Pál, a jewel in the crown of your inheritance.

As we approached the ferry crossing on the near shore, the ferryman's house and stable came into view, the horses that pulled the massive ropes and heavy boats across the water, the white stucco garrison house where the soldiers slept. On the far bank of the Duna huddled a few old men, burghers in somber black, bolstered by a not-insignificant number of soldiers in light armor. At first I wondered if the burghers of the city had come out to welcome my arrival the way the children had followed behind the carriage when, as a young bride, I had ridden across Hungary to my mother-in-law's house. But as we came closer I could see the grim looks on their faces, the way they rustled and shuffled their feet like priests at a funeral. It was clear that something here was out of order. Perhaps Mátyás had decided I had been asking too much in demanding the return of the money owed me by the royal treasury and now wanted to make an example of me. Or perhaps the city burghers, to show their loyalty to Mátyás, chose now to stand against me and my claim on Dévény. I swore under my breath. Thurzó would hear of this. The minute we arrived in Csejthe, I planned to write him to complain of it. What good was my friendship with Thurzó if his friend the king used his men against me, to keep me from my own property?

At the edge of the river, where the road turned and grew broad and flat and the smell of river water and reeds grew thick, we paused while the captain of my soldiers spoke to the ferryman whose job it was to take me across. From my place in the carriage I could see my man calmly sitting his horse, offering a fat purse he had been given for just this purpose, saw the ferryman shake his head and gesture at the river as if the river were the thing to blame. After a moment my man came back and said the ferryman was under strict instructions not to let us cross. "The city fathers are here to make certain he does so," said the soldier, a gray-haired veteran who had been the captain of my personal guard for years in honor of his service to my husband. His face betrayed a mixture of anxiety and weariness, as if I might ask him to fight the garrison stationed at the ferry, to battle and bully my way across. Instead I told him to stand his men down while I sent Gizela Modl to speak to the ferryman. Gizela, I thought, would be just the thing to convince the ferryman to let us pass. "Offer him double his usual fee," I told Gizela, handing her a second small purse filled with gold, a fortune to a man in his position. She would use all that ruthless charm on him, and if the money didn't sway him, Gizela would.

She spoke with him for many long minutes and then returned to the carriage with the purse still in her hand, the ferryman trailing behind her. "He says there is no price you can offer that he would accept."

I cursed the ferryman, his insolence, the burghers and the king. It was not I who had begun the rebellion, I said, nor supported it when it did begin. I had spent the winter in Bécs with Mátyás and Thurzó. I was a loyal subject to the king and to Hungary, and I had a right to my property. Did the rule of law no longer apply? I asked. Was it all to be set aside at the whim of a dictator? Perhaps Bocskai was right to take up arms against a king who thought nothing of the people he ruled, I said. Perhaps Bocskai should be king, and then we would all be better off.

A disagreeable-looking fellow with chipped yellow teeth and a jacket stained with river water and stinking of creosote, the ferryman had rough hands from holding the reins of the horses that pulled the rope across the Duna, but he looked so miserable as he glanced sidelong at Gizela that I thought he might let the carriage cross on his own back if the burghers weren't watching. "I'm sorry," he said, "but I would lose my head if I let you cross."

That the burghers would be so brazen as to deny me my rights as owner of the property was the highest possible offense. "The king will hear of this," I said, and with as much dignity as I could manage I opened the carriage door to reclaim Gizela. As we drove away

I could see the city fathers retreating on the far side of the Duna, a scattering of the Habsburgs' dung beetles running back into their safe little holes.

Traveling until long after dark, we rode farther downstream to find a Hungarian ferryman, one who was only too glad to take my gold and pull us across despite the late hour, but even when we were on the other side of the Duna I would not dare approach the fortress at Dévény. The burghers would be watching for me, for their master Rudolf—or was it Mátyás?—to reward them for denying me.

The Hungarian ferryman was amiable and garrulous, chatting the whole time about the news from abroad and showing a great deal of respect when he learned the name of the lady he ferried, lavishing praise on my dead husband, on my noble family name. "I served with your husband at the siege of Esztergom," said the ferryman. He had a scar through the meat of one cheek, and when I looked more closely, I could see he was missing several fingers on one hand. "A great man, a handsome and kind man, the best soldier I ever saw. Like one of the saints come to earth." The ferryman was still talking about poor Ferenc. "I grieved like I lost my own father when I heard that he died."

I rewarded him with the purse I would have used to bribe the German ferryman farther upstream, and he wept and said he would pray for me for a seat in heaven. Still, for a long time I could not remove the bitterness in my mouth over the encounter at Dévény, even as we passed into the empty plains, the miles and miles of grassland that had once—before Mohács, before the Turkish occupation, before the world had gone upside down—been the breadbasket of Europe, fields of wheat and barley and rye, uncounted fields from the Duna to the Carpathians. Nothing that had once been remained, and what was to come, I could not yet see.

# 12

After the trouble at the ferry at Pozsony, I traveled on to my own house at Csejthe, where I had first come as a young bride myself thirty years before. We spent a quiet summer there, in the calm that builds before a great storm, with a hushed sense of expectation and hurry toward the eventual release. I sent several angry letters to the king and some private, less strident ones to Thurzó, asking him to intervene in the matter of Dévény castle on my behalf, and he wrote me back that he would do what he could for me, but that I must listen to him for once and not anger the king further. *Remember your friends and your place,* he wrote, *and all will turn out right in the end.*

*My place,* I wrote back, *is with you. When are you coming?*

*Soon,* he wrote. *Soon, I promise you.*

Summer turned to autumn, and autumn to winter, but Thurzó did not come. I put aside my plans to return to Bécs for the winter, since Thurzó said he would not be able to return to the city that year to see me. Once a month or so he wrote to me, always saying the trouble with Bocskai was keeping him away, that the king had urgent commissions for him that took him far from his estate at Biscke, which was only a two-day trip from my own house at Csejthe. For my part I did my best to be accept his reasons for staying away, even as I looked forward to his company at Varannó that coming September, at the wedding of my daughter to young Drugeth. *Come early,* I wrote to him, *as my dearest friend and companion. Every day is a year until I see you again.*

*I will come as soon as I may,* he wrote back. *You can depend on it.*

So more than a year after our last meeting, still missing Thurzó, I made the trek across Hungary from Csejthe to Varannó to prepare for my daughter's wedding. Guests would begin arriving even in August, although the festivities didn't actually begin until September. As always I enjoyed playing hostess, seeing to the lavishness of the arrangements as once my mother and father had done at Ecsed, entertaining my many friends and relatives. Afternoons my ladies and I would ride in the countryside or organize fishing expeditions to the banks of the Vág, out of the earshot of men where we could wade in the river's edge with our skirts pulled up and eat cold chicken and cakes sweetened with honey. How pleasant it was in the afternoons when the sounds of bullfrogs and the feel of the cool water around my ankles gave refuge from the ordinary problems of minding my many estates, answering letters to this or that relative or friend.

Always, always, the need to keep the peace in my house necessitated the punishment of the maidservants, who had grown even more worthless in the time since my husband's death. That year I spent many grueling hours in the cellars of Varannó with the butt of a whip or the handle of a cudgel in my hand, seeing to the lazy, the insolent. One especially troubling week not long before the first guests arrived, I went every evening to the cellars, my arms sore from wielding my stick and my clothes ruined with blood. The young boy, Ficzkó, had to carry me up to bed because I could no longer walk from exhaustion. And every night Ilona Jó and Dorka brought more girls to me for punishment, mostly the ones who had shirked their chores or been caught stealing, but also ones who rutted with the stable boys, who had talked back to one or the other of the old women. The prettiest and most admired were also the most trouble. They thought beauty was their privilege, and it was up to me to disabuse them. Beauty was a curse to be borne, not a blessing.

Most endured their punishment well, recovering after a few days and returning to their duties with renewed humility, but sometimes there would be a sickly girl who would fall ill afterward and need to go to the churchyard. I did not pity them, since they saved me the time and expense of nursing them back to health. As before, I arranged the funeral rites and the singers, too, to send them to the next world. No one could accuse me of neglecting my Christian duty, though István Magyari, the longtime Nádasdy family pastor, had the audacity to threaten to go to the authorities if I kept up my nighttime activities. Desist, he said, or risk offending God. I told him he had better not risk offending me first. I made certain a few extra coins went into his coffers, and afterward I had the servants take our dead girls elsewhere for burial, where they would not fall under Magyari's watchful eye.

All this I had to endure without the help of my dear Darvulia, who that summer was afflicted with the onset of paralysis, a sudden attack one morning that left half her body limp, unable to walk or even stand. She took to her bed, and the others—Ilona Jó, Dorka, and Ficzkó—took over most of her duties. Every day I visited her and brought her the flowers she asked for from the fields and forests around Varannó, which she crushed and drank in a tea, though nothing improved her affliction. The skin on her face drooped soddenly toward her chin, like a cloth soaked with water, and her tongue too moved so slowly that she had trouble speaking. Only her inky eyes moved still the way they always had, making me think that at any moment she would shed this illness like an old cloak, just another disguise she had worn to confound the devil. She didn't know her age, but I had known the *táltos* for more than thirty years and guessed she had to be nearing sixty at least, as ancient a crone as I had ever set eyes upon. For weeks I pressed her old, gnarled hands to my chest and begged her to get better, but she only smiled and said there was no cure for what ailed her. "I will go to God soon enough," she said again and again, "and I'm not afraid of what he will say to me." Every day when I opened my eyes I expected someone to rouse me with the news that she had died in the night, tarnishing all the joyous preparations going on around us with a coating of dread. My happiness could not be happiness at all if Anna Darvulia could not have a share in it.

There was trouble with the servants once it became clear that Darvulia was not likely to recover, including a time when one of the little Sittkey girls, as scattered and flighty as any little bird, was caught *in flagrante delicto* with one of the stable boys, her skirts flung up around her ears. Dorka had the other girls gather stinging nettles from the fields and forced the Sittkey girl to sit on them, naked, in the courtyard for an afternoon, while she squirmed and wept and the stable boys laughed at her, even the one whose advances had caused all the trouble in the first place. I rewarded Dorka by placing her in charge of the servants during Darvulia's illness, and the servants soon began to respect and fear Dorka as they had once done Darvulia.

At Varannó I saw to the wedding preparations, hiring more than twenty wedding stewards, including the services of one Istók Soós, a thick-necked bull of a man whose job it was to spend the nearly ten thousand forints I gave him on capons and game birds and fish, butter and wine and cheese, oranges and citrons from Florence, cherries and dates from the orchards around my many estates. He did his job well. Wagonfuls of delicacies came daily. Artists came from Italy to paint the wedding hall with heroic murals of the groom, György Homonnai Drugeth, and of Ferenc Nádasdy. The softest new carpets were laid on the floor for the guests. All of Hungary was invited. The king would send his regrets from Prága, of course, but Báthorys and Nádasdys, Drugeths and Forgáchs, Zrínyis and Batthyánys from all over the old kingdom would be there. And, of course, György Thurzó, the man who loved me.

That summer I was forty-six, past the end of my childbearing and a widow of less than two years' duration, but I had begun to think that a marriage to Thurzó, which Ferenc had encouraged me to consider before his death and which I had resisted at first, might be something worth pursuing after all. Ferenc's will would not permit a stepfather to have control of his son's inheritance, of course, but the loss of status I might have to endure in giving up the management of the Nádasdy estates would be worth the protection of being Thurzó's wife. His love for me might be the comfort of my later years, and I awaited his visit with as much, or even more, anticipation as I had once done Ferenc. The master of the house—the master of my heart—would arrive any day now.

Certainly my friend had not been as discreet in his attentions as he might have been, for it was well known to the servants and retainers around Sárvár and Csejthe and Varannó that Thurzó and I were more than usually close, so that smiles and knowing glances accompanied any mention of his name. If I told the servants to prepare rooms for Thurzó's arrival, they gave each other sidelong glances. If I mentioned that he was planning to arrive on such and such a date, the maidservants giggled over their sewing, and even when I threatened to give them all a good beating if they didn't mind their work, the whispering continued wherever I went. The gossips would be watching everything we did, reporting back to noble houses all over Upper Hungary how Countess Báthory and Count Thurzó doted on each other. With his power on the rise in the kingdom, I relished the thought of walking into the wedding hall of Varannó on Thurzó's arm as I had once done with Ferenc Nádasdy. My enemies would fear and respect me then, that was certain.

In anticipation of Thurzó's arrival I expended many long, dull hours on my toilette. In the summer heat, unable to so much as slap a mosquito on my arm, sweat pouring down the back of my neck even as my ladies fanned me with little silk fans, I stood still as a madonna while the seamstresses pinned the fabric of new gowns on me, silk and velvet and brocade. Ilona Jó and Dorka stood on chairs to look through the hairs on my head, their fingers searching for errant strands of silver to pluck. I must look my best when Thurzó saw me again after an absence of many months, and that meant no gray hairs, no dry red skin. I refused the more dramatic cosmetics, having no need of such drastic gestures, but my ladies brought creams and unguents made with rose oil to rub into the skin of my face and hands, and perfume of honeysuckle to dress my hair, and mint for the dark bags under my eyes that came with the trouble of so great and public a celebration. There were new shoes of leather—red and yellow—and slippers of satin and velvet. The goldsmith made for me a necklace set with a large emerald brought from the Habsburg lands in the New World. Thurzó should not see me in anything I had worn before. Everything must be new again, everything startling and fresh. Only the bride herself would be permitted to be more beautiful, more admired.

For all this sewing—new dresses for myself, my daughter, and my ladies, fresh uniforms for my soldiers and retainers—Ilona Jó and Dorka scoured the countryside for seamstresses, bringing girls from Pozsony, from Kassa, wagons full of fresh-faced farm girls. They came with their sisters and their mothers on foot or by carriage, all following the whiff of necessity blowing from Varannó. They came with letters recommending their excellent skills and dispositions, their lively tempers, their modest charms. We took in cooks and chambermaids, laundresses and seamstresses by the dozens, often the younger daughters of lesser branches of the Báthory family, the Nádasdy family, relatives from every corner of the kingdom. As always, I did my duty and looked after them like they were my own daughters. I housed them and fed them, gave them rich clothing and good food, the chance for a little education and some decent society. It was my duty as a member of the senior nobility to be a mother to my people.

Soon the wedding stewards had the rooms ready, and the castle painted white inside and out. Kata glowed through the fittings for her dresses, the unpacking of the lavish jewels I had made for her, even finer and more costly than my own, the arrival of her friends and cousins who would be her bridesmaids and ladies now that she was to be a married woman. She had transformed, seemingly overnight, from the awkwardness of adolescence into the full bloom of womanhood, her gangly arms and legs growing rounder, softer, sweet and powdery as the down on a flower's stamen, and I wished at almost every moment to press my nose to her, breathe in her scent, as if, at the moment of her leaving me, I might retain a trace of her to wear into my future life. Unlike my Anna, who had seemed embarrassed by all the fuss and attention when it had been her turn, Kata smiled more easily than I had ever seen and threw her arms around my neck with as much affection as she had as a small child, when I would pick her up from her cradle in the early morning hours and rock her in my own arms.

In late summer the guests began arriving. My cousin Griseldis, still cloistered in her nunnery, sent me a letter with her remorse at not being able to attend. How could she, she wrote, when she had no carriage, no horses, no money to travel? The nuns forced her to eat the same poor food they did, and live in their frigid little cells, and clean and cook and sew all day long the way they did. How unfair was her treatment at the hands of her neighbors and the young men her two eldest daughters had married. How bitter was her old age. She said hardly a word about my Kata's own excellent match. When her daughters came to Varannó in their finery, with new slippers peeking out from their satin dresses, their mother's golden beauty and insincerity shining from their faces, I told them how sorry I was over the death of their father, how much his friendship had meant to my own dear husband. Of their mother I said nothing except that I hoped her health was good in her new circumstances. "She is the happiest she has ever been," said the eldest, and I expressed my gratitude to hear so. Then I sent them off with the steward, whose job it was to give them the smallest, most cramped quarters Varannó could boast. A petty revenge, perhaps, but satisfying all the same.

My friends came too—Margit Choron, Countess Zrínyi, my sister-in-law Fruzsina Drugeth in her widow's black, bringing her children with her from Ecsed. Each of them I embraced in turn, taking them to the fine rooms I had set aside for them, glowing under the lavishness of their praise for the house, the arrangements. It was a wedding, they said, the entire kingdom would envy. "And you, Erzsébet," said Countess Zrínyi, "look positively radiant yourself. One would almost think you were pregnant."

At this the other ladies laughed, for we were, all of us, beyond childbearing. But then Margit Choron sidled a glance at me and said, "Or else she's in love."

Silence then, and a significant one, too, as we went down the passage toward the guest quarters. Behind me Fruzsina Drugeth tittered like a bridesmaid herself. My friends did not need to ask the name of my suitor. No one did.

The best rooms, as always, I set aside for you, Pál, as you came from Sárvár accompanied by Imre Megyery and a few servants. I called out the household to welcome you. The servants lined up in rows, men on one side and women on the other, dressed smartly in their fresh new uniforms, and Kata and I went down to see you step out of the carriage. Do you remember? The door opened and a boy of eight, dressed in scarlet, stepped from the carriage onto the square of soft carpet I had asked the servants to lay out in the middle of the dusty yard. How much like your father you were, so serious and proper. You were handsome, too, with Ferenc's black brows and broad forehead, and my fine pale skin, my wayward mouth. I expected you to rush to me and throw your arms around me, as you always had done before, but this time you came forward with several shy steps to greet me as if I were a stranger. "Thank you for this warm welcome, Mother," you said, and bowed, so that I knew Megyery had been coaching you, probably all the way from Sárvár. Such formality from such a little one! When I scooped you up into my arms to kiss you, you blushed a furious red up into your hair, so that your suit and your face were all single a color.

"Darling," I said, "you look peaked. Are you well?"

"Very well, thank you," you said, your little-boy voice stiffened with shyness.

Your sister bent and kissed you on both cheeks. "It would not be a celebration without you, my dear little brother," she said, and you blushed again, as scarlet as the carpet you stood upon, and taking two steps back you retreated from us. Where had my little soldier gone? Where was the boy who jumped upon the back of his horse, who played soldiers in the yard with the other boys? In his place was a courtly little lad out of whom all the light had gone—a shy boy with white hands, more comfortable with books than his own family, pale and trembling like Megyery himself. My heart ached for you.

Over your shoulder I could see the tadpole, older now and more self-satisfied, his red mustache curling up around the corners of his mouth, smiling with condescension at my motherly affection. In a moment he, too, was before me, bowing and complimenting the mother of his young charge, saying how wonderful it was to see me again, how great was his honor, not a word of which I believed. Megyery bent to you and said that you mustn't forget to compliment a lady whenever you came upon one, even your own mother.

"His mother," I said, "finds her son's company the greatest compliment. She needs no other."

"Apologies, madam," said the tutor. "I meant no offense."

"Apologies, Mother," you said. "Megyery did not mean to offend. He only wants me to mind my manners, you see."

Suddenly the balance of authority had shifted, and I felt my hold on you, my only son, slipping away. A little more than a year in Imre's hands, and you felt like a stranger to me, no longer the happy little boy I had left in Sárvár after Ferenc's death. Your father had made the gravest of mistakes in choosing Megyery for your tutor, for the tadpole was making you in his own image, not your father's. It was a mistake I meant to rectify. Thurzó, to whose care Ferenc had entrusted me and all our children before he died, would find you a better tutor than old Imre. A more warlike man—less scholar, more soldier—would be better than old, dull, obsequious Megyery. I decided I would speak to Thurzó about it when he arrived. If anyone could make a man out of you, I thought, it was György Thurzó.

You bowed again and—oh, my heart!—stood back to let Megyery go before you. As if he were your father, instead of Ferenc Nádasdy. I stared daggers at the back of the tadpole's head as we went inside the house.

# 13

Thurzó himself arrived on the day of the fall equinox, when the length of the days and nights are equal—a good omen, I thought, for discourse between the sexes. He arrived on horseback, followed by a great entourage of carriages and servants. He was three years away from his election to palatine still, but one would never know it from the lavishness of his carriages, painted with gold and upholstered in red velvet, the gleaming black coats of his horses, or the great honor I did him in curtsying to him on his arrival in the full view of my servants and ladies. He returned the respect I offered him, bowing as if he were in the court of Rudolf himself. Crooking his arm, he escorted me inside the palace doors while his valets scurried upstairs with the trunks and carpets, the gifts of food and wine he had brought from Bicske. He had enough servants for a pasha, I thought, watching the men in their colorful finery scurrying through the halls of my *kastély*. Szulejmán himself had not brought so many men to the mouth of Buda.

We were momentarily hidden from the eyes of the house. "If you wanted to occupy my house as a conqueror," I said, tweaking a spot of softness near his belly, "you needed only to ask."

He laughed and brushed my hand away. "I will keep that in mind," he said. "For now, however, let us be at peace. I am glad to see you again. And when you have a moment, I would like to speak with you on a matter of great importance."

"Is there anything wrong?"

"No. That is, I hope not."

So he did have marriage on his mind still. I was sure of it.

Staying with him to settle him into his rooms myself, I waited for him to dismiss his servants so that we might have that moment alone. Again and again his thin-faced pikestaff of a valet came in with some question about the placement of this or that trunk, or when his lordship would like a glass of wine, or how his lordship wanted his bedclothes folded back. So many times the valet came back, in fact, that I shook my head in amusement and told Thurzó I would try to see him when he was less busy. He laughed and said he would come to me shortly, after he was settled into his rooms.

For the rest of that day and into the night, I waited. I sat in my room and read, or answered letters, or fussed over some little piece of embroidery I meant to give to Kata. Thurzó did not join me at supper but sent word that he preferred to eat alone in his room, that he would attend me afterward. I sent back word through Ilona Jó that I would wait on him if he were ill, but she returned with the message that he was quite well, but only had some matters of business that required his immediate attention.

So I waited. I waited until the house was asleep, and only the light of my single candle burned in the dark of the house.

After midnight, dozing, I heard a knock on my door, Thurzó whispering my name through the cracks. I let him in, standing back from the door while he slipped inside. He had not brought even a candle, so careful he was—I thought—to keep our secret still from the many guests in my house. I was about to embrace him when he held up his arm and told me it was not on bedroom matters he had come to me that night.

"What is it?" I asked. "György, are you feeling well?"

"Well enough. I have something delicate to discuss with you, Erzsébet. Some bit of trouble with the servants."

Again with the servants. I had half a mind to send them all out into the wilderness and let them fend for themselves. But I composed my face and only asked what they had done, had someone displeased him?

"No, no," he said. "But there have been reports of trouble among your servants. The maidservants especially. Megyery has written to the palatine and told him that maidservants by the dozens have been disappearing into your house for some months now, since Ferenc's death."

"I've been hiring girls to help at the wedding. Everyone knows that."

"What I mean is that he says the girls are dying. That there's hardly a family in Csejthe or Varannó who hasn't lost a daughter in your employ. How can I say this to you?" He coughed and raised his eyes to me, their expression unreadable. "He says you're murdering them, or your ladies are. He says you bury them in secret, without the Christian rites."

I stood back and folded my arms across my breasts, feeling my skin grow cold. What was Megyery up to? Trying to get himself declared master of the Nádasdy estates now that he had such enormous influence over my son? And now to be questioned by Thurzó was intolerable. This was not the Thurzó I wanted to see, in his shirt with the tails hanging loose and his feet in slippers, repeating the basest gossip imaginable. "Why are you telling me this?"

"I want to know if it's true. I wanted to ask you myself, and see the truth of it."

I protested my innocence. "Sometimes the maids have to be punished," I said, "but I am no murderer. You have your own house to run, György. You know how difficult it is to keep the servants in line when they steal, and get themselves with child, and disrupt everything and everyone around them. Sometimes they have to be beaten. There's hardly a noblewoman in the country who doesn't beat a servant now and then, and no one thinks the less of her. But to think I could murder with my own hands? How could you believe it?"

"Megyery is making a lot of noise. I wanted to warn you, Erzsébet. There is talk."

"There is always talk," I said, putting my arms around his neck, for I was ready to be done with this discussion. "The only thing that matters is what you believe. Do you believe it? That I am a murderer?" For a long time I waited for him to lean forward and kiss me, as he used to. I would have pressed my lips to the bags under his eyes and murmured my love for him as I did more than a year before. I would remind him how much pleasure we once knew of each other, and could again. "Come to bed. It's been too long."

But he peeled my arms off him and stood back a little, my two small hands clamped together in his own. "I wish I could. I have letters to write before the morning, and important business to attend to." He looked away from me, toward the door. "I hope you will be more careful. If there's trouble, I won't be able to protect you." He dropped my hands and went to leave, checking that the hallway was clear, and then let himself out, shutting the door behind him while I cursed Imre Megyery, the palatine, Thurzó himself, who dared to question me like a witness in a murder trial.

*I won't be able to protect you*, he'd said. Or was it, *I won't protect you*?

To this day, I'm not quite sure.

# 14

On the appointed day of the wedding there was a sudden downpour, a rush of thunder and wind that turned the dusty courtyard to a slough of mud and hay and sent a curtain of rain in through the open window of Kata's bedchamber, soaking her wedding gown. On silk the deep blue color of cornflowers a large brown water mark appeared. Dorka brought the servant girl who had left the window open down to the laundry and beat her soundly, ten or twelve blows with a stick until her back was blue and green. Afterward, remembering Thurzó's admonition, I had her kept in the cellars to recover until the guests were gone. The dress was still ruined. We decided to delay the wedding a day until the weather cleared to allow time for the mud to dry. The seamstresses were called back, whipping together a new gown, of Brussels lace and Venetian silk, in a frenzy of sewing that lasted until long after dark.

As they had thirty-one years before at my own wedding, farmers and merchants from villages all over the north of the kingdom gathered in the fields outside the walls of Varannó with no thought for the weather. They drank and sang by the light and heat of their fires the same as they would have at home, in front of their own hearths. The wedding stewards sent out pigs and cattle to roast over great open pits, and barrels of inexpensive but plentiful wine, and at each a rousing cheer went up from the crowd, toasting the Nádasdys, the Drugeths, the Báthorys. The people gathered were waiting to catch a glimpse of the faces of the noble families of Hungary, the warriors and statesmen whose names were known all across the kingdom. From my window I could see the lights of their fires and torches like a path of golden stars. From somewhere below the high, sweet voice of a young boy cut through the cold rain: "*Júlia is my two eyes / my unextinguishable fire / my infinite Love . . .*"

"Balassi," I said. "The old rogue. He was with my uncle when he was crowned king in Poland."

"Beautiful," said Kata, from where she sat next to her aunt, Fruzsina Drugeth, who was braiding her hair. "But who is Júlia?"

"We are all Júlia," I said. "Or at least we deserve to be, at least once in our lives."

A chant arose from the crowd demanding a glimpse of the bride, and I sent Kata to the window to wave and throw kisses at them, which they received with great cheers of approval. Kata said she did not understand why it was that the people were so eager to see a girl on the verge of marriage, what it was that they longed for. "They want a glimpse of the divine on earth," I said. "Today that is you. You may as well indulge them while it lasts, for tomorrow it will be someone else's turn." I urged her once again to raise her hand, and from the outside the sounds of cheers rose on the plains, and Kata blushed with pleasure to find herself, that day, like the Virgin being heralded by angels.

Inside the house there was enough merriment for a feast day. The gentlemen used the delay and the weather as a chance to get drunk, and the groom and his friends were up until long after dark, sending the servants scurrying for extra barrels of the good Tokaji wine that Thurzó had brought from his estate as a gift to me. I could hear them singing—not the romantic strains of Balassi, but old war songs—from the dining hall and knew they were linking arms, and telling stories, and that in the morning it would be all the servants could do to rouse them for the wedding ceremony.

The ladies gathered together to look at the wedding gifts, the cups of silver and gold, the carpets, the paintings. To my friends I gave fine gifts of clothing, of pieces of jewelry. My better friends linked arms with me and gave their most sincere compliments, but among the other ladies I could see a jealous countenance here and there—an older woman with a spinster daughter, or a poor relation from the east who had fallen on hard times. Did they believe the stories about me, the talk of dying girls and secret burials? They would turn on me when the time came, rejoice in my disgrace, but at the time all I saw was their envy at our good fortune. The greatest estates in the kingdom. Two daughters married, and my son nearing manhood. How close I came, in those moments, to perfect happiness.

At one point that night—do you remember?—you crept into my room, Pál, because you could not sleep, and asked me if you could go down to see the gentlemen. "Not yet, my love," I said. "You are still a child."

You seemed so crestfallen I almost relented. "But I am Count Nádasdy now, aren't I?" you asked.

"Not yet. Soon you will be a man, and then the gentlemen will come to you. You will be a great warrior like your father, or a great statesman like your uncle Thurzó, and your grandfather the palatine. But you must be patient until then."

"Perhaps I will be both," you told me, your black brows knitting together to form a single dark line. "A great warrior *and* a great statesman."

I laughed and kissed the top of your head, the sweet place where the bones had long since grown together. "Your father would like that very much."

Even with the delay, still Thurzó did not appear again at my door. He tried several times to speak with me at dinner in the evening or before the fire, but always someone interrupted us, a servant with some detail that needed attending to, a friend with a bit of news from far away. Thurzó would smile, but his face was grayish cast and ill-looking, I thought. I wondered if it were his digestion upsetting him and sent the new herbalist to him later that evening, but he sent her away again, saying he felt perfectly well. A lie. Something was troubling him.

The next day was clear and cool, with high, sunny blue skies and a skittering of pale clouds that blew past without a drop. The morning saw a stiff cool breeze, as it had the day of my own wedding, the banners caught high, but as if ordained by God, the wind died the moment Kata stepped into the courtyard with her ladies, all dressed in yellow silk like a carpet of buttercups. Kata's dress shone with fat pearls, some as big as duck's eggs, that caught and reflected the light, and lace so fine the ladies who made it complained of the cramping in their fingers. No one would know that only the day before she had planned to wear a different dress. Her rosebud of a mouth turned upward with pleasure when the groom's men stopped to greet the assembly, and the groom himself, in a blue velvet coat and black breeches, took her hand from among her maids and led her down the rich red carpets into the wedding palace. "Here is the lady," said young Drugeth, and Kata blushed with pleasure. Then the triumphant strains of music rose again, as the most eligible bachelor in all the land took my daughter into the wedding pavilion.

Just behind her, you escorted me inside. Instead of the black gown and veil of a widow, I wore red, the same deep crimson as the carpets, the flash of sunset painted on the walls. You blushed when you saw me and said you had never seen me look so beautiful. Always a good boy, to remember your mother at such a moment. The woman you marry will be lucky to have you, for the way a man treats his mother is the way he will treat his wife, and you were—are—the best son any mother could hope for.

We walked slowly, with the utmost dignity, even though I could feel you squirming, pulling on my arm. I whispered to you that a gentleman does not scurry but takes his time whenever he enters a gathering, especially a large gathering. "Hold your chin up," I said. "A gentleman does not look down at the floor, but up at his equals. Your father never looked at the floor in his life."

"But what if I trip over a bulge in the carpet?" you asked. "Wouldn't that be worse than looking down?"

"Be careful where you put your feet then," I said. "Quiet now."

Stately music played, the sweet strains of a lute strummed by an Italian in a feathered hat, and a boy of twelve or thirteen with a voice as piercing as a thrush's sang about the promise of new love. I scanned the crowd as we entered, looking for Thurzó, but I did not see him anywhere among the hundreds of dignitaries in the lushly painted pavilion, the light streaming in the windows like the finger of God. At the front your sister Anna waited with her husband, Miklós Zrínyi, the bulge of her pregnancy hiding underneath her garments. The place I had set aside for Thurzó, just next to that of my own dear family, was empty.

The priest began to speak, and with one eye on Kata, on the pleasure in her face, I looked over the assembled guests—the senior nobility in the front, lesser gentry toward the back. Everyone had outdone themselves in finery, in the brightest colors and best decorations—silver, gold, pearl. Most of their faces I recognized from other weddings, other celebrations, meetings of the diet at Pozsony, balls in Bécs, but here and there was someone whose face I strained to remember. A cousin, perhaps, by marriage or blood. Someone's grown-up son or daughter. There were Révays, Forgáchs, Rákóczis. Fruzsina Drugeth sat with her adopted daughter, my niece and cousin Anna Báthory, and her brother Gábor, nearly a man now, golden-haired and handsome, with the distinctive long Báthory nose and large, wide-set eyes. There Erzsébet Czobor, cousin to the Nádasdys, stood near the painting on the wall where my Ferenc was depicted on horseback, surrounded by light, heading into battle against the Turks. I almost did not recognize her. She had been a pale and sickly looking thing when she had come to Ferenc's funeral with her mother two winters before, and I had heard her mother say that she had been ill some months and was just recovered enough to travel. Some kind of trouble with a young man, the gossips had said, some young scion of a noble family who had rejected her for a girl with a greater fortune. Some even said young Drugeth had pursued her for a time, until learning how small her dowry was. And now here she was with roses in her cheeks, in a gown the color of honeysuckle, standing close to a middle-aged gentleman who had given her his arm. A tall gentleman with a long beard and deep bags under both eyes, dressed in a blue coat and brown breeches, his unhandsome face lit from within by some secret pleasure. György Thurzó himself.

The hall seemed to go quite dim, as if a cloud had passed over the sun. I clutched your arm a little more firmly than I meant to, so that you looked up in surprise and asked if I were well. Very well, I said. It would not do to faint there, in front of all my guests. In front of Thurzó, who was suddenly looking right at me. Damn him. He knew I would not make a scene in front of my guests, at my daughter's own wedding. How long had he been planning this surprise for me? How many times had I written him of my love, urging his coming, and all the time he was simply waiting for the right moment to push me aside?

I turned to face the young couple instead, but my vision was as black as the inside of a cavern. The priest's voice droned, and outside the wind caught one of the shutters and banged it against the sides of the wedding hall like a gun report. My hands were cold and felt nothing, not even your warm little arm as you tried to steady me. On the other side of the wedding palace, Thurzó wore a look of remorse—eyes beseeching, shoulders firm as if he were being upbraided in front of his Habsburg master instead of humiliating the widow of his closest friend. That he could even pretend to be sorry was outrageous. Immediately I looked away.

On the other side of me my nephew caught my other arm. "Are you unwell, aunt?" Gábor said. "Can I get you something? Here, sit on this cushion before you fall."

"No," I said, brushing off his hand. Kata's eyes caught mine for just a moment, widening, questioning. She should not be looking at me. The rest of the congregation turned to see what had caught her attention, and a whisper began to work its way through the crowd. Loud, now. Louder. "I am well, thank you," I whispered, forcing myself to smile. "I lost my balance for a moment. These carpets." I let go of Gábor, who was still trying to force me into a nearby chair.

"Mother?" you asked. When I looked down, your face was pale.

"It's okay, darling. Thank you. You are such a little man now, your father would be proud of you." Your arm clutched mine, and I managed to stand up a little straighter. Like Icarus, I went into the sea before a crowd of people—a ship under sail, a plowman, a shepherd—but no one saw.

# 15

The sight I had encountered in the wedding palace was no illusion: the gossips were all abuzz with the news that Thurzó planned to take Erzsébet Czobor as his second wife. The betrothal had been arranged the previous month after Thurzó had stopped for several days with the Czobors during his summer travels. Her mother had sent the girl to play hostess, serving Thurzó with her own hands as if he were the master of the house, strumming the lute for him in the afternoons as they lazed along the river in little boats. Before three days had passed, Thurzó had asked for her hand. Apparently he had told his friend Batthyány that he was so joyous at the prospect of the impending nuptials that he had asked the girl's parents to shorten the usual betrothal time. The small dowry her parents had saved for her was of little consequence to a man who had already married once, and been widowed, and secured his fortune and political career. A second wife, and a young one too, would give him more children. A blessing, the gossips said, on his lonely middle years.

In my room I sent out all my ladies, my daughters and friends—their words of condolence, their murmurs of shock and dismay, their nervous glances at one another—so that I might think in peace for a moment, without the eyes of the entire world upon me. Only before Darvulia could I let myself be free, so it was to my friend I went, startling her awake as I burst into the small room off the kitchen where she slept. The chamber smelled strongly of roast meat and the herbs she kept in little glass jars, arranged in a row on her window-sill. Darvulia sat up in bed in her thin white shift as I told her what had transpired in the wedding hall, how I had been passed over for a mere girl, a slip of a child with hardly any breasts, with no education and little money. I railed at the cowardice of György Thurzó in appearing at my daughter's wedding with his betrothed without the slightest word to me of the change in his affections. Everything Thurzó had ever uttered to me—everything we had said and meant to each other—was a lie. "I've become a laughingstock," I said. "He's made me the butt of a joke."

She looked tired but picked up my hands in her thin ones and rubbed the knuckles until I was calm again. The sight was nearly gone from her eyes, which were now the same cloudy blue-green color as the surface of Lake Balaton, but she still managed to fix me with a firm stare nevertheless. I should not have burdened her with my troubles, but I could not help myself. Who else had understood so well what Thurzó had meant to me? "You're only a laughingstock if it matters to you what he does," she said. "Does it?"

I took a breath. "I thought it did. It would have. Until this morning I would have given up everything I have for him. Now I would rather sleep with old fat Rudolf himself."

"Very well, then, you are both satisfied with where you find yourselves."

My mouth turned up in a small smile, all vinegar. "More satisfied than I was when I was with him, at least."

From her bed, my old friend laughed, and I shook my head at my own bluntness. I could say anything to Darvulia. She was failing—I could see it clearly now, how frail and thin she looked—and I knew I should have let her rest, but never did I need her as much as I did then, never. No one else must know the bitterness I was feeling.

"Wash your face, madam. Yes, do it. The cool water will take the puffiness out of your eyes and the redness from your cheeks." How she knew my eyes were puffy and my cheeks red, I did not know. "Afterward go down and greet your guests. Look pleased with everything. Do not let him or anyone else know he's hurt you, or you will become the laughingstock you fear."

As usual, Darvulia was right. I rinsed my face in the basin, arranging my face in the mirror into a semblance of disinterested calm. "Go," she said. "Enjoy your guests. When the party is over, come back and tell me everything that was said. You will feel better afterward, I promise." This last like a benediction. I embraced her and went out again.

The stewards and maidens scurried to and fro to the kitchens with plates of bread and fresh butter, wine in blown-glass Venetian pitchers. A great fire steamed at the far end of the hall, and the room filled with noise so that one could hardly hear the person speaking next to them. Yet the moment I entered all eyes turned to me, and the conversation died down a little, as if the room had drawn in its breath to see what I would do next. Thurzó came closer to speak to me, leaving the little brat who was his betrothed and her mother standing by themselves, looking ridiculous.

"Erzsébet," he began in a low voice. "Let me explain."

"There is nothing to explain. Where are your manners, György? Let me look at your lovely little bride." Immediately, in full view of the company, I approached Erzsébet Czobor and her mother. If Thurzó could debase himself with insincerity, so could I. I took the little simp's face in my hands and kissed her on both cheeks. Let everyone see how gracious I could be, how forgiving. "She is truly the gem of Hungary, Thurzó. You will be a lucky man."

The girl's mother likewise kissed me on both cheeks like a sister and praised the wedding arrangements. "No doubt we will be hard-pressed to offer so much when my own little beauty weds our friend here," she said. "I have never seen such a lively party. It would rival anything the Habsburgs themselves could muster." The witch. She knew Thurzó had loved me, and knew that in marrying her daughter Thurzó was spurning me. Now, in her moment of triumph, Lady Czobor had the audacity to offer me her paltry compliments as an olive branch.

"It is true that no one can compete with Countess Báthory for her gracious hospitality," Thurzó said. "The kingdom has not her equal as a hostess. You should send your daughter to her for a while, to make her better acquaintance. Under no one else could my betrothed learn the art of running a well-kept house better than the court of Mistress Nádasdy." I forced myself to smile at the compliment as if I found pleasure in it, wondering if he really thought I would make a good tutor, a friend for his idiotic child bride.

"Would you truly consider it, madam?" asked the wretched mother. "I would be so grateful."

I would be as likely to murder her with my own hands as I would make her my friend. Instead, I said, "Of course. Send her to me whenever you like. I always have need of ladies who can sing, and play, and dance, and entertain us during the long winter months. Send her to Sárvár and I will take her under my wing, at least until your anticipated wedding can take place. I understand there is some haste about it, but there should be some time for the girl to have a bit of education, and the friendship of other girls of her rank."

"We would both be most grateful," said Thurzó, ignoring my remark about the girl's rank. He took my hand and bent over it. I made myself stay perfectly still and accept his compliment. Around the walls of the wedding palace all eyes were on us. The room was a sea of music and light, and couples dancing to the strains of the lute, the guitar, the sweet high voice of the Italian singer, the smell of roast oxen and turkeys, and the intoxication of the best wine. Myself in the middle of it, my eyes so fixed on the middle distance that all I could see were the stitches in the seams of Thurzó's coat. As always, I presented the picture of graciousness and nobility and honor, duty and acceptance, as I fell into the sea with my legs kicking.

We were interrupted momentarily by the wedding steward, Istók Soós, who nodded his head to get my attention. I was so grateful I could have thrown my arms around his thick neck and wept. Instead I followed him away from the guests to a quiet corner where he complained that we were short of maidservants for the dinner, two of the girls who were supposed to have been serving having fallen ill earlier that day. "Ill how?" I asked.

"Dorka decided they needed some bit of punishment," said the steward, "but she beat them so badly they cannot stand, either of them."

"She should know better. They must be able to work still, even after their punishment. She is getting sloppy."

"There is still the matter of the dinner this evening. Two tables have no servant to wait on them. I spoke to Miss Modl and Miss Sittkey at the suggestion of Dorka, but Miss Modl said she would not wait at table since she is a married woman. Dorka says if she is, then it is news to the court, and she calls you to the kitchen court-yard to speak with Miss Modl yourself."

Now Dorka had overstepped her bounds completely, summon-ing me to deal with a serving girl in the middle of my daughter's wedding. She was getting a bit overambitious about her place in the house, and though I valued her help, she must remember that it was I who was mistress here, and not Dorottya Szentes. "Come with me," I said to Istók, and together we went out to the kitchen in the rear of the castle.

There the cooks were roasting a great oxen over a spit, and the servants whose jobs were done for the day were gathered to drink wine out of horn cups and wait for the cook to slice the meat. The pages had gathered there, and the seamstresses and chambermaids, released from their duties for the evening, assembled in clumps to gawk at the retainers of great men, to flirt and dance. A few old gyp-sies played music, and the smell of sizzling meat and charcoal, the smoke and closeness of the space, made me dizzy. Great piles of wood sat at one side of the roasting pit, while the head cook ordered more logs thrown on the fire to keep it hot. A whisper rose up through the crowd as I crossed the courtyard to find Gizela Modl sitting on a bench whispering with one of the chambermaids, laughing like anything and drinking cup after cup of wine.

"Miss Modl, Miss Sittkey," I said, "I'm glad you're here. I have need of two girls to wait at table tonight, since Éva and Aranka are ill. You can wear their clothes."

Gizela seemed surprised to see me there. "I can't, madam. I already told the steward as much." She was not only drinking, but drunk. Very drunk, in fact—her words slurred together so thickly it took me a moment to realize what she had said.

"Why won't you?" I asked.

"Only maidens wait at table."

"Are you not a maiden?"

"No, madam. I have a son."

"Since when do you have a son?" I asked. "I've never heard of this son of yours."

"You never asked."

"How old is your son? What is his name?"

"He is three years old, madam. His name is Ferenc."

"Is it."

"Like his father."

"Where is his father, then?"

"Dead. Dead nearly three years now."

Here and there the flames licked at the carcass of the dead ox, singeing the tail. The courtyard darkened, despite the firelight. I reached up and slapped the girl first on one cheek, then the other. She clutched her face, but her eyes blazed. "You will wait at table tonight," I repeated. "Now."

"No. I will not." She swayed and then steadied herself.

The courtyard went utterly still. The gypsy music died down, and the horn cups stilled in every hand as the servants, the pages and cooks and chambermaids who just a minute before had been celebrating the wedding of my daughter watched Gizela Modl defy my will. Drinking my wine, and eating my oxen, and sneering at me with every breath they drew. I would not have it. I would not.

The steward was behind me. "Very well," I said. "Pick up that log." I motioned to the woodpile. The steward walked over to the pile and chose one from the top, about the length of a man's thigh and as big around. "Now hand it to the girl."

"Madam?"

"Give Miss Modl the log, Istók."

The servant handed the girl the log. She did not dare refuse it, having refused so much else, but it was heavy, and it took both arms for her to hold it up. "What shall I do with it?" she asked.

"Since you are a mother, let me see your mothering. This is your child, my dear. What do you do with a child who has not yet been weaned?"

Her eyes grew wide when she understood my meaning. "You are mad," she said.

"Do it," I said, "or I will have Dorka take you to the laundry, where you will learn what it means to be obedient."

The girl's eyes widened, her mouth parting as if to speak, but she did not. A shadow crossed her face, the shadow of submission that comes with an extra dose of humiliation. She was entirely in my power, for the sake of her son and herself, for her mother and the family at home who could not take her in when there were so many of them, but she knew the servants in the courtyard would gape and jeer, and the little boys throw stones when she took out her breast and held the log to it. If she was so concerned with her dignity that she would not wait at the table, she would have even less if she suckled the log as if it were a child. "Do it," I said, "and I may let you stay here with your child and enjoy my home, and my protection. Do not and you will have to find someone else to put up with your insolence in the morning."

At last the girl reached up and with trembling hands opened the buttons of her blouse one by one, pulling the cloth aside. She had the dark nipples of a woman who had in fact borne a child, but her skin was milky, and it was all I could do not to imagine my Ferenc burying his face in her soft bosom, as he must have done nights while I slept only a few doors away. He always did have a weakness for servant girls, the prettiest ones, the basest and most ignorant ones. The Modl girl held the log to her breast, cradling it in her arms as if it were a suckling babe. Next to her the Sittkey girl, like an imbecile, began to weep. Gizela's expression shifted like the weather, now hot with anger, now with humiliation, and I waited until I saw her settle on a hatred for me so naked and fierce that I knew that the minute the guests left the house, she would not be able to hold her tongue. She would curse and damn me as she cursed and damned everything. She would call me every name she could remember, and I would be forced to teach her her own insignificance. She was not the kind of girl who learns a lesson once and is done with it. I would have to beat her until she couldn't stand. I would put my fingers in her mouth and tear the insolence out of it.

But for now she held the log to her breast. The men were already laughing and joking. I turned and crossed the courtyard and stopped to speak to the servant who had brought the girl's impertinence to my attention. "Make certain she doesn't cover up when my back is turned, Istók."

"No, madam. I wouldn't dream of allowing it."

He bowed, but a hint of a smile crept over his broad red face as he watched the Modl girl endure her punishment. He was enjoying it. The spectacle, or the girl's humiliation. Perhaps both. His mouth was more sensual than I had given him credit for, the lips large and red, and he licked his tongue over them once, then again. When he saw me looking at him, he bowed his head in submission. He was a man of very few words, unlike Thurzó, and unlike most of the men I had known in my life entirely dependent on my goodwill. I could see him weighing that goodwill now, and in a moment he dared to smile at me—a naked, immodest smile. If I had not looked at him before, it was only because I had someone else in my thoughts. But Istók Soós might be the kind of man I had been looking for all along. A servant could be very valuable as a lover, someone who would do my bidding when I needed it done and stay out of my way when I didn't. He was not Thurzó. He would not dare set me aside for a young girl with a firm backside and no education.

"I believe you are a man of some worth, Istók. Come to me later, and we will speak some more."

"Yes, madam," he said, smiling at his boots.

I tried to enjoy what was left of the evening, but when I went up again to the room off the kitchen, I found that Darvulia was gone.

She had taken a few things with her—a small bundle of clothes, a few bottles of herbs, a fine red cloak I had given her as a gift. But her bed was empty. Not even a note remained to tell me where she had gone, or how, in her blindness, she expected to find her way. I went to find Ilona Jó and asked if she had seen my dear friend. "She said she was going off alone, madam," said the old wet nurse, cowering as if she expected me to strike her for relaying such news. "She said you should not look for her, because you wouldn't find her. I told her you wouldn't like that, I said, 'She won't like that, Darvulia,' but you know how she is."

I did indeed know how Darvulia was. My death, she would have said, is no one's business but my own. A wise way to leave this life, I thought then, and I think so even more now. If I had been as clever as she, we might have gone together, Darvulia and I, into our futures, while they were still ours for the choosing.

# 16

*December 31, 1613*

Winter is upon me once more, and once more I feel the cold so deep that it reaches my bones. Three years now I have been in my tower, three years of loneliness and decrepitude, and this morning of all days I heard the halting notes of Ponikenus's voice outside my stone gap, the jumble of Hungarian and Latin and Slovak with which he tries to communicate with me. The pastor of Csejthe must think of these visits as his Christian duty, for otherwise he would not dare to show his face here. His real name is not Ponikenus at all but Jan Ponicky, which he changed to affect more importance than he is otherwise entitled to. This time he did not come alone, bringing with him a fellow pastor from Lešetice to witness what I could only imagine was a spectacle of great humor to them both: Countess Báthory in a cage. What the visitor wanted I could not guess, unless it was my immortal soul. They pulled up chairs before my stone gap so that their faces were visible to me and in thickly accented, halting Hungarian asked if my health was good, since they had heard I was ill. When I said my health was fine, they went on, exclaiming what a pleasure it was to wait upon me in my tower, how great was their honor that they could be of service to me. I laughed and said they may well think so, since they were the reason for my imprisonment.

"My lady," said Ponikenus, placing his hand oh-so-reverently over his heart, "you cannot think I did anything to harm you."

"We have never been friends, Ponicky, and I will not pretend otherwise. I know you went crawling to the palatine with your lies."

He said it was not true, that he always held me in high esteem. I know he flatters himself that he might be useful to me in my present distress, as if I would want help from the likes of him, but I knew I must be careful. Anything I said to him would be likely to get back to Thurzó, to the court. The visitor from Lešetice—one of Thurzó's minions, surely—said he bore me no ill will, that he too had heard of the greatness of the widow Nádasdy and only wished to serve me in my hour of need. His hands clutched at his shirt, plucking the fabric like the strings of a lute. A sudden weariness overtook me. I said I had misspoken, that I knew it was not the pastor of Lešetice who had sent me here. "But the pastor of Csejthe knows his guilt," I said, "since he used his pulpit to rail against me."

"I never did," said Ponikenus, searching for the right words. I would ask him to use Latin, but his vocabulary in that language is even more absurd than his Hungarian, and my Slovak is not up to the task of arguing with him. He said, "I preached the gospel. I preached humility and kindness. I never mentioned you by name. If your mind was troubled by what I said, perhaps I bit a little too close to your conscience."

Conscience, indeed. "It doesn't take much imagination to know that when you speak of the corruption of the nobility in the church of Csejthe, you are speaking against the family who owns these lands. Be careful, Ponicky. I have witnesses I can call when the time comes, and powerful friends still who will aid me."

He shook his head as if he did not understand, but I have known him to pretend to be ignorant of my language when it suits his purpose. I saw the tightening along the soft part of his jaw, the way he mashed his teeth together. He was not entirely certain of his position here. He wondered if my children or my friends would now be his enemies and remove him from his position at the church in Csejthe. Or something worse.

Then he controlled his expression and changed the subject, asking after the state of my soul. Did I pray, he wanted to know, and how often? He had spoken to the guards and heard that I sobbed in my cell at night, that I cursed God and begged for death when I thought I was alone. He felt it was his lot as pastor of Csejthe to protect me from temptation.

"Are you under the impression," I asked, "that I intend to murder myself?"

"Many prisoners have been tempted by the idea."

How exasperating is the tongue of any man inflated with self-importance, none more so than a man of God. "I could not even do the deed if I wanted to," I said. "Thurzó didn't leave me so much as a darning needle so that I might repair tears in my dress or a knife to sharpen my quills. The guards make certain my servants bring me nothing without their permission."

"You might find something else. Your dress for a noose, perhaps."

I smiled. "Now you are trying to give me ideas. Would it please you to see me hanging naked from the rafters?" He pretended to look aghast, but I waved away the words before he began to speak again. I would not let him blather more lies about how much value he placed on my life. "I can assure you I have no plans for self-destruction. Only a guilty woman would think of it, and I am not guilty."

Then the priest from Lešetice asked if I still believed in the divinity of Christ, in my redemption through the Crucifixion. Of course, I told him, though I refused to accept the prayer book he tried to give me through the gap in my stone door. I don't need it, I said. I know my prayers by heart, having spoken them every day of my life. "Ask Thurzó if he remembers his," I said.

We went on like this for some time, the two priests dancing around the salvation of my soul, the purity of my thoughts. I watched the hands of the two men perform an elaborate ballet in front of my stone gap, chopping the air for emphasis here, flopping in resignation there. Ponicky's hands were soft and fine, stained black with ink on the inside of the second finger, the hands of a scholar, of a man in love with the sound of his own voice. What would he do, I wondered, if he were denied the privilege of preaching every Sunday? Would he curl up and die like an old woman locked in her tower? After more than an hour I was weary and impatient with their visit, ready for them to be gone. I stood up from my chair and was about to bid them leave when Ponikenus came to the point at last: Who, he wanted to know, told me he was the one who betrayed me to Thurzó? Who spoke these lies against him?

A smile crossed my face. No one told me such, I said, except that he himself admitted it by asking me so.

"I never lied about you to anyone, madam."

"You lie to me now to deny it. I know you wrote to your superiors, who sent the letter to Thurzó. It was entered into the evidence against me. You made up stories about what happened to the Modl girl. You told people I murdered her at my daughter's own wedding."

"No one has seen the girl since then, my lady."

"Because I sent her home to her mother. She was flaunting her bastard child all over my house."

"Then why has no one heard from her since?"

"Whom would she write to, even if she knew how to write, Ponicky? You?"

"One of my priests saw her body on a cart that was headed out of Csejthe. Her face was gashed. It looked like someone had torn open her mouth."

"Your priests have been known to drink. They see the devil, too, I understand, when they've had a few sips of brandy."

"Under cover of darkness your man Ficzkó took her away toward Pozsony, with two or three others. Why would he take the bodies out in the middle of the night, if you were not trying to conceal your misdeeds?"

"The only misdeed I intend to conceal is the appointment of you as pastor in Csejthe. The Modl girl went home to her mother. The others died of the plague. The disease was all over the county in those months, and the bodies had to go out as soon as the girls died. Do you think I have enough strength to tear a girl's face in half? Do you think you can pass judgment on me? I supported your priests, all of them, as I would have my own children. Like a mother I made certain they had their education, their food and warmth. I welcomed you here after old Barthony died and made you pastor in his stead. Your ingratitude overwhelms me. Will you turn on the palatine, too, when he has outlived his usefulness to you?"

"I have never shown you ingratitude, madam. I remember you in my prayers every day. I ask the Lord to show you mercy and forgiveness for your sins, and once again make you prosperous."

"Oh, yes," I said, "begging for others' prosperity is the highest good there is. Congratulations, Ponicky. You must be a living saint to have the Lord answer your prayers thus."

He shook his head and spoke something low to his friend I did not understand. The Reverend Zacharias said he would come to me again, and we would speak some more. I told him not to bother, but he insisted, and afterward the two of them stood up and left. I heard their footsteps going back down the stairs.

I wonder why you do not come to me here in my tower, Pál, where I must suffer alone with priests, with fools.

# 17

After Kata's wedding, I passed a time of relative peace, traveling between the many Nádasdy estates once more to see that everything was in order—Sárvár to Bécs, Bécs to Keresztúr, Keresztúr to Csejthe. My health was sometimes poor—a lingering ague, which left me so hot that sometimes I stripped to my chemise and still I was soaked with sweat, sometimes so cold I froze in the heat of summer—but otherwise I had much with which to be content. Both my daughters were married, and you would soon be of an age to take up your father's titles. Istók Soós, who had come to my bed for the first time the night of Kata's wedding, remained all that time a trusted friend and confidant, useful in dealings with my tenants and menservants, especially the ones who thought me nothing more than a weak old widow, easy to defy. The other servants nicknamed him "Ironhead" because of his large skull and thick neck, and they soon set about currying his favor much as they had always done mine. He was stubborn in arguing his every advantage with them. What will you do for my lady, I often heard him ask, if I help you? I trusted him as much as the two old women and Ficzkó with the doings of the house when I was absent and rewarded him with new horses, a silver-handled dagger, fine clothes in which he swaggered like a rough little general. He did turn into a bit of a peacock, strutting in front of the others and earning himself some enmity, but under cover of darkness his soft red mouth was as sweet as any nobleman's. I was nearing fifty and less particular, perhaps, in my company than I had been in my youth, but I was truly fond of Istók, and after the disaster that was Thurzó I had no desire to sit around pining for one of the Habsburgs' toadies. Let Thurzó have his child bride, Erzsébet Czobor, and may they both be damned.

In the fall of 1608, after a power struggle within the Habsburg family, Mátyás was made king of Hungary, and the next year György Thurzó elected palatine. After he was confirmed, he took eleven villages belonging to one of his lesser neighbors by force and began harassing the widow of the former palatine, István Illésházy, into giving up some of her lands to him as well. Cementing both his power in the kingdom, and his wealth, by any means necessary.

We received the news at Csejthe with equal measures of shock and disgust. Istók Soós heard it from one of the tenant farmers, who had it from some of Thurzó's soldiers traveling the Vág road. Istók came and told me the news where I sat next to the fire, and I put down my book with the noise of the wind roaring in my ears, staring into the flames as if I could read the future there. I should have seen it coming. The way Thurzó curried favor with the Habsburgs princes, first Rudolf, then Mátyás, must have been calculated with just this design in mind. What had he promised Mátyás in regard to me, I wondered, to secure his position?

Two years earlier, when Thurzó had wed Erzsébet Czobor in Biscke, I had made sure to attend, dressing in the handsomest red velvet anyone ever saw, arriving in the most lavish carriage, so that Thurzó would know he had not broken my spirit. Thurzó gushed at the honor of having me attend his wedding. "Lady Nádasdy," he said. "I am so glad you could join us today. You look remarkably well. Only my own bride is more beautiful."

"She is," I said, forcing a smile. "The most beautiful bride there ever was. Congratulations, my dear."

The child clung to his arm, looking up at him with adoring eyes and simpering and smirking in my direction, unable to restrain her triumph. She murmured something low about hurrying the wedding night, so that Thurzó was forced to shush her in front of me and tell her to mind her company. I could barely hide my disgust. If this was what he wanted in a second wife, then truly he was better off without me. I wished them well and danced with my nephew Gábor, newly elected prince of Transylvania, or my son-in-law György Drugeth. I spoke with all my neighbors and friends, staying long into the evening and leaving only after the bride and groom retired to the bridal chamber. I did not want to seem too anxious to leave in front of the company of nobles, most of whom, if not all, knew that Thurzó had loved me once. I must look like their happiness affected me not at all, or as Darvulia had said, I would become the thing I despised the most.

After the honeymoon, as promised, I wrote to invite Lady Thurzó to stay with me for a few weeks, thinking she would decline, and that would be the end of my obligation to her. So no one was more surprised than I when the girl wrote that she would be happy to come to Csejthe for a little while that fall, that she looked forward to making my better acquaintance. I had the house turned inside out in preparation, giving her the best rooms, the ones Ferenc himself used to sleep in whenever we visited Csejthe. For all that she smiled and gushed and said how honored she was. "My husband tells me no one in Hungary runs a better house than Lady Nádasdy," she said, her eyes on the ground like a good submissive wife. "I hope that someday he will say the same about me. Please, I am your most devoted pupil. Teach me whatever you will." I would sooner have strangled her, but I bid her welcome and led her into the *kastély*, where the fire was burning, and set her down before it in Ferenc's own chair and served her a cup of wine. As she warmed herself and made small talk with Istók Soós, her face red in the firelight, I wondered what she was really doing there, what she had in mind, because I was quite certain our friendship, or lack of it, meant no more to her than it did to me.

As it turned out, Lady Thurzó had no interest in anything except playing the lute, which she was very talented at and which puffed her up with pride whenever she put her fingers to the strings. Every evening after the meal she would offer to play for us, in which enterprise I indulged her as a guest, until I realized that I could hardly get her to stop. She spurned all the other lessons her husband had asked me to give her, showing no interest in how to keep an accounting with her tenants, how to number and mark the family valuables to avoid theft by the servants, how to look over cattle or horses for disease to make certain the sellers were not cheating her. She preferred always to sit by the fire and chatter with her own ladies, to play and sing or take naps in the afternoons. She was poor company for me, too, for without enough education to have read the great books of our time, the religious tracts of Luther and Calvin, the astronomical treatises of Kepler or Copernicus, she had very little to offer in conversation except the basest gossip—what the king's mistress had said at court, who had worn an old dress to her wedding, who had grown so stout she had to have a trunk full of new clothes. Some days it was all I could do not to tell her to shut her useless mouth.

Yet for three weeks I did my best to teach the girl as her husband had asked, coaxing her to read the books in my library, to be present when I disputed with a tenant or spoke to the maidservants or the stable boys. She was all honey to my face, but in her letters home to Thurzó—which Istók Soós intercepted and opened for me before sending them on to Bicske—she complained that I was often cross with her. Once, she tattled, I had even slapped her fingers when she reached for a book on my shelf. My mother's copy of the Bible, actually, which I did not want the little twit touching with her ink-stained hands. She wrote Thurzó that I was a shrew, a cold, calculating woman who sported with the lowest of her menservants and whose inner circle consisted only of the basest commoners, former nurses and washerwomen, instead of the more refined ladies any other noblewoman would prefer. *Lady Nádasdy has a well-run house, as you always told me, my dearest, but it comes at a great price. The younger servants hate her and grumble about their treatment at her hands, and at the hands of the old women and the boy, the cruel one they call Ficzkó, who leers at me whenever the lady of the house is absent. They lord over the younger servants and abuse them, and the lady listens only to them, because they flatter her vanity, and tell her lies. Please, my only heart, let me come home again soon. I cannot bear to be even two days' journey from you and from our dear home at Bicske, where I truly belong.*

I did not see what admonishment Thurzó wrote to her in return, for Istok did not manage to get his hands on it, though the next letter she wrote her husband clearly showed that he had cautioned her about being so free with her accusations, at least in writing. *My most beloved, I was sorry to have displeased you and will be more careful in the future. We will speak more on my coming home about the old women, and the lady here. I will ask her to send me home in a day or two, since I am so missing you, and then I can tell you more in person, for I have learned much in my time away.*

It was no wonder I preferred the servants to noblewomen for my companions, with such friends as she. I should have known that the imbecile would betray the many kindnesses I showed her by tattling to her husband about my punishment of the servants, but I had no idea at the time she would turn on me so completely that in only three years' time Thurzó could believe me a witch, a vampire—the most appalling abominations imaginable. Dorka and Ilona Jó would never have betrayed me the way she did, either out of fear or because they could not write much more than their own names.

After less than three weeks' company I granted Erzsébet Czobor's wish and sent her home to her husband, to be rid of the very sight of her. I kissed her good-bye in the courtyard and bade her a safe journey home to Bicske. "Give my love to your husband," I said, and she smirked and said she would, and that was the last I had to endure the company of the new Countess Thurzó.

# 18

In the fall of 1610, Anna and Miklós came to visit, bringing their household with them, their servants and retainers, their horses and hunting dogs, trunks and carts and carriages, since I had decided to stay in Csejthe for the winter, in my own house. My *kástély* in Csejthe had never been large compared with the grander estates at Sárvár and the big house at Keresztúr, so we were all a bit crowded. To make some space, I had some of my maidservants and the younger men—including Istók Soós, who must not be seen to be too familiar with me while my daughter was visiting—sent up the hill to stay at the *vár*. It was only for a few weeks, until Anna and Miklós left to return home to Croatia and took their traveling staff with them. Istók grumbled about the decision, but he did not dare argue with me. I kissed him and told him I needed him there to make certain there was no trouble among the women. No one else, I said, would I trust with this most important task. He pursed his large red lips and said he would be glad to serve me however he may.

I sent Dorka up the hill as well to act as guardian over the maidservants, with strict orders that they were not to touch a drop of wine or go out of their rooms after dark. During Lady Thurzó's visit, I also had sent some girls up to the *vár* due to crowding at the manor only to find them drunk and rutting like dogs when it came time to call them back down again. Some of the soldiers had snuck into their rooms after dark, turning the servants' quarter into little better than a whorehouse. After Lady Thurzó's departure, I had the girls taken to the laundry and given a sound whipping, taking the strap myself to the most unruly. Still, it was as if they forgot these punishments the minute they were out of my sight. I would find them lazing about instead of doing their work and have to beat them again, and afterward there had been some trouble when Ponikenus told me he would no longer bury any of the girls who died in my house. He came to the *kastély* one afternoon chewing his fingernails and begging me to amend my ways, or risk my immortal soul. "If you continue to accuse your patroness of murder," I said, "you may need to look for a new position." He apologized, said he meant it as nothing but a testament of his concern for me, but I started having Ficzkó and the old washerwoman, Katalin Benecká, take the dead girls away for burial, bypassing Ponikenus and his puffed-up, self-important ways. He must not know too much, or have reason to interfere.

So when Count and Countess Zrínyi came to visit, I thought it best to set Dorka over the maidservants and send them up to the castle with fresh blankets and fruit, bread and cheese and wine. I said I would call for them if there was work to be done, but in the meantime they were to be good and honest girls, with no untoward activities with the soldiers at the keep. Dorka had bowed her head, coarse and red with age and hard living, and said there would be none. For a moment I wondered if it were a mistake to send her, but there was no one else whom the maids feared as much as her. I sighed. Just once I would have liked to be able to trust the women in my house. "I will hold you responsible, Dorottya," I said, "if I find there have been any improprieties."

Yes, madam, she said, and then I sent her out again.

When they were gone, I enjoyed the peace that descended on the house, the silence in the halls and the drawing rooms that came with the removal of the more troublesome girls, and waited for Anna and Miklós to arrive, the first I had seen them since the birth of their second child, a son to bear his father's and grandfather's famous name, heir to the *bán* of Croatia. The babe was home with his wet nurse, being too small to travel still, but I would be pleased to see my daughter nevertheless.

When the carriage pulled up to my door and revealed my lovely Anna, her eyes red, speaking in angry whispers to the boy she had once been so enamored of that I had worried for her virtue, I could not have been more surprised. Now they sat apart, their eyes never touching each other, young Zrínyi so pale that I thought he had been ill. I went toward them and took them both in my arms, first my stiff-backed daughter, then my son-in-law. "Thank you for having us," he said. There was no sense of what they had been arguing about so vehemently. My daughter smiled, all self-possession, and kissed me, and said she was feeling ill, and might she lie down for a little while, until she felt better? Of course, I said. I had the servants take her to her room straightaway, but when I stayed to ask her what was wrong, she only said, "I'm just ill, Mother, thank you," and so I closed the door and left her alone.

Late in the evening Miklós and I had a peaceful supper alone in the hall, with a crackling fire and some good red wine. Anna was still in bed with strict instructions to my servants not to disturb her. Miklós was quiet, and even when I asked if he wanted another piece of meat, some more bread, he simply sighed and said he could not eat another thing. A few times he looked up, his lips parted as if to speak, but then he would look down again into his plate. My son-in-law had something on his mind. Young Zrínyi had never been entirely easy with me, although we had known each other most of our lives. His mother, before her death, I had counted a good friend, one with whom I had shared the aches of labor, the difficulties of motherhood. The least I could do was to ease the boy's troubles, whatever they were. "And how do you fare lately, Miklós?" I asked. "You seem out of sorts."

"I'm sorry. I don't wish to be." He sighed and swirled the dregs of the wine in his cup. Above him the horns of a deer Ferenc had slaughtered years before hung over the mantelpiece, and beneath them two polished swords—my husband's and my father's—hung crossed.

"No need to apologize. But you know if you have something on your mind, you need only speak it."

"Thank you. I know." He took the last swallow of the wine and asked for more, drained the cup in one long drink. "I have hesitated to mention it, madam, but I suppose I could use your counsel on the matter. My father's estates have not done as well as they might have this year or last, and we find ourselves in debt."

"There will be Anna's inheritance as well. Some estates that she will receive upon my death."

He looked up. Above his head curled a thin veil of smoke. "I did wonder if you might not consider giving Anna her portion sooner rather than later."

"Now, you mean?"

"I hadn't planned to ask you, but yes. It would ease my mind to know that little Miklós would have his inheritance secured."

"I see. Yes, you would be worried for the child's sake." Despite the warmth from the fire, I felt a bit chill. "I will have to look into it, Miklós," I said. "I had not planned on doing it so soon."

"It would be the greatest kindness if you could," he said. "You are a mother, and you know how much worry there is in raising a child. As I said, I would not ask, except that it is on Anna's behalf, and your grandson's." Excusing himself, he went out again while I sat by the fire and brooded over what to do, the right course of action.

I was still brooding the next morning when Miklós said he planned to depart three days later, leaving Anna behind with me. He was stopping at Csejthe on his way to Pozsony, he said, where Thurzó had summoned him especially. My son-in-law stayed long enough to have dinner with us a few evenings, to sit with us before the fire on nights cool with frost. He shivered under a blanket, so that I asked Anna if he were ill. "I don't think so," she said. "Only he's preoccupied at present. Thurzó is pressing the nobles to declare openly their allegiance to the king, and swear to it in front of all the others, now that he's palatine. You know Miklós would prefer to do no such thing, but our uncle Thurzó is insisting."

"Yes, your uncle does insist on his way, doesn't he?" I said.

The morning he left I had Zrínyi sign his name as witness to my will. A scribe had made two copies of my original, one for Zrínyi to keep and one to take to Pozsony to give to young Drugeth, whom Thurzó had also called to take the loyalty oath and who had promised to meet Zrínyi there when they arrived. I thought it odd that

Kata's husband would not have time to stop at Csejthe on his journey, as my other son-in-law had done, but decided not to mention it. He must be pressed for time, and nothing more.

In the will I left everything to the three children and asked my daughters' husbands to be especially mindful of my son's rights, since he was still a child. Nothing was laid out in particular, nor did I want it to be. Young Zrínyi thanked me in most profound terms for the generosity of my will, saying how grateful he was to be part of such a grand family, how pleased his wife made him. I hoped rather than believed him to be sincere. Then he climbed on the back of his horse for the two-day journey with his valet and a few other servants and gentlemen for company, kicking up a line of dust as they followed the road north toward the capital.

As Anna and I watched them go I felt a wave of exhaustion wash over me, thinking of the disagreements and strife that would be going on inside the old town hall in Pozsony, the capital of what was left of the old Hungary. I felt a momentary fear that the men I had known all my life—good men, mostly, honorable men who with this or that scheme or allegiance had always hoped to restore Hungary to her former glory—were ultimately led not by national honor but their own greed for power and riches. The old Hungary, the one I knew only from stories, was indeed gone forever.

# 19

Anna and I spent some pleasant evenings in each other's company, but every night I felt myself droop after the wine, the game birds, the beef and dumplings, the goulash, the oranges Anna and Miklós brought as gifts from their orangery in Croatia. I went to bed early and got up late, with pains in my neck and shoulders, in my hands, and I was always, always too warm. I was exhausted in mind, exhausted in body. In the rain and growing cold an ache had begun to take root in my limbs, an ache like an unset bone. Over the next few days it grew and spread to my arms, my hips. I took to my bed from time to time to see if some rest would improve it, and Anna would sit with me all day, reading to me the love poems of Balassi and laughing with me at the old rogue's throbbing sincerity.

When my pains were worse after a few days, Anna mentioned that perhaps we might drive out to Pöstyén to take the cure there, along the banks of the Vág where the mud baths were known to restore people to health. We had gone there from time to time when she was younger, just a few ladies for company, all the formalities of daily life subsumed to the pleasures of the hot mud and steaming water, good food and easy company. My house there was small but comfortable, close enough to the banks of the river to walk to the baths. "Wouldn't it be nice, Mama," she said, rubbing my aching feet between her little hands, "to warm your bones in Pöstyén before the snow flies?"

So although the idea of a jolting ride in a cart between Csejthe and Pöstyén hardly appealed to me, I agreed that we both needed a change. For me the mineral baths would surely ease the aches that plagued me night and day, and for Anna they might help speed along another child. I told her to send for Ilona Jó to make the arrangements for us to leave in the morning. Anna went out to fetch her old nurse into my room. From down the hall I could hear the music in her voice, the joy of anticipation. "Ilona!" she called. "We are going to Pöstyén after all! Tell the others to begin packing."

In a moment there was some kind of noise from the dining hall, raised voices, and then Ilona Jó came into my room alone, carrying a tray with tea and hot soup for my midday meal. Her thin white face betrayed more than her usual amount of anxiety, the white knot of hair at the back of her head fairly quivering as her head wagged back and forth. No matter how many years she spent in my service, she never lost that sense I first had of her as a frightened horse about to bolt. "What is it?" I asked. "What's happened? Is it Count Zrínyi? Is there war?"

"No, mistress, but there is some trouble up the hill that I've just discovered," she said. She set down the tray, sloshing a little of the soup over the lip of the bowl and mopping it up quickly with the hem of her skirt. "The girls there are quite ill. Two have died already, and three others are so weak that Majorosné doesn't expect them to make it through the night."

"An illness? What kind?"

"I'm not sure, madam. I heard about it from old Majorosné when she came down to fetch some food and tea for the sick ones. She was shouting and clattering around the kitchen like anyone's business, and upset the cook."

"Go and find out what's happened, and come straight back to me. Dorka should have let someone know before now if they were so ill."

The old nurse curtsied and left, but nearly an hour later she returned with more disturbing news: it was not illness that had struck the girls at the *vár* but starvation. Two girls had died already and three others were at the point of death.

"Starvation?" I said. "I sent them up with a month's worth of food. How could this happen?"

"I don't know. I come up to the keep and the washerwoman, Kata Benecká, says that Dorka had the girls locked up in their room all week, freezing and naked, with no fire and no food. Dorka said she'd beat anyone who gave them a morsel to eat. Missus Benecká tried to give them some bread, and Dorka went after her with a broomstick so bad that she's been in bed for four days. The two that died are still chained to the three who are still living, and the smell is terrible."

Unbelievable. Dorka had really gone too far this time. I specifically told her there should be no trouble while my daughter was here, while the house was open to so many new people—my son-in-law's valet and servants and my daughter's maidservants—all of whom were strangers to our house, not used to our ways. "Have the cook send up broth for the sick ones, and have Istók Soós carry them to their beds if they can't stand. They're to have a fire immediately, Ilona, but don't give them too much to eat yet or they'll vomit it all up. A little broth for now, and then some bread."

"What should I do with the dead ones?"

There must be no gossip at Csejthe while Anna's servants were in the house, and Ponikenus had said several months back that he would not bury any more bodies for me in the churchyard at Csejthe. It would be difficult to remove the dead ones with Anna's servants in the house, since they might see. "Hide them. Kata Benecká should be able to help you take them to the laundry. Send Erzsi Majorosné to the others with food and tea right away, and tell Dorka to come down to me immediately. From now on, Ilona Jó, I'm leaving you in charge of the maidservants."

"Thank you, mistress."

"Are there any left to come with us to Pöstyén?"

"None that are well enough."

"Not even that fat little Doricza?"

"She's been moved to the laundry as punishment. For lechery, madam. She was caught rutting with one of the men."

"Which one?" I asked, astonished that any man would bed her. "Never mind. She will serve in a pinch. Send her back to me in the morning. She'll be glad to get out of the laundry, at least."

"I should imagine so."

"Thank you, Ilona," I said, indicating that I was finished eating and she could take away my tray. "You can send Dorka in as soon as she comes down. I'll give her a little reminder about who is mistress here still."

# 20

We left for Pöstyén with a small retinue of servants, only Ilona Jó, the new herbalist Majorosné whom I'd brought in after Darvulia left us, young Ficzkó, and the slow Doricza to wait on us. Dorka stayed behind as punishment for overstepping her authority, but for all that we spent a few pleasant days at the baths, going several times a day to the muddy edge of the river, Ilona Jó and Erzsi Majorosné each taking me by the arm so I would not stumble in the mud in my weakness. I hated the way my body felt, trembling and creaking like some kind of ancient ship under sail, but I allowed the ladies to help me, hoping that the mineral baths would provide some relief, as they had once done for Orsolya long ago. Age, it seemed, was finally catching up with me.

The waters smelled strongly of rotten eggs, but the servants scooped up cups of it for Anna to drink to improve her fertility and give her another child. She would hold her nose and swallow it hard, shaking her head afterward to rid herself of the taste. When she had drunk, we would sink down into the pools at the water's edge to warm and relax. The mud was as hot as the inside of a cauldron, bubbling and thick, and I smeared it like a paste onto my joints and across my breasts, sitting still while old Majorosné spread it on my back. When it was cold, I would wash it off and begin again. Majorosné said for the waters to have their effect I should sit in them from sunrise to sunset, but after two or three hours I would grow light-headed from the smell and the heat and ask to be taken back inside. The ladies would dress me on the riverbank and help me back to the house, and in truth I did feel less stiff in my joints, so that I did not need their help as much leaving the river as I did entering it. After the mid-day meal we would go back again, floating in the cloudy water and laughing like girls, until the heat and the smell drove us inside in the cooling dark of the evening.

Doricza was slow and lazy about her work, and often when we returned to the house we would find the beds unmade, the clothes wrinkled from being piled on the floor where we had dropped them. Often by the time she got ready the midday meal the soup would be cold, the bread burned, but she had much to do as the sole maid-servant in the house and I was not too hard on her, reprimanding her only when she ruined the dress I was going to wear at dinner by burning the hem with her iron. Ilona Jó and Erzsi Majorosné helped in the evenings, but during the day they had to attend to me at the baths, for I wanted their company as I sat in the hot springs and would not let them go back to the house with the girl. I had Ficzkó ask around the village if there were young girls looking for work, but he came back several times telling me that he had been unable to find any who would willingly come with him. Anna sometimes asked her own woman, Margit, to stay behind to help Doricza while we were bathing, and when that happened, at least then the meals were better, but the house remained a mess of clothes and towels, empty glasses and upturned books, from sunup to sundown.

After a week of this routine, despite the joy I had in my daughter, I began longing for home, for a well-run house where the food was always hot, for the sight of Istók Soós in my own bed, and so we made the return trip just as the first snow began to fall, wet and heavy, coating the upper reaches of the valley and the hills of the Little Carpathians. The fallen yellow leaves of oak and beech crunched under the wheels of the carriage. Anna chatted with Doricza, who was asking about Croatia, which she had never seen, and Anna regaled her with stories of summers in Dalmatia, of the deep blue of the Mediterranean Sea. Doricza said she should very much like to see it sometime.

"Perhaps if my mother could spare you," said Anna, "I might take you with me when I go, and you could see it for yourself."

I smiled at my daughter, at her thoughtfulness to the poor dumb creature. "You are very dear to offer, my love," I said. "But this one already has more work than she can handle. Maybe next year you can take her."

Doricza frowned and stared at her folded hands, and Anna reached over and patted the girl. "There, then, that will give you something to look forward to. We'll go early next summer, maybe, when the oranges are still small and green. I can give you a little tree of your own to look after. Would you like that?"

The girl looked up. Her face was round and ugly, pasty as unrisen dough, but I thought I read a hint of mute hope underlying the softness of her chin, the emptiness in her eyes. What she had to be hopeful about I couldn't guess. There was no likelihood I would let her go next summer, either. "I would," she said at last, and Anna sat back and talked to Ilona Jó instead, satisfied that she had shown as much kindness to the child as was merited.

Ficzkó had ridden ahead on his horse to let the servants know we were returning a week early, so as we pulled up to the *kastély* in the carriage Dorka and Istók Soós were waiting for us. Some sourness that hung in the air between the two of them convinced me that they had had a disagreement of some kind while we were gone, since it was with more than his usual gruffness that Istók offered Anna and me his hand to help us out of the carriage and then barked orders at the driver to steady the horses so he and his valet could get the trunks down. Dorka waited until I had a chance to take off my cloak and shoes and warm myself before the fire before she began the list of grievances that needed my urgent attention: the new stable boy had been caught peeking at one of the maidservants in her bath, and two of the horses had contracted some sort of lameness, and we were out of the good Tokaji wine. I told her to have Ficzkó beat the stable boy, to have the grooms wrap the horses' fetlocks in hot towels, and to order more of the Tokaji from Thurzó's steward, since it was his estates that produced the best vintages. "And how are the maidservants?" I asked. "The ones who were ill?"

"Those last three have died, madam," she said. "I do beg your pardon again on that account. I thought I was following your orders. When I caught them sneaking the soldiers into their rooms, I clamped down, just as you said, to punish them. So they remember their place and all."

"I understand that, but you can see what a predicament it left me in. There were no girls to take with us to Pöstyén, just that fat one who is so clumsy with everything. I've left you in charge before and seen you take matters a bit too much into your own hands. I can't be everywhere, so I've left Ilona Jó in charge for now. Until you remember to handle yourself a bit better."

"Of course, madam."

"That's all, then. Thank you."

When she was gone, I was joined at the fire by my daughter and Count Zrínyi, who had arrived just that morning, in time to embrace his wife. After the healthful waters of Pöstyén, Anna was more hopeful than ever of conceiving another child and eager to put the cure to the test. When she thought I wasn't looking, she whispered something into Miklós's ear that made him blush and glance at me in utmost embarrassment. "Not right now," he said in a low voice. "Surely you can wait until after dinner, at least." But he kept one arm tight around her waist while they warmed themselves in front of the roaring logs, and I was pleased to see the closeness return between them. Either the visit to Pozsony, or the generosity of my will—or both—had restored some of their former happiness.

We dined that evening on pheasant and capon and salted fish from Lake Balaton that the count had brought back with him as a gift for me. He talked of how the new palatine had set up his court, how mistrustful Thurzó seemed of his fellow Hungarians, insisting in the most strident tones that all the nobles swear fealty to Mátyás, especially any with close ties to the Báthorys. His eyes met mine across the table. "Thurzó knows that Gábor, as the new prince in Transylvania, is exciting the nationalists. He wants to be sure that we are in his pocket, at least in public."

"You will do as you must," I said. "Now the wind blows from

Bécs, but tomorrow it may blow from Gyulafehérvár. It's best not to make too many enemies before the storm hits."

"That is just what I said," Anna chimed in, yawning. Her wineglass was empty, but she waved away Istók Soós's offer to refill it and said she was going up to bed. She looked significantly at her husband, who blushed again—even in the firelight I could see the crimson spots on his cheeks—and said he would come to bed momentarily. He wanted to speak to me, he said.

"Oh?" I asked. The last time Zrínyi had wanted to talk to me, it cost me a third of my properties.

Anna gave her husband a look, but then she kissed me and took her leave, and Miklós and I found ourselves alone, sitting on the carved-back chairs before the fire. The servants were gone, even the shuffling of their feet stilled on the stones. Miklós took a great gulp and drained his wineglass, setting it back down again. A bit of red liquid clung to the sides and slid back down to settle at the bottom of the glass. I assumed my son-in-law had some questions for me about his dealings with Thurzó, or perhaps a message he wanted to send to Gábor in Gyulafehérvár without the palatine's knowledge. It was no secret that Miklós had dreams of increasing the glory of his illustrious grandfather's name, and if anyone could have offered Gábor Báthory an ally in Hungary, it would have been Miklós Zrínyi. But when my son-in-law opened his mouth to speak, it was not Gábor or Thurzó he wanted to ask me about.

He had been out in the woods around the castle hill that morning flushing game with his new rifle and the three dogs, he said, when the best of them got wind of something and took off through the woods. He called after the beast, but the other two were soon lost to his sight among the trees as well. When he came upon them, they had dug up from the shallow earth the mottled hand of a girl. Her skin was bruised and beaten, and around her wrists and ankles there were signs of shackles. As he was seeing to the first one, the dogs had uncovered at least three or four more. I pictured him in the fig orchard on the slopes of the hill, where the old washerwoman must have buried the dead girls, sitting astride his white horse and bending down to see what it was his dog had nosed. His revulsion when he realized what he was looking at, how he would have called to the dogs to leave the bodies. The carrion smell. Zrínyi told me how he had to pull the dogs off the corpses, to pull them snarling back to the house, where he asked Dorka why there were five girls buried in the orchard. The old woman told him they were plague victims who had died the previous summer and been buried in haste, so as to not frighten the people around Csejthe. Zrínyi hadn't believed the servant's explanation, especially since he could see for himself that the girls had not been dead more than a week at most. "Your servant looked," he said, "as if the devil had her by the throat. But I was determined to ask you about it first, my lady, because of my love for you. I would not want to assume the worst."

"Nor should you," I said. "The girls did die of the plague, Miklós, but it is as you say, they were dead only a week ago, up at the keep while you and Anna were staying here. We did not want to worry the village with the news. The poor things, they were so blackened when Dorka found them they were hardly recognizable."

"What of the marks from the shackles?"

"They were tied at the wrists, as usual, to remove the bodies. The servants could not lift them otherwise."

Miklós looked thoughtfully into the fire, swirling the dregs of the wine in his cup. A bit of sap popped in the fire, and the house grew still around us. Near the door I could hear the dogs settling down for the night, sighing with contentment, curling their tails around them. Zrínyi said, "Then it is what I thought. I knew you would explain it all." He stood, then bent and kissed my brow like a good son. "Of course I won't mention this episode to Anna. It won't do to upset her."

"Thank you, Miklós," I said, watching him turn to go. In the line of his back I could see a curl of distrust settle. I would have to watch him, young Zrínyi, to keep the peace in my house. God knows I needed no more troubles just then. "You're right, there's no reason to upset her over nothing," I said. Then I too took up a candle and made my way to bed.

# 21

At Christmas, when the snow muffled the sounds of the kites and hawks wheeling in the skies, when ice grew along the edges of the river like mold across old bread, I opened the house in Csejthe to my friends and neighbors for the celebration of the birth of the Christ child. The healing waters of Pöstyén had left me much improved in spirits, and in a jovial mood I sent for my children, my good friends, to join me. Thurzó wrote from Bicske that he was sorry he could not come, but his wife was nearing her confinement, and he wished to be by her side when the child, their first, was born. I was not sorry to miss them. My son and daughters all planned to come, as did my husband's uncle Kristóf Nádasdy and his wife. I had rooms prepared for all of them, moving the servants once again to the keep at the top of the hill, this time leaving them in Ilona Jó's charge, with strict instructions that there was to be no trouble of any kind while my family was with me. "The girls are to return as fat and fed as when they left," I said, looking significantly at Dorka, who stared back as if she did not know of what I spoke. If I needed the girls to return, I said to Ilona Jó, I would send Ficzkó up with the cart to fetch them down again.

The first to arrive at the manor house were you, Pál, and Megyery, on that bitter afternoon when the wind blew the snow hard against the shutters, driving it onto the sills and in the corners of old rooms like fine dust. Istók Soós and Ilona Jó and I had settled in before the fire for the day, convinced that no one would be foolish enough to come to Csejthe in this weather, when we heard the sound of someone pounding on the door and muffled voices demanding the house be opened to them.

I went to the door, pulling the fur of a silver fox around my shoulders, to see several white figures, men on horseback, moving in the courtyard, hunched and shivering in the cold, their mustaches and beards frozen and white. You were riding the little Arab mare I had given you as a gift, a creature I would have thought too delicate for the harsh journey between Pozsony and Csejthe, but she pranced and jangled as if a two-day journey through the Little Carpathians in a blizzard were nothing at all. You had grown since the summer, nearly as tall as me, so that I didn't recognize the snow-covered figure riding the little mare as my son at first, but then you swung down off your horse and flung yourself at me with great cries of happiness, and I took you in my arms. You were wrapped in a red fur-trimmed cloak and wore a high black bearskin hat round as a drum, but when I embraced you, I could still feel how cold you were, how you shivered. The others came to the door stamping the snow from their boots and brushing it from their mustaches, their faces the color of new-pressed wine. I scolded Megyery for risking the roads on such a terrible day. "You should have stayed at Pozsony until the weather cleared," I said.

The old tutor bowed and murmured one of his usual apologies, but you spoke up for him. "It wasn't Imre's fault, Mother," you said. "The snow didn't start until we were halfway here, and he wanted to turn back, but I said that with half the distance covered already we may as well finish the journey. I made him keep going, because I was so anxious to see you."

I looked to the tutor, whose eyes remained on the ground, but I knew the tadpole had more on his mind than he was willing to say. If Megyery had truly wanted to turn back, you would not have been able to convince him otherwise, Pál, but I said nothing. I would not argue with your friend and make you suffer. As before, it worried me that my own son felt always the need to lie to protect the tutor from my displeasure. If old Imre were to ask you for a dukedom, I knew you would not be able to refuse him. It made me afraid for you and makes me afraid still. If something should happen to me—if I die before you reach your full majority and can be reasonably emancipated—there will be no one to counter your guardian's influence over you. After the frail health I had suffered for a little while in the fall, I had begun to be more aware that the number of days ahead of me might be fewer, far fewer, than those behind.

"Very well," I said, "but we should get you inside before the fire. You look half frozen, my love."

"I'm not cold, Mother," you said. "Did you see me riding Sabina? Master Bálint says I've become as good a rider as Papa ever was."

"I believe he's right. Your father would be proud. Now let me have Deseő bring you some soup, and let's get you out of those wet clothes before you catch cold."

"Megyery needs some soup and dry clothes too."

"Yes, Megyery, too. I'm sure we can set another place for him." I took you by the shoulders and marched you in front of me into the house. "Now tell me what you have been reading lately."

# 22

On Christmas we met in the dining hall to gather round the long wood table, to eat and drink. György Drugeth and Kata, who just that summer had converted to the Roman faith after an intense campaign by Bishop Pázmány on the pope's behalf, did not join us for the morning services in the church but instead held a small mass in the chapel with their own priest, who had traveled all the way from Homonna with them. They invited me to join them as well, but Ferenc had converted these lands to the reformed church, and I was not about to discard the faith that my husband had chosen for them. When I said this to my daughter, she smiled and nodded and said nothing, but when her eyes met mine, an understanding was there, a kind of apology that said she would much rather have come to services with us than endure the formalities of her husband's well-timed Catholic conversion. "You are welcome to use the chapel at the *vár,* if your priest doesn't mind," I said, by way of excusing them. "Old Ponikenus is likely to pollute the congregation with the wind of his fetid breath, but it wouldn't do for me to be absent on Christmas morning, of all mornings."

Kata laughed, placing her hands on her round belly, for she was expecting her first, and I could tell she was a little green this morning, for the child was making her ill. "Go to bed with two tablespoons of honey and brandy," I said. "If you must stay behind from services, the good Lord will understand you are only doing your duty as a mother." Kata thanked me and went back to her room. Then I put on my hat and cloak and went up to the church arm in arm with you on one side and Anna on the other, in the path that the servants had cleared for us. Ilona Jó and Dorka followed behind, each dressed in new velvet coats, my Christmas gifts to them for the loyalty they had shown me all year.

I did not often attend Sunday services at the church with the townspeople, since Ponikenus's sermonizing usually exhausted me, but I had made it a tradition that at Christmas I would join the people of Csejthe in the church, sitting among them and listening to the nativity story read aloud by the priest. Afterward I would pass out gold and silver coins as gifts to the parishioners. In the past few years, it had become a great event in Csejthe. Commoners, especially women, came from miles around to greet me and speak to me about this or that matter of business, or to introduce to me daughters whom I might take into my service, or just to touch my sleeve as I passed by them on my way out the door and pressed a coin into their hands. It was always the mothers to whom I gave my money. Mothers would not gamble it away or drink it up in taverns or spend it in whoring. Mothers would make certain it went where it was most needed. It was always the mothers I searched out when I passed through the crowd—the eyes wide with need, the belly empty so that her children might have bread. I would take out my heavy purse and press as much into her hands as I could spare—copper, silver, gold.

The townspeople were singing as they came up the hill toward the church, which looked gray in the new snow despite its coat of whitewash, but the bells were ringing and the air was fresh and cold. The silvery chimes of the bells rang across the hills and echoed back at us. Fathers came bearing their little sons and daughters on their shoulders, breaking paths in the snowfall for their wives and older children to follow in, smiling, rosy-cheeked. I recognized the butcher's family and returned his bow with a smile. The townspeople were dressed in their best clothes, everything clean and pressed, fresh embroidery shining on jackets and waistcoats, cloaks and hats like a spring garden of new flowers, red and yellow and blue. They stood back to let us pass without a murmur.

At the doors of the sanctuary Ponikenus himself waited to greet us, bowing and uttering something polite and bland in his awkward Hungarian, taking the free arm I offered him to lead us into the sanctuary. Our eyes needed a moment to adjust to the inside dark. Beside me, you stumbled and nearly took me down with you onto the stones. The priest caught my other arm. "Thank you, Ponicky," I said.

He frowned. "Please, more care, my lady."

Ponikenus led us to the place of honor at the front of the church, where the carved wooden pulpit looked out over the gathering congregation of faithful, where lit candles and fragrant boughs of fir and pine made me remember, for a moment, the death of my father, and how much I had longed for my elder brother to turn and look at me, for my mother to take me in her arms. How long ago that was, and yet so deeply did my limbs remember that mother ache that for a moment the light in the room blurred and dimmed. "Are you all right, Mama?" you asked. "Did I hurt you?"

"Not at all, my love," I said, and touched your soft black hair.

When the bells stopped their ringing, the service began, the readings from the Gospels of how the Virgin had bowed her head in submission to the will of God and conceived a child. How the sacred family went down to Bethlehem, to the city of David, where the Virgin gave birth in the stables of an inn, among the donkeys and sheep and cattle. How the greatest of all was born in the humblest of circumstances to be the light of the world, how kings and potentates from the east came to bring him rich gifts and pay homage to the newest star in the firmament, the one that named him King of All. Dorka translated for me, since Ponicky spoke not in Hungarian but the local dialect, the only language most of the people there understood.

When he was finished reading, his voice like an avalanche, Ponikenus stood at the carved and gilded pulpit and looked for a moment out before the congregation of townspeople from Csejthe, from Felsővisnyó. It was a long pause, long enough to hear the cough of an old woman from the back and a small child crying until its mother shushed it. Beside me Dorka shifted in her seat. He was a fan of theatrics, was Ponicky. He was looking directly at me, and I was about to ask Dorka what was taking so long when at last he began the day's sermon. He talked of the beauty of the Christ child's humility in allowing himself to be born in a stable, in the lowliest of the lowly places in the world, how if he had chosen it for himself he could have come to us all clothed in silks and satins, in spun gold, but that the corruption of material things mattered so little to him that he shunned them all even from the moment of his birth. How the greatest king of all lived like a beggar and a pauper among the great nations, even in the time of Caesar, to be an example and a vision for all to follow. Ponikenus paused and took a breath, his eyes still on me. Then he began anew, with a new note in his voice, brass instead of silver. He said how the corruption of wealth and power had turned Hungarians into slaves of the Habsburgs, of the Turks, of their own ambitions and greed. How money and power turned good people to evil, forgetting their brothers and sisters, demanding only more and more.

A murmur went through the crowd, a ripple of fear and anticipation, and one by one the people stopped and looked at the place
where my family and I sat. Dorka had stopped translating, her eyes
flashing anger at the priest.

"What else does he say?"

Her voice was choked with anger. "I don't wish to repeat it. He
tells the filthiest lies."

"What else does he say?" I demanded again.

He says, she told me, that the humility of Christ cannot touch
those who are corrupted with wealth and power, who forget their
duty to the widow and the orphan, the sick and injured. Who take
and take and never give a thought for those they take from. Who
murder the low ones and hide their sins in plain sight.

It was me he was speaking of—denouncing me in public, on
Christmas, in view of my family and friends, and all the ones I loved.
I who had taken him in and given him a position on my estate, who
had brought into my house widows and orphans, who had given them
food and clothing and shelter, a dowry, an education. I whom he
named a murderess and a criminal, in hearing of all the townspeople
of Csejthe. It was, I thought then, an outrageous act by a scheming
little toad puffed up with his own self-importance. I didn't realize
then it was the opening shot of the battle that would be waged against
me, that it was the beginning of trouble, rather than the end.

Beside me you and Miklós Zrínyi were standing up to leave,
pulling me after them. Zrínyi said the priest had gone too far. "We
won't sit here another minute and listen to his filth," he said. He led
us out of the church—Anna and you and myself—back down to
the *kastély*, the coins in my purse jangling because I had not given
them out to the townspeople. From behind me I heard a woman's
voice hiss "murderer!" But when I turned to look, I could see nothing but a blur of faces, none of them recognizable as the speaker of
such an abomination. My head was filled with red light, and I would
have thrown myself on them all in a fury, would have screamed the
place down, but Zrínyi had me by the elbow, Zrínyi was dragging me

away from the scene of my humiliation, and I nearly stumbled trying to keep up with him. "He has not heard the last of this," said my son-in-law. "Can you send him away? Complain to his superiors?"

"How can he say such lies about me?" I said when I could speak. "I never harmed him or denied him anything he's asked of me."

"He must know that you cannot let the incident stand," said Megyery.

"I most certainly will not," I said, taking off my cloak, but my hands were shaking with anger. To denounce me in front of the entire congregation, and at Christmas, too—either Ponikenus had taken leave of his senses, or he had found a new patron, someone else to stuff his coffers. That it could have been Thurzó did not occur to me, not even then.

# 23

Before dinner I sent Zrínyi and Drugeth and Megyery together to speak with Ponikenus about what had transpired at the church, to warn the little toad that he was treading on the most dangerous ground. Anna and Kata and you and I ate a cobbled-together lunch of lukewarm soup and yesterday's bread while we waited for them to return, and Dorka kept coming in with questions from the cook, who was wondering how long I would keep dinner waiting. Since the church was hard against the walls of the *kastély*, I couldn't imagine what was keeping the men so long, and as dusk began to fall gray and lonely and a thin snow began to fall, I was about to send Ficzkó out after them when they arrived back at the door, stamping snow from their boots and brushing it out of their mustaches. "I have spoken with the priest, madam," Zrínyi said. "He will join us shortly before dinner to offer his apologies."

"That's not enough," I said. "He will denounce the remarks he made today in the church and publish his disgrace to the neighborhood the way he published his lies."

"He will," said Drugeth. "He promises that Sunday next he'll retract every word."

"Sunday is still five days away. Until then he's not to set foot in this house," I said, turning to old Deseő. "Do you understand?"

"I do. What shall I tell him when he arrives?" asked the steward.

"He can make his apologies out in the snow. I will listen from the doorway and forgive him, if he's sincere. But until he's restored my good name in the neighborhood, I cannot forget what passed today."

Deseő went out to relay my instructions to the rest of the servants not to let Ponicky through the door.

We sat down to an uneasy supper of dressed game birds and dumplings and bread hot from the oven, still on its baking stone. Kata and her husband had learned what had passed in the church and sat close to me, my daughter reaching out every once in a while to pat my hand and say that old Ponicky could not have meant what he said, that there must have been some mistake. Anna looked pale. The servants rushed in and out of the dining hall with their plates and cups, pouring wine and taking the dirty dishes in utmost silence, as if to speak would break the glass under which we found ourselves. The clink of silver on gilt, the sounds of wine being sipped, were broken only when you dropped your glass and shattered it on the floor. "Oh!" you said, apologizing to me over and over, although I kept telling you it was unnecessary.

All that night I hardly spoke, but the girls kept up their end of the chatter so that it did not get too quiet. My family seemed to have lost its appetite, and much of the food, so carefully prepared, went uneaten. When the final courses arrived—fruit dressed with honey, or dipped in brandy and set afire—you and Drugeth took little bites, but the rest of us sat looking at the platters with our stomachs full of lead. I had the servant girl, Doricza, come in and take them out again, and not long after, I stood and announced I would retire for the evening. The truth was that I had had quite enough of everyone, and I wanted nothing more than to be alone for a little while.

Ilona Jó came and helped me get undressed and into bed. Outside the dogs were barking, and we paused for a moment, thinking that it might be Ponikenus approaching the house, but then they stopped and paced, whining, outside the fence. "Probably just an old cat," Ilona said, undoing the tight laces of my waistcoat. When they were loose, I took a deep breath, the first of the day. The candlelight chiseled her angular jaw into less severe relief. It appeared that Ponikenus would not come that day for his apology.

The longer he made me wait, the worse it would be for him.

I was settling into my chair to have Ilona Jó brush out my hair when Dorka came into the room, muttering and shaking out a skirt I had torn that morning in all the excitement and that one of the seamstresses had just repaired. She handed it to me without looking at me, so that I had to stop her and find out what was the matter, why she was so agitated. "Doricza, my lady," she said. "I just caught her in the servants' quarters with the dish of spiced pears, the ones that were left from dinner this evening, handing them out to the maids. I asked the cook, and she said she'd set them aside and thought I'd taken them. I told her, I said, if I had taken them, you would've known about it. She stole them, just took them eager as you please, and the plate, too."

Stealing on Christmas, of all days—how could she do such a thing, and with my daughters and son in the house too? The cow. If she had asked me for the pears I would gladly have given them to her, but simply to take them for herself was out of the question. At every turn I was surrounded with incompetence, every day of the year, every year of my life. Since I was a young girl I had never had a moment's peace with my servants, not a single day in which there was not some kind of trouble that needed my attention. What I wouldn't do to rid myself of every last one of them, their nattering voices, their insolence, their greed.

In a moment I was out of my chair and moving down the hall

under the torchlight toward the dining hall where the steward and some of the menservants were still at their supper, and across to the servants' quarters in the half dark, where I could hear the maids chattering and laughing as I went toward them, and my feet on the stones were loud so that as I drew close a hush fell over the room, the maids sitting on their beds in a half circle of candlelight. The smell of cinnamon and cardamom and nutmeg was thick in the room, the plate of pears Doricza stole hastily pushed under the bed, glinting a little in the light, the gold and silver gleam of the tray that held them, about as long as my arm and twice as thick, with scrolls of lions and birds worked into the metal. My inheritance, that tray, a gift from my mother when I left for Sárvár as a new bride long ago. Not only pears, then, but something more valuable. She was a thief, a lazy little wretch. More than once she'd been punished for gluttony, for taking others' bread, and for lechery. I had tolerated her slow lazy way with her chores, her mute anger, her clumsy shuffling walk. I had taken her to Bécs, to Pöstyén, had taught her letters in my carriage, and given her coins as presents, and this was how she repaid me—with thievery.

The fat girl's eyes went wide, shimmering with unshed tears. I pulled the treasure out from under the bed, spilling the pears and the sticky sauce all over the bed, and held the tray over her head, so that she crouched and cowered and covered her belly with her hands— her belly that was more than fat.

"Who," I asked, letting the tray fall, "is the father of your child?"

Immediately she dropped her hands, but I had already seen. "I'm not with child, mistress."

"Tell me, or it will be worse on you, I swear."

"I—" she began. I could see her weighing her answer. Truth versus fiction. At last she said, "The steward, madam."

"Old Deseő?" I asked. "You're joking."

"No, madam. The other, the wedding steward." Istók Soós, then.

I looked down at the girl from all my height, from a distance that seemed to grow and stretch. The longer I looked at her, the uglier she became, her pink skin taking on the hue of a sow's, her mute eyes damp and comprehending. Laziness and greed and thievery and licentiousness, all in one awful package. If she had been loyal, I would have gladly given the tray to her. I would have given her a fortune in new clothes and treasure for a dowry and found her a husband. But she was fat and stupid and useless, more useless than an old cow, who at least could be slaughtered for our supper. I would not even be able to marry her off now.

The room was dimly lit and full of faces, faces that seemed always to be mocking me, laughing at my misfortunes, searching out ways to rob, to lie. Dishonesty and deceit were the only virtues among the people whom I had tried always to help. I had offered them employment, education, the refinements of good food and good company, a chance to distinguish themselves, but not one of my maidservants had proven herself worthy, not in all my long years. Whores and bandits, *hajdúks* in my midst. Their excuses and apologies seemed to reach me as if from a long way off, and their tears were the tears of actors, of the most abject liars and cheats. I put my hands over my ears and would not listen. I would not listen, I said, to another filthy lying word.

What happened next is something I can only recall dimly, as if in a dream. I called for Ficzkó, who with Dorka gathered up the gaggle of offending girls and ushered them into the cellars before me, weeping and clinging to each other, the backs of their heads in the lamplight like the manes of a herd of unruly horses. Something was in my hand, and I lashed out at them again and again with it, driving them before me. Someone cried out. Ahead I could see fat Doricza turn and, with the whites of her eyes showing, say something I didn't hear or don't remember. My blood was so hot in my veins I thought it would boil. *Save me*, it said.

At last we came into the cellars under Csejthe, where the wine barrels were kept and where Dorka had held the ones who had so offended her earlier that autumn. A strange smell was in the air, rotten and cold. Five of the girls were tied together and sent out of the room with Ficzkó to wait while Dorka stripped the fat one naked to the waist. Her pearly white skin was so like the flesh of a pig, so rounded and rippled and pink, and when the first blow of my cudgel struck her on the back a pig's noise too rose from her mouth, and a pig's pink blood. The room was very cold and still and smelled strongly of copper, a stony, mineral smell. I struck her again, and each time the room went completely black, my vision obscuring and clearing again. She was weak, she was worthless. A few moments later, she slumped to the floor with the marks of my fingernails in her neck.

My vision cleared. The cellar came back into focus, dim in the torchlight, and the sounds of girls crying from out in the halls, and at my feet a pile of flesh that might once have been a girl, pink and red and rippling, but she was breathing; she would live.

Ficzkó asked what he should do with her.

I told him to leave her where she lay, and then to bring in the others and chain them there. As a warning, I said, and went back the way I'd come, into the *kastély*. Ilona Jó helped me change out of my soiled dress and crawl at last into my own bed, where I fell into a deep and dreamless sleep and did not wake until midmorning the next day, when the first rays of the sun fell slanting across my face, and I woke fresh, and feeling better than I had in many months, better than I had after the baths at Pöstyén. A new day dawning.

# 24

Ponikenus did not come to apologize to me all the next day, or the next. For two days I dressed to expect him, and every evening when I went to bed, I told Ficzkó that the priest would not be welcome when he arrived. But still I expected him. I set dogs at all the doors, and guards, and told them that they were to turn him back the moment he approached the house. That I would not see him if he were struck ill by the plague. I kept to my room and read my books in the thin winter light, not remembering a word of them and seeming always to hear footsteps in the halls, on the stairs.

My son and daughters and sons-in-law left Csejthe on their return journeys, so that they might make it to Pozsony before the worst of the snow began to fly. I parted with them with many tears and wishes that they might stay, but they had their own estates, their own families and business to see to, and before long the winter roads might be impassable. Anna needed to be home with her little ones, and Kata to return to her comfortable house for the end of her pregnancy. You and Megyery were making your way back to Pozsony, then Sárvár. The gentlemen had not been good company the past few days at any rate, restless and bored and going out in the afternoons on long rides along the river valley to hunt, staying out nearly until dark, looking guilty when they returned. Wolves had been seen in the woods around the keep, and Megyery had an urge for a wolf pelt, so the others were taking him to look for one, they said. The idea of the old tadpole taking down a wolf was laughable to me, and secretly I wondered if the gentlemen weren't visiting the tavern down in the village instead, looking for the company of other men instead of staying in the house with a gaggle of ladies. But I had said nothing of my suspicions for the sake of my daughters and for you, my son, who loved them.

When they were gone again and the house quieted, Ilona Jó and Kata Benecká and I spent the afternoon around the fire playing cards and reading out to each other some Latin poems that I had been teaching them. The house had sunk into an unusual state of calm and quiet, even the great white dogs at the door snoring and kicking their legs, dreaming of the hunt. But I felt an intense agitation, a mute anger that threatened always at the backs of my eyes, the palms of my hands. I found myself shouting frequently at Dorka, at Ficzkó, over the smallest infractions. Istók Soós would hardly come near me since I discovered that he'd got that stupid Dorizca with child—up at the keep while Anna was visiting, it must have been—for in my bitterness I could hardly set eyes on him without making accusations. His thick bull-neck and his red face, his arms so broad that he almost could not put them down at his sides. Why had I never seen how coarse he was, how stupid and greedy? I could not believe that he, of all people, could turn on me after everything I had done for him. What was it about her you loved best? I asked him, again and again, my voice nearly breaking with animosity. I followed him from room to room waiting for an answer. Was it her stupidity, her laziness? The soft rolls at her belly? What?

Her silence, he said at last.

We were in my room, the room I had shared with him night after night for nearly three years. His words were still hanging in the air between us like smoke from a burnt-out candle. Silence, he had said. If he wanted silence, I would give it to him in abundance. He stood near the door, waiting to see what I would do, if I would fly at him, if I would collapse at his feet and weep. Once again I had been passed over for a younger woman. It occurred to me to have him taken to the cellars himself and whipped and beaten, but who among my servants, now, was strong enough to stand up to him? Who could I rely on except for Ficzkó, who was a dwarf next to Istók, and a bunch of old women?

I told him it would be best if he started looking for a new place. He would not be welcome in my home any longer. He seemed about to say something else, something he knew he would regret. Then he seemed to reconsider, set his great bull of a neck more firmly on his shoulders, and turned away. Left me there, alone, not even bothering to close the door after him. I watched him turn his back on me, sat at the window to see when he would leave. In an hour or two, just long enough for him to pack up his few things and saddle his horse, I heard hoofbeats retreating from the *kastély*, and after that I refused to hear his name spoken by anyone in the house. It would be as if Istók Soós, the wedding steward, had never existed at all.

It was four days after Christmas. The girls who had been taken away for stealing and kept in the catacombs under the hill continued to protest their innocence. I had Dorka and Ficzkó whip them a couple of times a day until they reconsidered and asked my forgiveness, and report back to me on their progress, but so far there had been none. They still insisted they had done nothing wrong.

The night Istók left I went down to the passages that led from the manor into the cellars of the castle. They were dark and stony, with dripping white teats of limestone growing down from the ceiling. We passed small antechambers where barrels of wine were stored, and ice cut from the river in the winter kept buried in sawdust. Sometimes a white handprint or bit of writing smeared with age betrayed the long history of the place, and I wondered about the women who had lived here before, and all the ones who would come after. The smell of earth and damp was everywhere, and underneath it something sour and decayed, as if the stones and earth themselves had gone rotten. Ficzkó, who went in front of me, had trouble at times finding the way among the many passages and dead ends. Several times we had to double back to find our way, until I slapped his ear and told him to watch where he was going, that I did not have all day to wander around in the dark. After that we made our way with little difficulty.

In a little while we came to the room where the girls were tied up, chained to the wall and clutching at each other, naked and shivering, smeared with dirty handprints on their faces where Dorka and Ilona Jó and Ficzkó had slapped them, and bruises along their buttocks and under the shackles that bound their wrists. The room was wet along the floor, smelling of piss and blood, and cold, so that our breath came out in little white clouds. There was hay piled in the corners, and ash on the floor to soak up the wetness, and the smell of living things in close proximity—the smell of barns, and childbirth rooms. A frightened, animal smell. The torchlight flickered and gave everything a furtive look, as of things only half witnessed.

When they saw me, the chained girls began to wail and protest their innocence. They had done nothing, they said. They had taken nothing. Mercy, mistress, they said. Mercy, please, for the love of God. The fat Dorizca, her pregnant belly showing, the stripes on her back crusted from where I had beaten her, pulled at her chains and tried to cover her nakedness, whimpering.

The flesh of her back bunched into little folds almost like a second set of breasts, the skin of her thighs bulging together at the top, at the place where Istók Soós had so willingly buried himself. I imagined them rutting in my room when I was out of the house, defiling the white bed where I had spent so many pleasant nights with him. She wrapping her fat legs around him, he burying his soft red mouth in her breasts. Laughing at me, and telling each other stories about me. Turning all the many kindnesses I had showed them both into less than nothing, into excrement.

Now I took the whip from Dorka's hand. Doricza whimpered, and looked at Ficzkó as if to plead, but the boy wisely decided to say nothing. "Will you ask forgiveness," I asked, "for what you have taken?"

"I did not take the tray, my lady. It was only the pears. I was going to bring the tray back to the kitchen when the pears were gone, I swear it."

She swore she had taken nothing, but I myself had seen the tray in her room, I said.

The cook had given her the pears, she said.

I said the cook was the one who had accused her of stealing.

At this she began to cry. "I never did," she said. "I never took anything from your ladyship, I swear it. Don't you remember," she said, "don't you remember when we went to Bécs, and the other girl, the one who died, you remember you gave me that coin? You gave it because you liked the work I had done. You promised that I would be rewarded. You promised my mother you would try to find me a husband, but I have lived here six years and have never heard of a husband yet. You promised my mother, when she brought me here, and I have done nothing but be loyal to you and treat you with kindness. I only wanted a pear." Her face was blubbering with snot and tears. *Save me.* "It was Christmas, and I wanted a pear. That's all. Just the pear. I was hungry, and no one was eating them, why couldn't we have them?"

"If you had asked me," I said, "I would have given them to you."

"I did ask," she said. "I asked Istók Soós if we could have them. Ask Istók, he will tell you. I asked permission, and he said we could have them. He gave me the tray, I swear it."

"Istók Soós is gone," I said. "He left this morning. He took his horse and rode away, and left you here with me."

Her blubbering echoed in the underground caverns and infected the others, set off a chain of wailing that assaulted my ears. The girl had been nothing but incompetent since the first I had taken her into my home. She had been less than worthless at Pöstyén, at Bécs. I could not have thievery and dishonesty and incompetence among my maids, and now she had lain with Istók Soós, whom I had been obliged to send away. Once again a young girl—a simpleton, a whore—had come between me and a man who loved me. Once again I had lost the comfort of affection, and pleasure, to one I had trusted, to a girl of no education, no breeding, no worth.

As if in a dream, I raised my hand and put the lash across her back myself, over and over. Her back was a mess of stripes, the yellow fat showing through the wounds. The floor sticky, my clothes. There was blood on my hands, my face. The room went dim again, and cleared, and dimmed, the slow beat of my heart in my ears the only sound, though I could see their lips moving, I knew they were saying something to me, imploring me for something, but I did not know what. *Save me.* The girl slumped forward, curled on the ground like a pig that had its throat cut. Silent.

From behind me I hear, as if from underwater, the sounds of weeping, perhaps my ladies themselves, perhaps the girls still chained together to witness the punishment of Doricza. Perhaps it is myself. It comes to me from very far away, like a horn, like a clatter of hooves. The girl is naked on the cold stones and her eyes are closed, and I think, she must be cold, we must get her off the floor before she freezes, or she will be no more use to me. I tell Ficzkó to cut her down and have Ilona Jó tend her wounds. There is spiderweb, I say, and plaster to make her well. The women look at each other. Ficzkó bends and picks her up under the arms, but she is bigger than he, and he stumbles. "She's dead," he says.

"What did you say?"

"Countess, the girl is dead," said Ficzkó. "Plaster and spiderweb won't help her."

Somewhere behind me someone begins to cry. There is another voice, raised, shouting, one of the chained girls. *Škrata*, it says. Witch. A bit of spittle flies out and lands on my cheek. Anger. White anger, and cold.

I raise my hand and the heavy end of the whip—a lead bludgeon wrapped in strips of leather—and bring it down on the head of the one who spoke, the one nearest me, who is so filthy I can't make out who she is. A cracking noise, like the breaking of stone, and the room grows dim before me, blackens. I am alone in the darkness, and then, as if from a great distance, colors come back to me, sounds, light. There is a girl in front of me, a girl crying. Her nose is bright with blood, and her eyes tear, making tracks in the dirt on her face and the blood. There is something about her eyes that is familiar. Her eyes are green and watery, like someone else's I knew long ago. I recognize her, I think. A cousin I took in a few years ago when her mother wrote to me that the young men of her village had all died in the Turkish wars. I had promised to get her a husband, I wrote the mother. Éva, the name comes back to me now. Éva Cziráky. A pretty little thing, with a sweet singing voice and a mass of yellow curls, like my cousin Griseldis long ago. How small she looks, how frightened. For a moment I wonder what her days are like, what love there is for her, whether she feels fear, or anger, or pity, or love. Whom does she love? What have those she loves done to her? There is blood on her face, running off her chin in little spins and rivulets. I'm not sure how it got there. My hands grow numb; something falls to the floor. There are raised voices and shouting, and the barking of dogs, but it's all a distant roar, like thunder heard from underground. My heartbeat slows and steadies; my skin is damp. There is blood on it.

Someone is taking my arm, someone is speaking in my ear. I cannot hear them, I don't know what they're saying.

A rough hand spins me around until I am looking into the red face of Ficzkó, bending toward me, shouting. I cannot hear him. My ears are full of water. He shakes me once, then again, harder. "Countess!" he says, urgent, almost fearful. "The palatine is here. He's come for us. We must leave now, or else." He pulls on my arm but my feet are rooted to the ground like old trees, deep into the underground of Csejthe, my home.

In a moment he is gone, Ficzkó, back down the tunnels we came from, toward the manor house, where the palatine's men are already waiting for him. From the *vár* above come the voices, deep and drowned, the cries of my servants and the girls in the room and the smell of death everywhere. I have never felt so alone. There are soldiers, the shine of metal, and dimly, in the lamplight, I recognize the face of young Zrínyi, the face of young Drugeth, the face of Megyery.

They have betrayed me, then. The face of Thurzó himself coming toward me, swimming toward me, his deep-set eyes, his unhandsome, disloyal mouth, ordering his men to unchain the girls. How could I ever have loved him? How could I have shared my bed with him, he who loved no one except himself?

Arrest her, he says, pointing at me, and the guards come closer with their hands on their swords, and I drop my whip—my hands are numb—and the men are coming toward me, shouting, but the palatine stands back in the darkness, away from me, he will not look at me, but on his face—I will swear it to my dying day—I see his mouth turn up in a smile.

# 25

Outside my tower walls Csejthe has stilled in the heat of another summer, the hawks turning slowly in the air to search for mice in the fields, long black snakes sunning themselves on bare rock below, curled there like question marks. There are tracks in the dust outside my tower, the cloven footprint of the devil himself, whose stamping impatient feet I hear again and again beyond my door. I will meet him soon enough. The guards bring me my daily tray of food, and whatever letters come to me from the world outside, and complain that the rooms are too close and too hot, though I am always cold. "Look," I tell them. "Look how chill my hands are. Look at how I freeze." They only shrug and go away again.

More than three years I have traced the patterns of light on the walls as spring turns to summer, summer to winter. The summer solstice has passed, but these are still among the shortest nights of the year. The air coming through my window turns sodden with the scent of rain, but still I can see little outside except the hills that roll away from me, toward Poland, toward Moravia, toward the world I will never see again.

Once a week the guards bring me fresh clothes, and each time I beg them for a mirror. A little piece of mirror, I ask, so that I might look on a friendly face at least once before I die. Today one of them brought me a broken shard with jagged edges, a fragment left behind in some corner of the keep. The weight of the mirror in my hand makes me a bit calmer. I often found something soothing in a mirror, in the lines of my countenance, which changed throughout a long lifetime from the round, pink-cheeked flush of youth to the firm clear lines of maturity. My visage has been my constant companion these many years, even as family and friends have failed me, or love turned to disappointment.

When I look in the mirror now my hair is wild and streaked through with more gray than I remember, especially at the temples. Unbound, without the pearls I always wore in it, it falls in waves to my waist, looking heavy and rough as a horse's tangled mane. My normally pale skin is marred by dark, ashen pockets that have sprung up under my eyes and in the hollows at my temples, and between my brows a crease has developed from sleeplessness and worry. At the corners of my eyes webs of lines grow deeper, making me look like an ancient crone who has spent her life herding goats in the hot sun instead of a noblewoman of fifty-four who has cared for her beauty like a monk with a cherished icon. How quickly beauty spoils, how final is its demise. I put the mirror away again carefully, shaking my head. I do not want to weep, not here, in front of my jailers. There will be plenty of time for that later.

I undress. Exposed, my body is a thing I do not recognize. The skin at my belly, stretched from the pregnancies and births of six children, hangs under my navel, webbed with white stretch marks and so loose I can gather it in my two hands. My breasts hang limp and empty as wineskins, and the flesh at my neck is crumpled, mottled red and brown, my feet calloused and tough. Up and down my legs are spidery veins, blue and green, that divide my new self from the old like borders drawn on old maps, conquered by time and indifference.

I put on the clean clothes, but they hang loose from my shoulders and gape open at my wrists. I have grown thin in the past three years, fed on porridge and fatty meat, bits of undercooked pork or overaged cheese, the sour wine left behind in the cellars. It is as difficult to take pleasure in food as it is to take pleasure in breathing. It is just as well you do not come to me. I wish you could see me as I once was, Pál—my cheeks pink and blooming, my bosom plump over the tightly laced waistcoat, my hair glossy with health, my smile as sure of a man's love as any woman ever was. Now my skirt hangs about my waist because there are no ladies to tie the cords, nor are there ladies to iron the lace frills of a new collar into stiff little points, to serve my face upon it like a platter, as my mother's ladies once did for her. I do the best I can with the ties but still nothing fits properly. I push the sleeves up my wrists, bunch the blouse under the waistcoat. When I am dressed, I take a moment to rub sweet almond oil into my hands, my face. A little berry juice on my lips and cheeks gives them a little of the old life back, rose and cream. A few drops of ink help to cover the streaks of gray at my temples. When I look in the mirror again, I see a little of the Erzsébet who arrived at the house in Sárvár as a new bride, who danced with Thurzó in the moonlit halls of Bécs. I touch my face, feeling the old bones under the flesh. I once laughed at the vanity of women of forty and fifty who wore cosmetics to balls and parties, who whitened their ruddy old skin with lead, but now I know such salves are not disguises for old crones who wish to catch a young husband. Instead they are only a mask we wear so that we can, for a little while, still recognize ourselves.

Now that my nephew Gábor is dead—murdered in Transylvania by his own men—the palatine will no longer have any reason to think of me at all. I am no more use to him now in my prison tower, just another old woman with failing health, hands that ache from cold even in the hottest days of summer. What my mother said to me long ago was true, that a woman who does not marry is at the mercy of the world, but equally powerless is a widow with a young son, a widow hidden away in a forgotten corner of the house, a relic from an earlier age. When you are a man, when you are old enough to understand what I have written in these pages, I hope you will remember your old mother and how she loved you, Pál, what she sacrificed for you.

Kata has promised to visit soon, but she is expecting again, and naturally she is afraid to travel far in her condition. It does not seem likely I will see her before the snow flies in the winter, and if not then, then not until the roads between Pozsony and Csejthe clear in the spring. The worst news, however, is that after her latest miscarriage, Anna has taken to her bed, and though the doctors come to her again and again nothing seems to improve her spirits. Miklós writes to let me know how she is doing, for the poor girl cannot even hold a pen herself. I know that if I could only go to her, I could nurse her to health again. I worry for her. She is still young and could be happy, but the death of the child has blighted her spirit, and she withers as much as her old mother does in her prison tower. I fear I have not been fair to Anna and left her without the resources she might have needed to weather this storm. But there is no turning back now, nor, perhaps, should there be. The sins of one's youth need only be repented once, as my guest Rev. Zacharias tells me during his visits. "For God's mercy is everlasting," he says. I don't tell him that even if God forgives you, you do not forgive yourself. You live in your sorrow like a room of mirrors that reflects on and on to eternity.

If confession and confinement could bring forgetfulness, like drinking the water of the Lethe, then how fervently would I fall once more to my knees and lay bare my soul to the Almighty and grow to love these narrow walls. What relief it would be to feel even a moment's peace. Writing down my sad memories has only made them bolder, more vivid. It brings back the faces of my lost loved ones, my mother and father, especially when I have no fresher faces before me. István, Zsofía, Klára. Darvulia, Ferenc. I have outlived them all, and two of my own children besides. The Greeks claimed they would call no man happy until he was dead, for until then he was not happy, only lucky. I have lived fifty-four years in this old world, enough to see my hair turn gray and my beauty fade, enough to bury my husband and my friends, my mother and father and sisters and brother, my children, and I know that I'm the unluckiest person left on this earth. Death alone will be my consolation, when it comes, and yet I dread it. I dread what waits for me on the other side of the curtain, what new heaven, or new earth, is in store for me.

At times I think of the girls who died, the ones who bore the brunt of my anger and jealousy. Judit, Amália. Gizela, Éva, Doricza. All the ones whose names I never knew. There are times when I think I would give back every one of their lives, every lash or blow, to see you again, my son. All of them together are not worth the loss of you.

If I could have one wish for my old age, besides to walk out of this tower and ride away from the cold heights of Csejthe *vár*, it would be to return one more time to the marsh at the family seat in Ecsed where my brother and sisters and I played as children among the lichen-covered stones of the fortress, where my mother and father, my family, were once so happy together. Perhaps I would stand at the window in the moonlight and hear again the voice of the gypsy man condemned for selling his little daughter, the way his strange accent cracked on the Hungarian words like a hammer on stone. *Save me*, he said. Perhaps there I might be visited by the ghosts of all my dead ones, my parents and siblings, my husband, my children, my friends, all the dead Báthorys and Nádasdys who have gone before me. And the others, the ones who died at my hands, whose faces I see now always coming in through the cracks of my walls, the stone gap at my door. Was I wrong to treat them thus? Was it not my right, as the mistress of the house, to punish them as I saw fit? I have lost my children in payment, my fortune, my good name—everything. Their lives did not seem worth much to me, but I would give them all back, every one, for one more day with you, Pál, with your sisters. *Save me*, they said, but I would not. It will not be long now before I join them.

Soon they will take the wall down and carry me out into the light. They will carry me down the hill of the *vár* to the vault in the church at Csejthe, far from my family crypt in Nyírbátor, far from your father's resting place in Sárvár. I will watch over you then, my son and daughters in their different corners of the kingdom. Anna, Kata, Pál. My other daughter, the vanished one. I will touch your cheek with my hand that will not be my hand. I wonder if you will hear me call your name.

I keep my trunks packed, so that when you or your sisters come to tell me I am free, I will be ready.

I watch the horizon for the sun to rise. Every day, I watch and wait.

# READING GROUP GUIDE

1. The book opens with a quote from "Snow White": "Just then a young boar came running by. He killed it, cut out its lungs and liver, and took them back to the queen as proof of Snow-White's death. The cook had to boil them with salt, and the wicked woman ate them, supposing that she had eaten Snow-White's lungs and liver." Many historians think this fairy tale might have its origins in the legends of Erzsébet Báthory and the atrocities she committed against young women. How is the Báthory in *The Countess* different from the Báthory of legend? How is she the same? What other legends or fairy tales might have similarities to her life story?

2. The letter from Father Zacharias, which serves as the prologue of the novel, explains that the manuscript is a letter Báthory wrote to her young son, Pal, justifying her actions in light of the social and political pressures she was feeling at the time. How does Father Zacharias's letter to his superior influence our thinking about the rest of the story?

3. The novel—like some other recent "retellings" (*The Mists of Avalon, Wide Sargasso Sea, Wicked, Grendel*)—lets a notorious character tell her story from her own perspective. How does the first-person point of view change how we see her? What does she reveal, and what does she conceal, and why?

4. When Erzsébet is a child, her mother teachers her crucial lessons in being the mistress of a household. What does she learn? How does it influence the rest of the story?

5. What kinds of relationships does Erzsébet have with the men in her life—her father, her husband, her son, her lovers? How are those

different from her relationships with women—her mother, her sisters, her cousin Griseldis, Darvulia, her daughters, her maidservants?

6. Starting with the punishment of Judit, the girl who stole the skirt, Erzsébet learns (with Ferenc's help) that she can inflict torment and humiliation on the servants without repercussion. In fact, every time Erzsébet suffers a romantic setback or humiliation, she takes it out on one of the maidservants. How does she view her servants in those moments? What is their role in her household, and how does it change over the course of the novel?

7. Countess Báthory is infamous for bathing in the blood of virgins to keep her youth and beauty. Although those rumors turn out to be false, what role does beauty and aging play in Erzsébet's thinking in the novel?

8. Erzsébet is born at a crucial moment in religious history, the Reformation, when the rise of Protestant religions was displacing the old Catholic order. The Catholic Hapsburgs, who controlled the crown of Hungary, often ran into trouble with the largely Protestant Hungarian nobles. Erzsébet's own son-in-law later converts back to Catholicism during the beginning days of the Counter-Reformation. How might the plot of the story be influenced by these religious tensions? What would the Catholic Hapsburgs and their loyal palatine, György Thurzo, have to gain by having Erzsébet arrested and imprisoned? What would her sons-in-law have to gain?

9. In the final pages of the novel Erzsébet begins to have a hint of her own mortality. Does she look back on her life with regret? Is she even capable of regret? Why or why not?

10. They say that history is written by the victors. How have the novel and Erzsébet's legend been influenced by the fact that she was *not* the victor of her own story?

# ACKNOWLEDGMENTS

Many thanks to Richard Abate, Suzanne O'Neill, Emily Timberlake, Louise Quayle, Ray Ventre, Catherine Knepper, Michelle Falkoff, Colette Sartor, Stacey Shrontz, Aubrey Ryan, Melissa Cottenham, and all my family and friends, as well as my colleagues in the English departments at Northern Michigan University and DePaul University for their invaluable support during the writing of this book. Special thanks also to Amy Hickey for help on the spelling and pronunciation of Hungarian words and names, and to Chet DeFonso for pointing me in her direction.

For research on the life of Erzsébet Báthory and the world she lived in, I am deeply indebted to Tony Thorne's *Countess Dracula: The Life and Times of Elisabeth Báthory, The Blood Countess* (London: Bloomsbury, 1997) and Katalin Péter's *Beloved Children: History of Aristocratic Childhood in Hungary in the Early Modern Age* (Budapest: Central European University Press, 2001).